Dear Reader,

We women have always understood the feminine power of just changing your mind. A major shift in direction lifts your spirits and somehow makes anything possible. So our theme in Harlequin Duets this month is women on a mission, makeovers, girl power!

In *Great Genes!*, our creative but klutzy heroine takes charge by designing her own baby by finding a hero who has all the qualities she lacks. Then Nell Phillips of *Make Me Over* transforms herself into a killer babe—only to fall for the man who teaches her how. (Harlequin Duets #13)

Margo Haskell definitely doesn't want to marry a cowboy in *Sex and the Single Cowpoke,* but once she turns herself into a Texan, the idea of making the cowboy a permanent part of her life begins to feel right. Then Dru Logan, a woman for whom career definitely comes first, finds herself under the influence of a love potion in *Lovestruck*—and loving it! (Harlequin Duets #14)

Lift up your spirits with Duets!

Malle Vallik

Malle Vallik
Senior Editor

Sex and the Single Cowpoke

Mary Beth had lied to him.

Wyatt stopped in the middle of Fifth Avenue. Ever since Mary Beth had pushed him off the monkey bars in third grade, knocking the wind out of him, he'd assumed they would get married.

Wyatt's thoughts were stopped cold by the sensation of someone ramming full tilt into his chest. "Hey! Watch where you're going!"

Wyatt looked down. The woman had bounced off him and stepped clear out of one of her shoes and dropped her briefcase. "Whoa," Wyatt said, steadying her.

The woman stiffened. Wyatt found himself peering into the most beautiful eyes he'd ever seen. "Whoa?" Her tone brimmed with disbelief.

Wyatt translated. "I meant careful there."

"Listen, Tex, you can't run around grabbing people after you slam into them." She grabbed the briefcase from him. "You need to watch where you're going." Before he could respond, she disappeared into the horde at a brisk walk.

For the second time in Wyatt's life a woman had knocked the wind straight out of him.

This time he wasn't going to let her get away.

For more, turn to page 9

Lovestruck

"What are we going to tell Dr. Peel?

"After all, it's two o'clock," Dru continued, pulling her sweater self-consciously over her head. She couldn't help the awkwardness she felt dressing in front of Pierce this morning. But she'd had no trouble *undressing* last night. "He'll be wondering why we haven't surfaced before now."

"Don't be embarrassed," Pierce said as they started down the hall. "They think we're a newly reunited married couple."

"Who've been doing it like bunnies for the past fifteen hours. You go in first."

Dru peeked around the door as Pierce went in and greeted Dr. Peel. He seemed to have the situation under control—until the doctor's assistant quickly poured him a glass of water. "Here, drink this. You're probably dehydrated."

Dehydrated? What the—?

Dr. Peel rose from his easy chair and came to stand beside Pierce. "So, my boy," he said, patting him on the shoulder, "how did you like my little love potion?"

For more, turn to page 197

HARLEQUIN DUETS

ISBN 0-373-44080-4

SEX AND THE SINGLE COWPOKE
Copyright © 1999 by Elizabeth Bass

LOVESTRUCK
Copyright © 1999 by Susan Goggins

This edition published by arrangement with Harlequin Books S.A.

® and TM are trademarks of the publisher. Trademarks indicated with
® are registered in the United States Patent and Trademark Office, the
Canadian Trade Marks Office and in other countries.

Visit us at www.romance.net

Printed in U.S.A.

LIZ IRELAND

Sex and the Single Cowpoke

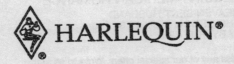

HARLEQUIN®

TORONTO • NEW YORK • LONDON
AMSTERDAM • PARIS • SYDNEY • HAMBURG
STOCKHOLM • ATHENS • TOKYO • MILAN • MADRID
PRAGUE • WARSAW • BUDAPEST • AUCKLAND

Dear Reader,

I love to make things up. Always have. If reality didn't suit me, I could always imagine something slightly more exciting (I would like to think this partially explains my low scores in math). Part of the problem was that I grew up in a small rural town where not a whole lot happened, so imagination was a vital possession (especially in those pre-satellite dish days). But every once in a while, when I was a youngster, a friend of my parents who was a federal D.A. would pay a spur-of-the-moment visit to our farm. You can just guess what these occurrences did to a kid whose imagination was already on overload!

So I suppose you could say *Sex and the Single Cowpoke* stems from autobiography, except this federal D.A. is an uptight city girl dropped in from New York, and the hero is a Gary Cooper-type cowboy, and believe it or not, Armadillo Bend is a regular metropolis compared to my hometown. But like I said, I love to make things up.

Liz Ireland

Books by Liz Ireland

HARLEQUIN DUETS
5—THE BEST MAN SWITCH

HARLEQUIN AMERICAN ROMANCE
639—HEAVEN-SENT HUSBAND
683—THE GROOM FORGETS
767—BABY FOR HIRE

MANHATTAN
MAVERICKS

Not quite home on the range

1

WYATT LAMAR COULDN'T believe where he found himself. It was like something out of a movie. Heck, it *was* something right out of a movie—a whole slew of them, all the way from *King Kong* to *Sleepless in Seattle*. The Empire State Building!

He'd nearly walked right past it but now he stopped, standing stock still in the middle of the sidewalk on Fifth Avenue. He felt obliged to push back the brim of his Stetson and just stare up at the thing. It was one of those moments he'd heard sometimes happened to people—like the time his Uncle Roscoe was struck by lightning, survived, and decided to dedicate his life to perfecting his chili recipe. Here he'd had been, alone in New York, his heart as heavy as a bucket of bricks...until he just happened to glance up and there it was one of America's most inspiring landmarks. It wasn't the sort of thing that happened to a person every day. Especially not to someone who had spent his whole entire life in Armadillo Bend, Texas.

He craned his neck, straining to see all the way to the very tip top of the famous spire. There was something magical about the place, really. He was getting a lift just from looking at the sleek, majestic edifice, and felt all his own piddling problems slipping away. For at least a moment, it was easy to forget that Mary Beth Sumners had lied to him and had actually been living with an accountant in Queens for eight whole months, and that his hopes of becoming a married man before the week's end had been dashed.

In fact, maybe the whole situation wasn't so darned tragic after all. He'd set quite a store by Mary Beth. Ever since she'd pushed him off the monkey bars in third grade, knocking the wind out of him, he'd assumed they would get married. He'd been drawn by her brash thumb-her-nose-at-the-world attitude, and the way she'd been more sophisticated than the other girls in Armadillo Bend. While other girls at Sam Houston High School had worn jeans and T-shirts, the same as the boys had, Mary Beth had always dressed like she'd just stepped out of *Cosmopolitan* or *Vogue*, or at least Luanne's Dress Shop, the very best women's store in town. Mary Beth had seemed like a one in a million type gal.

Or so Wyatt had thought.

But heck, *all* the women in New York City were so brash and sophisticated, you'd swear every podunk town in America had sent its own Mary Beth out to populate the place. For two days he had watched these city women trooping down sidewalks in their no-nonsense business suits, shouldering their way like linebackers onto crowded subway cars and city buses, power lunching at expensive restaurants. These women were a breed apart—sleek, fast, and independent. All this time he'd assumed that Mary Beth was unique and irreplaceable, that he'd never find another one like her and that he'd just have to fly out to New York and haul her back home.

Mary Beth, happy with her accountant, wasn't budging. But for all her treachery, she had inadvertently led him to make an earth-shattering discovery. There wasn't only one woman in the world for him, as Wyatt had believed since third grade. There were millions! New York City was teeming with them! Why, all he had to do was reach out and—

Wyatt's thoughts were stopped cold by the sensation of someone ramming full tilt into his chest. For a second the collision knocked the wind straight out of him.

"Hey! Watch where you're going!" a voice brayed in annoyance.

Where *he* was going? Perplexed, Wyatt looked down and saw that a woman, a little tornado of a woman, had slammed into him so hard that all sorts of things had happened at once. First, she'd bounced off him and stepped clear out of one of her shoes, which explained why she was hopping around on one foot, backwards, trying to retrieve it. She'd also dropped her briefcase, which had been kicked open by another passerby. The papers that had spilled all over the sidewalk were now marked with footprints. And the last thing he noticed was that one of her stockings, which just so happened to be covering one of the most shapely legs he'd ever had the pleasure to lay eyes on, had snagged on the concrete.

She noticed it, too, just as she was trying to shove her foot back into the wayward pump. "Oh, terrific!" She twisted around to see the ladder racing up her calf and nearly stumbled over her briefcase.

"Whoa," Wyatt said, grabbing her shoulders to steady her.

The woman stiffened and her head snapped up. Suddenly Wyatt found himself peering into the roundest, bluest, most startlingly beautiful eyes he'd ever seen. *"Whoa?"* Her tone brimmed with disbelief.

Wyatt translated. "What I meant to say was, careful there."

By the way her mouth pinched up he could see that his drawl had not gone undetected. "Listen, Tex, you can't run around grabbing people after you slam into them."

Assured she wasn't going to tumble over, Wyatt freed the woman and bent down to retrieve her briefcase and the scattered papers. "Pardon me, ma'am," he said, smiling affably.

The smile seemed to ruffle her. "You need to watch where you're going," she repeated, but the phrase lacked the punch it had carried before. She combed a hand through her hair.

"But see," he explained, "I wasn't even going anywhere. I was just standing here—"

The woman grabbed the briefcase and papers from him hurriedly and interrupted his explanation. "You shouldn't just stand around here, either. This isn't the Grand Canyon, cowboy."

Wyatt guessed she'd noticed the hat, too.

Before he could respond, she was moving again, disappearing into the hordes at a brisk walk. Wyatt stared after her, his mouth still open to respond—but now it loosened into something like slack-jawed amazement. Everything had happened so fast! He hadn't been able to get the woman's name, or tell her his. Shoot, he hadn't even had time to notice what color her hair was. Some kind of brown. Or check to see if she wore a wedding ring.

He just remembered those eyes—blue like crystal blue pools of water on a hot July day back home. Never in his life would he forget them. For the second time in his life a woman had knocked the wind straight out of him. But this time he wasn't taking anything for granted.

This time he wasn't going to let her get away.

"NUTTY TOURIST!" Margo Haskell muttered. That was the trouble with New York. All these people who didn't belong here, lumbering down the sidewalks like lost souls, clogging traffic and causing confusion, doing damage to the innocent residents who were just trying to go about their very important business.

She careened into Macy's and made a beeline for the hosiery department. With only twenty minutes to get all the way downtown for a pretrial hearing, she'd already been pressed for time. Now, thanks to Buffalo Bill, she was running really late.

Of course, if she stopped to think about it, she was always running late. But that was to be expected for a busy assistant district attorney. Much as she wished it would, crime didn't take holidays, and neither could she. It seemed like two years since she'd even taken a coffee break. Then again, if she'd wanted coffee breaks, she could have stayed in her hometown of Tallulah, Ohio, and yawned herself into an early grave. But she'd decided at an early age that she wanted something more exciting for herself than some humdrum existence highlighted by weekend trips to Wal-Mart. No, this was the life she had worked hard to achieve, and busy was the way she liked it.

Margo veered into the rows of panty hose and quickly started making selections. While she was here, she might as well stock up, she thought, snatching up stockings to match every color of suit in her closet. Her job didn't leave her a whole lot of time for shopping. On her rare days off she preferred watching a video or reading a book in the relative peace of her apartment to battling the crowds in the department stores.

There was even a certain satisfaction in buying a million pair at once, because now, for the first time in her life, she had the money. After years of scrimping, saving, working lousy waitressing jobs, and having credit card companies refuse her applications with hearty belly laughs, the rush she received from handing a store clerk her platinum card was almost sinful. She was almost glad to have been poor so she could fully appreciate having money.

Almost.

"Excuse me, ma'am?" drawled a familiar voice next to her.

Margo cocked her head to look up at the man, who doffed his Stetson and smiled amiably down at her. The sight of that hat nearly made her groan. Oh, no! The cowboy again.

The *very good-looking cowboy.*

She blinked. Lord, he was tall! And she hadn't noticed quite how handsome he was, either. Maybe it had something to do with the lighting, or the fact that when walking on the streets of Manhattan she found it best not to look too closely at what was going on around her, but inside Macy's, she found herself staring up at a definitely good-looking face with a strong jaw, shaved close, soulful brown eyes, and black hair cut short and neat.

He had a very Gary Cooperish way about him that made her smile in spite of the fact that she was running late, and that he was the prime reason why. Prime being the key word. What woman could help grinning at such a dreamy male animal?

"I kind of felt bad about what happened back there," he said. "You didn't give me a chance to apologize."

Margo hugged her panty hose to her chest, feeling awkward. Now that the scene replayed in her mind, maybe it wasn't actually this guy's fault they'd collided.

She had been thinking about her court appearance that afternoon.

Which reminded her, she didn't exactly have the leisure to sit around mooning at Mr. Cooper all day. "Don't give it another thought," she said, backing out of the hosiery aisle and heading for a cash register.

"But see, I was wondering whether I might be able to make it up to you. I'd be most obliged if you'd go with me on a date."

At the sound of that unfamiliar word—*date*—Margo tripped, sending fifteen pair of panty hose flying into the slipper display.

Date? Was this guy some kind of crackpot? She hadn't been on a date, a real date, since pimply Lon Shiberta had escorted her to the junior prom back in Tallulah! She bent down to collect her hosiery and sent a sidelong glance at the man as he followed her lead in gathering up the packages. Maybe he wasn't even a Texan at all, but an escaped nut from Bellevue who stood outside famous New York landmarks pretending to be an innocent aw-shucks type and hitting on women.

"I seem to have upset you," the man said. "I hope I didn't say anything wrong."

"Listen, Tex, people just don't—"

"It's Wyatt," he said, thrusting his free hand forward for her to shake. "Wyatt Lamar."

Tentatively, Margo let him wrap his big paw around her hand and pump it heartily. "Listen, Mr. Lamar, people in New York don't date. They do lunch, or meet for coffee, or drinks. But it doesn't really matter, because I don't go for guys who are into picking up women at Macy's."

His eyes widened as her words sank in. He looked appalled and embarrassed, with just a pinch of offended thrown into the mix. "Now wait a cotton-pickin' minute. I wasn't intending anything shady here—I just wanted to take you out to dinner."

Margo stood and started walking brusquely to the cash register. Wyatt strode along behind her.

"Thank you very much, but I don't do dinner," she said, slapping her hosiery down on the counter.

He reached for his wallet.

"Oh, no!" Margo protested, guessing his intention. She dug into her purse to whip out her American Express card. In almost perfect unison, they thrust their plastic towards the startled saleswoman on the other side of the register.

The elderly woman pushed her glasses up to the bridge of her nose and shook her head, looking from one card to the other. "Which?"

Margo turned on Wyatt with a huff. "Please, this isn't necessary."

"It's the least I can do after our little collision."

"You don't have to do anything," she said. "It was just an accident."

He shook his head. "I'd feel a heap better if you'd just allow me to do this little thing."

"Little!" Margo exclaimed, her voice an octave higher than usual as she pointed to the pile of hose she was buying. "That's eighty dollars' worth of hosiery!"

The saleswoman nodded. "At least. Then there's tax." Her brows raised in speculation.

"But since you won't go out to dinner…"

She rolled her eyes. Her arm was getting tired of being held at a right angle, but she wasn't going to back down. "I don't have time to eat dinner."

His jaw dropped in surprise, and he asked, "Never?"

"Well…hardly ever. I have a very busy life, and it's

easier just to run out for a late lunch. You know how it is.''

By the concerned expression on his face, he didn't. "I haven't skipped a dinner since I came down with chicken pox when I was four. It's not right. Don't you eat at home?''

"You mean, as in, cook?'' When he nodded, she admitted, "Well, I have a toaster, a coffeemaker, and a microwave. I can work them.''

Wyatt was so horrified that he almost dropped his credit card. "Microwave!'' he drawled in distaste. "Pardon my bein' so bold, but that kind of food isn't fit for human consumption. Now you've got to let me take you out for a real meal.''

"But I...'' Margo glanced down at her watch and felt a wave of panic. She just didn't have time to be standing around arguing with this character, who had a particularly stubborn strain of chivalry. She needed to get back to work, pronto. "Okay, okay,'' she muttered in resignation, "put your card away, Tex. I'll go out to dinner with you.''

"Tonight?'' he asked, his VISA still thrust at the Macy's saleswoman.

Margo gave up all pretense of a fight, and laughed. "All right, all right. Whatever you say.''

Smiling, the saleswoman took her card and began ringing up the purchase.

Wyatt returned his own card to his billfold and leaned against the counter, looking her up and down in a way that made her very uncomfortable. He was grinning that lazy smile of his, and she felt a little shiver of awareness at having all that male appreciation aimed at her. It had been a while since she'd had an admirer. A long while.

"Where would you like to go?'' he asked.

She looked into his smoky brown eyes and felt her heart catch. Good lord, what was she doing? What had she agreed to? "I don't know," she said, shrugging. "Wherever you'd like."

The woman handed Margo's card back to her and said, "May I suggest Tavern on the Green? It's just the place for special occasions. My father used to tend bar there!"

"Well now!" Wyatt exclaimed, as if she'd just informed him that her father had been President of the United States. "What was his name?"

"Boris Tovetsky."

"And you're...?"

"Myrna, Myrna Tovetsky."

Wyatt shook her hand like a head of state meeting a foreign dignitary.

Margo signed her sales slip while Wyatt chitchatted with Myrna about Tavern on the Green. Was the guy for real? He certainly looked too good to be true. Could a man with movie-star good looks actually have the heart of Mr. Rogers?

Did she really want to find out?

When Myrna, still yucking it up with Wyatt, handed her a Macy's shopping bag, Margo took it quickly and turned on her heel to go. Wyatt darted out a hand to catch her arm so he wouldn't lose her.

"Nice meeting you, Myrna," he called to the saleswoman. Then he turned back to Margo. "Nice lady!" The man seemed genuinely to enjoy listening to saleswomen talk about their fathers.

He paused at the front door and held it open for Margo. Then he kept it open for another woman pushing a cumbersome baby stroller. Then he held it for two older women laden with packages. Margo, mindful of the time and unable to wait for the stream of needy females to die down, hustled to the edge of the sidewalk to hail a cab.

When Wyatt finally joined her, she shook her head at him. "You're an oddball in this city, Tex."

He looked surprised. "Why? Good manners are appreciated anywhere."

"You obviously haven't tried the subway yet."

He laughed, a deep throaty sound that practically made her toes curl. She slanted an admiring glance at him, then stopped herself. What the hell was she doing, talking to a stranger like this? Ogling him, even! Her instincts, honed to a sharp defensiveness from years of living in a big dangerous city, told her that she needed to be on guard. But one smile from Wyatt Lamar seemed to storm through that tough wall of imaginary bricks and mortar she'd carefully built to shield herself from the rougher aspects of Manhattan.

"Honestly," he said, still holding her arm gently at the elbow. "We don't have to go to Tavern on the Green."

Margo blinked. She didn't really have time to eat dinner this evening. She needed to go over some old depositions in the Johnny Garcetti case, and since she was due at court in a matter of minutes, the only free time to do her research would be this evening. Which left her little time for Lash LaRue here.

Which was probably just as well, considering the fact that she didn't know the man. He could be anybody—an ax murderer, for all she knew. What would her friends say if she told them she was even contemplating going out with a tourist she'd bumped into on the street! To Tavern on the Green, no less—tourist heaven!

On the other hand, now that she thought about it,

she'd always wanted to eat at Tavern on the Green, ever since she'd first heard about it when she was a little girl. It sounded so sophisticated, so quintessentially New York, but somehow, since moving to the city eight years ago, she'd never had the opportunity to go there. Oh, she'd walked by it on the occasional Sunday stroll past Central Park's sheep meadow...but eat there? No. Maybe because she'd never had the money. Or an escort. Now was her big chance.

She looked into Wyatt's eyes again, and was mesmerized. "Tavern on the Green sounds fine."

His smile broadened, dazzling her with its friendly glow that seemed to blot out all the teeming humanity bustling around them. Lord, he was good-looking! The man probably had scores of women clamoring to get at him back in Texas.

Or maybe he was married. She glanced down at his left hand to check for a ring. He didn't wear one. But what did that prove? Married men came to New York all the time, telling their wives they were off "on business."

She had no way of knowing who Wyatt Lamar was. The man might not even be a Texan! Any lunatic could don a Stetson and start talking Bonanza-speak. Her nerves began to jangle a warning. Maybe Ted Bundy lured women with some kind of John Wayne howdy-do-little-lady drawl, too!

Why, why, why had she ever said she would go out to dinner with him?

Margo dragged her gaze away from the man's handsome face and, gathering her wits about her again, darted her hand out to signal for a cab. A whole slew of yellow vehicles were barreling down Broadway.

"Where should I call for you?" Wyatt asked her.

"What for?" she asked suspiciously.

He blinked. "For our date."

There was that word again! It made her even more jumpy the second time around. Maybe because her vague memory of the term reminded her of awkward conversations and uneasy good-night kisses. And instinct told her that a kiss from this cowboy could keep a woman up nights, remembering.

"Never mind." There was no way she could go out with this guy. She didn't know him. She didn't have time. Naturally she felt guilty for leading him on when she knew she'd never have the nerve to actually go to dinner, but if she didn't lead him on, she doubted he would ever let go of her elbow. "Why don't we, uh, meet at the restaurant?"

He didn't seem pleased with this suggestion. "Here," he said, reaching into his back pocket for his wallet. He pulled out a business card and quickly scrawled something across it. "I'll give you the name of my hotel and its number, in case you need to get in touch with me or can't find the restaurant."

"Tavern on the Green doesn't get lost very often," she told him, trying to avoid taking that card. Trying to avoid looking into those soulful eyes.

Thank heavens, a cabbie finally saw her outstretched arm. Margo dashed into the street to meet the sedan as it practically flea-hopped over two lanes of busy traffic to screech to a stop inches from her.

Wyatt opened the door for her—of course—and shoved the card into her hand. "What time?"

Margo blurted the street coordinates for the downtown courthouse to the cabbie, then turned back to Wyatt, who was still holding the door open. "What?"

"What time should we meet?"

"Oh, um…" Clearly, he wasn't going to let the door go until she named a time. Meanwhile, she had a court date to get to—and the cab's meter was already running. "Eight?"

Guilt, guilt, guilt.

He shot her that dazzling smile again. "Eight it is. It's been nice meeting you…" He laughed. "I don't even know your name."

"Margo," she said, but before she could say anymore, the Thirty-fourth Street light turned green and the cab leapt to life. Wyatt was forced to close her door, leaving her in the vinyl cocoon of the Ford, slightly disoriented. As she glanced back and watched Wyatt recede into the distance, she tried to look philosophically on their chance encounter.

He seemed like a genuinely nice guy, and he was certainly handsome, but she just didn't have the time or the inclination to pursue a relationship—especially a risky one like a flirtation with a tourist. She didn't like to lie, but sometimes it was the easiest way to deal with people. Her biggest regret was, she'd always wanted to see Tavern on the Green from the inside.

And, she admitted shamelessly to herself, she'd always dreamed of kissing a handsome cowboy like Wyatt Lamar.

IT WAS WELL PAST EIGHT when Margo wobbled out of the courthouse that evening. For weeks she'd been living on little else besides caffeine and nerves, but the exhaustion was worth it. This was the first time in her career that the District Attorney, Robert Thomasson, had handed her a real assignment—not just research, not the kind of grunt work case most lawyers tried to avoid like the plague. Beginning in two weeks she was going to present the bulk of the physical evidence against one of the most notorious crime bosses in the city.

The Garcetti gangland murder trial was a make-or-break moment of her career, a gig that perfectly suited her vision of herself as a crusading public defender. If she was lucky and did the more-than-competent job she knew she was capable of, it might also mean that her main rival in the assistant D.A.'s office, a smug little jerk named Barry Leiberman, would stop nipping at her heels all the time. If nothing else, a good showing would be a chance for her parents, who had sacrificed so much for her, to see that three expensive years in law school had finally paid off. The trial was going to be featured on Court TV.

Margo tried not to think too hard about that. Organizing the evidence and witnesses was already using up most of her gray matter; worrying about whether the camera would love her would be mind-boggling. Yet the idea that she was about to achieve her lifelong dream of really making her mark in the world put a self-satisfied spring in her step. Not much small-town, small-time veneer left on her! Finally, finally, she had gotten about as far away from her Tallulah roots as humanly possible.

She felt the slightest stab of guilt for bad-mouthing her hometown, even if it was just in her own head. Tallulah wasn't *that* bad...if your idea of a good time was grabbing an Icee at the local skating rink. But for some reason, Margo had been one of those people who'd grown up wanting more. She'd never found a soul mate in Tallulah, and she probably never would have if she'd stayed there till she was a hundred. Even her parents, who she loved to death, hadn't ever understood her need for adventure, for expanding her horizons. Even after seventeen years of living with her, they'd seemed almost

shocked when she'd applied to out-of-state colleges and
escaped to New York.

Where else? To her mind—which, naturally, had been
prejudiced by what she'd seen in movies—New York
was a fairy-tale place where the daughter of a laidoff
factory worker from Talullah, Ohio could start fresh and
with hard work make a rip-roaring success of her life.
And hadn't she proved herself right? Sure, she lived in
an apartment as big as her mother's pantry, and maybe
her job was a little too high-pressure. And, okay, maybe
she hadn't found her soul mate here, either…but that
didn't mean she wouldn't. In fact, in a town of eight
million, surely the odds were better than anywhere else
that she would find the perfect person for her.

A block away the subway stop globe glowed. The
downtown streets were fairly deserted at this time of
night, and a rain from earlier that evening—which, holed
up in the law library as she had been, she naturally
hadn't even noticed—lent the air a gritty humidity and
the streets and sidewalks an unnatural shine.

She couldn't wait to go to bed. Maybe she would fix
herself a hot cocoa when she got home, and soak in the
tub for a while. Really treat herself. With the trial so
close, who knew when she would have another almost-
entire evening to relax?

As she clipped through a puddle of light thrown by a
streetlight, she noticed a car coming her way. Not a cab.
Darn. Normally she tried to be frugal and take the subway, but as long as she was going to spend the rest of
the evening pampering herself, why not start now by
saving herself from a bone-rattling ride on the A train?

Beyond the closest set of headlights, she saw, mirac-
ulously, a yellow car coming her way—and its ceiling
lamp was lit to show it wasn't occupied. She stepped

into the street to hail it. Margo felt like whooping for joy, and might have, had it not been for that first car, nearest to her, which was going way too fast. In fact, it almost looked as if it were heading straight at her.

Margo froze. For a split second, she couldn't believe her eyes. The black sedan with tinted windows barrelled along at breakneck speed, careening recklessly down the slippery street. She couldn't have said why—she couldn't even see the driver of this out-of-control vehicle—but she suddenly felt as if she were the car's target. In fact, standing alone in the light on the deserted street, she was a regular sitting duck.

When the speeding car was no more than a hundred feet away, she knew her crazy instinct was right. Heart pounding, she turned on her heel and ran. But where could she go? There was no barrier around—no trees, no bus stop. Just as the car was coming at her heels, so close she could feel the drops of water kicked up by the tire's treads, she ducked to the side and ran behind a street mailbox.

To her horror, the car didn't stop. It collided with the mailbox, filling her ears with the sickening sound of metal scraping metal. Terrified, she sprang as far and as fast as she could, and half slipping she began dashing the rest of the way towards the subway stop. She expected to hear a car door open and footsteps running after her. Already, her life was passing before her eyes.

But about the time she reached third grade again, she came to a sudden realization. Behind her, tires squealed as the car peeled off down the street. No one had gotten out of the car. She was safe.

But for how long? She looked around in time to see the sedan turn the next corner. *Oh, Lord—what if it circled around the block to finish her off?*

She wasn't going to be here to find out! Skating across the slick sidewalk, she slid out into the middle of the street on shaky legs and waved her arms, purse, and briefcase frantically at the oncoming cab. If it didn't want to stop, it would just have to mow her down.

Thankfully, it did stop, and Margo wasted no time throwing the car door open and diving inside. The cabbie, a man in a turban, gaped in amazement at the red, white and blue mailbox that the car had crumpled like a tin can. "Crazy drivers! Crazy people!"

Amen to that, Margo thought feverishly. Who would try to run her over with a car? It had to be one of Garcetti or his men.

The cabbie stared into his rearview mirror at Margo, who was collapsed on the backseat, hyperventilating. "Where you go, lady?"

Her mind was a blank. She couldn't even recall her home address—not that it mattered. She was too freaked out to go back to her apartment alone. If someone was trying to get her, that would be the first place they would look.

She should go to the police...and tell them what? That she was *almost* run over by a car? New York cops would barely raise an eyebrow at that. Probably a drunk, they'd say. An accident, a coincidence. And maybe it was.

But she didn't think so.

Where else could she go? It wasn't likely that any of her friends would welcome putting her up for the night if goons in unmarked cars were after her. Maybe she should go to a hotel?

"Lady?" the cabbie repeated.

She sat up. And suddenly, an answer came to her. She needed to go someplace bright, where there were lots of people. Someplace where she couldn't imagine anything really bad happening to her. And where there would be a long, tall Texan with big muscles to protect her just in case anything bad did happen.

"Tavern on the Green," she instructed the cabbie.

2

"WOULD YOU LIKE to try some soup, Wyatt?" Mrs. Morrissey bestowed a motherly smile on Wyatt. Like her travelling companion Mrs. Walters, Mrs. Morrissey was sampling the soup of the day.

"No, thank you, ma'am."

Mrs. Walters patted the handle of his fork. Or was she Mrs. Morrissey? The two drama teachers from Iowa were practically identical, except that one had a blue rinse in her hair, and the other was a natural gray. But Wyatt wasn't positively certain which was which now. He was normally good with personal detail, but he'd been so distracted.

"You eat up, Wyatt. Goodness! A tall man like yourself must have to rack up a lot of calories just to keep himself going."

Wyatt nodded. "Back home at the Lonesome Swallow, it's awful easy to eat enough—more than enough most times."

"All that beef," Mrs. Walters guessed.

"Yes, ma'am."

The way the two ladies were focussing their gazes on him, he felt obligated to eat more of his dinner, a very elaborate crabmeat crepe with enough sauce for a whole shoal of crabs to swim in. His appreciative grunts brought beatific smiles from the ladies, but his heart wasn't in his meal.

He forced himself to smile back. In fact, he'd had the same friendly grin plastered on for so long now that he feared his face was going to crack. When he'd asked the two women to dine with him, he hadn't thought it would be awkward; he usually was able to gab pretty well with strangers. But he hadn't figured his mood into the equation. He kept thinking about Margo. Kept wishing that, somehow, those two ladies would turn themselves into Margo and he'd suddenly be having the dinner he'd dreamed about all day, with the woman he'd dreamed about all day.

He wondered what had happened to her.

But then again, he guessed he knew. What woman in her right mind would meet a complete stranger at a restaurant, on the basis of one sidewalk collision? Probably he should have been more worried about her if she *had* shown.

"Have you seen any Broadway plays since you've been in town?" Mrs. Walters asked politely.

"No, I haven't exactly had time." Between hunting down Mary Beth and getting over his disappointment over Mary Beth, he hadn't felt like taking in a play. And this was his last night in town. "I guess I might have gone tonight..." If it hadn't been for meeting Margo.

"Oh, no!" Mrs. Walters—he assumed she was Mrs. Walters— exclaimed. "Everything's dark tonight."

How fitting, Wyatt thought glumly. First Margo, and now another disaster. "You mean that there's some kind of blackout going on?" The restaurant seemed bright enough.

The ladies chuckled again. "No, no—that just means it's Monday night. There aren't any shows on Monday nights!"

"Oh." He took another bite, but found his appetite

lacking. He couldn't get Margo out of his head. Of course, he would have to, since he'd never see her again.

The strange thing was, he was seeing her—coming through the doorway of the huge dining room. He decided he must be going crazy. Why would Margo show up at all, much less nearly an hour late? Surely she didn't think he'd wait for her all that time.

But as he shook his head to clear it, he felt his heart leap in recognition. It was Margo! She looked exactly as he'd thought of her all day, only more limp and ragged, as if she'd really been through hell. She was wearing the same creamy beige suit she'd been wearing that afternoon, though it appeared splattered and even streaked with mud in one place. But the woman was still so beautiful she made his heart race. He pushed his chair back and shot to his feet so fast that the two ladies in front of him jumped in alarm.

Margo, who was being headed off by the *maître d',* saw Wyatt and made a beeline for the table, her progress hampered by her heavy briefcase and equally large pocketbook that was banging against tables, chairs, and even diners as she passed. Close up she looked disheveled, anxious—but very glad to see him. When their eyes met, a broad smile spread across her face.

"Hi!" she said, zipping right up to the table. "Sorry I'm a little late." It wasn't until she'd dumped her things on the floor that she suddenly noticed he had company. "Oh... I'm sorry, I didn't know..."

Wyatt jumped in to reassure her. "Margo, I'd like you to meet Irene Morrissey and Jane Walters. They're drama teachers from Iowa."

Margo still looked confused. "I thought you were from Texas," she told Wyatt.

"He is," one of the ladies explained. "We just met

Wyatt while we were here waiting for a table. He had a reservation, only it seemed that his date had stood him up and...oh dear.'' Her cheeks turned a bright pink.

"I'm sorry," Margo repeated, as she planted herself in the free chair. "I was, uh, unavoidably detained but I'm certainly glad you didn't wait. And that you found some company." As she reached over to retrieve her napkin, her hand nearly knocked her water glass over. "Oops!"

Wyatt sat down. Maybe he was just imagining that Margo was anxious. Heck, maybe she was just the high-strung nervous type. She'd seemed a little jumpy when they'd met that afternoon, too.

But even in her work clothes and stressed out from what must have been a bear of a day at work, she was still a sight for sore eyes. He drank in her blue eyes and shoulder-length chestnut hair and suddenly felt at peace with the world. Life didn't seem nearly so gloomy now. In fact, the whole place seemed brighter. All at once he noticed the visual splendor around him—the walls of open windows looking out on shrubs lit with colored lights, the burnished wood panelling and elaborate chandeliers. It was almost as if Margo's very reappearance had blinked him back to life.

"We saw *Phantom* last Friday. Now that's an excellent show!" Mrs. Morrissey was exclaiming to Margo.

Their waiter arrived at the table and, peering at Margo down the bridge of his nose, asked her if she would like anything for dinner. He apparently didn't approve of patrons arriving nearly an hour later than the rest of their party. Especially ones who were untidy with their water glasses and left big wet splotches on the tablecloths.

Margo shook her head. "No, no thanks. I think I'll just have coffee."

Mrs. Morrissey asked. "Would you like to have some

of my soup? Cream of mushroom—much better than Campbell's.''

Margo smiled. "Oh, no, I couldn't," she said, taking a deep gulp of water. Her hand shook a little as she raised the glass to her lips, making the ice cubes rattle melodically against the crystal. "I don't usually eat dinner, anyway, and tonight—" She shivered. "Well, I just couldn't eat a bite."

Her words, in Wyatt's world, were tantamount to blasphemy. He pushed his crepe over to her. "You've got to eat," he told her. Maybe it would get rid of that pinched nervous look on her face, and calm her nerves. She seemed awfully jittery. He picked up her fork and placed it in her hand. "Dig in."

She dutifully dunked her fork into the crepe and took a bite. Wyatt smiled. He knew he was being a mother hen, but he couldn't help himself. He liked to see folks eat.

"Do you like the theater, Margo?"

Margo swallowed. "Sure, I like it. My work doesn't leave me a lot of time for plays and other entertainment, though."

"What is it you do?" Wyatt asked.

Mrs. Morrissey and Walters looked at him quizzically. "Don't you two know each other?"

"Oh, no!" Margo exclaimed just before shovelling in a mouthful of crabmeat dripping with sauce.

"I just met Margo this afternoon," he explained.

"Oh…" The two women exchanged looks. "Oh dear, this is a little awkward… If you two would like us—"

"The more the merrier!" Margo said quickly, interrupting them. Her gaze darted nervously to the door. "And to answer your question, I'm an attorney. An assistant district attorney."

The ladies were duly impressed, as was Wyatt. No wonder she'd been in such an all-fired hurry to get downtown. She had a pressure-cooker job to get back to.

The ladies, though obviously finding her job interesting, were still stuck on the previous topic. Namely, the nature of Wyatt and Margo's relationship.

"Then this your first date?"

Wyatt didn't know how to answer. If he said yes, Margo might get a little defensive. She didn't seem to like that date word. Then again, saying no would be a lie, wouldn't it?

Margo saved him by barely looking up from the plate she was quickly devouring and answering vaguely, "We're just having dinner." She glanced around, suddenly noticing that she was the only one still eating. "Or at least, I am. I'm sorry." She smiled at Wyatt. "Were you still working on this?"

"You go right ahead," he told her. The more she ate, the more he liked her. "There doesn't appear to be a food shortage here."

The ladies chuckled, but they were still stuck on the date thing. "Are you sure you wouldn't like to be alone?"

Margo shrugged as she continued to empty her plate. For someone who'd claimed not to be hungry, she was sure packing it away. "It's no big deal. We just ran into each other this afternoon. You know how it is."

Wyatt grinned and said with a nonchalance he certainly didn't feel, "Just one of those love-at-first-sight type deals."

Margo's water glass was almost knocked over again.

Within ten minutes, the drama teachers were gone. As gone as Wyatt's crepes.

"That was veeeeery good," Margo pronounced, sitting back in her chair and taking a deep breath. "I'm stuffed!"

Wyatt grinned in triumph. Nothing pleased him more than hearing those words, and it was good to see Margo looking a little more relaxed. "How about dessert?"

If she went for the dessert, he really just might be in love.

"Oh, no, I couldn't," she said with a moan.

He thought for a moment. "Well then, I guess we could hit the street and walk somewhere."

Suddenly, her whole demeanor changed. Her blue eyes widened, her body tensed up, and her gaze darted around the restaurant in search of their waiter. She lifted her hand to flag him down. "On second thought, I've heard you can get an incredible crème brûlée here. I might have a few of those before we go!"

A few? Lord, she was so tiny, it would be a miracle of physics if she managed to choke down one, especially after that dinner she'd tucked away. But Wyatt was more than willing to oblige her in the attempt. "I'm in no hurry," he said, smiling.

She grinned back. "That's good."

They ordered dessert and as they sipped coffee, she asked, "So, Tex..."

"Wyatt," he reminded her.

"So...why are you in town? Surely you're not a drama teacher, too."

"No, I'm not. Actually, I came here to look up...well, an old friend."

Her face seemed to relax a little, and she grinned. "An old *girlfriend*, you mean?"

"How did you know?" Maybe that stuff about

women's intuition wasn't as much hooey as he'd always thought.

"Because of the pause," she pointed out. "You hesitated before you called her 'an old friend.' If she'd really been just an old friend, you would have referred to her as an old high school pal, or college buddy, or something more specific, more familiar. And you wouldn't have hesitated to admit it, would you?"

"Are you always this analytical when you make small talk?"

She smiled. "You're avoiding the question. It was a girlfriend, wasn't it?"

He nodded. He could see how Margo might be a good person to have in a courtroom. On your side. "She was my high-school sweetheart. Now she's living with a man in Queens."

"You didn't know? And you came all this way?"

He didn't want her to think he was a chump, or a rube. "I guess you can tell by now that I'm sort of impulsive. I just wanted to see her and find out what she thought about moving back to Armadillo Bend."

"Armadillo Bend!" Margo exclaimed. "What on earth is that?"

"It's the town I come from, in Texas." He smiled fondly. "It's quite a place."

Margo nearly choked on her crème brûlée. "I'll bet." Her tone oozed skepticism. "Haven't you heard that old chestnut about not being able to keep someone down on the farm after they've seen Paree?"

"Well, Paris, sure," Wyatt allowed. "But should the same hold true for Queens?"

She laughed.

"Don't you like small towns?"

"Heavens, no!"

That didn't bode well. "Have you ever lived in one?"

She lifted her head proudly. "I'm a New Yorker, through and through."

He sighed. Of course, it was her sophistication and self-assuredness that had first caught his eye. It seemed he'd been born with some congenital defect that doomed him to be attracted to a type of woman who was incompatible with Armadillo Bend.

"Armadillo Bend isn't a hot spot or a metropolis, but it's got loads of character, plus everything I want. The Lonesome Swallow Ranch, my old Gramps and a slew of other relatives, the house we Lamars have owned since 1902."

Margo took a sip of coffee and eyed him sharply. "But they don't have the girl you want."

"Woman," Wyatt corrected. "I might be from a small town, but I am a man of the nineties."

"You're avoiding my question again."

He smiled and admitted, "No, the woman I want doesn't seem to be there. Most females around those parts just think about leaving, and I guess I can't blame them. Aside from Bingo night at the senior citizen's center, there's not a heck of a lot of action in town. But the people are nice, and the land is one-of-a kind. There's an unhurried pace to life there that you just don't find many places anymore. And if you do crave more action, there are large towns nearby. Austin, Kerrville..."

Margo chortled. "I bet that's comforting!"

"Okay, so maybe Kerrville isn't much to boast about." He was beginning to feel a little silly. "You probably think I sound like I'm from the Chamber of Commerce."

Margo stared at him thoughtfully. "No, I think I get the picture. What you're telling me is that your ideal woman is some sophisticated city chick who can appreciate this hiccup on a road map that you call home.''

Wyatt nodded. "That's right.''

She barked out a laugh. "Good luck, cowboy!'' And she kept on laughing.

Wyatt ducked his head. Guess it did sound pretty improbable, at that. Wasn't Mary Beth living proof? "Of course, that's not *all* I'm looking for,'' he said in his own defense. "Intelligence, imagination, a good sense of humor.'' And it would be nice if that humor weren't all at his expense.

Margo tried to quiet her chuckles. "No offense, Wyatt, but I think you'd better go home and get yourself married to a nice female from Armadillo Heaven, or whatever you call it. Otherwise, you might waste your whole life just hunting for the perfect woman—like those nuts who spend their lifetimes searching for Bigfoot and the Loch Ness monster.''

Now she thought he was a nut. Wyatt sighed. Maybe he *was* nuts. Because deep inside, he had the gut feeling that he already had discovered his elusive prize; but he doubted Margo would care to be informed that she was his Bigfoot.

He flagged the waiter down for the check. Margo looked jumpy as he pulled out his credit card and adamantly refused all her offers to help pay.

"But you never finished dessert, or even your coffee.''

She didn't seem to want to leave. Taking that as a good sign, he ended up swallowing down the remains in his cup while Margo scarfed down the rest of his crème brûlée. She looked like an angel and ate like a trucker, which made her even closer to being his dream woman than he cared to admit.

Finally, however, there was no more food and nowhere to go but out. Margo seemed strangely hesitant to hit the streets. In fact, once they were out on Central Park West, she took on that jittery, anxious look again, the one she'd had when she first entered the restaurant. He'd hoped all that food had taken the edge off her nerves. Apparently not.

"Would you like—" Wyatt looked around and noticed he'd lost Margo. Then he turned full circle, and found her directly behind him. "Would you like me to take you home?"

She jumped. "Home?"

He moved a hand to her arm to calm her, but his quick movement only seemed to scare the living daylights out of her. "I'm sorry, I didn't mean to startle you."

"Oh, no!" she exclaimed, her voice a squeak. "Home, did you say? Isn't it rather early to be going home?"

He didn't want to part company with Margo...then again, he didn't know exactly what to do with her, either. "Well, it is past ten."

"Ten? That's nothing! This is the city that never sleeps!"

"The city might never sleep, but frankly you look like you could use a rest," he told her. "I assumed you had work tomorrow."

She pooh-poohed the very idea. "Why, I can do that old job with my eyes closed. By all means, it's your last night in the Big Apple—let's go somewhere. Quick."

He squinted at her, not quite understanding where all this sudden gaiety and energy was coming from. Maybe he just wasn't used to the frenetic tempo of life that people in New York took for granted. He began to acclimate, however, as they jogged toward Columbus Avenue.

When they reached the bustling thoroughfare, he was winded and Margo looked like she was just warming up. ''Mind if we take a break? It's been a while since I've run a marathon.''

Margo laughed nervously. ''Sorry. I just thought you might want to see everything. There's Lincoln Center.''

He squinted towards where she was pointing and saw that, sure enough, two blocks away was the fountain and buildings familiar to him from years of flipping past public television.

''Well I'll be,'' he said, discovering that he had to twist around again to talk to her. Funny, this afternoon he hadn't noticed her unnerving habit of standing almost behind a person. ''Is something wrong, Margo?''

''No, goodness, no! Now where would you like to go?'' Her gaze darted to inspect the faces of the people who passed them on the sidewalk.

''Well, I always sort of wanted to...'' Wyatt stopped, suddenly realizing that he was talking to himself. Where had Margo gotten herself off to this time? He turned and caught sight of her down the street at a sidewalk stand, trying on scarves.

He strolled over to her. ''Maybe next time you might warn me before you decide to go maverick.''

''Sorry.'' She held out both a scarf and a floppy wool hat to the stand owner and coughed up the amount of money he named for both. Then she quickly donned her new woolens. ''Do I look funny?''

''Well...'' Actually, the hat-scarf combination brought to mind something his Aunt Eulalie might have concocted, but somehow he didn't think Margo would appreciate his comparing her to an eighty-year-old woman who'd never stepped foot inside a department store.

She guessed anyway. "I look like a bag lady, don't I?"

He laughed. "Do bag ladies carry briefcases?"

"In this town, it wouldn't surprise me one bit," Margo said, but kept her new purchases on. "Let's get a cab."

Wyatt was just ambling over to the sidewalk to hail a taxi when he noticed that Margo had already jumped into the middle of the street, flagged one down, and was opening the door. "C'mon," she said, beckoning impatiently.

He followed her into the vehicle's backseat.

"Where to?" asked the driver, though Wyatt noticed that not knowing where he was going hadn't kept the driver from roaring down the avenue already.

"Where to?" Margo asked Wyatt. "This is your night. Live it up."

He smiled. "There is something I've always wanted to do...but I never dreamed I'd be lucky enough to have a female companion to do it with."

Margo shot him a nervous glance. "Oh, wait a second..."

Smiling, he leaned forward to the clear partition between the front and back seats. "South Ferry," he told the driver.

AT FIRST MARGO had thought a ride on the Staten Island Ferry would be an excellent way to kill time and avoid going back to her apartment. Now she had doubts. Every movement she caught out of the corner of her eye she was positive was her would-be assassin. And she was trapped. The only way off the boat was a swan dive into New York Harbor.

"Are you anxious about something?"

Margo jumped.

"There you go again," Wyatt drawled. "Acting like you swallowed a bedspring."

She swung around, almost bumping him. "Huh?"

"Means you're jumpy."

"Oh!" Sometimes, it seemed the man spoke a different language entirely. "No, I'm fine."

Wyatt crossed his arms. The cold wind off the ocean seemed to wrap its frigid arms around the boat. "Maybe we should go to the lower level, where it's covered and heated."

She shook her head. Though her teeth were chattering, she preferred being out in the open to being trapped in the lower decks. From here, at least she could make that swan dive if worst came to worst.

"Don't you think it's prettier up here?"

They were approaching the Statue of Liberty, which was lit up spectacularly against the night. The statue who had greeted millions of immigrants and even more tourists was more impressive than it looked in pictures or even in the movies. Margo wondered fleetingly why she'd never come out here before.

Maybe because it was so darn cold.

"The view's a lulu," Wyatt said, taking in the landmark with awe. "I'm just worried about you. You keep looking over your shoulder."

After he'd bought her dinner and had been so nice to her, Margo didn't have the heart to tell Wyatt that the main reason she'd sought out his company was that she was scared stiff that there might be someone trying to kill her. Of course, that fact might make Wyatt a little nervous, too, if he had any sense.

Sometimes Margo wondered if he did. Talking to saleswomen, buying drama teachers dinner at Tavern on the Green, taking women he barely knew on romantic moonlit trips on the Staten Island Ferry... What kind of man did these things? No one she'd ever known. She wasn't certain whether Wyatt was a truly one-of-a-kind wonderful guy or some kind of kook.

One thing she didn't have to wonder about was her response to him. The man was unbelievably good-looking. And it wasn't just his height and sturdiness that made her think so—although she felt well protected when he was around. Calmer, though at this point in the day, calm was a relative term. There was something appealingly charming about Wyatt. With his movie-star smile, and those very sincere puppy-dog eyes, the man probably had to beat away the women in that town of his with a stick.

"I'm just not used to going out on ferryboats with strange men." She wasn't used to having people attempt to mow her down in unmarked cars, either—but she left the thought unsaid. She was trying to banish the incident from her mind, after all.

Yeah, right! Just forget about almost being killed.

Although, if anything could make her forget that somewhere in the city there was a hit man after her, it would be Wyatt's liquid brown eyes.

"It's not something I do every day, either."

"What do you do every day?" Margo still didn't know, which was understandable. She'd been rather preoccupied this evening.

"Oh, I've got a place called the Lonesome Swallow," he said. "It's been in the family for a long time."

She nodded, and as she pictured him sitting proud atop a horse, doing whatever it was cowboys did, a thought occurred to her. Maybe in Texas, Wyatts weren't so rare. Maybe the whole state was full of guys like him. She looked up at his strong jaw and felt something flutter deep inside her. For all his aw-shucksness, the man was surprisingly sensual. Funny, she'd never gone for the Boy Scout type. But with the mob on her tail, a six-foot-plus Boy Scout seemed like a good thing to have around. "Do you know anything about guns?"

This time, he looked startled. "Why?"

"Just curious... I guess I just think of every man in Texas coming out of the womb with rifle in hand."

He chuckled, a sound that seemed to rumble even in her own chest. Meanwhile, the boat chugged toward Staten Island.

"I guess that's not far from the truth," Wyatt admitted. "I'm not big on hunting, but I have a heap of relatives who are. Uncle Roscoe's a collector."

"You mentioned a grandfather," she said, not feeling the usual strain of making small talk with a stranger. Wyatt was an easy person to talk to. "He's still alive?"

He nodded, laughing. "Gramps is immortal. As long as the Lonesome Swallow makes money, he'll want to be there to do the books. Product of the Depression."

She laughed. "He sounds interesting."

"Actually, most days he makes my life a misery." There was a smile on Wyatt's face. "He'd make yours one, too. Gramps has a thing against lawyers."

"Him and everyone else in the world," she moaned.

"Trouble is, he hates lawyers but can't stop watching that channel...you know, the one that shows all the court cases."

Her heartbeat picked up. "Court TV?" She thought

about telling him that she was about to be on Court TV, but she didn't want to brag. Plus, the way things were going she wasn't certain she'd live long enough to make her television debut.

"That's the one. Gramps is a character." Wyatt shook his head. "The Lonesome Swallow wouldn't be home without him."

The love in his voice when he spoke of his ranch made her go all dewy-eyed with nostalgia...and she'd never even seen the place. "It must be great to like your home that much," she said wistfully. As if she could ever feel wistful about Smalltown, USA! Of course, right now she felt a yearning to be anyplace where there weren't mobsters lurking behind every street sign.

"Don't you like New York?"

"I love it," she said emphatically, then added, "I really love it when I see it in movies."

He nodded. "Well, I guess every place seems better at some times than others."

"Except Armadillo Bend," she joked. "You seem to think your hometown's perfect all the time."

He looked at her, his face serious. "You really ought to see Armadillo Bend someday, Margo."

She laughed. "I don't get down to Texas very often."

"Well, I'm telling you here and now, you've got a standing invitation to come to the Lonesome Swallow."

She couldn't imagine a reason on earth why she would ever take him up on his offer, but all the same was touched at his making it. "You don't even know me, Wyatt."

He smiled that warm smile of his at her, the one that made her heart flutter and her toes curl. She'd never known a man who could affect her so with just a twitch of the lips. But then, she'd never met anyone on earth quite like Wyatt. He made her feel warm inside, and a little anxious.

"Say...that love at first sight business—that was just a gag, right? You didn't really mean it." No one really believed in hokey stuff like that anymore.

Did they?

Wyatt cleared his throat. "This might sound a little crazy to you, Margo, but ever since we first bumped into each other, I felt drawn to you. Like..."

"Like a magnet?" She folded her arms and eyed him skeptically, fighting the puddle of mush his words were threatening to turn her into.

"That's right, like a magnet." He thought for a moment, as if it were of the utmost importance that he describe the experience in just the right words. "Or, actually, like something stronger—as if there was an energy connecting our lives, like the tug of the Earth on the moon. Far apart, nothing alike, and yet destined to move together."

No man had ever tried to seduce her with cosmic alignment analogies! And yet, corny as it was, it was working on her. A little. Maybe it was the setting—the movement of the boat, the dazzling Manhattan skyline as a backdrop... Or perhaps it was just the fact that she was a nervous wreck, and so desperately needed this knight in shining Stetson. When Wyatt bent to kiss her, she didn't make a move to stop him. In fact, she stood on tiptoe to meet him halfway.

She didn't regret it, either. The moment their lips touched, she felt transported. Like the man himself, his lips were warm and giving, strong and tender. There were no groper tactics at work here, though she could feel the coiled strength of his lean body in the sinewy muscles of his arms and shoulders. Her body seemed to melt into his, seeking its protection, seeking comfort, seeking to find out whether he was right, and there was something magnetic and special between them.

Lost in the sensual world of his kiss, it certainly seemed that there was. Revelling in the feel of him she lost all track of time. He was so solid, so male. They might be standing on the Staten Island Ferry, but her senses were swept away to another realm entirely, where men smelled of whiskey and old worn leather, where ravishings were an everyday occurrence. She'd always dreamed of being kissed by a cowboy, and Wyatt didn't disappoint her fantasies of what a long, tall Texan's lips could do to a woman.

God knows her heart was stampeding like something off an old episode of *Rawhide*. Warmth pooled in her middle and she wrapped herself just a little more tightly around him. She sensed that they needed to stop, that if she didn't put an end to this she might be the one doing the ravishing. And yet she couldn't force herself to be sensible when so many wondrous feelings were swirling in her. Closeness. Sensuality. Safety.

When he pulled away from her, Margo didn't know if they had been kissing for five seconds, or for five trips to Staten Island and back, but she immediately wanted to step right back into his arms.

"We're almost to Manhattan again," he said, regret in his tone. "I guess I'll have to take you home now."

Just the thought of going back to her empty apartment made her boneless body go rigid. "Home?"

"Where else would you like to go?"

She looked into his eyes and it didn't take her more than a second to come up with the answer. Those eyes were like pools of calm in a churning sea of chaos. "How about your place?"

3

WYATT KNEW THINGS WORKED faster in the big city, but he hadn't expected this!

He tried to keep his voice steady. "My hotel?"

Margo nodded. "Do you mind?"

Mind? He would have to be out of his mind to mind! At first he'd just thought that Margo was his ideal type—beautiful, confident, sophisticated. But the more he got to know her, the more beautiful she was to him. And stranger still, she seemed completely unaware of that fact. She didn't overdo her makeup, or dress to calculate seduction. In fact, her fashion sense almost went against the grain—like that scarf-hat combination she'd picked out. Yikes! Yet it was strangely endearing. And her brashness, he could tell now, hid a striking vulnerability that brought out all of his protective instincts. As for her sophistication... Well, she was worldly, and funny, and wry. He liked a woman who could make him laugh at himself.

Mind? Heck, here he'd been, sad that this was his last night in New York, thinking it was probably his last fifteen minutes with Margo...and now this!

"I'll admit to being astounded, but I certainly don't mind."

She smiled up at him and took his arm. "Good. Let's go." They disembarked from the ferry and, at Margo's pace, did the hundred yard dash to the street to catch another taxi.

"The Grammercy Park Hotel," Wyatt told the driver.

It wasn't far, but to Wyatt, the cab ride seemed to take hours. He felt strange escorting a woman to his hotel room—a woman who he didn't even feel comfortable scooting over next to. Of course, between Margo's purse and that huge briefcase of hers, it wasn't really physically possible to snuggle. But if he didn't feel right putting his arm around her in the backseat of the taxi, what was he going to do once he got her up to his room?

The obvious answer came to him, and he felt as if someone had punched him in the stomach. Land's sakes! He hadn't blushed since he was a kid, but Lord help him, just thinking of Margo and that body of hers made him tense. As anxious as he'd been his first time. Thank goodness it was dark in that cab.

They got out at the hotel and started up to his room. All during the silent elevator ride, however, his doubts multiplied. In fact, the closer they drew to his floor, then his room, all the while not speaking, not even making eye contact, the more anxious he became. This just wasn't right. He'd never had a fling before. Oh, he'd had his share of girlfriends, some of them quite serious—he and Mary Beth had been off and on for fifteen years. But never in his life had he taken a woman he'd known for less than a day up to a hotel room for the express purpose of making love to her when he knew full well he might never see her again. He was returning to Texas tomorrow!

Yet he just couldn't find the words to put the brakes on the situation. And if he did find them, he didn't know if he could make himself speak them.

He put the key into his door and opened it. His room wasn't much—just a double bed, TV, nightstand and bureau—but as Margo stood in the center of it and turned, taking in the faded yellow decor, she looked as impressed as if she'd just entered a room at the Plaza.

"Not bad!" She dropped her things, sank onto the bed, and bounced. "Mmm...a soft mattress. That's good."

Wyatt stood frozen, gasping for air. Margo on his bed was causing his hormones to hit warp speed. He searched quickly for a distraction. "I, uh, think I'll...brush my teeth. You just make yourself at home."

She smiled at him—a sweet, tired, teasing smile that nearly made him leap onto the bed and make love to her then and there.

He fled into the bathroom, picked up his toothbrush, and began to brush. And brush, and brush. What the heck was he doing? Here he'd found his ideal woman, and he was just going to have a *fling* with her? It seemed so insubstantial! Like sitting down in front of one of his Aunt Clara Mae's homemade peach cobblers and only having one itty bitty piece. It would be unsatisfying, leave you craving more. And given the fact that Margo lived in New York City and he lived in Armadillo Bend, what more could there be?

The trouble was, he was already half in love with the woman. Given his druthers, he wouldn't just want a roll in the hay with her. That wasn't his way, and besides, Margo deserved more of a courtship. Maybe she was used to slick guys who were fast operators, but he wished he had the time to show her how nice it could be another way, to actually go on a few dates, get to know each other. To kiss, and dance, and kiss some more, and then, after they absolutely couldn't imagine not making love, to take her to bed with him for about a week or so.

But the fact of the matter was, there was a delectable woman out there on his bed, and how the hell was he going to resist that temptation?

Quickly, he jabbed his toothbrush into the holder, splashed cold water on his face, and gathered his courage to face Margo and tell her that, no matter how much he wanted to in this particular situation, he just didn't do one-night stands. It just didn't feel right.

When he opened the door, however, and saw Margo sprawled across the bed, her beautiful silky hair loose and flowing around her pillow, her jacket off, her skirt riding up her thighs and her blouse revealing more than a hint of cleavage, he decided that it did feel right. So damn right that he groaned at how much he wanted her. All that dating and dancing and getting-to-know-her business flew right out of his mind. All he wanted to know was how it would feel to have those shapely legs of hers wrapped around his body when they made love.

There was only one hitch. Margo was asleep.

He could tell by the way she appeared to have fallen in her traces that she was out like a light. And he just didn't have the heart to wake her. He didn't even want to creep up on the bed, for fear of rousing her. She was so completely sprawled across the thing anyway, it wasn't as if there was a lot of room for him on there. Double beds, for Wyatt, always seemed aptly named— he practically had to double up to fit in the darn things.

Instead of bothering Margo, he sneaked a pillow off the bed, grabbed the extra blanket from the closet, and stretched out on the carpeted floor. He was reminded of the stories his Gramps used to tell him, about early days before the Lonesome Swallow went bust, and cowboys riding herd used to sleep out under the stars. Gramps always said having only the hard ground for a mattress was mighty uncomfortable.

But here he was in New York, not the prairie; and it wasn't the ground making him uncomfortable so much as the thought of Margo just an arm's length away.

MARGO WOKE WITH A START. Where was she?

Just before she'd jolted upright in the strange bed, she'd dreamed she'd been standing on the sidewalk in front of work again, with that car coming at her. Only this time, when she'd tried to move, her legs had felt like lead.

They didn't feel like lead now, though, as she swung them over the side of the bed and jammed her feet into her mud-splattered pumps. The clock said eight-thirty—she was already late for work! And not only that, she was still in her dirty clothes from yesterday, frazzled, and not at all certain how she would present what had happened last night to her boss. Should she demand protection? Or brush the incident off as nothing?

She would have to think about it on the trip downtown. She jumped up and took a glimpse of herself in the mirror. Her mouth involuntarily dropped open. She looked like lunch meat. Though her hair was still askew from being stuffed in that silly hat, then slept on and not styled, she could safely say that it was going to be much more than a bad hair day. It was a bad everything day.

She snatched her purse and briefcase off the floor and went skittering towards the door—then screeched to a stop, remembering. *Tex!* Where was he?

She glanced around the room and craned to see into the bathroom. "Wyatt?"

No answer. Had he gone out for a paper or something?

If her brief acquaintance with the man were any indication, he could be anywhere. Knowing him, he might have decided to stroll to New Jersey before breakfast. He'd probably made five new friends already.

Still… She hated just to run out on him. Sighing, she fished through her purse for a pen and went over to the bureau, where there was a piece of hotel stationery. For a moment, she considered what to write. Should she give him her full name? Her address? Remembering his gorgeous brown eyes and that toe-curling kiss on the ferry, she was tempted. She didn't meet very many men who fulfilled the qualifications of being both heart-poundingly sexy *and* nice. Besides, he was leaving today. And he'd been awfully kind to her.

For a moment, the small town Tallulah in her warred with big-city brusqueness. All her life she'd dreamed of finding a man who could be both white knight and friend, lover and champion, and she plain just didn't want to give the brush-off to a guy as handsome and sweet as Wyatt. Then again, exchanging personal information would be pointless. The man lived half a continent away, and there just wasn't a reason in the world why she should lead him on into thinking that she would ever be seriously interested in a man from Armadilloville. As if she hadn't spent half her life trying to escape from that kind of a moose trap!

Besides, she didn't have time for a long-distance romance. She had a life here. A busy career. She was going to be on Court TV, for heaven's sake!

She bent down and scribbled a quick goodbye note—trying not to think about the curiously glum feeling that weighed down her heart as she scrawled the words across the page.

Wyatt,
Thanks so much for an enjoyable evening. Sorry I
had to run.
     Happy trails!

                                        Margo.

WYATT READ MARGO'S NOTE for about the fiftieth time,
then finally crumpled it in his hand. Damn.

He'd gone out early this morning to buy gourmet coffee, those perfect New York bagels, and a paper, and
she'd disappeared. Just his luck. A romance done in by
his quest for better quality food. He should have just
made do with the hotel's room service, crummy as it
was. Or he should have scribbled a note before he'd
left—with strict instructions to write down her full name
and address if she had to leave.

He frowned, watching the dizzying parade of neigh-
borhoods fly by as the yellow cab raced towards the
airport. Of course, it was more than likely that her note
had purposefully given him all the information she cared
to provide. In which case, her message came through
loud and clear. She didn't want to have anything more
to do with him.

After Mary Beth he should have had more sense than
to go chasing after Margo, hoping the near-impossible
would happen in one single night. He shouldn't have
risked another love wound so soon.

Not that he *was* wounded. He hadn't been that carried
away. He'd just got his hopes up. Margo had bumped
into him on the rebound—just as he was bouncing off
the backboard, actually. That's what accounted for his
disappointment.

But instead of being disappointed, or bitter, he knew

he should try to take a lesson from this lost weekend.
The cost of a fare-saver ticket and a few nights in a hotel
wasn't a bad swap for a much-needed dose of reality.
After this weekend, he vowed to be more practical.
Hadn't Margo said it herself? She'd told him he should
settle down with a Armadillo Bend girl and forget about
city women, and he was about ready to take that advice.
The Lamar family was known for being down-to-earth
and adaptable, after all. When the Lonesome Swallow
Ranch had gone bust during the dustbowl, they'd transformed the whole outfit into the most popular restaurant
in the county.

Oh, sure. He could be practical. From this point on,
city women were a thing of his past. It was an Armadillo
Bend girl or bust. Which left him with one problem, but
it was a doozy.

There just weren't a whole heck of a lot of women in
Armadillo Bend to choose from.

THE BULLET MISSED HER by inches. One minute Margo
was hustling up the courthouse steps next to her boss,
D.A. Robert Thomasson, and the next, she heard a shot,
then was pushed to the concrete. Her heartbeat fired in
her ear like a jackhammer.

For days, she'd been on guard. Every car that came
toward her she was certain would be *that* car, the one
with her name on it. Every time she sat down at a restaurant, she requested a table far from the windows, remembering the method by which gangsters were sometimes gunned down in Little Italy. And whenever she
went home, she dashed into her building, double-
checked to make sure no one had followed her, locked
all three of the dead bolts on the new steel door she'd
had installed, and then cravenly peered into each closet

and beneath every piece of large furniture before allowing herself to relax.

But relaxation wasn't what it used to be. She hadn't felt calm since that day when she'd almost been killed and spent the night in the hotel room of that handsome Texan. For some reason, she considered the two events as being equally responsible for turning her life upside down. All during this frantic time, Wyatt Lamar had never been out of her mind. Thinking about the kiss they'd shared just added to the turbulence in her life. Oddly, she'd missed him—missed the warm way he looked at her, his insistent, reassuring presence, and his smile. Just thinking about him made her feel hollow inside, and shaky. She could have used his strong shoulder to lean on there on the courthouse steps.

Though no one was hurt, the mayhem caused by her unseen would-be assassin's bullet didn't die down before the six o'clock news. That night, every station reported that an attempt had been made on the life of the District Attorney, Robert Thomasson. And though Margo had told him about the car that had tried to run her over, Thomasson didn't refute their report that the bullet was aimed at him.

Margo wondered about that—especially since the police were never called in to question her about nearly getting run over. She felt almost as though her boss were attempting to make her invisible, or at least shrugging off her concerns for her safety.

Not until later that night, after all the local news reports had aired, did it occur to her that something else entirely might be going on. At a late conference of the attorneys on the Garcetti case, the D.A. put his feet up on the oblong mahogany conference table in his office, laced his fingers behind his head, and levelled his dark, hawk-sharp gaze on Margo.

"We need to get you out of town, lady," he announced. "I can't have someone trying to unnerve me by picking off my staff."

Margo was stunned. Never mind that he'd just told the press that the bullet had been aimed at himself. Unnerve him? How did he think it felt to be the one being picked off? "But I just can't leave," she said, glad at least that he wasn't shrugging off safety concerns anymore. "Can't we just arrange for some protection till the trial's over?"

He shook his head. "I care too much about my staff to let them risk their lives."

Nice speech, but she wasn't buying it. In fact, as she stared at the sharp planes of his face, and remembered his brave performance on the nightly news, a possible reason for her boss's getting rid of her popped into her head. The whole world was looking at him as the brave D.A. standing up against mobster assassins out to get him. Maybe what Bob Thomasson didn't want to risk was someone killing her and taking the spotlight off him.

Margo had no intention of getting killed, naturally. But neither was she going to turn tail and run. "Look, Bob, I'll admit I'm worried, too," she said, playing along with the fiction that he actually gave a hoot about what happened to her. "But I just can't leave town now, not with the case next week."

"I'm taking you off the case."

Margo's jaw nearly hit the mahogany table, and for a moment she gasped for air. *Off the case.* She could have sworn he'd said that she was being taken off the case. It was like someone telling her that she was about to be deprived of oxygen. In fact, she felt light-headed. "I beg your pardon?"

"Leiberman can present the forensic evidence at the Garcetti trial."

Margo looked from the D.A. to Barry Leiberman, her fresh-out-of-Harvard rival, and felt her blood begin to boil. Barry, whose lips were turned down in a concerned, sympathetic frown, nevertheless managed to look smug beyond belief. Coincidentally—or maybe not so coincidentally—the two men with their slicked-back hair and their sharp, dark gazes, were practically Twinkies. She should have known Barry would buddy up to the boss. She wondered whether he hadn't come up with the idea of getting her out of town and whispered it into the great man's ear.

"But that doesn't make any sense," she pleaded on her own behalf. "Even if you send me away, what if the mob goes after Barry? You can't let yourself be intimidated into taking everyone off the case."

Immediately, she knew she'd made a key strategic error. Telling the District Attorney, or even insinuating, that he was allowing himself to be intimidated was not the wisest move. "No one has gone after Barry so far," he said coldly. "Just you. So as of tomorrow, I'm giving you leave to pay a visit to your family in Toledo."

"Tallulah?" She nearly shrieked at the injustice of it. Here she was on the verge of being a key player in putting the city's most notorious, ruthless crime boss behind bars, and he wanted to send her back to Tallulah? The injustice of it—the indignity! All her hard work, the sleep-deprived months...all down the drain. Instead of her parents being proud of her, they would only see that she had gotten herself into some sort of muddle. A very dangerous, mob-related muddle.

Which was another problem. She couldn't go home if there was a killer after her! Granted, the danger would probably end the moment she was taken off the case and left New York, but she couldn't be one hundred percent positive of that fact. She knew too much. And she wasn't about to risk putting her parents' lives in danger. "I can't go back to Ohio!"

"Fine. Take a vacation. Go anywhere—Puerto Rico's nice this time of year."

Margo gaped at him, flabbergasted. Was he insane? Her skyrocketing career was going down in flames, and he was telling her Puerto Rico? Was she supposed to lie on the beach while lazy, slimy Barry stole her thunder? Barry didn't know the first thing about the evidence against Garcetti. He'd been sweating over a meter maid corruption case!

"I don't want a vacation," she insisted. "I want to present this evidence, Bob. I've been working my tail off for months. I know the case inside and out. If you take me off now..."

Glare was too kind a word for the look her boss shot her. His arms were folded across his chest, his lips were turned down sourly. Margo didn't finish her sentence. She didn't say the words *you'll jeopardize the case.* But he guessed them. Oh, boy, could she tell he guessed them!

Nice going, Margo.

His thin upper lip twitched angrily. "Hand your files over to Barry tonight," he instructed her, as Barry smirked happily. "Then call the travel agent and book your flight. Keep an expense account. And Margo?" He lifted one of his sharply delineated dark brows at her.

She gritted her teeth. "Yes, sir?"

His lips flattened into a humorless smile. "Bon voyage."

THREE LONG YEARS she had sweated through New York Law School, the toughest in the state, in preparation for her career. When she'd landed her job in the D.A.'s office, she'd thought she was well on her way to achieving her dream of carving out a name for herself, and making a difference in the world. Now her dreams were being ripped out from under her.

Barry Leiberman! Taking her place on Court TV!

Fuming, she returned to the broom-closet-sized room she worked in and proceeded to gather her Garcetti files. She felt angry and sad and helpless, like a kid being forced to hand a pet over to an animal shelter. Who knew what would become of her baby. Was she going to have to watch Barry bungle all her hard work?

She carefully culled manila folders, each laboriously categorized. One, containing documents submitted by the DNA specialist who had gone over the blood evidence, she couldn't find. She proceeded to search her whole office for the missing file, but it wasn't there.

She frowned, trying to remember. She'd had it just that afternoon, was carrying it...during the shooting...

Her mind flicked through the events prior to and after the shooting. In the heat of panic, she'd dropped the things in her hands, but had gathered them quickly afterwards. The only person she remembered being near her in that short expanse of time was Bob Thomasson.

A cold shiver ran up her spine. This was weird! But maybe Bob had it in his office. She went down the empty hall and searched through his darkened office, but didn't discover the file there. Nor was it anywhere else in the building that she looked. Margo began to feel a little more frantic. The documents from the DNA specialist were essential—they could make or break the case. Who could have taken them?

Again and again, her mind returned to her boss. But why would Bob Thomasson take her file? Why?

She remembered his ho-hum reaction to her near-death by speeding car, and then his public assumption that the bullet this afternoon had been aimed at him. Could it be that her boss was shrugging off these attempts on her life because he didn't want them stopped? Was her boss trying to get rid of her?

Nonsense, of course. She was just being overly emotional, surely.

Then she remembered. He had gotten rid of her!

Margo paled, as a dread realization began to creep up on her. Bob was getting her out of town, putting the near-incompetent Barry Leiberman in her place, and even before she left, key evidence was disappearing. Could Bob be on the take from the mob? Could the D.A. himself be attempting to undermine the Garcetti trial?

Heart thumping, she made one very clear decision. She needed to get out of that building! Quickly, she stuffed everything she possibly could into her briefcase, purse, even her gym bag that had been gathering dust in the corner of her office for three months. She loaded herself down with every one of the most useful files she could find on the Garcetti case and ran out the door before she could absorb the extent of her folly. Maybe that gunfire had rattled her brain. What she was doing was unprofessional, unethical, and quite possibly illegal.

Or maybe it was salvaging a case in jeopardy from within the D.A.'s office.

When she arrived home, she dashed up the stairs to her apartment. She had to move fast. As soon as they realized that she had left without giving the files to Barry, and worse, had taken the files she was supposed to have handed over to him, they would track her down.

She had to hide out long enough to devise a plan. If nothing else, if she stayed hidden for a week, she could make certain Barry wouldn't have enough time to review her files before the trial; that way, maybe Bob would be forced to allow her to present the evidence, or risk looking incompetent. If she could just make it into that courtroom, she was certain she could win that case, even with Robert Thomasson trying to sabotage it.

She could hide out in a hotel. She thought of the Grammercy Park—Wyatt's hotel. If she used a fake name, and changed her appearance a little bit, perhaps no one would be able to find her. She pushed her key into the door, prepared to fly around the apartment throwing a few necessities into a suitcase, when suddenly she was stopped cold.

She hadn't had to turn her key to push the door open. And her apartment looked like a hurricane had gone through it. Someone had turned over every piece of furniture. The couch had slashes in it, and pieces of foam stuffing blanketed the floor like yellow snow. Every single drawer, from her lingerie drawer in her bedroom right down to the utensil drawer in the kitchen, had been pulled out and upended, the contents spilled and scattered.

Slowly, from the marrow of her bones, she began to quiver, until her whole body was shaking. She'd never felt so violated. Not taking a moment longer to think, she skittered through the apartment, snatching up items willy-nilly—a bra, several shirts, old sneakers—giving no thought to whether they matched or would be useful. She stuffed them into her gym bag along with the files, turned, and ran back out of her apartment. She didn't want to stick around the place even long enough to call the police. Not if Garcetti's men might be sticking around, too.

She flew down the stairs and hit the sidewalk running, and didn't stop until she reached the corner of Amsterdam Avenue. Then she hailed a cab and jumped in. She was still shaking.

Where to go? The police station—with her hot files and her wild story about the D.A.'s ties to the mob? To the FBI, who would immediately contact the D.A.? Even the Grammercy Park Hotel didn't seem as safe as it had. Nothing seemed safe, here in New York.

"Where to, lady?" the driver asked.

Good lord, she didn't even know if she had enough cash on her to pay the cab fare, much less rent a room anywhere! She would have to stop at an ATM. She reached into her pocketbook and pulled out her billfold, tugging at her plastic cards with shaking hands. Bank cards, library cards, ID cards and even business cards were all so tightly embedded in the little billfold slits that she couldn't dislodge any of them.

"Lady?" the driver repeated impatiently. "Where to?"

Finally, she tugged at about five at once, sending all of them flying around the backseat.

"Omigosh!" she cried, ducking down to retrieve the cards from the floor. She grabbed up several, then noticed a business card in the seat next to her. She picked it up and recognized it at once. On one side was written the number of the Grammercy Park Hotel. On the other was engraved the name Wyatt E. Lamar, along with address and phone number for the Lonesome Swallow Ranch in Armadillo Bend, Texas.

Wyatt E. Lamar... A week ago she would have shuddered at the idea of what that E stood for. Now she took comfort in the strong, Western lawman ring of it. She clutched the card in her hand and for a moment felt a wave of calm hit her. And clarity. Why should she risk getting gunned down by the mob here when there was no reason that she should stay in New York—and good reason that she should get far, far away from it. Say, as far as...

"Texas," she said aloud.

The driver turned and shot her an exasperated look. "Look, lady, if you want to tell jokes I'll take you to Caroline's Comedy Club. Otherwise, give me a break."

She shook her head. "I meant, LaGuardia Airport, please."

4

"GRAMPS, WHAT WOULD you think about adding crème brûlée to the menu?" Wyatt asked, glancing over at him.

Gramps was perched atop his customary stool by the bar. "I'd think no one should ever go to New York City. It puts all sorts of cockamamie ideas in their heads!" he said shaking his silver-haired head in disgust.

Tuesday nights were generally slow at the Lonesome Swallow Ranch, the restaurant Wyatt's grandfather had started during the Depression when the actual ranch went broke. At first the restaurant had done little better than a soup kitchen, and through some lean years had barely managed to hang on, but in the past decade, under Wyatt's stewardship, when it seemed no one had time to cook in their own kitchens anymore, people flocked to the Lonesome Swallow for the down-home fare they'd been serving up for sixty years—meat and potatoes, soup, corn bread, biscuits and any kind of vegetable in season. Mention of an out-of-season vegetable—a tomato in January, say—would send Gramps on a tirade.

It was beginning to look as if crème brûlée would have the same effect on him. "Listen, son," he said, "you just need to get that place and that woman out of your head. I never did like Mary Beth, but I was all for you givin' a stab at dragging her back to Armadillo Bend if you could. Heck, why not at least try?

"But now you tried, and the woman wouldn't be

dragged back, and there's no sense trying to drag back crème brûlée instead. Our customers don't want it and cookin' it will probably just remind you of New York and that woman and make you gloomy all over again. Best to let the whole thing go.''

Seeing his grandfather, who looked like a stooped slightly shrivelled version of Wyatt, gazing eagle-eyed at him, he looked away in discomfort. Big mistake. Half the wait staff, including Stacy Stewart, a blond waitress Wyatt was mostly certain had a crush on him, were standing around listening to his grandfather's rant. Not that Wyatt's private life was any secret around the Lonesome Swallow. Gossip travelled at the speed of light around these four old ranch house rooms, and he was certain everyone already knew that his gambit to fetch Mary Beth had failed miserably.

What they didn't know was that he'd gone to New York City to fetch one woman and had come back pining after another. *Margo.* Just thinking the name made him sigh.

Gramps tapped his fingers impatiently against the old cigar box that still served as the restaurant's cash register. Then he leaned in and told Wyatt, a little more quietly, ''What you need to do is set your sights on another woman. Get that Mary Beth person clear out of your head. She's been lodged in there too long anyhow. It's not natural!''

This, coming from the man who had married his highschool sweetheart when he was eighteen and stayed married for forty-seven years and never looked at another woman since she'd passed away! But Wyatt didn't argue. How could he? Margo had already dislodged Mary Beth anyway.

But how was he going to dislodge Margo?

Beckoning him closer with a knobby finger, Gramps said confidentially, "If I were you, I'd ask Stacy out. She's been after you for five years."

Wyatt flicked a glance at Stacy, dawdling nearby. She nearly dropped a tray of chicken fried steaks when he caught her eye. She steadied herself and scurried away to one of the ten tables still occupied.

There were several problems with Stacy. Sure, she was pretty. Very pretty—though with her heavy makeup and blond-from-a-bottle hair, Wyatt couldn't really tell whether she was aiming to resemble Marilyn Monroe or Courtney Love. But looks weren't everything, especially since Stacy's personality could make a Tasmanian devil seem sweet in comparison. And even beyond personality, the real trouble was that she was the apple of Wyatt's best friend's eye.

"I couldn't ask her out, Gramps. Tom's been sweet on Stacy for years."

Tom was their second cook, and was probably runner-up to Jesus for nicest man who'd ever walked on the planet. His undying love for Stacy was a secret to no one but the woman herself; or perhaps she knew and just wasn't interested. Wyatt didn't understand that at all. Tom was handsome and hardworking, and even owned the house that his parents left him, which made him a pretty good catch for Armadillo Bend.

It was the curse of the small town, he supposed. Mix too few people with the normal percentage of stubborn hearts, and you ended up with a town chock-full of love disasters. The state of romantic affairs in Armadillo Bend was always pitiful, but it kept the tongues wagging down at the Chat-n-Curl, and the bar tabs high at the Long Neck downtown.

Wyatt crossed his arms. "Maybe I just wasn't meant to get married."

"Not meant to get married!" Gramps practically hooted, drawing surprised stares from diners and an especially startled one from Stacy, who was on her way back to the kitchen.

Wyatt winced. "Do you have to be so loud?"

"Do you have to be so lamebrained?" Gramps shot back. "What do you mean you aren't meant to be married? You think there's only one woman in the world for you?"

"I'm not sure." He remembered his Empire State Building revelation, when he realized that there was a whole world full of women he might be interested in. In the next moment, though, he'd met Margo. And now it seemed she was the only woman in the world he could possibly be interested in. He'd never even felt that strongly about Mary Beth, and they'd been on and off for fifteen years.

"Of course there's more than one! And what are you waitin' for?" His grandfather slapped the polished wood bar. "I don't know if you've realized this, but I'm gettin' a little old here. Be nice to know that my name and the business I worked so hard for all my life weren't going to come to a screechin' halt after I meet my reward."

Wyatt rolled his eyes. They'd had this conversation before, so he knew Gramps was serious. His own son had died in Vietnam in '72, and since then, Wyatt had been his sole hope to carry on his legacy. But he didn't want to talk about it. Mostly, he didn't want to even imagine what life at the Lonesome Swallow would be like without Gramps sitting at the bar, insulting people as they walked in the door.

"You've never been sick a day in your life," he pointed out.

Gramps thrust out his chin. "I didn't say I was meeting my maker tomorrow. I was just saying it might be nice to see you hitched before I go."

"You don't have to sell me on the idea—I don't want to be a bachelor forever. I want kids and grandkids and the whole bit. That's why I went to New York, if you'll recall."

"All right, so you went to New York! Now just think how nice it would be to have a girl who actually liked living in Armadillo Bend. Hell, she even works at your restaurant—that's potential free help, son. And she won't be flittin' away the next time the wind shifts."

Wyatt frowned. Hadn't Margo been telling him the same thing? Settle down with a nice Armadillo Bend girl, she'd advised. Brush-offs didn't come much more bald-faced than that!

At that moment, Stacy's husky laughter rang out from the other side of the room. She was lively, even if she did show occasional divalike bouts of temper.

"But what about Tom?" he said, agonizing.

Gramps looked fed up. "Let Tom tend to his own romancing. He hasn't been doing any better than you have! Maybe giving him some competition will light a fire under him."

"But that would still leave one of us out in the cold."

"This isn't mathematics, Wyatt. There isn't ever going to be a surefire way to check your homework and see if everything came out even. What's that expression you idiot kids are always tossing around? *Get real!*"

Wyatt clenched his jaw to bite back another sigh. Maybe Gramps was right. He just needed to take some kind of action. And maybe it would be good to have a witness as well. To that end, he called Stacy over. She arrived at his side in a split second.

"Yeah?" she asked, smacking a piece of gum against her molars.

Wyatt hesitated. All that blond hair! She seemed Technicolor bright to him all of a sudden. And energetic. And oh, lord, what on earth did they have in common? What would they talk about? All either of them knew was Armadillo Bend!

Gramps quietly tried to crawl off his stool.

"No, you stay right there," Wyatt instructed him, gathering his courage. "I want you to hear this."

Stacy's brows drew together, and her green eyes clouded in confusion. "Say, are you feeling all right?"

He didn't know how to answer that truthfully. Everything about this seemed wrong. In fact, he had a queasy feeling that he was making the worst mistake of his life, but maybe all men felt that way when they finally decided to find an appropriate woman to settle down with. Fifty years looking into Stacy's pretty green eyes first thing in the morning could hardly be called a fate worse than death, after all. She was competent, headstrong, and full of energy.

He'd need that energy, too, because right now he felt his own spirit being sucked right out of him. Really. It was as if his whole personality were seeping right out of the soles of his feet. But maybe that was just nerves. That's why he'd told Gramps to stay. With an onlooker, he couldn't back down.

He took a deep breath. "I was, uh, just wondering whether you'd like to go out sometime this week."

Stacy's face went blank, and her gum-smacking jaws fell silent. Wyatt wondered whether he and Gramps and everyone else hadn't misread the woman completely. As far as he knew, no one had produced a direct quote of her saying she liked him.

She blinked twice, and her mouth dropped open. "Wyatt, let me get this straight. *You* want to go out with *me?*" Her tone was laden with disbelief.

This wasn't getting any easier. He shifted his feet and nodded, beginning to feel like a first-class idiot. "If you're interested, sure."

"Interested?" Suddenly, her face broke out in one of her biggest, sunniest smiles. "*Interested?* What do *you* think?"

Right now he thought that if she'd refused him, he'd have a lot less to worry about. Tom, for one. He hadn't really wanted to horn in on another man's territory. And romances weren't so easy. They were a lot of pressure, especially in the beginning. You had to think of things to do, and remember to perform nice little duties like sending flowers, and you had all sorts of new dates to remember, like month anniversaries and birthdays and, oh, it just went on and on! He wasn't at all sure he was ready for this. No, not at all. But now he'd done it, there was no turning back. He couldn't uninvite her out.

Especially not with Gramps looking. Darn it.

He forced his lips into something resembling a smile. "How about Thursday?"

"Oh, great! That would be great! Thursday's my night off!"

"Yeah, I know that."

She laughed and slapped him on the arm. Hard. "'Course you do! You're the boss."

Wyatt rubbed the stinging spot on his arm. He didn't have the least idea what to say next.

"So...Thursday!" she said, beaming like a thousand-watt bulb. "Great!"

He nodded, backing out of her swinging range. "Well. Good." What more was he supposed to say? "I'll...uh, pick you up at your apartment. Say, seven-thirty."

"Great!" She was still planted in front of him.

Wyatt cleared his throat. "Well then." If she said great one more time, he might weep.

She didn't. Instead, she winked. "We'll have a lot of fun, Wyatt, you'll see."

He nodded, and was relieved when she finally turned and half walked, half skipped back to the table that held the glasses and the water pitcher. Wyatt felt low as a worm as he watched her practically dance around the room rehydrating the customers.

He turned back to Gramps. "Lordy, this is going to be a disaster!" the old man predicted gloomily.

Wyatt tossed up his hands. "I did just what you told me to!"

"Did you have to sound like you had a gun to your head?"

"If I did, it was you holding it," Wyatt said. He watched Stacy waltz through the batwing doors leading to the kitchen. High-pitched, excited voices drifted out, followed by the sound of a cast iron pan dropping to the floor.

"That would be Tom, finding out," Gramps guessed, his tone positively funereal.

"Oh, Lord," Wyatt muttered.

"Don't blame me. I was just talking off the top of my head—throwing out ideas," Gramps said, all innocence as he made change for Marlie, their other waitress.

Marlie, who was older and funny and unfortunately already married, gave Wyatt a hostile stare.

"I guess you heard Wyatt asked Stacy out," Gramps

said, disapprovingly, as if he hadn't stirred all this up to begin with.

Marlie pursed her lips. "I'm not saying a word."

But she didn't have to. Disapproval was also written all over her face, and Wyatt could guess why. Marlie was the mother hen of the staff, and Tom and Stacy were like her baby chicks and she'd been trying to convince them that they couldn't live without each other. She plucked the change out of Gramps's fingers, sent Wyatt a last glare, turned crisply and stomped away. Her stiff back and gleaming red hair beamed her fury at him.

Gramps grunted. "Can't blame her for being angry." He sighed. "Well, maybe it wasn't such a good idea, Wyatt."

Maybe? He was acting as if this were all Wyatt's doing—and Wyatt supposed it was, but... "What happened to all your talk about continuing the legacy of the Lonesome Swallow? I thought you'd be glad!"

His grandfather kept shaking his head. "Well of course...if you find the right girl. But Stacy?" He made a tsking sound. "Nope, not a good idea. There's gonna be trouble."

Wyatt rolled his eyes. "Well, it's only one measly date."

Gramps frowned. "Dating!" he hollered, as if he'd just discovered the term. "What will they think of next!"

Wyatt laughed. "They thought that one up a long time ago." He looked towards the kitchen with dread. "Guess I'd better go help out." He straightened his shoulders and marched off to face Tom.

POOR WYATT! Gramps remained perched on his stool and started doing a preliminary count of how much money they'd brought in that night.

He'd never realized finding a wife could be such a difficult proposition. Back when he was a young buck, he'd met Loretta, decided he liked her, and married her. Coincidentally, she'd liked him, too. Loved him. Amazing!

He sighed, trying to concentrate on counting. He liked to squirrel away the bigger bills every so often in case they were robbed. Hard to believe, right here in Armadillo Bend, but they'd been burgled seven times. Seven times since 1933. That's why it was absolutely essential that he keep his eye on the cigar box.

As far as full-time jobs went, watching a box could get a little tedious. During the day, he kept the TV on— for Jerry Springer and Court TV mostly. At night Wyatt believed it was better to just play music. Less distracting to groups of diners, he said. Gramps had agreed—this was Wyatt's show now—but he still kept strict control of what went on the jukebox. None of this namby-pamby Garth Brooks whiny stuff. Or LeAnn Rimes, for Pete's sake! He still favored real country music. Milton Browne, Bob Wills, Hank Williams and Patsy Cline. Oh, that Patsy!

Right now Johnny Cash was playing. Johnny was all right every once in a while. But Gramps's mind drifted back to Patsy Cline. Maybe all this love talk with Wyatt was making him nostalgic, but he felt like hearing her. He pilfered a quarter from the cigar box, climbed off his stool, and shuffled over to the jukebox. He punched in A-6, which was "Crazy" and "Walkin' After Midnight." Then he climbed back onto his stool and waited.

He'd known Wyatt and Stacy weren't right for each other, but ever since that New York trip, Wyatt had been walking around the place in a lovesick fog. Gramps had felt he needed to jolt the boy, stir things up! He wanted Wyatt to be happy.

Like he'd been with Loretta.

Patsy was just easing into the opening strains of "Crazy" when the door opened and someone walked in. Gramps flicked the woman an annoyed glance. She had a briefcase as big as her suitcase, which appeared to be one of those gym bag thingies. Lord only knows why she didn't leave all that stuff in her car! Maybe she was meeting someone. She was wearing a rumpled but still expensive looking suit, with matching stockings and pumps that brought her almost up to his eye level.

Gramps took in the question in her blue eyes and nodded toward the sign that read in big bold letters, Please Seat Yourself. There were at least twenty empty tables in the place. Still, the lady didn't seat herself. Instead she shuffled her things awkwardly and finally chose the most moving moment in the song, when Patsy Cline was just crooning her pretty little heart out, to clear her throat.

Gramps turned on her. "Read English?"

She blinked. "Oh, yes…"

"What's the problem then? Don't like any of the available tables? You want sterling silver flatware?"

She shook her head frantically. Gramps always got a good chuckle out of flustering the ladies. Young ones, especially. This one put down her bags to free up her hands so she could gesture with him—sign language. Some people thought because he yelled at them he was deaf. Ha!

"I'm not here for dinner," she explained, waving her hands in front of her face.

"Well you're too darned late for lunch and too early for breakfast," he snapped back.

This time the waving was accompanied by some violent head shaking. "I don't want to eat, period. I've just come in from New York City. I'm looking for Wyatt Lamar."

At that precise moment, Wyatt himself pushed through the batwing doors, followed by Stacy, who held a tray of steaks aloft. That tray didn't stay aloft for long. Wyatt stopped in his tracks, his jaw nearly dropping to the floor. And at the sound of the woman's voice saying the words "New York City" and "Wyatt" in the same sentence, Stacy's gaze immediately honed in on the intruder who'd caught Wyatt's eye. And she obviously didn't like what she saw: perfect figure, sophisticated clothes, pretty face with beautiful blue eyes.

After "Crazy" ended, the next sound heard in the Lonesome Swallow was the clatter of three top chop platters crashing to the floor.

EVEN WITHOUT THE broken plates and Wyatt standing before her in an apron, Margo was confused. *This* was the Lonesome Swallow Ranch? A *restaurant?* So much for brawny cowboys risking their lives to protect her from maverick mobsters! The most fearsome creature in *this* cowtown was the old man perched like a vulture at the bar by the door.

He and every other person in the place were gaping at her as if she were a Martian—and it wasn't exactly a comfortable feeling. As for how she was going over with her public...well, those weren't exactly waves of love radiating out from that blond waitress standing by Wyatt.

As for Wyatt himself, apron or no apron, the man was drop-dead gorgeous. How could she have forgotten? He was staring at her a little disbelievingly, but she couldn't blame him for that. After the way she'd snuck out on him that morning in New York, he probably thought he'd never see her again. She'd been kicking herself during the entire flight to Texas, then during the preposterously long taxi ride to Armadillo Bend, for running off to hide with a man she'd known for less than a day. How did she know she could trust him any more than she could trust her boss? Who on earth could she trust?

But now, looking into Wyatt's warm brown eyes, she was reassured about her snap decision. He looked as strong and solid as she remembered from their brief encounter. She felt safe.

Finally gathering his wits about him, he rushed to her. "Margo!"

She laughed, a little nervously. "Hi, Wyatt. Hope you meant it when you extended that invitation."

"Why sure, but I didn't expect you'd take me up on it." He frowned. "Not that I'm not delighted."

The old man cackled. "Oh, we're *all* delighted."

Wyatt flicked him an irritated glance, then looked back at Margo. "I guess I'm just surprised to see you."

She owed him some sort of explanation of her sudden appearance. But how could she possibly tell him what she'd been through? If she did explain that she was being hunted by the mob, Wyatt might not even want her there, and she wanted to be there so desperately. Where else could she go?

Her mind groped for something to say that wouldn't have her on the first plane back to Garcetti-land. She decided flirting a little couldn't hurt. "I guess first I owe you an apology for running out of your hotel room like I did that last morning, Wyatt." She batted her lashes as best she could. It wasn't exactly an art she'd practiced over the years.

"Oh, well..." Wyatt stammered incoherently for a moment, while the old wiseacre by the door snorted with laughter. Nearby a water glass shattered.

That blond waitress must be a klutz!

"We don't have to go into all that," Wyatt continued.

"But you were so nice to me," she said, "even letting me stay in your bed! And you'd only met me that afternoon. I just had to—"

Before she could utter another word, Wyatt took hold of her arm and wheeled her towards a secluded table. Cackles from the old man followed them.

"Who is that guy?" Margo asked.

"Oh, that's Gramps."

Gramps? That old curmudgeon?

She'd almost forgotten about the grandfather Wyatt had told her about so fondly. And no wonder. That night in Manhattan seemed years ago, not a mere week. Yet when she sat down across from Wyatt, it was hard to believe she could measure the time she'd known him in hours, not years. His eyes were that combination of sexy and reassuring that had first drawn her to him. The memory of their moonlight kiss flitted through her memory, sending a shiver of awareness through her.

"May I get you anything?" Wyatt asked.

She shook her head and looked with interest around the old restaurant, which still bore all the markings of a stylish old ranch house. The floor's wide pine planks gleamed from polishing. Exposed ceiling beams loomed overhead. On the opposite side of the room from the oak bar, there was a fireplace with a stone mantle. One door led to a kitchen, another had been widened so that she could see additional dining space nestled adjacent to this room. There was another door, marked private—an office, she supposed, or supply room.

"I can't believe it!" she said, taking it all in. "You never told me you ran a restaurant, Wyatt!"

He looked surprised. "I didn't?"

"I thought you were a rancher!"

He laughed. "Not me. Gramps was, back in the old days."

She understood now something that had puzzled her when she'd first met Wyatt. "No wonder you were so offended when I told you I didn't like to eat dinner!"

He grinned, and she felt her elbows, which were propped up on the sturdy wood table, go noodly on her. "I'd be equally offended if you refused to have dinner now. Have you eaten?"

She shrugged. "Pretzels on the plane."

He winced, and didn't even bother showing her a menu. Instead, he pulled a pad out of his apron and began scribbling.

"What are you writing?" she asked.

"You'll see," he said, then strode over to the kitchen. Before he could make it back, however, an older red-headed waitress bustled past her boss on the way to Margo's table. The woman was carrying a tray practically sagging beneath the weight of food. She set it down in front of Margo just as Wyatt walked up, a quizzical expression on his face.

"Tom heard about the arrival of the good-looking New York lady and made up a tray for her. Guess he wanted to give her a warm welcome."

Margo's stomach rumbled at the sight of a big bowl of tomato and rice soup accompanied by a hunk of steamy homemade wheat bread. Next to it lay a thick, mouthwatering steak accompanied by roasted new potatoes and buttery carrots, a tossed green salad, and the largest slab of steaming fresh peach cobbler she'd ever seen in her life. She laughed giddily at the sight of so much food—she hadn't realized how hungry she was.

Later she could try to explain to Wyatt why she had travelled halfway across a continent. Right now she just wanted to chow down.

"Is this all for me?" she asked hopefully.

The waitress turned to Margo and sent her the biggest, friendliest smile she'd received since setting foot on Texas soil. "Sure is, hon. Compliments of our lovesick chef."

5

MARGO WANTED TO STAY at a hotel, but Wyatt wouldn't hear of it. He'd been willing to allow that perhaps he'd behaved rashly when he was up there in New York City, and maybe he shouldn't have believed that what he felt for Margo was love at first sight. Even though they'd spent a few pleasant hours together, and despite the fact that Wyatt knew some intimate details about her like the fact that she kissed like an angel, had a panty hose fetish, and snored slightly when she slept flat on her back, after he'd come back to Texas he'd had to admit she'd given him no indication that she wanted to further their acquaintance.

But now, here was Margo, in Texas, looking more heartbreakingly desirable than ever, and hard as he tried, he couldn't think of any other reason why she'd be here if it weren't for him, at least on some level. This time, he really wasn't going to let her out of his sight.

Still, there was something peculiar about it all. At the Lonesome Swallow Margo had told him rather vaguely that she'd just wanted to get away from it all. But when they got back to the house he shared with Gramps, it became apparent that Margo hadn't packed for a week of pleasure. In fact, it looked like she'd left New York in a rush. In that big gym bag she was carrying, she hadn't thought to include a toothbrush, or a pair of pajamas, or even a pair of jeans. Furthermore, for a woman

who protested that she wanted to leave the rat race behind for a few days, she'd brought enough papers with
her to keep a workaholic busy for a year at least. Mighty
peculiar.

But even so, Wyatt wasn't discouraged. If he'd
learned anything in his life, it was that the course of true
love never did run steady...and Margo was the one
woman he'd met he was willing to make the confusing,
winding trip with. In fact, he couldn't imagine a more
pleasurable occupation existed for any man than spending about fifty or so years trying to romance Margo.
Now he just had to convince her—with however much
time he had—to take that journey with him. Having her
agree to stay at his house, which she'd done after much
arguing, was a first step towards that end.

Though there was no earthly reason why he shouldn't
go ahead and go to bed, Wyatt sat in the living room,
listening to the quiet all around him. Gramps had gone
out on one of his customary midnight strolls, and Margo
had hit the hay long ago. But the last time Wyatt had
circled the house for signs of life, a strip of light under
her closed door indicated that she was still awake.

Restless, he decided he might as well poke around
outside for a minute. Gramps had built the rambling
ranch house a mile from the Lonesome Swallow in the
fifties, once the restaurant started turning a profit. It had
four bedrooms, two bathrooms, one of the biggest kitchens Wyatt known to man (given what had happened to
his last house, Gramps just called it planning ahead) and
a wraparound porch with custom-carved oak rockers facing every direction.

Wyatt paced around the porch, not quite registering
why he felt so restless until he rounded a corner and
nearly slammed right into the reason herself: Margo, her

small frame swimming in a pair of pajamas he'd borrowed for her from Gramps, was standing at the porch railing, looking out at the night-darkened hills. The pajamas covered her so thoroughly she had to roll up the legs and sleeves until they bunched around her ankles and wrists. With her face fresh scrubbed and her hair combed out, she looked almost like a teenager at a sleepover.

Wyatt's heart flopped over about six times before he finally managed to speak. "I didn't know you were out here."

She smiled. "It's so quiet, I can't sleep."

It had been so loud in New York City Wyatt had wondered whether urban ills weren't really rooted in a massive case of sleep deprivation. "I guess I could park my pickup under your window and honk the horn for an hour or so. Maybe that would make you feel more at home."

She laughed. "The city dweller's lullaby." Then she shook her head, and looked out in amazement at the clear sky studded with bright fat stars. "I thought all that talk about stars being big and bright in Texas was something dreamed up by a bureau of tourism."

"No, out in the country it's still true."

She gazed at the surrounding hills. "And I thought Texas would be flat!"

"There are plenty of places where it is, but this is the Hill Country." He grinned. "So I guess you're disappointed. You want your Texas to be noisier, darker and flatter."

Her smile lit up the porch more than the thousand stars above their heads could. "No, I wouldn't change a thing. Except that I really should be staying in a hotel."

Wyatt sighed. "I thought we'd settled that. Besides,

a hotel wouldn't be able to loan you fashionable duds like Gramps's jammies.''

She flapped an arm to demonstrate the oversize fit of the pajamas, which were an unsightly beige and white pattern. ''They're very comfortable. They've almost convinced me to take my name off the Victoria's Secret mailing list.''

''Don't do that,'' Wyatt couldn't help advising quickly. He would adore watching Margo lounge on a porch rail in a potato sack, but the mental image of her curves encased in fluttery silky stuff was too tantalizing to deny. When she registered surprise at his urgent tone, he fumbled for a logical excuse why he should care what catalogs came to her home. ''I only meant...those pajamas are one-of-a-kind. In fact, I bet that stripy pattern was discontinued around 1960.''

She laughed. ''Maybe that's why your Gramps didn't want to part with them.''

It was true; Wyatt had practically wrestled the night-clothes out of his grandfather's hands. Especially when he learned his donation would go to clothe a lawyer.

Wyatt edged a little closer to her, near enough to catch a whiff of a perfume in the air. The flowery scent hit his senses like a drug. ''Gramps tends to be a little cranky with strangers.'' Heck, he was cranky with everybody.

Margo looked up at him, unsmiling, her blue eyes large and plaintive. ''I shouldn't be imposing on you, Wyatt. Maybe I shouldn't have come here. It's not like I planned it or anything. I just—''

He put a hand on her shoulder. Big mistake. The fist-ful of soft warmth made his mouth go dry so that he had to swallow even to croak out his intended reassurance. ''Whatever your reasons, I'm glad you're here.''

In the darkness he detected two bright stains of color

on her cheeks. "But I somehow didn't calculate the fact
I might be in the way. If I could do something for
you..."

He smiled. She was already doing all sorts of things
to him, but he doubted she'd take it too kindly if he told
her that all she needed to do was just be her pretty little
self. Even if he meant it sincerely, that kind of comment
had gone out with the stone age—or, in Texas, the eight-
ies. This was an educated, liberated woman, after all.
Used to being appreciated for her mind as well as her
looks. And she was accustomed to being busy. In fact,
maybe the best way to keep her here with him wouldn't
be by flattering her or pursuing her, but by keeping her
occupied.

"You could," he said matter-of-factly.

His reply perked her up. She smiled. "Really?"

"Ever wait tables?"

"For about seven years." Her voice radiated pure dis-
may.

"We're shorthanded at the Lonesome Swallow."

She looked at him doubtfully. "I should have said, I
was the *world's worst* waitress for seven years. Plus, that
was back when I was in school."

He laughed. "The job hasn't changed much."

"Oh, but..." She stopped her protest in mid-sentence
and thought for a moment. When she looked back up at
him, she looked in a mood to bargain. "I'm not sure
how long I'll be here. It might only be for a week or
two."

Wyatt's heart filled with hope. If he she could just get
to know Armadillo Bend for a little while, and the people who lived around here, she might get to like it a
little. If she could only discover that this small town had
as much to offer her in its own way as a place as big as

New York City, he might stand a fighting chance with her. "We have a big wedding reception coming up in five days. We could really use you."

She tilted her head, still unsure.

"Think of it as a way to barter for your room—and you can keep your own tips."

Suddenly, her lips broke into a big bright grin, and she held out her hand for him to shake. "Deal."

Her hand was small and warm, but her shake was businesslike. When he looked down, their entwined hands had disappeared underneath the rolled cottony cuff of her pajamas, so that it looked as if there was just one continuous arm joining them together.

Wyatt hoped that was a good sign.

IT DIDN'T TAKE Margo thirty minutes on the job to discover that she was not the most popular person in Armadillo Bend. Especially not with the waitress named Stacy.

At first, she thought the time when Stacy had bumped into her, causing her to spill a Coke on a customer, had just been an accident. Heaven knows, she herself was prone to those. And the incident where Stacy mixed up the orders for three different tables of Margo's she chalked up to being a little initiation ritual; waitress hazing, in which she was supposed to prove her mettle. So she gritted her teeth and fixed the orders and tried to be a good sport. But when the butter pats magically appeared on the floor while Stacy was on break, and Margo ended up skating and wobbling across the slick wood and losing a whole platter of chicken fried steak specials—one of which landed on a very nice woman named Selma, who also happened to be the wife of the Baptist preacher—Margo was hopping mad. She hurriedly reposted the orders, cleaned up the mess, then went stomping towards the back of the building where the staff usually took their breaks.

Maybe she'd stepped on Stacy's toes, or antagonized her in some inexplicable way. Margo was grateful to Wyatt for offering her something to keep herself occupied while she hid out in Texas, though of course she had no intention of pouring her heart and soul into this job. But neither did she intend to spend her week in Armadillo Bend being tormented by a hostile waitress with a crazy grudge.

Midway to her destination, she was stopped by Gramps, who was chuckling at her. "Ever hear the one about the three lawyers at St. Peter's gates?"

She rolled her eyes. Ever since Gramps had discovered she was a lawyer in another life, he hadn't given her a moment's peace. He was convinced that all lawyers were crooks, and given what had happened to her at the D.A.'s office back in New York, she wasn't particularly inclined to defend the honor of her chosen profession. But she'd been enduring his lawyer jokes all morning, and was beginning to lose her sense of humor.

"As a matter of fact, I have," she retorted. "I also know how many lawyers it takes to change a lightbulb, and where good lawyers go when they die, and the punch line to any O.J. Simpson joke you care to toss my way."

Gramps pinned her with those hawklike eyes. "Weeeelll," he drawled in a half sneer, "aren't we the touchy little filly today!"

That was another thing! She didn't know if she would ever get used to being compared to livestock, which happened a lot here. She had heard one table discussing a mean boss referred to as "that tough old rooster," and a woman called a "pretty little heifer." Of course, if she had to be mentioned in the same sentence as a farm animal, perhaps she ought to be grateful to be compared to a filly and not a cow.

Hanging above the bar and pointed directly at Gramps, a television blared out Court TV, adding to her exasperation. It was so distracting. Margo had been watching it out of the corner of her eye all morning, halfway following the trial of a man who had allegedly pushed his aged mother down a flight of stairs. Next week, she thought, she might be up on that screen—if by some miracle everything worked out for her.

She still didn't know exactly how she was going to make lemonade out of the very sour lemons she'd been handed in this circumstance. If she went to the FBI and started telling them stories about her corrupt boss, would they believe her? She had no real evidence. All she had were files that she, technically, had stolen.

She'd been uncomfortable hiding the hot files at Wyatt's house. What if Gramps started poking around her room? She had decided she'd feel better if she placed the files somewhere she wouldn't have to look at them every night, so she'd brought them in this morning and hidden them away in the root cellar out back. No one would think to look for legal documents under a pile of onions, and now she wouldn't have to spend sleepless nights next to the reminder of the rash action she'd taken.

Lord only knew how it would all turn out, but just having the TV turned to that channel reminded her of how much she could lose. "For someone who professes to hate lawyers," she told Gramps, "you certainly do spend a lot of time staring at them."

He snorted. "That's how I can dislike them so—all

those slick operators up there on that screen, defending crooks.''

''Some of them are prosecuting crooks,'' she pointed out.

He wasn't swayed. He leaned forward, informing her confidentially, ''Ever tell you that my brother used to be a lawyer?''

She shook her head. But considering the fact that she'd still been in Armadillo Bend for less than twenty-four hours, this was hardly surprising.

He sat back. ''My older brother, Roscoe. He was the last lawyer that we ever had in Armadillo Bend.''

''What happened to him?''

''He got hit by lightning.''

Margo hadn't expected that. ''How terrible!''

Gramps looked at her as if she were dim-witted. ''He didn't die,'' he explained testily. ''*That* would have been forgivable. Instead, he had to go and horn in on my business.''

Confused, she blinked at him. ''You mean the ranch?''

''Heck, no! He opened his own restaurant, right in downtown Armadillo Bend. Roscoe's Chili Parlor and Bar-B-Q. Surely you saw it!''

Margo had to confess she hadn't. ''It was already dark when I drove through last night.''

''Well heck, Roscoe's got a neon sign,'' Gramps told her. ''You couldn't have missed that!''

Armadillo Bend wasn't exactly a metropolis, although Margo was certain Gramps didn't want to hear her tell him that. The whole downtown consisted of two strips of old brick buildings bordering Main Street. Blink and you missed half the town. To avoid aggravating him more, she asked, ''Have you seen Stacy?''

He chuckled. "Going to chew her out for throwing those butter pats on the floor by your tables?"

Margo's jaw dropped. "You saw her doing it?" And people said New Yorkers weren't helpful!

"Stacy was just blowing off steam," Gramps explained.

No kidding. "She obviously resents my being here, but I'm at a complete loss as to understand why."

"Ha! Because she'd finally got her hooks into Wyatt before you sashayed through that door."

Margo felt the pit of her stomach drop about ten feet. Somehow, she'd never considered the fact that Wyatt might have a sweetheart here. Back in New York, he'd sounded as if he was stuck on some woman in Queens. He surely had replaced her quickly! "Is Wyatt... serious...about Stacy?"

"I guess so! Leastways, he seemed serious about wanting to settle down and have babies. And he asked her out for Thursday."

Thursday! Margo felt sick.

Of course she had no hold over Wyatt, and really had no right to an opinion concerning who he wanted to go out with. But...*babies?* With Stacy? She didn't seem his type at all! Wyatt was so sweet and patient and kind, while Stacy... Well. Margo didn't want to sound vindictive, but the woman had proven herself to be a vicious butter pat tosser. "I don't see why my arrival here should change things," she said with a sniff.

"Maybe because Stacy saw the way Wyatt looked when you walked through that door," Gramps pointed out.

Margo frowned, trying to recall that moment herself. She could only remember the way she'd felt, looking at Wyatt, and realizing how glad she was to see him, and how much handsomer he was in person than he'd been even in her dreams. And he'd been pretty darned handsome in those dreams. "How did he look?"

"Like he was a kid and you were the Easter bunny."

More animal references, but she got the idea. "That's preposterous." She tried to stamp down the little thrill that was snaking through her. "I only knew Wyatt a few hours in New York!"

"Long enough to share his bed?"

Her face reddened. "Oh, no—it wasn't like that. Wyatt slept on the floor. He was a perfect gentleman!"

An iron gray eyebrow shot up skeptically.

"Honest!" she said.

He smirked. "Lord have mercy! No wonder I don't have any great-grandchildren."

"I never would have come here if I thought everyone would get the idea that Wyatt and I...that we..." She stumbled for words, but there was no way she was going to use the phrase *were lovers* in front of Gramps.

The old man crossed his arms and hunched forward in thought. Then he chuckled. "Poor Stacy! She's been strung out tighter than barbed wire all morning."

That was easy enough to clear up. "I'll just go tell her that her worries are for nothing. Why, even if Wyatt and I did have a little something between us—which we don't, we absolutely don't—it would never work out. I'm a city girl."

Even if she no longer looked like one. She wore a work shirt with the Lonesome Swallow logo above the breast pocket, and a pair of Wyatt's jeans, which she'd had to belt and roll up beyond all recognition. There was room enough for two of her in those dungarees. She was glad for the pair of sneakers she'd snatched out of her apartment; the one practical item she'd packed. Her hair, which she usually wore swept neatly to her shoulders, she tied back in a simple ponytail—something she hadn't done since she was a kid. In fact, all morning she'd felt flashbacks to her youth. Maybe it was her outfit, but sometimes it was like she'd never left Tallulah.

Of course, she still longed to go back to New York. She wasn't immune to Wyatt's charm. She'd even thought he might kiss her last night out on the porch. But their relationship could never go beyond a brief flirtation. Wyatt clearly belonged here, in this town, running his beloved Lonesome Swallow. After having sampled his bacon and eggs this morning, she could attest to the fact that he was as good a cook as he was a kisser. And of course, she belonged back in the big city, with her work. That is, if she wasn't fired and tossed into jail the moment she stepped foot back in the Empire State.

Besides the geographical barrier between her and Wyatt, there was also the matter of her not being entirely on the up-and-up here. She hadn't confessed the real reason she'd come to Armadillo Bend. Garcetti probably couldn't trace her here—Bob Thomasson, either—but even so, Wyatt might not appreciate even the remote possibility that she could have lured mobsters into his peaceful Texas town. Besides, the fewer people who knew her whereabouts, the less likely it was that she'd be found, either by the Mafia or her boss.

"I'll go set Stacy straight right now." Margo told herself she didn't want to stand between Wyatt and happiness, but most of all, she didn't want to be having to watch her back during every shift for the next seven days. It was bad enough worrying about mobsters without having to look over her shoulder to check to see what Stacy was up to at all times.

Just as she was walking out the back door, however,

a hand clamped down on her shoulder, stopping her. She pivoted, half expecting to see Stacy lobbing a custard pie towards her kisser. Instead, she found herself face-to-face with Wyatt.

HE COULDN'T LET Margo talk to Stacy.

Wyatt wasn't blind; but even if he had been, there could have been no missing the tension at the Lonesome Swallow all morning. It was thick enough to cut with a knife. As thick as butter, you might even say.

Startled, she whirled on her heel and looked up at him with those blue eyes of hers that seemed to have shadowed his every conscious thought now for a solid week. She lifted her shoulders innocently. "Can't a person go out for some air?"

He reached down to grab the doorknob before she could, then sidled in between her and the exit. He didn't want a confrontation between Stacy and Margo. Stacy might let on that there was more between him and her than there really was. "Is this your break?"

"No, but..." She crossed her arms in front of her and tapped her foot impatiently. "I don't recall your telling me I needed your permission, your highness of the gas grill."

"Your break couldn't possibly have anything to do with telling Stacy to climb a rope, could it?"

Her lips spread into a thin smile. "Now what makes you think that?"

"I cooked up the three extra chicken fried steaks myself, but I intend to make sure no fur flies. Good help is hard to find around here, and don't forget, that wedding reception is coming up. I need every hand I can get."

"I've never had a cat fight in my life."

"You've never met a tigress like Stacy," Wyatt

warned her. "She's perfectly sweet most of the time—but when she feels threatened, her insecurity comes out in the darnedest ways."

Margo pursed her lips into a wry smile. "And what does she have to feel insecure about?"

Wyatt clenched his jaw. He didn't want to tell Margo that he was somehow involved with another woman. That's what he'd dashed over to avoid having her hear. "Well, um, her job. You're such a good waitress."

Margo cackled at that one. "Not to sound overly modest, Wyatt, but I don't think my performance this morning would intimidate anyone."

"That's because of Stacy's sabotage."

She grinned and stepped forward, so close that he could smell her intoxicating mixture of soap and perfume and French fries. One dark eyebrow arched tantalizingly. "Don't you think Stacy might feel jealous because you and she are trying to start a relationship?"

A bead of sweat trickled down his temple. Wyatt hadn't noticed how hot the restaurant was until just now...when he found himself within inches of the woman who had been the leading lady in all his dreams. "I wouldn't call it a relationship."

"Gramps told me you two have a date tomorrow night."

Darn it! He sighed raggedly. "It's not what you think."

"Gramps said something about settling down and having babies," she went on.

Wyatt emitted a limp laugh. "It's about time—the man's eighty if he's a day."

"I think he meant you," Margo clarified. "Honestly, Wyatt, I'm already imposing enough on you—I don't want to undermine any romances you have brewing."

"Nothing's brewing," he assured her. "Stacy and I are just going out on the town one time. I swear it."

Margo shrugged. "It makes no difference to me. I just don't want to get in the way."

How was he supposed to tell her that he wanted her in the way? How had his love life, which had been about as fertile as the Gobi desert for these many years, suddenly gotten so mixed-up? His mind whirred aimlessly, trying to come up with the exact words that would express all the things he felt for her, all the hopes in his heart that she might come around to feeling the same way about him, but his tongue remained hopelessly tied.

"Margo, I—"

Oh, heck. He knew the dark rear door behind the kitchen, which was lit by a bare forty-watt bulb and the exit sign, wasn't the place to get lovey-dovey, but he couldn't help himself. The most perfect moment he'd ever experienced in his life was the time he'd held Margo in his arms, and somehow he thought if he could only recapture that moment, everything would fall into place. So instead of wasting a lot of time stuttering out phrases that probably wouldn't make much sense, he reached forward, grabbed Margo by the forearms, pulled her to his chest, and kissed her.

She let out a breathy gasp, then a little moan of pleasure. Her mouth was as wonderfully sweet and yielding as he remembered, and while he drank in the delectable nectar of her lips, they might not have been in the Lonesome Swallow, or in Armadillo Bend, Texas or even planet Earth as far as he was concerned. The kiss carried them to somewhere timeless, where few others had gone before. And most of the ones who had been there were fiction. Romeo and Juliet. Antony and Cleopatra. Rick and Ilsa from *Casablanca*.

Slowly, as his hands worked their way down her back, molding her to him ever more closely, his mind hit on a disturbing realization. Romeo and Antony and Rick hadn't come out so well, in the end.

Were his feelings for Margo likewise doomed?

Using lunging wolf tactics wasn't doing much to help fate along. Gradually, the world started encroaching on him, and he realized that he probably should have used some aftershave this morning, or at least taken off his grease-splattered apron before running over here half-cocked and pulling her to him like a barbarian. The locale could have been better, too—much better—especially now that someone was pounding on the door which he was jammed firmly in front of.

"Hello? Can somebody let me in?"

Wyatt heard the muffled plea, followed by a startled moan from Margo, whose lips were still locked beneath his. He broke off the kiss, and found himself staring into Margo's bright blue eyes, which mirrored his own feelings of befuddlement and raw desire.

Someone pounded on the door at his back. "Oh, Lord—Stacy!" he whispered, noting that Margo's pink lipstick was smudged on one side of her mouth.

The moment he stepped forward to hand her his handkerchief, however, the door behind him pushed open and Stacy slipped through, combing her hand through her thick blond hair in frustration. "Good grief!" she drawled. "I was knocking and knocking! What's going on—"

She stopped fussing long enough to finally take in the sight of Wyatt and Margo standing awkwardly and guiltily next to each other in the bare hallway, shuffling their feet and wiping lip rouge off their mouths.

Stacy's face reddened as she drank in their abashed

expression for long, seemingly endless seconds. Then at last she abruptly spun on her heel and went running through the kitchen. Even from the corridor, Wyatt could hear Tom's heavier footsteps taking off after her. Their charge through the restaurant was sure to provide high drama for Lonesome Swallow customers.

Wyatt turned to look into Margo's eyes for reassurance that he hadn't insulted her, too. After all, he was her employer, and she was staying at his house, and he'd just taken advantage of her. Of course, she hadn't exactly seemed to be an unwilling participant in that kiss.

That was the one bright spot he could see in the whole situation. "Margo, I don't know what to say."

She shook her head, allowing a wry smile to touch her lips. "I wouldn't say anything, Wyatt. If I were you, I'd just be prepared for a lot more broken plates."

6

"DON'T YOU WORRY, Margo. Audrey's very gentle." Wyatt grinned up at Margo, who was perched atop the sweetest horse this side of the Mississippi. Audrey was the perfect mount for novices.

Margo smiled reassuringly. "Don't sweat it—I can manage a horse better than a tray of lunch specials."

Wyatt checked the girth and the stirrups. He wanted Margo to have fun during her stay, and she'd said she wanted to ride a horse, but he didn't want her to break her neck. That's why he'd saddled up Audrey for her. For a beginner, Margo seemed overconfident, which could lead to problems. And accidents.

"You don't have to spur her like they do in John Wayne movies," he told her, holding her sneaker to demonstrate. "Just a light tap, and maybe cluck your tongue a little."

She laughed. "Don't worry, I can handle myself."

He wasn't so sure. "But if you aren't used to riding—"

"Actually," she interrupted him, "I have ridden a few times."

He was surprised. "I didn't think there was much equestrian opportunity in Manhattan."

Her lips pinched into a wry smile. "Oh, I haven't lived my entire life there." She cleared her throat. "I went to summer camp once."

Even that made him feel a little better about letting her ride out into open pasture. "As long as you're comfortable."

Her smile was magnificent. "Don't be such a worry-wart!"

He tilted his head, remembering how she was when he'd first met her. "Back in New York, I thought you looked like a worrier."

She swallowed. "Oh? Why?"

He shrugged. "You had a sort of frantic way about you."

Two bright red spots appeared in her cheeks. "Well, of course. That's why I had to get away from it all. And now I'd better get a move on, as you all say."

"We also say y'all."

"I don't know if I'm ready to go that native yet, but I'm ready to give the old gray nag a spin."

He smiled up at her, lost for a moment in those blue eyes. The memory of taking her in his arms that afternoon flashed through his mind; he would have liked nothing more than to pull her off Audrey and kiss her again until they were both breathless.

Those blue eyes blinked. "Wyatt?"

He shook his head, clearing it. "Yes?"

"You'll have to let go of my foot."

He looked down, realizing that he still had a hold of her shoe. He stepped away, embarrassed. "Sorry."

"No problem." She laughed. "Tallyho!"

She and Audrey rode off at a trot. Wyatt watched them recede into the distance, and backed up slowly until he bumped against the wood fence behind him. He heard a familiar chuckle and whirled quickly to see Gramps staring after Margo, too.

"How long have you been here?" Wyatt asked.

"Long enough." His grandfather eyed him know-ingly. "Thought I'd come out and see what kind of ac-tivity would draw you away from work on a Wednesday afternoon."

Wyatt shrugged. "Business was slow, so I thought I'd..."

"Come give Miss Big City Lawyer a riding lesson!" Gramps finished for him. "Only it seemed that you were mostly tongue-tied, and the Manhattan maiden didn't need your tutelage."

Margo was cantering across a hillside, her hair blowing free behind her. "She said she'd learned to ride at summer camp."

Gramps shook his head. "What do you know about this woman, Wyatt?"

"Just that I like her."

Gramps grunted. "So nothing you know about her would explain why she's hiding something in the Lone-some Swallow's root cellar?" He folded his arms across his chest proudly, as if he'd just dropped a bombshell.

"What are you talking about?"

"This morning when you drove to the restaurant, she had that gym bag of hers with her."

Wyatt shrugged. "So? Maybe she was using it as her purse. Lots of women haul half their belongings around with them."

"But most women don't bury their belongings under a pile of onions." He aimed a sharp look at Wyatt. "Doesn't that just prove she's up to something?"

"Maybe."

"Gol-darn it, Wyatt! Do you think that gal's here un-der some kind of ulterior motive?"

He laughed. "Yeah, I think she travelled two thousand miles to enjoy your company."

Gramps was astonished. "You act like you don't care!"

Wyatt nodded. "You're right, Gramps. I don't."

"What if your lawyer lady is on the lam from the law?"

Wyatt laughed. "You watch too much shock TV."

"You can't say for sure that she isn't," Gramps pointed out.

"No, I can't." Wyatt stared into Gramps's face, trying to relay in one look how much conviction he had in Margo's honesty. "I'm just going to trust her, because I believe in my heart she's a good person."

"You mean because you love her," Gramps said.

Wyatt didn't answer. He wasn't sure he could. The way his heart swelled when he looked at Margo felt like love. But was it really possible to love someone so quickly? And someone he knew so little about?

"What about Stacy?" Gramps asked. "What are you gonna do about her?"

"I'm taking her out tomorrow night, just as I promised. It's just a date."

Gramps grumbled. "I say we go storm the root cellar and find out what's in that bag!"

"Nothing doing. That's her business."

"Don't you want to know? If you like her so much…"

"She'll tell me," Wyatt said with assurance.

He *hoped* she'd tell him.

His biggest fear wasn't what Margo was doing here, or what she was hiding. Ever since they'd met, gut instinct was telling him they belonged together. And if some mishap had brought her to Armadillo Bend, who was he to say that wasn't part and parcel of their destiny? His biggest fear was that Margo would disappear as quickly as she'd appeared. He wasn't sure what he'd do if that happened.

Gramps poked his hat brim off his forehead and let out a sigh as he watched Margo come loping at them. "If Peter Minuit were alive, I'd like to strangle the fellow."

Wyatt laughed. "What for?"

"For buying New York City from the gol-darned Indians!"

"LET'S SAY WE PAINT the town red, Margo."

Margo, who was just gathering up her purse to go home on Thursday night after closing, looked up in surprise as Tom donned his cowboy hat and sent her an inviting grin.

Gramps, who was putting on a pair of Nikes in preparation for one of his famous late-night walks, let out a cackle. "Well, now! That should take you and Dale Evans here all of five minutes."

Ever since her horseback ride that afternoon, Gramps had been calling her Dale Evans. She frowned at the old man. "What else can I do? You won't let me accompany you on your walk, will you?"

Gramps looked panicked. "'Course not! You'd only slow me up, and I need my nightly brisk constitutional to keep my complexion soft." He ducked quickly out of the restaurant.

Laughing, Margo turned to Tom. "Let's go!"

Even if touring Armadillo Bend did only take five minutes, it would be five minutes she could put off having to go to bed and ponder the one thing that had displaced the Mafia from her mind—namely, Wyatt's kiss. Tonight she would undoubtably toss and turn, wondering whether he was kissing Stacy.

Not that that should matter one bit.

She liked Tom a lot. He was a little on the shy side, but unfailingly polite to her. She even thought he was good-looking, though not half so handsome as Wyatt. Where Wyatt's height could be considered hazardous to low-flying planes, Tom was merely tall. He obviously lifted weights or participated in some vigorous activity, because his was not the usual short-order cook bod. In fact, he had the wiry frame of a wrestler. His brown eyes, which were magnified by a pair of wire rim glasses, were kind. And he was scrupulously neat—short trimmed brown hair, clean, unwrinkled jeans, and always polished boots. Always.

All in all, he was not a shabby escort, the one drawback being the fact that he was head over heels in love with Stacy. Nobody had informed Margo of this fact; it was simply as obvious as Stacy's yen for Wyatt. As they locked up the restaurant, Margo had to wonder what he was wasting his time with her for, but perhaps he, like herself, simply felt like stepping out.

They got into his truck, which, unlike Gramps's 1966 Chevrolet, had air-conditioning and a stereo. He turned the radio to a country music station. "Music!" Margo exclaimed. "And something besides Hank Williams."

Tom laughed. It was a well-known fact that Gramps guarded that jukebox like a lioness guards her cubs. "Last year when I tried to sneak a LeAnn Rimes song on there, he almost had a stroke."

Margo nodded. "I like to hum Rolling Stones songs under my breath whenever I'm around him. He starts looking as though he might come apart at the seams." In fact, she was beginning to enjoy needling Gramps as much as he liked needling her.

They drove into downtown Armadillo Bend, which

was two miles down the highway from the Lonesome Swallow. Uncle Roscoe's neon sign was dark, so there was one possibility barred to them. Margo was almost disappointed. She would have liked to see Gramps's face go beet red when she told him that she'd partaken of his brother's chili. But next to Uncle Roscoe's was the Long Neck Bar, which, judging by the dim light inside, was still open.

They got out and went in. The bar didn't have a lot to boast about, except if you counted character. The long, narrow, smoke-filled room had a high ceiling of molded tin, and pine plank floors like those at the Lonesome Swallow. Aside from the long bar lined with stools, two of which were occupied, and the single table, which looked as if it was never occupied, there was a pool table in the corner.

Margo hadn't played in years, but at one time she'd fancied herself the Minnesota Fats of Tallulah, Ohio. "How about a game, Tom?"

He looked at the table doubtfully. "Oh, I don't know."

"C'mon, it'll be fun." And there didn't appear to be a lot of other alternatives, entertainment-wise.

The two men at the bar, one as skinny as a zipper, the other a glum-faced man, pivoted and stared at Margo as if they'd never seen a female before. "You two gonna play pool?" the skinny one asked.

"You want to join us?" Margo asked. "We can play teams!"

"Oh, well now..." Tom glanced at his watch. He looked antsy to be somewhere else, but he was a good sport and put up with her rusty playing.

Luckily, Tom himself was quite a good player. After

he'd drunk a beer and hit a few balls in, he almost looked relaxed.

Margo was having fun. The glum guy, Clarence, she discovered was actually an artist. A welder. He made decorative trellises and belt buckles and all sorts of odd things. As he described his work to her, he actually grew almost animated.

"Say…" Nick, the skinny fellow, said as he watched them deep in conversation. "You guys aren't paying attention to the game!"

"Sorry," Margo said, taking her turn. She scratched.

Nick laughed. "Clarence here scratched the last time, too. You two need to keep your minds on the game and off your little flirtation."

Tom glanced up. "Margo's Wyatt's girl."

The two men clammed up as Margo turned on Tom, fuming. "I'm *what?*"

Nick jumped in between them. "Oh, well, we'd heard you were visiting Wyatt, but…"

"I am," she clarified, shooting Tom an annoyed glance. "And I'm working at the Lonesome Swallow. But as far as I remember, I haven't signed any contract of exclusivity."

Had word gotten around about that stolen kiss at the Lonesome Swallow…or was Tom just engaging in some wishful thinking?

The four of them finished their game more amiably, and then Tom started pulling her towards the door. "Sorry," he said once they were outside. "I didn't think we'd get trapped in there with Clarence and Nick."

Margo laughed. "I had a great time! I haven't played pool in years." Not since she'd left Tallulah. Her life in the intervening years hadn't left her a lot of time for fun and games. Or for riding horses, or for meeting people who weren't lawyers or somehow involved in the law.

She looked down Main Street, which for all its smallness, suddenly seemed like a fairyland. For the first time in years, Margo realized, she felt relaxed. And back in the pool hall, she'd been laughing, really laughing, until her stomach hurt. And she'd met people who weren't lawyers or crooks. How long had it been since she'd just goofed off and had a good time?

"We should check out the Tasty-T-Freeze," Tom said.

The little ice-cream parlor was open, and surprisingly full of kids for this late hour. But it was summer, and the early summer air was already a little steamy even at night, so ice cream seemed a natural. Margo ordered herself a soft-serve cone and sat down to eat it.

"Wouldn't you rather walk?" Tom asked just as she was easing her bone-tired body into a Formica booth.

"Aren't you tired from a long day on your feet, cooking?"

He shrugged. "I thought I might show you the rest of Armadillo Bend."

She didn't want to be a killjoy. "Sure," Margo said, reluctantly hauling her butt out of the booth. "Great."

She licked her cone as they walked down the old sidewalk past buildings a century old. As Tom gave her a quick history of the town which never quite recovered from being passed over as the county seat and missing the railroad, Margo couldn't help comparing it to Tallulah. They weren't much different in size. But Tallulah's insult had come more recently, when the shoe factory that had been there since the Twenties closed down. Ever since the closing, the lifeblood had slowly been seeping out of her hometown, as kids left as soon as they could and the population steadily grew older. Tallulah, which she'd always considered a typical small town, was a shell of its former self. But Armadillo Bend was another matter. This scrappy place was still holding on, clinging to a rocky hill on a highway with the delicate ferocity of a wildflower.

There was one bank still in its original building, but everything else seemed a little confused. The place marked ''mercantile'' in brick lettering now had a sign in the window proclaiming itself to be a coffee shop. A used bookstore and a craft shop bordered it, and on the other side of the street, there was an old movie theater whose marquee read Antique Mall.

''Lots of craft people come here now,'' Tom told her. ''There's even an art gallery open here on weekends, over in the old drugstore. And in the spring we have a big rodeo in the old fairgrounds near here. It's a lot of fun. I rope bulls.''

That would explain the wrestler look about him. She had to laugh at Tom's boosterism. It was almost as if he were trying to sell her on Armadillo Bend. ''What are you? The mayor?''

He chuckled. ''I just wanted to show you the finer points of the town,'' he said. ''It's really a nice place to live...especially if you're tired of city life.''

Margo slowed her steps, suddenly realizing that this little tour was more than just an escape from boredom, it was a sales pitch. It was also a reconnaissance mission. She took another lick at her cone and studied Tom's profile more carefully. His jaw was set, and his eyes scanned the streets distractedly. He was watching out for somebody. And it didn't take a rocket scientist to guess who.

Suddenly, in front of the last building in town, which

was the senior citizen's center, he stopped on a dime and turned to her. "Well lookie here! It's Bingo night—I'll bet you haven't played Bingo in a coon's age." He appeared to like Bingo a lot more than pool.

"Since third grade, as a matter of fact," Margo replied.

The reason behind Tom's curious enthusiasm for Bingo became crystal-clear when she stepped foot in the hall crowded with full tables and found herself staring straight at Wyatt. And next to Wyatt sat a glaring Stacy. People were milling around the hall, especially around a concession stand set up in back, indicating they had caught the place in between games.

"We're just in time to catch the start of a game," Tom observed.

Margo forced her anxious gaze away from Wyatt. "I don't know about this..."

Paying no attention to her protests, Tom dragged her up to the big table set up front and plunked down money for more cards than they could possibly keep track of, then he hustled Margo back to Wyatt and Stacy's table and sat across from them.

"Fancy meeting y'all here," Tom crowed by way of greeting. "Margo and I just happened to be passing by and thought we'd pop in for a quick game. Isn't that right, Margo?"

Her lips twisted wryly. "Something like that."

She couldn't take her eyes off Wyatt. She never could. She'd never known a man before who drew her gaze like he did. He straightened up and aimed that dazzling smile at her, the one he'd first shown her while she was hopping around on one foot in front of the Empire State Building.

Next to him, Stacy was also staring at her. No smile there.

"I was trying to give Margo a taste of Armadillo Bend nightlife," Tom explained.

"I'm sure she was overwhelmed," Wyatt said. "Even before she got to the Bingo hall."

Margo laughed.

Tom turned to her accommodatingly. "Can I get you something? Corny dog? Frito pie?"

She shook her head, experiencing a powerful Tallulah flashback. "No thank you."

He made the same offer to Stacy, who answered by crossing her arms and slanting a thin-lipped frown at him. Tom, who was as wound up as a kid at his first State Fair, didn't seem to notice the hostility being aimed at their side of the table. But Margo sensed that she was the last person Stacy wanted to share Wyatt's company with, and she could well understand why.

There was no denying the electricity that snapped between herself and Wyatt. Margo tried her hardest to fight it, but every time she looked at Wyatt, she felt herself reliving each moment he had held her in his arms. Which wasn't exactly an appropriate channel for her thoughts, since he was officially out on a date with someone else…and that someone's eyes were shooting daggers at her. So instead of looking at Wyatt, the minute the Bingo caller stepped up to his dais, Margo buried her head in her cards.

She had to remind herself that she had a high-powered job in a district attorney's office, that mere days ago she'd been dodging bullets in Manhattan, and that she was a self-made urbanite through and through, because the fact of the matter was, when the caller shouted out "B-5" and it was right there on her card, she actually found herself getting into the spirit of the moment. And there was the added benefit of the company. Wyatt was amusing the table by pretending to be locked in fierce competition with Tom. The two were practically tearing their hair out, though neither was close to winning.

"Did you get B-5?" Wyatt asked, leaning over to examine Tom's cards. Beneath the table, one of his long legs jostled against Margo's. She steeled herself to keep her gaze on the cards.

Tom quickly covered his cards with his hands. "Mind your own business!"

Wyatt buried his head in his hands, making Margo giggle. You'd think he was Gary Kasparov going up against Big Blue.

"O-72!" the man at the head of the room yelled.

Margo looked down at her card and felt stunned for a moment. Then she shrieked. *"Bingo!"* She might have been a grand prize winner on *The Price is Right,* given the stir she created. People from surrounding tables craned their necks to watch as she double-checked her card. And all the while, she was grinning like an idiot, feeling an adrenaline rush all out of proportion to the actual achievement.

Wyatt laughed at her, then pretended to glare. "I think you cheated."

"You've won fifty dollars, miss," the man at the front called.

She ran up to collect her winnings, then ducked into the ladies' room.

"Lucky gal!" a pink-cheeked lady coming out of a stall told her.

The weird thing was, Margo felt lucky. For the first time in weeks. Maybe years. It was as if a million tons of pressure had been lifted off her shoulders. She loved her job, and New York City, she really did, but she was amazed when she looked in the mirror and saw her flushed cheeks and bright eyes. Why, this was the first time, work aside, that she'd been out past eleven in mixed company in...she couldn't remember how long.

And then she remembered. The last time had been while Wyatt was in New York. Before that, it had been at least a year.

For a ridiculous, giddy moment, she let herself bask in the simple pleasures of Armadillo Bend. Everything seemed so straightforward. She didn't have mobsters chasing her down, or a crooked boss undermining her hard work. She didn't have to worry about her apartment being tossed, or being terrorized. Imagine. People were handing her money for playing a silly kids' game. And in Armadillo Bend, when a man liked you, he didn't play silly kids' games, he just pulled you up against his strong chest and kissed you smack on the lips.

For some reason, back when she lived in Tallulah, things like that hadn't seemed so important. But back in Tallulah, she thought dreamily, she hadn't had a Wyatt.

With a crash, the bathroom door banged open, and Stacy rushed forward. Her face was beet red, and she was breathing hard. At first Margo had thought she was behaving so oddly because she was sick, but now that she was nose-to-nose with the woman she saw that Stacy was just madder than spit.

"I'm fed up with you!" Stacy declared hotly. "I'm tired of you chasin' after Wyatt."

It sounded so preposterous Margo almost laughed. "Me? I've never chased anybody!"

"Ha!" Stacy's fists balled at her sides. "You followed him down from New York, and talked yourself into staying at his house, then cornered him at the restaurant and kissed him. And now you show up here, too!''

Margo lifted her shoulders helplessly. "It's not what you think. I didn't mean to follow him or kiss him or any of that— it just sort of happened."

Tears of frustration welled in Stacy's eyes. "I saw the way he looks at you!"

"But that's *him*," Margo assured Stacy. "Wyatt means nothing to me. I'm from New York City, for heaven's sake. And he's...well, you know. A cowpoke."

Stacy watched her for a moment, taking in ragged, heaving breaths, fighting to regain composure. Margo was beginning to think she might have calmed the girl somewhat...at the expense of the truth. Because even though her statement might have been true a week and a half ago, she certainly didn't think of Wyatt as a cowpoke now. Besides, given her excitement over a simple night of Bingo, she was beginning to wonder whether her own urban sophistication weren't fading like a Labor Day suntan.

Too late, she noted that Stacy's anger had hiked up a notch. "Then you've been leading him on! And you don't even care for him at all!"

Margo waved her hands in front of her face, trying to find the words to clear up all the confusion. "Of course I care for him—"

"Ha!" Stacy yelled.

And before Margo could qualify just how much she did like Wyatt, which was far from being clear in her own mind, the whole conversation was brought to an abrupt end when Stacy swung her purse back then slung it right at Margo.

It was such a surprise! The split second after the heavy

leather bag made contact with her nose, Margo staggered back against a sink, almost too shocked to feel any pain.

Stacy gasped, like someone who didn't know her own strength. "Omigosh, you're bleeding! I'll run and get help!"

As she left, Margo reassessed things. Maybe simple small town pleasures weren't so simple after all. The romance situation was a serious tangle. And she was willing to bet that Stacy could give the New York mob a run for its money.

MARLIE, WHO WAS the only waitress with breakfast patrons in her station the next morning, whistled when she took a look at the white bandage on Margo's nose.

Wyatt felt something inside his chest hitch. Poor Margo! What a night it had been. Because of the set-to, Margo and Stacy were both banned from Bingo night for the next three months.

"Weeeelll," Gramps drawled. "You New York gals sure know how to stir things up."

Tom poked his head out from the kitchen. "Need potatoes from the root cellar."

Stacy was, blessedly, off on a break somewhere, giving the restaurant a fifteen-minute window of peace, so Wyatt headed for the door. But Margo slipped up to the exit before he could reach it. "Aren't you needed in the kitchen, cowboy?" she asked with a smile, looking pointedly at the hat on his head.

After she'd disappeared outside, Wyatt looked over at Gramps, who was nodding sagely, as if Margo's not wanting Wyatt to go to the root cellar meant something.

Did it?

Wyatt self-consciously took off his straw cowboy hat, which he'd forgotten he was wearing. Ever since arriving at the Lonesome Swallow this morning, all his attention had been focussed on Margo. She hadn't said a word in his pickup on the way to work this morning. Just fiddled with the radio dial and laughed at the Washington scandal of the day on the news.

"Don't say it," he told Gramps.

"All right, I won't even mention that gym bag under the onions." Then older man shook his head in amazement at Wyatt.

Wyatt scowled, especially when Marlie patted his arm in a maternal, sympathetic way, and handed him a glass of tomato juice. "Drink this, Wyatt," she said. "It's got vitamins—good for love stress."

For Pete's sake! Wyatt thought grimly. It seemed everyone in town was watching after him, studying him like he was some sort of rodent in a lab. This morning it was easy to imagine the whole town of Armadillo Bend standing around in spectacles and white coats, anticipating how he and Margo and Stacy would all act around each other.

Margo seemed to be the person under the least strain, despite having been popped in the nose. He was as nervous as a frog in a frying pan. And Stacy...

As if direct sync with his train of thought, Stacy skulked back into the restaurant through the back door just as a couple came through the front. Not missing a beat, she gathered up two menus and made a beeline for the customers.

Gramps snorted as she went past. "Well, if it isn't the Rocky Marciano of the waitressing set!"

Stacy glared at him. "My purse just slipped, that's all." She seated the couple at a quiet corner table.

Gramps shot Wyatt a skeptical glance. "You buying that explanation, cowboy?"

Wyatt shook his head. "Purses usually don't slip up to nose level."

Gramps contemplated the issue and allowed that it didn't sound likely. He tilted a questioning look at Wyatt. "You ever going to ask that New York girl what she's doing here?"

Wyatt rolled his eyes. "The girl is nearly thirty, Gramps. And she told me that she just needed to get away from it all."

His grandfather didn't look convinced. "There ought to be some other explanation—people just don't want to get away from nothing. Did she break up with a boyfriend? That often causes women to go berserk. You see 'em on Jerry Springer all the time."

Wyatt frowned. "She never told me about a boyfriend." Somehow, he'd never considered the possibility that she might have a prior attachment. Although, given what happened with Mary Beth, he should have.

"What about something involving her work?" Gramps asked. "Some case she's working on."

"No...if anything, it sounds like she's tired of her work. She never wants to talk about it."

"And why would she come here?" Gramps asked insistently.

"I asked her to come," Wyatt reminded him.

"But why would she actually take you up on it?"

Wyatt shrugged, and admitted in his quietest voice, "I was kinda hoping she liked me."

Gramps's leathery face settled into a sour frown. "Seems like if you two wanted to have a romantic rendezvous, she could've suggested flying off to Cancun or something like that. Armadillo Bend ain't exactly the romance capital of Texas."

With every word his grandfather spoke, Wyatt felt his

heart sinking a little closer to his boot heels. Maybe Margo's being here didn't make a lot of sense theoretically. But whenever he looked at her, her presence seemed perfectly logical. She was here because he was crazy about her.

He sighed, and absently took a gulp of tomato juice. "The trouble with you, Gramps, is you think too much."

He slammed the juice glass down, and, deciding he needed to take a break himself—at least from his grandfather's pessimism—he ambled out the back door. Directly behind the restaurant was an acre and a half of land where they grew their own tomatoes and whatever else Gramps had a fancy for. The land always had a calming effect on Wyatt, and today was no different. As he stared out over row after row of tomato cages covering healthy plants, he felt himself smile. Hard to believe that during the Depression this place had been considered a failure. It just proved how much things could change.

Maybe Margo would change, too. For a city girl, she'd seemed to be having a lot of fun last night. At least until she'd gotten bonked on the nose.

Slowly, as he continued looking out over the land, he became aware of a sound. A banging. Pounding. He turned, trying to locate the source of the noise. And then he spied it. The root cellar door. Margo!

As he ran toward the cellar, he began to hear her voice. "Hello? Is anybody up there?"

Wyatt threw the heavy wooden hinge on the cellar door and yanked it open. Margo tossed out a large burlap bag, then scrambled out just as fast as she could. She looked pale and shaken. "I thought I was going to suffocate in there!"

He held her by her shoulders as she took a few deep gulps of breath. "Are you all right?"

She frowned. "Yes, I guess so. I can't imagine how the door got stuck, though." She turned and inspected the latch, but it only took a few seconds for her to know that her being locked in couldn't have been an accident. Two-by-fours couldn't be blown into a latched position by a gentle breeze. Margo crossed her arms and shot Wyatt a look.

He felt his jaw working as he remembered Stacy coming back in from her break just after Margo had left for the root cellar. "I can't believe she'd do this. I'll have a talk with her."

"That sounds very Ward Cleaver."

Wyatt wasn't in the mood for jokes. Margo wouldn't have really suffocated in the cellar, but it wasn't something he wanted going on at his place of business. "If she keeps carrying on like this, she's going to be fired."

Margo looked alarmed. "You can't do that."

"Why not? Butter pats on the floor were bad enough, but locking people in cellars in June..."

"I don't want anybody being fired on my account," Margo replied quickly. "Besides, it really wasn't that terrible. Really, I've had worse things happen. And don't forget that wedding reception. You need all the help you can get."

He weighed the matter for a second. "If it were only one incident."

"But after all, I'm the one who doesn't belong here."

"Why do you say that?" Wyatt asked, alarmed. Did this mean she was ready to leave Armadillo Bend? He felt he'd barely had time to speak to her, much less try to persuade her to stay.

"I came here with an open mind, but I'm too much

of an urbanite,'' Margo said. ''Let's face it, I don't even own a pair of jeans.''

He grinned. ''But you look mighty good in mine.''

She rolled her eyes and inspected the cinched-in waist of her pants. ''My only fear is, if I stay here and keep eating your and Tom's cooking, I'll actually fit into them.''

He laughed. ''Blue jeans aren't the litmus test of country living, you know. My mother never wore anything but dresses.''

She eyed him skeptically and pointed to her bandaged nose. ''Yeah, but I bet Ma Lamar never looked like Jack Nicholson in *Chinatown,* either.''

''That was Stacy's doing, too,'' Wyatt said.

''True,'' Margo acknowledged, ''but for some reason, I provoked her. In fact, I seem to have caused you a lot of trouble since coming here. I just don't think Armadillo Bend and I get along.''

He frowned, then stepped forward. She tried to side-step him, but he pulled her a little closer to him and looked into those blue eyes that never failed to draw him in. ''Armadillo Bend is a place. It doesn't have an opinion. What matters is what you think of it, and of the people in it.'' *One person in particular,* he added silently.

She swallowed. ''Wyatt, you shouldn't hold me like this.''

''Why not?''

Her cheeks flushed. He couldn't forget their kiss Wednesday, and how Margo had felt in his arms. Heck, he'd thought about little else for twenty-four hours now. All last night he'd stayed up, dreaming of ways to keep her here. Armadillo Bend wasn't full of incentives.

Maybe he should have thought of the lock-her-in-the-cellar trick.

"Because you know and I know that it's a prelude to a kiss."

"And...?"

For a moment, she looked torn. Her gaze fluttered down to his lips, just as her tongue darted out to lick her own. Then, setting her jaw stubbornly, she took a resolute step backwards. "And I have to get these potatoes to Tom."

"Okay." He released her reluctantly. "I'll go find Stacy."

"No!" she said. "Let me talk to her."

"Every time you two get together, feathers fly."

"Yes, but you said yourself the first night I came here that help is hard to find. Before you do anything rash, let me try to patch things up."

He considered for a moment, then plucked the potato sack off the ground himself. "All right," he agreed. "Though I worry that you're taking a risk."

She laughed, tilting her nose at him. "But this time I know what I'm up against."

7

IN SCIENCE FICTION novels, time travellers always had to be careful not to change history. In Armadillo Bend, Margo felt the same pressure not to affect the events around her—no matter how much she liked Wyatt, she knew it would be doing them both a disservice to pretend there could be a future for them. But keeping out of his life was difficult, considering her own inappropriate feelings and the fact that for some reason she seemed to be Wyatt's type.

When the solution to this problem finally occurred to Margo, it hit with such gale force that she nearly poured hot coffee on Abe the pharmacist's lap. What if Stacy became Wyatt's type?

"Whoa there!" Abe exclaimed. "My coffee cup's beginning to look like Niagara Falls!"

Margo jerked back her coffeepot and quickly began sopping up spilled coffee with a napkin. "Sorry, Abe, my mind was somewhere else."

The man nodded generously. "That's okay. I'd rather have it on the table than on my pants."

She laughed. In New York, most of the time a waitress would get hassled for making that kind of an error. But here, people seemed to take things in stride. Her nose, for instance. Everyone had been real friendly about it. Then again, the regulars had probably all heard the saga of her getting socked long before they wandered into the Lonesome Swallow this morning.

She marched right over to where Stacy was making a new pot of coffee and leaned one elbow against the counter. "I need to talk to you."

Stacy sent her a sideways glance and huffed impatiently. "Okay, okay, so I'm sorry about your nose. Go climb a tree."

Margo sighed, realizing that she might not have the easiest task ahead of her. "I wanted to talk to you about something completely different."

The waitress's mouth pursed skeptically. "I got nothing to say to you."

"Even about Wyatt?" Margo whispered confidentially.

Stacy's eyes narrowed. "What about Wyatt?"

Margo smiled, knowing she'd hooked her fish. "Not here. We can drive over to the Tasty-T-Freez after our shift."

"How do I know this isn't a trick?" Stacy asked, looking at her suspiciously.

"To prove my good faith, I'll split my tips with you today."

Stacy couldn't refuse such a deal. "Okay," she agreed reluctantly. "But if this is some kind of a joke..."

"It's not," Margo assured her, and watched Stacy slink away, still suspicious.

What she needed now was a very specific plan. In fact, she needed to approach this undertaking much as Rex Harrison transformed Audrey Hepburn in *My Fair Lady*. A good starting point would be on superficials. Hair. Clothes. She had to make Stacy look like Wyatt's ideal.

She grinned, ready to give Rex a run for his money.

WYATT HESITATED at Margo's door. He didn't want her to think he was pressuring her by stomping into her bedroom at all hours. If he did that, he feared she would scamper off to a hotel, or worse, take the next flight back to New York.

But he figured just this once might not hurt. He knew she wasn't asleep yet, because he'd just seen Stacy's car drop her off at the house. He would have paid good money to know what those two had been up to all day long. They'd left the Lonesome Swallow together after their shift. What could they possibly have done that would take the entire afternoon and the best part of the night? He'd been gone a while this evening himself, and had expected to find Margo home when he'd gotten back. Instead, he'd beat her back to the house by two hours.

Margo answered his knock in half a second. When she spied the shopping bag he carried, her dark brows arched inquisitively. "For me?"

Wyatt stood there, trying to hold back a goofy smile he felt building inside every time he looked at her, as well as a rush of desire. Not that Gramps's pajamas had improved any in the past few days, but ever since Margo had landed in Armadillo Bend, his hormones had been on overdrive. The accumulated tension of the several days she'd been here, sleeping just rooms away from him, was beginning to wreak havoc on his nerves.

"Actually, yes."

"You shouldn't have done anything like that!"

He held up a hand. "It's not much, really. I just wanted to give you a little bonus, for helping at the store."

She ushered him inside the spare bedroom, where she had managed to put her personal stamp on the space in a few short days. He couldn't help noticing that the room looked dusted and clean, with an old glass milk bottle of freshly cut wildflowers on the dresser. A glass of water and a mystery book by Agatha Christie were on the nightstand. He liked mysteries, too.

Margo perched on the edge of the bed and looked up at him, her arms folded. "Do you go out buying things for the other waitresses?"

He nodded. "On their birthdays. I have no way of knowing if you'll be here for your birthday, so I thought I might as well hedge my bets and get you something now. You mind?"

She seemed surprised by the weird logic of his spontaneous answer. He was, too. "When you put it that way, how could I?"

He nodded, then handed her the shopping bag. He smiled as she peeked in the first clothes box.

"A pair of jeans!" she said, laughing. "And they actually look like they might be my size." She held them up to herself to admire them, and he was pleasantly surprised at how close he had eyeballed the fit of the jeans. They would be a little roomy, but not by too much.

"I thought they'd be more comfortable than mine," he told her.

"They sure will!" she agreed, sitting down again. "You shouldn't have!"

He shrugged. "Open the other one."

She did so without hesitation, and leaned back, shocked, when she looked into the larger box. A brand spanking new pair of shiny boots gleamed back up at her. She gasped in delight. "Real live cowboy boots!"

He chuckled. "Not live, I hope. Here, let me help you."

Kneeling next to her, he helped push one of the

pointy-toed boots on for her. It seemed almost an instinctive thing to do, but once he was sitting there, holding her delicate little foot in his hand, he somehow quit breathing. All his life he'd heard about weirdos with foot fetishes and never understood how strange desires like that came about. Now, just for a split second, he began to have an inkling. Margo's was the sexiest little foot he'd ever laid eyes on.

Deciding that if he continued down this path much longer he might just spend the rest of his manhood in a padded cell, he quickly jammed the other boot on her left foot and stood up. "There!"

"This is too much!" Margo got up and traipsed around the room, proudly marching from one end of the bed to the other, lifting her pajama bottoms to admire her new acquisitions. "Aren't they great? Don't I look absolutely authentic?"

Anyone peeking through the window might have said she looked a little like a lunatic, with her threadbare pajamas and her shiny new boots. And who knows what they would think of him, staring at her as if she were the greatest thing since Cindy Crawford. Maybe they were both a little nuts; he knew he was about her.

"You look great," he said.

She laughed. "I can't believe you did that! How sweet!" She crossed over to him and gave him a big hug.

He shrugged modestly, steeling himself against the desire that coursed through him as their bodies made brief contact. He needed to get out of that bedroom. "It was really nothing. If you don't like them, or if they don't quite fit, you can take them back. They came from right here in town."

If possible, she looked even more amazed. "Right here in Armadillo Bend?"

He nodded. "The store's behind the ice-cream parlor." As she studied her boots more carefully, still smiling like a kid on Christmas morning, he cleared his voice. "Speaking of ice-cream parlors..." He couldn't conceal his curiosity on one point. "I heard you and Stacy went there this afternoon."

"Uh-hm."

He glanced at her doubtfully. "Nothing bad happened?"

"Of course not!" She laughed. "What did you think? That Stacy and I duked it out in public again?"

"No, I saw her car drop you off a little while ago, safe and sound."

"Well then," Margo said, still smiling. "You should know that everything's worked out—otherwise we wouldn't have spent a moment longer than necessary in each other's company."

That was what had him puzzled. He waited a moment, hoping she would volunteer more information, then, when she failed to do so, finally asked, "What were y'all doing together all this time?"

She looked up at him sharply. "Nothing."

He knew that couldn't be true, and the look he sent her said as much.

She giggled. "Oh, all right. I might as well tell you that I have a surprise planned for you."

"A surprise." For some reason, that word sounded more ominous than it should have. "What is it?"

She rolled her eyes. "I'm not going to tell you."

"Does this have anything to do with your being here?"

Her eyes focussed on him questioningly. "What do you mean?"

"Well, I was wondering if it would have anything to do with how long you intend to stay."

Her face fell. "You want me to leave…"

Wyatt practically fainted. "No, Lordy, no! Stay as long as you want."

"Gramps wants me to go, I know that."

"I think you're wrong about him. You might think he's cranky to you, but he's not singling you out."

She waved a hand. "Oh, I know that. But sometimes I feel him watching us—you—protectively. Like he thinks I'm a predator."

In her oversized pajamas and red boots she looked about as predatory as a teddy bear. "Gramps always thinks I choose the wrong women."

Her gaze became guarded, and he could have kicked himself. He'd made it sound as if he'd chosen her…which, of course, he had. From the moment he'd seen her, he'd known Margo was the woman for him. But he also knew she was as skittish as a newborn colt, and he ought not to be telling her things like that. He raised his hand to allay any protests she might make. "Please don't say anything, Margo. I know you don't feel that you belong here, but—"

She stood and clomped towards him in her new boots, cutting off his words. To his shock, she took his hands in hers. "Whatever you have to say, Wyatt, just wait until tomorrow. After tomorrow, I'm willing to bet things will look differently to you."

He tilted his head curiously. "What happens tomorrow?"

"My surprise." She grinned, unconsciously making her lips look far too kissable. Wyatt wasn't nitwit enough to follow through with the impulse to feel his lips beneath hers, but she must have read his thoughts, because in the next instant her sexy smile disappeared and she took a stumbling step backwards.

"I'd better go to bed now," she said.

Oh, how he would have liked to follow her right into that bed and under those covers! He nearly ached with wanting to. And from the dark smoky look in those blue eyes of hers, and the color in her high cheekbones, he could almost have sworn that the same thought had rushed through her mind.

Before he made a damned fool of himself by asking, he took a step back through the doorframe, to the safe side of her bedroom. She moved to close the door, and he just stopped her from shutting it with his hand. "You mean, after tomorrow you'll listen to what I was about to say just now?"

"If you still want to tell me."

Wyatt nodded, turned on his heel, and strolled back to his own room, where he was sure he would spend another night tossing and turning in his lonely bed.

In his head, he was having very un-Western, non-rugged male thoughts. Specifically, he was thinking about what he was going to wear. Because if tomorrow were his day to make his declaration, he wanted to look his best. In fact, he might have to break out the cologne Marlie had given him last Christmas and really do the thing up right. Get up early and polish his boots.

Tomorrow was courtin' day.

"I NEED A LAWYER."

Margo nearly dropped a plateful of biscuits. "I beg your pardon?" she asked, sure she had misheard

Gramps. Then, more loudly, she asked, "You? A lawyer?"

"Shh..." He flapped his hands at her to tell her to pipe down.

Wanting to be at the Lonesome Swallow early today to beat both Wyatt and Stacy, Margo had bummed a ride off Gramps, who always drove himself. She, Gramps, and Tom were the only ones at the Lonesome Swallow so far. Tom was in the kitchen and couldn't possibly hear their conversation, and Stacy hadn't come in yet. Margo glanced around the room at all these imaginary people Gramps didn't want to hear them and grinned broadly. She was going to enjoy this. "You want *me* to help *you?*"

"You heard me right the first time," he grumbled.

But she would have savored hearing him say it again. It was so rare for her to have the upper hand around here. "What can I, a mere crooked attorney, and a troublesome New York female to boot, possibly do for you, Mr. Lamar?"

His lips pursed into a frown of distaste. "I would have asked somebody else, but there isn't another lawyer in town, 'sides that brother of mine."

She crossed her arms, and tapped the toes of her new boots in delight as Gramps squirmed on his stool. "What do you need a lawyer for?"

He almost answered, then her shiny new footwear caught his eye. His eyes widened in shock and he let out a howl of surprise. "Where on earth did you get those blasted things?"

She smiled and pulled up the legs of her new jeans to better model her boots. "Wyatt gave them to me."

"Oh, Lordy!" he hollered. "Givin' women shoes! What'll he think of next?"

She laughed. "What was it you wanted to talk to me about?"

His gaze kept travelling doubtfully from her face to her boots, almost as if he didn't want to confide in her, now that he knew that his grandson was giving her footwear. "If'n I tell you, will you explain what your intentions are?"

"Intentions towards what?"

"My grandson, that's what! What in heck are you up to?"

She thought for a moment. "No."

At her blunt answer, he recoiled. "No, what?"

"No, I don't think I will explain."

He slapped his hand on the bar. "That's not fair!"

"Why not? Why should I have to offer legal services and tell you about my private life? I should at least know what you want me to do first."

He finally grumbled, "Well, if you must know, I want to write a will."

Immediately, her smile faded and she stepped forward, worried. "A will! Why now?"

"Never mind that," he said testily. "I just wanna know can you help me."

"Of course," she said. "You know I'm not licensed to practice in Texas, but for that matter you don't even need a lawyer to write a will."

His gray eyebrows arched in surprise. "I don't?"

She shook her head. "All you need to do is write it in your own handwriting, sign and date it. As long as it's in your own writing."

He blinked. "You sure?"

"Positive. Of course, if you want to have it witnessed and notarized—"

"But if'n I wanted you to look everything over to

make absolutely certain that the wording's right so it can't be contested, then you would do that?''

"I couldn't take money for it," she said.

"An honest lawyer—now I've seen everything!" He eyed her squarely. "Then would you do it...as a friend?"

She slipped up onto the stool next to him, amazed. "Of course." But she worried about Gramps. "Are you feeling all right?"

He waved a hand dismissively at her. "Oh, sure. Nothing wrong with me. Despite what that fool Doctor Grigsby says, my ticker's still got another decade left in it at least. In fact, it's probably in better shape than yours, with you livin' in all that smog all your life. Plus, I take my nightly constitutional."

"Right." She wondered about those midnight walks of his. Did he take them because he was so worried about his health?

"I'm not planning on checking out any time soon," he assured her, then he laughed and knocked on the wooden counter.

She tilted a sharp gaze at him. "I hope your writing a will doesn't have anything to do with my arrival here."

Two iron-gray brows rose in surprise. "Why should it?"

"You could always put a codicil in saying that if Wyatt married someone of whom you didn't approve—say, a New York lawyer woman—he wouldn't inherit the restaurant."

Even faced with only a hypothetical barrier, one she had pulled out of thin air, she felt herself writhe in indignation.

Gramps's beady eyes narrowed on her. "You thinkin' of marrying Wyatt now?"

"No...I was just thinking of examples."

He chuckled. "The air's gettin' pretty thick around here, I've noticed."

It wasn't half so thick here as it had been in her bedroom last night. After Wyatt had given her the boots, she'd been sorely tempted to step into his arms for another demonstration of his expert kissing technique...and maybe more. With that bed nearby, which his gaze had flicked to with unconcealed speculation, it was hard not to get ideas. Her dreams about Wyatt were definitely becoming more carnal in nature. But the better she knew him, the more she was certain that Wyatt wasn't any more the type than was she to have one-night stands or loose-ended relationships. If her days in Armadillo Bend had shown her anything, it was that her years of city living hadn't shaken small-town romantic notions of her youth.

Which only proved that she needed to get him and Stacy together...and get herself the heck out of Armadillo Bend soon, out of temptation's path. The trial would begin next week. Next week! She needed to decide when would be the best time to call the FBI, or take the files back to New York. She had to do one or the other.

Funny, anything happening in New York seemed slightly unreal to her now. If it weren't for Gramps watching Court TV all day long, and their previews of the Garcetti trial, she would have forgotten about the place entirely. Without meaning to, she'd been completely swept up in the lives of the people here. Namely, one person.

Gramps cleared his throat. "I believe you really like him."

"Wyatt?" Margo asked, astonished. "Of course I do!"

"But do you love him?"

Her mouth dropped open, but no sound came out. Love? That was a serious word. Of course she didn't love him. She couldn't!

So why wouldn't her lips form the simple word no?

"Well, never mind," Gramps said, reluctantly getting back to the real topic at hand. "To put your mind at ease, the will has nothing to do with you. I'm worried about Roscoe."

"Your brother?"

He nodded. "I want to make sure Wyatt is full owner of the Lonesome Swallow after I'm gone."

Margo bit her lower lip as she thought through this puzzler. Roscoe was Gramps's older brother, and had to be ninety-five if he was a day. "Isn't it more likely that you'll outlive Roscoe?"

Gramps eyed her squarely. "I wouldn't put anything past that brother of mine! I haven't trusted him since he opened that barbecue joint, tryin' to steal my business."

She tried not to laugh.

"Anyways, this place is the closest thing to a gold mine we got in Armadillo Bend. Why, on the weekends we get people in all the way from San Antonio. Last year we made *Fodor's*."

She could understand why. The food here was great and the atmosphere was as thick as the steaks. She didn't bother telling Gramps that Roscoe's Chili Parlor and Bar-B-Q was also prosperous and that his brother probably had no interest in stealing the Lonesome Swallow from his nephew.

"If you want, we can get started on it tonight."

His eyes widened in astonishment. "Tonight, hell! We'll do it today."

"But I've got to work..."

He waved away her protests. "Pshaw! You call that exercise in confusion and dropping things work?"

"Well, but I'm scheduled for today..."

He laughed. "That's okay. I told Marlie to come in today." He reached behind the bar and brought out a yellow legal pad. "Now, where do we start?"

She heaved a sigh. A whole day hammering out a will with this ornery old man wasn't going to be a cakewalk. Nevertheless, what choice did she have? "Well, first thing you should write is 'I, then your name.'"

He nodded, started writing, then stopped when he got to the place for his name. "If I tell you my name, will you tell me whether you're in love with my grandson?"

She chuckled. "Why? Is your name a secret?"

"Only Roscoe knows." He grinned. "If I told you, that would make two."

She shook her head, resisting the temptation. "You're going to have to write your name on a legal document, Gramps."

He lifted a brow. "My name's a humdinger, I promise you."

"Then you'd be let down if you traded it for the information that I'm not in love with your grandson." She said the words with a conviction she didn't actually feel. "In fact, after Stacy comes in, you'll understand that I'm trying to make sure Wyatt is cured of his fixation with me."

"What are you up to?"

"Never mind. It's a surprise."

As she and Gramps worked, the rest of the gang began to show their faces. First Marlie, then Wyatt strode through the door. When she heard the sound of Wyatt's bootsteps, Margo made a point of not glancing up, even when Gramps nudged her. Finally, she heard Marlie's long, low whistle.

Margo finally looked up and felt her heart stop momentarily. Standing just in front of her, Wyatt was holding the biggest bouquet of roses she'd ever seen in her life—in every color. Pink and orange and peach and red. The whole room reeked of their singular perfume. She had to get beyond the intoxicating smell before she realized there was something about Wyatt, besides the roses, that was different. His hair, for one. He'd trimmed it. And he was shaved as clean as a whistle...and if she wasn't mistaken, some of the smell wafting around the room was men's cologne. The dark blue material of his shirt was so new that it still bore the fold marks from the store. And he was also wearing a tie—not his custom at work. His jeans were tidy as always, and his boots were polished to a high shine.

And he was staring at her with an intensity that made her decidedly uncomfortable. Not that she hadn't seen that particular glint in his eye before. The last time had been just last night, when he'd come knocking on her door. But he'd never sparkled at her so obviously in public before—at least, not in front of this public. Gramps and Marlie and now Tom from the kitchen were all staring at her, as if she'd done something.

Gramps let out a whoop. "Whoo-ee! Wyatt, looks like you won a beauty contest." He sniffed. "Smells like it, too!"

Wyatt flicked his grandfather a long-suffering glance then turned to Margo, holding the roses out to her. "I brought you these."

No kidding.

She took them—all thirty-six of the darned things. It was ridiculous. There were too many to hold in her lap, and they flopped over the booth, covering Gramps's will, and practically covering Gramps, too.

Margo attempted to swallow past the dry lump she felt in her throat when she looked into Wyatt's eyes. Something terrible was happening to her—something she had been fighting hard not to feel. She was feeling way too much for this love-struck cowpoke. But that was wrong—all wrong. She had plans...the trial of a lifetime back in New York...

As she stared mutely at Wyatt, her throat still too tight to speak, she heard the Lonesome Swallow's door open and the sound of footsteps. Then, abruptly, the footsteps stopped. Tom was the first to stare at the newcomer, and his eyes beneath his glasses were dewy with adoration. Then Marlie looked, her jaw dropping in amazement, then Gramps. Margo didn't have to glance over to know who was standing there, taking in the scene, rose by rose. But look she did.

Stacy was a knockout. They had dyed her hair from its usual dark-rooted platinum to light brown—her real color, Stacy had informed her with distaste. The new color softened her, made the fine bones of her face seem less pointy and stubborn and more classically beautiful. Her green eyes appeared less beady when they weren't obscured by layers and layers of gloppy mascara, and her eyeshadow had been toned down, too. She wore a light pink lipstick that matched the conservative dress she wore. Anyone who looked at her would think she was a Madison Avenue office worker, rather than a tough, scrappy Texas waitress.

Then she opened her mouth. "What the hell's goin' on here?"

She hunched her shoulders defensively, planted her fists on her hips, and glared at spiffed-up Wyatt and then at all those roses in Margo's lap. For long uncomfortable seconds her gaze travelled between the two of them. Wyatt, for his part, looked up at Stacy, blinking in surprise, but didn't say anything. He just smiled, faintly, and looked back at Margo for her reaction.

Gramps grinned at Stacy. "Wyatt brought Margo here some flowers."

Margo felt like hiding. This wasn't going at all as planned! Why wasn't Wyatt looking at Stacy? Didn't he notice how sophisticated looking she was?

Stacy stared at the garden of roses sprawled all over the booth, then fixed the world's most withering glare on Margo. Then, without another word, she turned on her demure two-inch heels and sprinted right out the door she'd just come in. Tom was right on her trail.

Marlie shook her head. "What was that!" She stared in shock at the door that had just slammed shut.

Gramps shrugged impatiently. "Heck if I know! What's gotten into Stacy? Did she change her hair or something?"

"She changed her *everything*," Margo said, her voice filled with indignation. She glared at Wyatt. "Didn't you notice?"

He nodded, but he didn't seem to be paying a lick of attention to what they were talking about. "Oh, sure. She looked different."

"More attractive?" she prompted.

Wyatt appeared confused. "Well...I didn't look that closely."

"We made her over completely!" Margo shouted at him in frustration.

His lips parted in a smile. "Really? You're a real miracle worker, Margo."

Terrific. Just what she didn't need—more praise from Wyatt. She sank a little deeper into the booth and breathed a heavy, rose-scented sigh. Somehow, instead of solving the Stacy problem, she seemed to have exacerbated it. Margo groaned silently.

Wyatt glanced curiously around the room, then looked back at her, still grinning. "So, where's that surprise you were telling me about?"

8

STACY SLAMMED A WASHRAG into the sink. The wet cloth hit the porcelain with a hearty *thwack!* just as Margo walked in. Red marks stained Stacy's cheeks where she'd scrubbed off her sedate makeup. She had taken out her own cosmetics and was now going about reapplying her old look with a vengeance. She narrowed her eyes at Margo through the mirror. A dark streak of emerald green was brushed angrily across one eyelid. "Thanks! Thanks a whole lot for making a big fool out of me! He barely looked at me!"

Margo winced. "I'm sorry."

"I'll bet! He gave *you* roses!"

"I didn't ask him to."

That didn't seem to be the right thing to say at all. Stacy's cheeks reddened a shade darker than her bright apricot blusher and she planted her hands on her hips. "I guess you think you're too good for Wyatt. You think you're too good for all of us, Miss New York woman!"

"I do not," she said, startled by the accusation.

"You're just like that Mary Beth!"

Margo opened her mouth to defend herself, but she didn't know where to begin. Her first instinct was to deny that she was anything like the treacherous Mary Beth, but really she didn't know the first thing about her.

"What don't you like about him?" Stacy huffed. "It's been plain as day from the moment you walked into the restaurant that Wyatt was wild about you. Why isn't that enough for you?''

That was the three-zillion-dollar question, as far as Margo was concerned. Wyatt was romantic, funny, hard-working. The perfect man. If he lived in New York. Or she wanted to live in Nowheresville. But she didn't, she reminded herself. She'd spent her entire life trying to build something meaningful for herself, a career in a city she loved.

''If you don't want Wyatt, why don't you just go back to where you came from and stop pestering us down here!'' Stacy shouted at her.

Because someone there wants to kill me. Margo, tired after her long day, suddenly felt whipped. She'd thought coming to Texas would help her gain perspective, and solve her problems. But from Armadillo Bend, everything in New York seemed far away, and even more difficult to figure out. She'd been hashing the matter over for days but still couldn't settle on a plan of action. Would the FBI believe her hunch about Bob Thomasson, or would they slap her in jail for stealing files? After all, it was her word against his. If they slapped her in jail, then her work on the Garcetti trial—not to mention her entire career—went down the drain. In which case, maybe she should have stayed in New York and sat on her hands while she watched her boss undermine the trial.

She sagged against the sink. She'd thought she was doing the right thing—but it seemed all of her best laid plans were doomed. ''I can't tell you how sorry I am, Stacy. I'd turn back the clock if I could.''

Stacy pivoted away from the mirror, peered into Margo's face, and scowled. ''You look pale. Have you eaten today?''

Margo shook her head. That was the trouble with waitressing. All that food made her hungry, but she was always too busy to eat. The hungrier she got, the worse her waitressing was. Which made her feel as if she didn't deserve to take a break.

"I guess I'll try to catch a ride back home," she said.

Stacy wasn't making any offers. "Sorry I can't drive you. I'm waiting for Tom to finish his shift."

"You're going out with Tom?" Margo asked, perking up a little. "That's great."

"What's so great about it?" Stacy shot back. "Tom's nothing special. But at least *he* doesn't act as if I'm invisible!"

Tom would have moved a mountain for Stacy—though heaven only knows why. People in Armadillo Bend seemed to form attachments in just such a way to make life as hard as possible.

Margo left to try to bum a ride back to the house. And who should she bump into but Wyatt, who sensed her transportation needs without her even asking. "Want to ride with me?" he asked as soon as she walked out of the ladies' room.

She nodded. "Thanks."

They went out to Wyatt's pickup. "You look all done in."

"I am," she said, with a slight chuckle. "Now I know why I became a lawyer. Less stress."

He nodded sympathetically. "You need to eat something. You didn't have a bite all day."

"How did you know?"

He shrugged. "I notice these things. For instance, for lunch, Marlie had the fried chicken with okra. Gramps had his usual hamburger with extra pickles. Tom just settled for coffee and a garden salad because he's trying to trim down to impress Stacy, and Stacy had two chocolate milk shakes, a cheeseburger, fries, onion rings, and two pieces of strawberry rhubarb pie.''

Margo's stomach responded to all of the eating that had gone on around her with a vociferous growl. "And what did you have?"

He smiled. "Not much. Like you, I was saving up for dinner."

She shook her head. "I'm just looking forward to a hot tub and bed."

"You have to have supper," he insisted.

"Maybe a sandwich."

"I was thinking barbecue." He looked at her and smiled. "How about it?"

"I'm too tired to go out."

"I know the most relaxing place in the world," he said. "Very low stress. You can catch a catnap while we wait for our food, and I promise you it's got one of the best views in all Texas. You'll even discover the answer to one of the secrets of the universe," he promised.

That caught her attention. "What kind of secret?"

He waved a finger at her. "You'll have to come along to find out."

She considered his offer. On the one hand, she knew she was being bamboozled. Wyatt was sexy as all get-out and dressed to kill and playing on her weakness. For him.

But she really was hungry. And she hadn't had any barbecue in Texas yet. She couldn't leave without sampling some. Besides, she hated the fact that someone might understand a secret of the universe while she was left in the dark. "Oh, all right," she agreed. "But can I take a shower first?"

He nodded. "Of course. It's your night."

HIGH ON A HILLTOP with only the lights of a small cabin winking in the distance, Margo felt as if it really were her night, specially ordered up by Wyatt for her enjoyment. He'd spread a blanket over the tailgate of the truck, on which she now reclined, looking at the thick canopy of stars shining overhead. Crickets and birds chirped, and the air was thick with the smoky smell of barbecue, which Wyatt was cooking up nearby.

He must have been planning this evening for some time, Margo decided, because he had the meat marinated, the coleslaw shredded and ready to go, and his own potato salad at the ready. Of course, the latter he'd stolen from the Lonesome Swallow—but he must have been pretty sure that she would agree to this outing to think to bring it home with him.

She frowned. Was she that much of a pushover, or was Wyatt that sure of his powers of persuasion?

She glanced over at him and grinned. He was circling the charcoal grill with a huge fork in one hand, eyeing the sizzling meat cautiously. Van Gogh painting sunflowers couldn't have been as intense. "The trick is to get it at just the right stage of doneness," he said. "Right before the last vestiges of pink have disappeared."

"Why don't you cut into it and check it?"

"That's cheating!"

She laughed. "I'm sorry, I forgot I was speaking to the Van Gogh of the pit grill."

She lay back and stared up at the stars that hung above her like a thousand sparkling bulbs. "Why did you pick this place?"

Before she knew it, she was looking straight up into

Wyatt's face...or, rather, he was looking down into hers. She hadn't even heard him move away from the fire.

"You'll see," he promised.

It must have something to do with that mystery of the universe he'd been talking about. She propped herself up on her elbows and smiled. "We could have just gone to your Uncle Roscoe's for barbecue."

He shrugged. "That's okay. I use his recipe."

She laughed. "Does Gramps know?"

"Of course not." He stepped back over to the grill and poked at a piece of meat. "Did you want to go to Uncle Roscoe's?"

She shrugged. "I'll admit I'm curious about him."

"Good, because in a way, I did take you to Roscoe's." He nodded down at the cabin down the hill. "That's his house."

She whirled and squinted at the simple frame house. "Oh! I assumed he lived in town, near his restaurant."

"We're really not that far from Armadillo Bend," Wyatt replied. "We just had to take a winding road to get up to the top of this hill. Actually, we're about halfway between my house and town."

Margo squinted off into the distance, trying to get her bearings. But there wasn't another light on the ground. "Everything's so spread out here. I'm not used to being so isolated, but I have to admit it's peaceful."

"All this quiet doesn't still make you nervous, like it did your first night here?"

"Not as nervous as walking downtown at night in New York City." She remembered the night she'd come out of work into the damp, empty streets, and almost had a car crush her like a bug. The memory made her shiver. That incident seemed so long ago, it was easy to forget the threat was still out there.

Wyatt frowned at her. "Anything wrong?"

She shook her head, and forced a smile. There was no use in thinking about Garcetti and his mob now. They would never find her here. "Just hungry, I guess."

Wyatt grinned and with a flourish picked up a platter he'd brought from home. After he'd loaded it up with food, and set two plates on the tailgate, he lit a citronella candle behind them in the bed of the truck. Finally, he poured two glasses of wine for them.

His brown eyes glinted at her as he clinked his glass lightly against hers. "Thanks for humoring me," he said.

She took a sip of wine and felt its warmth spread through her. Hot as it was during the day, the nights in the hill country were pleasant, almost cool. The drop in temperature gave a person time to recover before the next blistering day.

She took a bite of the meat Wyatt had lavished so much attention on, and nearly fainted. Maybe it was just because she was so hungry, or because she knew it had been lovingly prepared especially for her, but Margo had never tasted anything so delicious. A moan of pure pleasure escaped from her lips. "This is fantastic!"

He nodded. "It's Roscoe's marinade."

Whoever was responsible, the food tasted like manna from heaven, and Margo ate until she was afraid she would pop. When she finally finished glutting herself, all she could do was lie back, almost feverish from her feeding frenzy, and wish that she were back in Wyatt's size thirty-six jeans.

He rested his back against the side of the truck bed, laughing softly at her. As his gaze bore into her and his smile faded into an expression more serious and searching, Margo felt the change to the very core of her being.

"So what do you think of Armadillo Bend?" he asked her.

"Oh, it's a hotbed of excitement."

"I mean really," he said, not laughing along with her.

She tried to think about the matter honestly. The truth was, she had expected something completely different. Something like Tallulah with a Texas accent—a sparsely populated wasteland. Even though Armadillo Bend was a Bingo and barbecue kind of place, it wasn't at all the one-horse, tumbleweed town she'd anticipated. It had character, and had a liveliness all its own, and yet it was isolated from big city problems. She'd grown to like the people there—with a few exceptions—and even looked forward to going to work in the morning and chewing the fat over coffee with their early bird regulars.

But most of all, when she thought of Armadillo Bend, it was impossible to separate her impressions of the town from her feelings for Wyatt. "I like it...very much."

Too much. She gazed into his eyes and felt her heart do an Olympic-caliber, gold medal flip.

He smiled and touched her arm lightly. "You know, I never thought there was anything lacking in Armadillo Bend till I met you. I like it much more, now that you're here."

The simple contact, the simple words, sent a lightning bolt of awareness through her, and she straightened, forgetting her full tummy, forgetting everything except the torrent of emotions roiling in her. She tried to remind herself of the wine she'd drunk; that surely had a lot to do with how tempted she was to boldly offer her lips to Wyatt. Alcohol always affected her more strongly than it did other people. But the strange thing was, when she looked into Wyatt's eyes she felt relatively clear-headed.

I want him. The declaration echoing in her head was so simple, so elemental. So seductive.

She was no novice when it came to sex and relationships. She'd had her share of heartbreaks; though when she'd started her pressure-cooker job at the D.A.'s office, she decided that the hassles of romance weren't worth the headache. It had been a wise decision, allowing her to remain targeted on what was really important to her: her career. But what had led her to Armadillo Bend if not her faltering career?

She was astonished when an answer to that question actually popped into her head: Wyatt.

The truth was, she could have gone anywhere in the United States and hidden out in a roadside motel. Doing so would have been a lot easier, in fact. She wouldn't have had to bus tables and handle ornery grandfathers and deal with aching feet at the end of the day. She wouldn't have had to dodge jabs to the nose and worry about getting locked in potato cellars. But she wouldn't have been with Wyatt, either. And that's what had really brought her to Armadillo Bend. The memory of Wyatt's kisses and his strong, protective embrace. Her feeling that nothing bad could happen to her under his watch. Even now, when she felt storm-tossed by conflicting emotions, his gaze was warm, reassuring, comforting.

He pulled her to him, and as their lips came close to touching, the declaration in her mind became a roaring demand. Want him? She was dying for him. Stampeding wild beasts couldn't have broken her from his embrace.

She didn't wait this time to be kissed. Instead, she twined her hands around the nape of his neck and pressed herself against him. They probably had some kind of word for this brazen behavior in Texas, she thought idly as she pressed her lips full against his. What would Louis L'Amour have called her?

A *hussy*. Attacking a man while half reclining on a tailgate of a pickup probably put her in that category.

But she didn't remain the aggressor for long. As soon as he got over the initial shock of her bold kiss, he turned the tables on her, pulling her into his lap. His hands settled on her hips, rubbing her against him in such a sensual way that she was instantly aware of his arousal. She felt a shiver work down her spine all the way to her toes. She'd never been locked in such a masterful embrace before; when he started working little gentle, expert kisses down the length of her neck, she felt like putty in his hands.

Never had her body seemed so weightless—so weightless and so full of desire. Her whole being seemed composed of nothing but nerve endings responding to Wyatt's every move and touch. Where his lips kissed, she felt a trail of fire that led right down to the molten core of her being. When he bent, she moved with him, until finally they were lying flush against each other across the blanket.

The next minutes flew by in a whirl of physical sensation—taste and touch and sounds of pleasure. Clothes were askew. She couldn't say just who had unbuttoned what, or when; she wasn't even aware of anything except Wyatt's lips against her newly exposed skin. Her bra straps were pushed back, exposing her bare shoulders. The bottom of her shirt was hiked up, and as Wyatt reached up to cup her breast, instantly bringing it to an aroused peak, the rational world slipped away quickly.

Instinctively she realized that her modesty was hanging by a buttonhole. It was do or die time. Time to put on the brakes or go full steam ahead.

Margo was all for steaming. Quivering with need, she bent and kissed the crown of his head, revelling in the piney male scent of him. He looked into her eyes again, his gaze so intense, so passionate, that she almost wept.

"I want to make love to you, Margo."

The words, spoken in a whiskey-soft whisper, melted whatever reserve she had left. Though her head might have cautioned her otherwise, her heart, not to mention other equally sensitive parts of her anatomy, was swept up in the moment. She wanted Wyatt with a fierceness she'd never felt before. The power of it stunned her.

"I want you, too."

The man needed no more encouragement. They tasted, explored each other compulsively, completely, and sometimes maddeningly slowly. Just when Margo thought she was at the point of being completely aroused, Wyatt would pull back, taking his time, as if they had all the leisure in the world. As if morning were something light-years away. He tried her patience wickedly.

As long as she lived, Margo thought, she would always remember the singular smell of their mixed colognes and the scent of barbecue. It acted on her like the most exotic aphrodisiac. She and Wyatt moved together as if they were born to be together. As if this was fated.

Ridiculous. A New Yorker and a long, tall Texan? Yet when he pulled away from her, she felt as if she'd lost a half of herself. She lay tense, anxious. What was he doing? Her body didn't relax again until she heard the muted sound of a small foil packet being ripped open. A grin of anticipation touched her lips. A long, tall, cautious Texan.

He sent her a smile that was tentative and loving and so sexy she felt as if she might just leap on him like an urban jungle tigress. But she was too slow for him. He pulled her on top of him, nestling her body against the stiffness of his manhood so that she moaned with unquenched desire. And then, in the next moment, he was inside her, and the world around them seemed to spin away until there was just them, barely anchored to the bed of that pickup, and the stars overhead, and the whirlwind of pleasure to be had in each others' arms when the night stretched before them like a promise.

"I LOVE YOU, MARGO."

At first Margo thought she was dreaming. But when she turned stiffly, and felt the cold steel of a pickup bed beneath the little wool blanket, she knew a dream would be kinder.

She bolted up to sitting, blessedly taking the blanket with her. Good Lord—she was naked! She'd almost forgotten... But of course, how could she forget the most incredible lovemaking she'd ever experienced in her life?

Wyatt had put on his clothes. In fact, he'd cleaned up the whole area and appeared ready to return home, so maybe she'd heard him wrong. Perhaps he'd said something like, "Let's go home, Margo."

But when she looked into those eyes of his, the sincerity in them left no room for doubt. "I love you," he repeated, with even more conviction in his tone than the first time he'd said it.

For a moment, if felt as though an iron band were squeezing her heart. God, she felt so mixed-up. Of course she liked Wyatt—more than liked him—but everything was happening so quickly. One minute they'd been eating barbecue, then they were making love, and before she knew it, she was half-asleep with a man proclaiming his love. And not just any man—Wyatt E. Lamar, who just a week ago she had considered some sort of Lash LaRue crackpot.

"But you can't," she argued as she quickly started snatching up her clothes and putting them on. "You barely know me. We just met a week ago!"

He smiled, and reached out to help her tug one bra strap back into place. "It didn't take me a week to understand what I felt for you. It didn't take me a day, or even an hour. When I met you, it knocked the wind clear out of me."

"But that's because I ran into you—we collided."

He nodded. "Don't laugh, but I think it was fate."

She wasn't laughing. She was too busy trying to remember. No, it hadn't seemed like fate, or love at first sight, or anything like that to her. She'd just been late, and preoccupied, and hadn't been watching where she was going. But somehow, to Wyatt, he'd equated the experience of her crashing into him as some sort of kismet.

And then she remembered. When they were making love, the possibility of fate had crossed her mind, too. Their bodies fit together so well it seemed as though they were meant to be.

"That's ridiculous," she declared, arguing with herself as much as Wyatt. "It was just an accident."

"Was it an accident that you followed me back here?"

She blinked, disturbed by the flash of discovery thundering through her being. Because it was strange that she had bumped into Wyatt just when she needed a place to go. For the first time in her life, Margo had needed a pair of strong arms for protection, and she'd run smack into them.

But she couldn't give in wholeheartedly to such a shaky superstition. If she and Wyatt were fated to meet and fall in love, where did that leave all that she'd worked so hard to become? She was a lawyer, not a waitress. She was a New Yorker, not a Armadillo Bender—if not, her flight from Tallulah would have been in vain. And what about her ambitions? The odds of success might be slim, but she still had a prayer of fulfilling her Court TV dreams. She couldn't pursue those in Armadillo Bend.

And she couldn't separate Wyatt from Armadillo Bend. It would be like...like pulling the Statue of Liberty out of New York harbor.

What was she going to do?

What had she done?

His gaze still enveloped her. "Margo, you don't have to say anything now. Maybe I shouldn't have, either." He smiled reassuringly. "But I couldn't just make love to you and say nothing. I had to let you know how I felt."

She swallowed past the dry lump in her throat, and became aware of the hollow ache inside her. Heaven help her, she wanted him again. And yet she'd already behaved so rashly, without thinking about the consequences, without thinking about how Wyatt might interpret making love. Not that she took such things lightly, but...

He looked off towards the little house in the distance and smiled wistfully. "I would like to have kids someday. Three, I think."

Children! Heavens! As usual, Wyatt was galloping way ahead of her.

"Don't you think three's a good number?" he asked.

She crossed her arms over her chest, willed herself to

breathe, and cleared her throat. "Two's better. Otherwise, the parents will be outnumbered."

The deep rasp of his chuckle worked through her like a tranquilizer. She, too, began to look at the warm cabin lights in the distance, and ruminated silently on babies. Though she'd always known she would have a family someday, she couldn't have said how she was going to achieve this feat: she certainly hadn't taken steps to search for a mate. She'd been too caught up in her job. And living in the crowded city didn't exactly encourage the procreative urge. Housing was expensive; schools were a mess; just everyday living was a struggle.

But raising kids in the country was different. Her own free-ranging small-town childhood made that sort of lifestyle easier to imagine. She liked the idea of a child having lots of space to have adventures in, and the opportunity to do fun things like riding horses and ramble around the countryside, unfettered by city fears. She smiled, just able to imagine two tall, Wyattish youngsters roaming around these hills.

Wyatt was watching her again. Without looking at him, she was aware of his slightest movement, his every breath. It was as if she'd suddenly been granted a sixth sense. So she tried all the more not to pay attention to him, concentrating all her thoughts on that little cabin.

Just then, an outdoor light blinked on, and the back door opened. She squinted. "Looks like your uncle has company," she observed, as a figure of a man appeared on the back doorstep.

"I know." Wyatt didn't even glance down at the house—and she didn't have to look at him to know that his gaze was still on her.

When the back door closed again and the man disappeared, she looked at Wyatt. "How do you know?"

"Because Uncle Roscoe has the same visitor several times a week."

"Who?"

"Can't you guess?"

Margo's jaw dropped as realization struck her. "Gramps!" Now she understood what those nighttime walks were all about!

"They have a bi-weekly domino game, and have had for years."

She shook her head. "That crazy old fellow has the whole town snookered!"

Wyatt laughed. "They must think it's good for business to have everyone believe they're arch rivals."

She thought about Gramps's planning his will to guard himself against his brother and laughed. "He certainly had me fooled."

So why had he wanted her to help him with his will?

"That's the secret of the universe I was telling you about," Wyatt said. Then he grinned. "Was it worth the trip?"

She couldn't meet his eye, and instead busied herself with folding up the blanket. Their love nest. She didn't give a hoot about Gramps, and she could barely remember the meal she'd stuffed herself on. But making love with Wyatt...that had been worth the trip.

Not that they would ever be able to do that again. There was too much standing in the way. Her work. His home. Perhaps the FBI, if her boss had turned her in yet for stealing files.

But at least this night would give her something to dream about when she was back in New York...or in federal prison.

9

NAPKIN FOLDING DUTY had the distinct advantage of not requiring any contact with customers, and since Margo had been in a funk all morning, she gratefully jumped at the chance to do something other than apologize to people for confusing orders, which she'd done three times already. Try as hard as she might to concentrate, her head wasn't in the job.

It was back on that moonlit hillside, looking dreamily into Wyatt's eyes. She let out a sigh, remembering the feelings and emotions that had flooded through her like a raging river.

The noise brought a chuckle from Gramps, who worked beside her. He was a faster folder, even when he was absorbed in Court TV. "We'll never get these napkins ready for the reception tonight if you don't stop mooning after my grandson." She swung her startled gaze on him, causing him to laugh again. "Oh, it wasn't hard to guess. I had a little romance myself once, you know."

She blinked. "There's no romance between me and Wyatt."

"Uh-huh," he said. "That's why every time Wyatt's in the kitchen, you're looking around for him, and whenever he's around you, your face goes as red as one of my Big Boy tomatoes."

Was she that obvious?

"Kind of like now," he said, chuckling as he glanced up at the antacid commercial on the television.

She felt another blush spread over her cheeks and bent over her napkin stack with renewed vigor. She needed to get out of here. She would have before now, except...

Except she had been lulled by the goings-on in Armadillo Bend. And by her flirtation with Wyatt. At least, she'd always considered it a mere flirtation...until last night. After their picnic, there was no denying that she and Wyatt were involved. Unwittingly, she'd fallen for all that laid-back charm. Without conscious thought, she'd made a shift from simple dalliance to serious smittenness, something she had no right to feel for someone whose life was so different from her own.

She sighed, overwhelmed by all that had happened to her, so unexpectedly.

Without looking away from the set, Gramps spoke. "I thought you said you didn't love him."

"I..." She didn't want to answer that. She couldn't. So she changed the subject. "I thought you said you were having a feud with your brother!"

He swung around. "What are you talking about?"

She folded her arms and grinned. "I found out the secrets of your walks, Gramps. You faker!"

He slapped a folded napkin down on the bar. "Nosy New York women! What will the world think of next?" He peered closely into her eyes. "Bet you still don't know my name, do you?"

She crossed her arms. "I suppose Rumpelstiltskin would be too easy."

He cackled. "You'll never guess. Not if you're here a million years."

And for the first time, he sounded as if he wouldn't mind if she actually stayed that long. She felt a rush of triumph. Gramps liked her! She didn't know what she'd done to win the old curmudgeon's seal of approval, but it was something she would cherish as much in its own way as her law degree.

As if taunting her, the television chose that moment to return to the New York studio, where they were previewing the Garcetti case.

Gramps grinned in anticipation. "That's going to be a good 'un."

Margo looked up, and then felt the blood drain from her face as her picture flashed up on the corner of the screen. In the foreground, a grim-faced announcer stood in front of the courthouse in downtown Manhattan.

"Inside sources have released some startling new developments about this case. One of the assistant district attorneys in the Garcetti case, Margo Haskell, has disappeared under mysterious circumstances. A colleague, Barry Leiberman said that Ms. Haskell either walked out of the D.A.'s office with some important files, or was abducted with them while they were on her person. There has been some speculation that she might even be working in collaboration with Garcetti's men."

The room was spinning. It was almost a minute before the world around her registered again, and Margo realized that the sounds of the diner behind her were going on as usual. People were eating, and Marlie was bantering with one of their late-morning regulars. Hank Williams was so lonesome he could cry. No one had been paying attention to the television; no one ever did.

Only Gramps. She couldn't look at him.

"You care to explain this to me?" he asked, his kindly teasing tone of moments before gone. Completely gone.

Slowly, she turned to face him. His blue eyes were fastened on her with eagle-sharp intensity.

She swallowed, then admitted, "I wasn't abducted."

"Are you tellin' me you stole the missing files?"

Sick, she nodded. "Please...it's not how it looks. I'm not working with the mob—that's preposterous! It's just that Barry Leiberman hates my guts. He was trying to undermine my career there."

Gramps let out a bark. "So you tried to save it by heading for the hills."

Her cheeks reddened. "Only because my life was threatened. I would have stayed in New York, but Garcetti's men were trying to kill me. In fact, I'm almost convinced the D.A. himself was in on some kind of plot." She realized that her ranting probably sounded like pure gibberish.

"So *that's* what led you here," he guessed. "You were running."

She nodded miserably, feeling craven and foolish. And disloyal. She should have told them, all of them, why she was here.

Gramps appeared only slightly sympathetic. "You've just been using this place as a hideout—it had nothing to do with Wyatt at all."

"That's not true." She ducked her head. "Well, it wasn't at first. But now...well, I don't know."

Gramps was silent for a moment, but his silence spoke volumes. He thought she'd been leading Wyatt on, which just wasn't true. Was it? If she had been, the plan had backfired.

Of course, her plans usually did.

"All I can say, missy, is that you'd better skedaddle back to where you came from, and try to clear up your mess."

"I will," Margo agreed quickly. "The next flight out."

He frowned. "Make that the first flight out tomorrow. There's the wedding reception tonight, and we're short-handed as it is. You could at least show Wyatt that courtesy."

"Of course," she repeated. She felt so guilty she would have agreed to crawl back to New York on her hands and knees if he'd told her to. And to think, just last night she'd been in Wyatt's arms, thinking about fate and children...it seemed so unreal now. So wrong. How could she have forgotten that her real life would yank her back to New York, away from this quiet little community?

"First thing tomorrow morning I'll drive you to the Austin Airport," Gramps said.

She nodded numbly. Tomorrow. That was so soon!

But she had no choice.

Suddenly, she was faced with less than twenty-four hours left in Armadillo Bend. Time to go back and face the music...the mob...and to tear her heart away from a certain good-looking Texan.

NORMALLY, STACY DIDN'T watch Court TV, especially at home, but the jury was out on the murder trial that had been going on at work for weeks now, and she just couldn't bear not knowing how it all came out. That annoying station had her more hooked than a soap opera, and she couldn't stand those stupid soaps. She had enough unrequited love and romantic anguish in her life without having to watch it on the darn television.

She didn't actually turn up the volume on her set until she happened to glance over and see Margo's face on the television. The sight brought a gasp from her. At first she thought her eyes were playing tricks on her, but that was Margo all right!

She turned up the volume as the man on the screen was saying something about Margo's having disappeared. Disappeared? And it looked like she'd taken some stuff with her—important stuff. And that maybe she was hiding it for the mob!

That sneaky liar! No wonder she'd showed up out of the blue! Stacy had always known that there was something weird about her. She grabbed a pen and wrote down the name of the man at her office in New York. Barry Leiberman. Did she have a thing or two she could tell him!

She was considering telling Wyatt a thing or two, too—like that his dream girl was playing him for a chump, using the Lonesome Swallow as some kind of mob hideout. But then she thought better of it. She didn't want him to think that she was exposing Margo out of jealous spite, 'cause that wasn't it at all. It was for all their safety. Why, if Margo stayed on in Armadillo Bend much longer, there was no telling who would show up next.

Besides, this way, once Margo was hauled off to jail and everyone realized it was Stacy who had saved the day, she would be a hero. Maybe then Wyatt would take a little notice of her!

Smiling, she picked up the phone and dialed information.

THE LONESOME SWALLOW had never been so festooned with crepe paper, flowers and candles—or so filled with raucous, happy people. Every inch of the place was packed, and in the center of the swirl of all the activity was the bride, Leslie, a friend of Wyatt's since childhood. Heck, practically everyone in the room was a friend of his since childhood. But Leslie was the only one standing on a table doing a bridal striptease to Peggy Lee's "Fever."

The staff was nonstop busy, none more so than Wyatt, who had also been a guest at the wedding. But he wasn't so busy that he didn't notice the way Margo was watching him covertly. He was wearing a dark suit and tie, but Margo, like the rest of the staff except Marlie, who had also been a wedding guest, were in their usual uniforms of jeans and long-sleeved shirts. To Wyatt, Margo in blue jeans looked sexier than any other woman in the slinkiest designer dress. Those jeans hugged every contour of her petite figure, and the shirt, with the Lonesome Swallow logo above the pocket, covered a body that he knew now was beyond perfection. He ached every time he thought about their night in the bed of his truck. In fact, he'd been trying to put the incident clear out of his head, at least until Margo was more sure of what she wanted.

Trouble was, it was almost as if he was outfitted with a homing device…and Margo was home. Wherever she was, he tended to gravitate. Whenever he looked up, his eyes instinctively met hers for a fleeting instant before they both looked away. And whenever he found himself momentarily unoccupied, her voice floated over the din of the crowd to taunt him, and make him wish he were the lucky son of a gun getting to talk to her.

She might be trying to put a little distance between them, but the truth of her feelings had seemed clear to him last night, when she was in his arms. High up on that hilltop with Margo alongside him and the stars above them was as close to heaven as Wyatt had ever been. Margo had surprised him; she was usually so skittish around him, he hadn't expected her to let her guard down. But now that he'd gotten a taste of Margo uninhibited, he couldn't imagine a future without her in it.

Today she'd been avoiding him as best she could when she was usually just half a room away. Maybe she was embarrassed. Maybe she was as overwhelmed as he was at how far they'd come in so little time. Maybe she needed reassurance that a relationship between them wasn't as untenable as she feared.

Heck, he was worried about their differences, too. From New York to Armadillo Bend was a hell of a leap for anyone to make, especially a woman used to all the action of a big city. But if they didn't try, he knew he would always regret it. And after last night, he was certain Margo would, too.

Fate had brought Margo here, he'd about decided. But now it was up to him to convince her to stay.

Marlie almost ran into him with a pitcher of margaritas in one hand and a bottle of champagne in the other. "Sorry, boss man." There was almost no way to move around the packed room without bashing into someone. "The last character I bumped into asked me when I was going to throw the bouquet."

Wyatt looked down at her and grinned. "Hard to believe that the sedate church wedding we attended turned into this." He gestured across the room, taking in the full complement of inebriated wedding participants, ending with the groom, who was hauling his bride off a table in her slip. In three hours, the gathering had gone from heartfelt toasts to heavy partying. Over on the other end of the room, chaos was about to break out because someone had sneaked in a boom box and was attempting to play Celine Dion. Gramps's howls of protest soared above the hum of conversation.

Marlie looked over the raucous mess, then at the bride and groom, and smiled. "Nice to see a romance go right for a change."

At that moment, his homing device kicked in. Wyatt's heart hitched in his chest as he stared into Margo's beautiful face. She was laughing at something going on by the kitchen, but when she caught him watching her, two rosy blotches appeared in her cheeks and she pivoted away.

Marlie gave Wyatt a shove with the champagne bottle. "You might not have noticed, but that milling crowd over by the door is dancing." He looked down at her, clueless, and she laughed. "Ask her, Wyatt."

He swallowed. "Oh, well, maybe later."

"Later, my foot," Marlie declared. "There's no reason for you not to march right over there, take her hand, and sweep her off her feet, you dense cowboy chef. Heck, this crowd is so oblivious it's the next best thing to being alone."

And the prospect of being alone with Margo was too seductive to resist. Wyatt grabbed the champagne bottle out of Marlie's hands, poured two glasses, and worked his way across the room. When he reached Margo, she whirled, as if she'd known all along he was there.

"Break time," he said, handing her a glass.

She shook her head. "I'd better not."

He nodded, put the glasses on the nearest table, and took Margo's hand, leading her into the milling crowd. Behind him, she let out a string of protests, but for once, he wasn't listening. Then she dug in her heels, and he dragged her the rest of the way to the dancers. On one side, Johnny Cash was singing "If I Were a Carpenter," and on the other, Celine Dion was singing the love theme from *Titanic,* punctuated by Gramps's angry brays. Wyatt turned a deaf ear to it all and simply pulled Margo into his arms.

"I love weddings, don't you?" He grinned. "You know, they say that weddings produce more weddings."

"Like mushrooms releasing spores," she quipped.

Wyatt looked into her blue eyes. "Have you ever thought about getting married, Margo?"

"No," she lied. He could guess she was lying by the way her cheeks changed from pink to pale in nothing flat. "And if I were you, I would worry about how to get these wedding guests home rather than thinking about on the next wedding."

He ignored her words, as well as her attempt to tug away from him. "Myself, I've been thinking about marriage a lot."

She finally gave up the struggle and settled in to the hybrid two-step shuffle that was all the small space allowed. "Wyatt, there's something I need to tell you."

"If you're going to say that you don't belong in Armadillo Bend, I've thought all that out. You could hang a shingle and practice law. After all, Gramps needed your services."

Her lips twisted into a wry smile. "That will business was just a ploy of your grandfather's to scope out my feelings."

Wyatt was surprised. "About what?"

"About you."

She could have knocked him over with a feather.

"I knew it when I saw him visiting his brother last night," Margo said. "He told me that he was worried about Roscoe taking the Lonesome Swallow away from you."

Wyatt tossed back his head and laughed. But Gramps

attempting to get the New York lawyer lady to stay? He was surprised by that.

"If Gramps is on good terms with his brother, he obviously knows that Roscoe doesn't have designs on the restaurant."

"So did you tell him what your feelings were?" he asked. It would be helpful if somebody knew.

When she caught his gaze, her blue eyes darkened with unmistakable passion. If he hadn't been standing in the center of the entire population of Armadillo Bend, he would have kissed her right then and there. Then again, maybe it didn't matter who saw. Stacy had dropped a platter the moment she saw them together. Marlie knew instinctively that there was something between them. Even Gramps had known. They had never fooled anyone.

"Wyatt, there's something I've got to tell you." Margo's tone was grim.

Wyatt felt his heart beating like mad, and steeled himself for unexpected bad news. "You're married," he guessed.

She blinked in surprise. "Well, no—of course not!"

He waggled his brows, thinking of the worst revelations Jerry Springer had to offer. "You're really a man."

She barked out a laugh. "No!"

"I didn't think so...after last night."

Her whole body seemed to flush. "Wyatt, we shouldn't talk about last night."

"Why not?"

"Because we both lost our heads. It was a...a..."

For some reason, it pleased him that the word mistake eluded her lips. He had no intention of supplying the intended word for her, either. "A revelation," he said instead.

She stared straight ahead, at his chest, and he put his thumb to her chin and lifted her face to his. "You're like a jackrabbit who hears a car backfire, Margo. You're going to keep running and running until you're plum worn-out. Then you'll realize that there was never any danger to begin with."

She looked into his eyes, her brows knitting together, and considered his argument. Gramps's voice thundered somewhere behind her, still trying to turn off that boom box.

"Jackrabbit? What are you talking about?"

"I'm talking about all the differences between us. About your fears of leaving the big city for the first time in your life. If you stopped and looked around you, you would realize how well you get along here."

Her cheeks colored again. "Okay, it's confession time," she said. "Now would you just listen?"

He frowned. "Of course. Don't I always?"

She rolled her eyes, but said quickly, "First thing, I'm not from New York."

It was as if the whole room went silent. "You're not?"

She shook her head. "I misled you about that. I'm from Ohio—and not from Cleveland or even Akron. I'm from Tallulah, Ohio, population four hundred and twenty-three. And falling."

Wyatt was shocked by her confession, but not completely surprised. "Then you are a small-town girl?"

She sighed. "Through and through, I'm afraid. Believe me, I haven't been misleading you half as much as I've been misleading myself. But the truth was, I could ride before I got here. My first job was slinging hash—badly—at a country diner. And the first time I ever kissed a boy, it was in a hayloft."

"I'll be damned," he breathed.

"I'll even admit I like the country. And I like this place." She gave him a warning glance. "But that's not the end of my deception, Wyatt, so don't get your little cowpoke hopes up."

"Sweetheart, I don't care what you've done," he said. Suddenly, the gulf that had always been gaping between them closed up. Whatever hurdles they had to clear next would be a snap. She had to love him, even just a little, to make these confessions. "I knew it! It was fate."

She shook her head vehemently. "Would you listen? There's something else I need to get off my chest."

"Me too," he said. He reached inside his jacket and brought out the little Ziploc baggie he'd been carrying around all day. He'd meant to wait until the exact right moment. But now he couldn't help himself. He held out the baggie in front of her. "I got this out of the bank vault today," he told her.

She peered through the clear plastic and let out a gasp. Inside the baggie was his mother's wedding ring, which Wyatt's father had left to him when he died. It had always been Wyatt's intention to give it to the woman he decided to marry.

She took the bag in her right hand, examining its contents. "How beautiful!"

The ring was a sapphire surrounded by tiny diamonds. "It was my mom's," Wyatt explained. "And probably the most expensive item my father ever bought in his short life."

Margo squeezed her eyes shut. "Oh, Wyatt, put it away, quick!"

He laughed lightly, then willed her to look at him. He didn't want there to be any doubt of his sincerity. "The only place I want to put this ring is on your finger, Margo.''

She blinked. Her lips trembled. Then she pushed away from him, firmly. ''You're being impulsive.''

He nodded. ''I know.''

''You haven't been listening to me,'' she said.

''There's nothing you could say that would make me change my mind,'' he replied. ''I don't care if you're in the Witness Protection Program. We'll work it out.''

She sighed. ''Well, you're getting warmer, at least.''

He frowned. It couldn't be that bad. What could Margo have done in her short life to make her so afraid of the future?

Unfortunately, before he could find out, all hell broke loose.

Across the way, someone screamed. ''Wyatt! Come quick!'' A crowd surged around the jukebox.

Wyatt pivoted, trying to see what the commotion was about. Then Marlie appeared, and was pulling him across the crowd, which parted for his benefit, towards where his grandfather had been arguing with the Celine Dion faction. Now, as the room fell silent, he saw Gramps lying on the floor, his face ashen.

10

MARGO'S LAST NIGHT in Armadillo Bend was one of the longest nights in her life. After the ambulance arrived and Wyatt sped off after it, Margo had caught a ride with Tom back to the house and waited. And waited.

And while she waited, she'd wept, and worried, and prayed.

Finally, she'd called the hospital and wheedled a nurse into telling her Mr. *Archibald* Lamar's condition. Margo had almost laughed when the nurse spilled the beans about Gramps's name, and she actually did laugh—for joy—when she heard that he was in stable condition and alert...and cranky.

She wondered how Wyatt was doing. The look on his face when they'd wheeled his grandfather out of the Lonesome Swallow on a stretcher was something she'd never forget, a horrible mix of worry and sorrow and cold fear.

At about one in the morning, Wyatt had called and told her that Gramps was fine, and they both would be spending the night at the hospital. Gramps had suffered a heart attack—a minor one, if there was such a thing— but doctors assured him that he would soon be minding the cigar box at the Lonesome Swallow again. Wyatt told Margo to try to get some sleep.

As if.

By the time she'd walked to the Lonesome Swallow

the next morning, her feet were killing her and she was exhausted. Her boots were definitely not made for walking. Much as she wanted to wait around to see Gramps again and say goodbye, she figured the best homecoming present she could give him was not to be there when he came back. She hoped one of the truckers who were breakfast regulars at the Lonesome Swallow would give her a ride into Austin, where she could catch a cab to the airport.

At the Lonesome Swallow, she was able to walk right in the front door, indicating that she was not the first arrival. The employees parked on the other side of the building, so she couldn't see whose cars were there. Apart from Gramps's '66 Chevy, there was only a lone white Ford out front, a rental that was probably one of the guests' from last night—someone, no doubt, who had overindulged and had caught a safe ride home.

She sniffed the air, hoping that Marlie had arrived and had put on a fresh pot of coffee. She could use a stiff slug of caffeine.

But there was no aroma of java in the air. The dining room was silent and her boot heels echoed eerily against the wide plank boards of the floor as she strode past the bar. "Hello?"

She stopped, listening. She thought she heard a sound coming from the kitchen, but she wasn't sure.

It occurred to her that maybe in all the hubbub of last night, with the party breaking up and Gramps's attack, everyone had forgotten to lock up. In that case, maybe she was the first one here.

Still, she remained frozen to the spot, concentrating on the absence of sound so intently that the loudest noise to her ears was the thumping of her own heart. A chill of awareness swept through her, and the raised hairs at the nape of her neck gave her the distinct impression she was being watched. She didn't know what to do next; if she left the restaurant, there wasn't a pay phone for miles. And if she did call the police, what on earth would she tell them? That she had a creepy feeling?

Slowly, so very slowly, she began backing towards the bar, where there was a phone under the counter. Heel, toe, heel, toe were placed down ever so gently. Tension coiled inside her like a spring. When finally she was almost to her destination she threw caution to the wind, turned, ran behind the bar and grabbed the phone.

"Drop it!"

The man's voice startled her so that she did better than drop it; she instinctively threw the phone at whoever had spoken. Unfortunately, it missed the gun-pointing black-clad figure in the ski mask who hovered in front of the swinging kitchen door. Margo batted her eyes in disbelief. The menacing robber looked so out of place in the homey room, with its checkered curtains and sturdy wood tables.

"Get out from behind that counter, Margo," the ski mask ordered in a raspy voice.

She jumped. Oh, lord, he knew her name! As she followed his instructions, she tried to place the voice. It didn't sound Southern, like any of her customers...but maybe someone passing through had remembered her from her name tag. Or maybe this was the mob hit she'd thought she'd escaped from.

When she circled back around the counter, the man moved forward quickly and grabbed her arm. It twisted painfully, causing her to shout in pain. Instinctively, she kicked the robber as hard as she could in the shin. She was recovering her wits enough to be angry, but not enough to be wise.

"Who do you have in the kitchen, you scumbag?"

He wrenched her arm again, shutting her up and practically bending her double. "Two ladies, who will be fine just as soon as you give me what I'm looking for."

"None of us have access to the restaurant safe," she reasoned with him angrily. "You won't get anything from us."

"It's not money I'm looking for, Margo."

The voice was less raspy this time, and more sneering. More like how she was used to hearing it—in the offices and corridors of the D.A.'s office in Manhattan. A cold wave of recognition washed over her. "Barry!"

The hard metal of his pistol jabbed into her side. "Shut up!"

It was him. Barry Leiberman, her rival at the D.A.'s office—her nemesis. He'd turned out to be more dangerous than she'd ever guessed.

"Are you insane?" she asked.

"Were you, when you stole those files?"

"Is that why you're doing this? For the files?"

A pair of hard, shiny eyes peered at her through the eye slits of the ski mask. "That's what I want, all right. And after I get them, I'm going to make sure you're out of my way for good."

For a split second, her heart stopped beating. Out of the way? For good? The only way he could be sure of that was if he killed her. "Barry, that's nuts! I'll *give* you the files."

"Damn right you will."

"You don't have to hurt anyone! Let the others go!" She could only hope that Marlie and Stacy were okay.

"I wouldn't worry about your co-workers, Margo. They'll be fine."

She swallowed. Beads of sweat were starting to trickle down her temples. "This is crazy. You'll be caught."

"Me?" he asked with malicious glee. "Why would anyone come after me? If anything happens to you, everyone will know that Garcetti had it in for you." He laughed. "You looked pretty funny, Margo, thinking that you were running from the mob."

Her blood ran cold as she remembered the night the car had almost hit her...the afternoon someone had shot at her...and that same day, when someone had tossed her apartment, going through even her most intimate belongings. She felt sick, and foolish.

No one in Garcetti's mob had been trying to kill her. It had been Barry all along. He'd been insanely jealous of the progress she was making at the D.A.'s office, especially after the D.A. announced that she would be presenting the forensic evidence in an important, televised case.

"You convinced Bob that I needed to be sent away for the duration of the trial," she said.

"I didn't think you'd be so cagey as to take off with evidence." His eyes regarded her flatly through the ski mask. "I don't know if you're very smart or very stupid."

She feared she would soon be very dead. "But why did you start stealing files before I left if you thought I was about to be sent out of town?"

"Bob was dragging his heels, that's why! I was afraid he wouldn't replace you, so I stole the file from his office so I could make you look careless, as if you'd lost it. But you were gone before you could look incompetent.

Imagine my joy to discover that you did me one better by appearing to be a thief.''

She tried to ignore his sadistic laughter. "How did you find me?''

He nodded towards the kitchen. "Over the phone yesterday little Miss Waitress in there said you were hiding out here.''

Margo was shocked. "Stacy told you?''

He laughed. "I can see you're as adept as ever at making friends among your co-workers.''

She scowled. Stacy must have seen the same report she and Gramps saw. She should have known someone would.

"Those two think this is just a garden variety robbery,'' Barry said. "I was waiting for you—but if you don't tell me where those files are, you'll all have to die.''

Margo shrank back. "Why should anyone get hurt, Barry? I'll give you the files—and when you go back and tell Bob what I've done, my career will be history. You'll be a hero. Isn't that enough?''

He smirked. "It would be if I trusted you not to be able to fast-talk your way out trouble. Bob always liked you best!''

Good grief, he was acting like a jealous sibling—now she *knew* he was nuts.

She didn't want anything to happen to Marlie and Stacy, but then again, she wasn't in any hurry to end her own life, either. If she could just keep Barry from the files for longer…long enough to come up with some kind of plan.

She stepped backwards towards the bar. "Let me see…'' She shook her head. "If I could just remember…''

The gun barrel butted her in the side again. "Quit stalling."

"I'm not," she lied. In her mind's eye, she envisioned the gym bag hidden under the piles of onions in the dark root cellar. That wasn't anywhere she wanted to go with a gun-toting madman.

She was just trying to imagine how many places inside she could have him search before starting outside when she heard the sounds of wheels crunching on the gravel on the drive in front of the restaurant. Tom—or was it Wyatt? The thought of either man walking in on a man with a loaded gun made her sick with dread. At this point, Wild West heroism could end in tragedy. Her mind reeled as she tried to think of what to do next, then she heard a second truck drive up and around to the side. Both of them!

"What's that?" Barry asked.

She stiffened. She couldn't bear to think of anything happening to Wyatt, especially because of her. If he walked in unsuspectingly on the scene, it would be so easy for Barry to lose his head and simply shoot.

Barry's eyes narrowed and he muttered a curse. "How many people does it take to run this dinky place!"

"We'll have to hurry," she told him. "Out the back."

She felt almost nauseous as he dragged her past the rest rooms to the back exit. It was here Wyatt had kissed her once, she thought inanely. Oh, why had she ever come here? In terms of bad life decisions, it ranked right up there with stealing office files. She never imagined that her actions would have such terrible repercussions for everyone, especially Wyatt.

Wyatt! Suddenly, she remembered that in her jacket was the baggie with the engagement ring he'd been trying to give her. She'd planned to leave it for him this morning, with a note. But now...

The fields of vegetables behind the Lonesome Swallow were drinking in water from their irrigation sprinklers, and the gentle morning sun reflected off the dewdrops on the plants was breathtaking. Margo tried to keep her mind on their beauty and the gentle hiss of the sprinklers instead of the cold fear seizing her as they moved silently towards the root cellar. She could just see the edge of Wyatt's pickup. He would be coming in the front door of the restaurant now. Maybe he would have just noticed that eerie silence.

They reached the root cellar and she threw open the door. "Quick," she instructed Barry, who looked strikingly weird in that ski mask outdoors in the seventy-degree warmth of morning. "My bag's under that pile of onions."

"You first," he said, giving her a little shove.

This was it. Margo looked down the steep steps in a panic. Maybe she could figure out a way to turn the tables on him. Her mind reached back to the self-defense course she'd taken when she first moved to New York, but none of the little simulated exercises they'd done there covered the situation of being poked down a flight of dark steep stairs by a nut with a gun.

She sent up a silent prayer and took her first shaky step. She would wait to make her move until they were deeper in the dark and she might catch Barry off guard.

The next step she took, however, coincided with a metallic thud. Then Barry was pushing her. Oh, God! Panicked, she tripped down several steps, then managed to angle to the side, grabbing the wooden railing, hoping to trip her captor. But to her shock, as she held her leg out, Barry was already falling, and tumbled past her, landing at the bottom, face forward on the earthen floor.

Margo stood frozen in surprise, then pivoted and glanced back up the stairs. At the mouth of the cellar stood Wyatt, backlit by morning so that he appeared to have a halo around him. Another person was also up there—Tom, who was holding one of the kitchen's extra-large cast iron skillets in his right hand. Her rescue, it turned out, was a triumph of culinary skill.

Margo let out a yelp and dashed back up the stairs and hugged both men. "Oh, thank heaven! I'd about given up hope!"

Wyatt held his arms protectively around her, and she felt safe. Blessedly, gloriously safe.

When he spoke, there were equal parts relief and recrimination in his tone. "We found Marlie and Stacy in the kitchen. What the heck were you doing bringing that maniac out here for?"

"There was something down there that he was looking for," Margo confessed. "Something that belonged to me."

He frowned, then held her away, searching in her eyes.

"We'd better get our man good and locked up," Tom said, interrupting. "That bump on the head won't keep him out long."

They ran back down the steps, and while Wyatt checked to make sure Barry was breathing, Margo unearthed her gym bag. Tom retrieved the gun and let out a long, low whistle. "Lady, this could have done you some serious damage."

She looked up at the thing and shivered.

Just as they were locking Barry in the cellar, Stacy burst out the back door of the restaurant. She ran full tilt towards Tom and nearly knocked him over. "I've called the police!" she said, hugging him tight. She looked into his eyes with a melting stare. "Thank God you came in time, Tom! You saved my life!"

Two splotches appeared in the new hero's cheeks.

Margo smiled. "Tom clunked the lunatic over the head."

Tears rolled down Stacy's cheeks. "Oh, Tom, did you?"

Slowly, it appeared to dawn on Tom that his dream was coming true. His act of heroism had clearly brought him the admiration of the woman he loved. In a daze, he nodded.

"You wonderful, wonderful man!" Stacy stood on tiptoe and planted a kiss on his lips.

Margo looked at Wyatt. He was grinning, but his brown eyes were still filled with concern Soon she would have to explain all about her being here, and about the files, but she didn't want to ruin this moment for Tom and Stacy. Someone, at least, was having a good morning.

The county police arrived and seized a groggy Barry Leiberman from the cellar. In the Lonesome Swallow, Barry immediately started spurting out accusations against Margo. She let him blow off steam, then began to explain the situation to the officers. The cops didn't know what to think of the allegedly stolen files, but they did know one thing—Barry was the one who had threatened to kill people. They hauled him off to jail.

Margo sank against her chair where she'd given her statement and felt incredible relief as they dragged him away. Barry had been the culprit. She'd been wrong to steal the files, but as long as she got back with them to New York, pronto, maybe she would be able to convince

Thomasson that she had freaked out and taken the files for a good reason. If so, she might still be able to salvage a little of her reputation. After all, she'd been menaced from within the D.A.'s office, and when she'd told him of her brushes with death, Bob had done nothing to find out where the threat was coming from. Of course, mentioning that she thought it was Bob himself might not be good politics.

Boot steps stopped next to her and she grinned up at Wyatt, unable to hold back a flush of triumph, and gratefulness. In fact, she felt as beholden to Wyatt as Stacy did to Tom. Without him, she might have been the crumpled form at the bottom of those cellar steps.

He sat down next to her. "All this about the files... I guess it's true what you told the police."

She frowned. "What do you mean?"

He took a deep breath. "You just came out here to hide out."

She couldn't lie anymore. "Yes, I did."

"I never guessed," Wyatt said. "Not even when Gramps tried to hint..."

She sucked in a breath. "Gramps! How is he?"

Wyatt nodded, and for the first time she noticed how weary he looked. "Fine. He was the reason I came in to the Lonesome Swallow. This morning he told me that you had promised to leave." His gaze was accusatory. "Weren't you going to tell me?"

Margo swallowed past the sandy lump in her throat. "I tried, but it didn't work out. Gramps had his attack, and then, over the phone..." She hadn't been able to tell him over the phone.

Wyatt's jaw clenched. "You must think I'm a class A sucker."

His words, his tone, startled her. She shook her head,

but felt a flush of guilt seep into her cheeks. Somehow, she'd expected him to be hurt, not angry. "That's not true. I never meant to mislead you—it just…"

He smiled grimly. "It just happened that way."

She nodded.

"Margo, people just don't happen to wind up in Armadillo Bend. You have to work at it."

"I know, but—"

"When I asked you why you came here that first night, why didn't you just tell me straight out? Why did you lead me to believe you wanted to get to know me better?"

"I did!"

He stood and began to pace in front of her. "You used the Lonesome Swallow as your hideout, and for recreation, you used me."

"That's not true!" She shot out of her chair. "I love you!"

The words were out of her mouth before she could think twice. And she was glad. She lifted her chin defiantly, as if daring him to contradict her. "I love you," she repeated. It felt even better the second time. She smiled. She expected him to take her into his arms and give her the kiss of her life.

But that didn't happen.

His lips thinned to a flat line. "You love me. *Now* you love me. Last night you didn't seem to."

She was speechless. "Last night…" Last night seemed ages ago. But she did remember that he'd given her the ring…and she had been on the verge of giving it back when Gramps had had the attack. "But last night was different."

"Last night you still had ideas about running out on me," he reminded her.

How could she make him understand? "I was going to leave because I felt so terrible for lying. Everything was such a muddle, I felt I had to go back to New York to straighten it out before I could deal with all that had happened between us."

"Why didn't you just tell me the truth? Did you think that I wouldn't be on your side?"

She blinked. She hadn't thought about having someone, especially a virtual stranger, help her. All her life, she'd had to fight her own battles. She'd never considered leaning on Wyatt or anyone.

Her head hung low. "Oh, Wyatt, I'm so sorry. I've handled this all wrong."

His expression didn't change. "I asked you to marry me."

She nodded. He wasn't repeating the question. And he was looking at her as if he wouldn't trust her farther than he could throw her.

"What were you going to do with the ring?"

Her cheeks filled with heat as she remembered. She pulled out the baggie. Inside was the ring and the note that she'd slipped in, explaining why she was running away. "I was going to leave it in the cigar box for you."

His lips turned down. "I see."

She breathed out in frustration. "Don't be like this, Wyatt. This has all been so mixed-up. I started us out wrong from the beginning."

He took her hand. "Maybe that's the first truthful thing you've ever said to me. But there's one way to unmix it," he said. "Stay here. Let's straighten things out, as of now."

He was giving her another chance! Her heart soared—then plummeted just as quickly. "Stay in Armadillo Bend? Now?"

He nodded.

"But I can't! The Garcetti trial starts in three days!"

"I thought you said your boss had taken you off that."

"But with Barry gone I might be able to vindicate myself. Don't you understand what this means? I've been working on this case for months!" As she spoke, her old fervor for her career overtook her, even as some deep recess of her mind told her that every word was undermining her best shot at happiness. "I'm going to present forensic evidence that will finally jail a vicious gangster who has eluded the law for years and years."

He dropped her hand and stared at her, his face expressionless. "It's quite an opportunity."

"But it doesn't mean we're through," she told him.

A wry smile touched his lips. "Neither of us can be both places at once."

"But…"

But he was right. She couldn't have it both ways. It was either back to New York and her life's work or chuck everything for life in Armadillo Bend. There was no middle ground.

Her heart was being tugged in opposite directions, and the physical pain nearly caused her to drop in the chair again. But she lifted her chin stubbornly. The Garcetti trial! Wyatt didn't understand. She'd risked her life for this opportunity. She wanted this one success more than anything else in the world. It wasn't fair for him to ask her to choose.

"I can't make any decisions now." She crossed her arms. "I have to go back to New York. It's my job."

"That sounds like a decision to me, Margo."

It was, she realized.

The disappointment in his eyes was unmistakable. Almost as unmistakable as the final ripping of her heart in two. "All right," he said. "I'll have Tom drive you to the airport."

"MEMBERS OF THE JURY, do you find the defendant, Giancarlo Garcetti, innocent or guilty of the crime of first degree murder?"

"Guilty."

A roar of murmurs burst through the courtroom, followed by the sound of a gavel pounding. Meanwhile, the merciless camera zoomed in on Garcetti's grim face.

Gramps pivoted from his perch in front of the television to gaze at Wyatt. In fact, Wyatt felt as if every pair of eyes in the Lonesome Swallow were focussed right on him. "What do you think of your girlfriend now?"

Wyatt shrugged. "She did a good job, didn't she?"

"Good?" Gramps yelled at him in disgust. "She was great! And I should know—I watch this durn channel all the time!"

She was great. Wyatt felt equal parts pride in Margo for her expert work in putting away a notorious criminal, and shame for having tried to pressure her to stay in Armadillo Bend. After her story had gotten around, Margo had become the town's most talked-about citizen…absentee though she was. Now she'd made a minor splash nationally, and he felt ridiculous for ever hoping that she'd settle for his little small-town dreams. Especially since she'd told him that she'd clawed her way to success from that little town in Ohio. Anyone who'd gone so far in life wouldn't want to backtrack.

Though Margo would stay in his heart as the woman of his dreams, he guessed maybe he hadn't known her. Not really. Now the only thing he actually regretted was the manner in which they'd parted—the way he'd seemed to begrudge her this once-in-a-lifetime opportunity. He wished he could have the chance to see her again and apologize for making leaving Armadillo Bend hard for her, and tell her what all the time they'd shared meant to him, no matter what she decided to do with her future.

"I think we should all write her a card," Gramps said. "You, me, and the Lonesome Swallow crew, and take it to her."

"Take it!" Wyatt exclaimed. "To New York City? All of us?"

Gramps sent him one of those sharp-eyed level looks of his, the intensity of which hadn't diminished since his illness. In fact, he was fit as a fiddle again now, and as irascible as ever, though he did admit that in future he would bend a little on the subject of what music would be allowed in the jukebox. His one heart-wise concession.

"Not all of us, dumb cluck!" Gramps said. "Just you."

Wyatt snorted. "Nothing doing. She wouldn't want to see me anyway."

"How do you know?"

He shrugged. "I wasn't exactly sunshine and roses when she left."

Gramps nodded. "You wanted her to stay here. That's natural."

"But look at her," Wyatt said, pointing to the screen although Margo wasn't there. Only two commentators remained, summing up the trial. "She's worked hard to get where she is."

His grandfather dismissed that argument with a wave of a wrinkled hand. "Son, that's what they used to call in the movies—the good 'uns before the amateurs took over—a hollow victory. She's not happy.''

Wyatt laughed. ''No?''

''Couldn't you tell? She looked drawn. I don't think she's eating right.''

Wyatt stiffened instinctively. She had looked thin! And now that he recalled, when they'd first met she'd said she didn't know how to cook—except in a microwave. Terrible! Especially if she was under stress. He needed to call her, to tell her to...

He finally caught the direction his thoughts were racing, and realized that Gramps had used nutrition worry to panic him. He folded his arms. ''I'm sure Margo knows how to feed herself.''

Gramps grunted. ''She's lost nine pounds since she got back to New York.''

Strange that his grandfather would pluck such an odd number out of thin air. ''How do you figure nine pounds, exactly?''

''I don't figure,'' Gramps retorted. ''She told me.''

Wyatt's jaw dropped. ''When?''

''This morning.''

He couldn't believe his ears. ''What were you doing talking to Margo?''

''I called to wish her good luck,'' Gramps replied, as if that were the most normal thing in the world. ''She sounded more upbeat than usual, but I think that was because she felt fairly certain of the outcome.''

Than *usual?* ''How many times have you talked to Margo?''

Gramps thought for a moment. ''Let's see...she's been gone for twenty-nine days, so I guess that would make it...'' He grinned. ''Twenty-nine times.''

Wyatt was shocked. ''You've been calling Margo

every day?'' He himself hadn't spoken to her since she'd left!

Gramps shook his head. ''Well, not exactly. In the beginning, back in the hospital, she called me. To see how I was doin', you know. Now I call her and tell her how you're doing.''

He couldn't believe his ears. ''I don't believe it!''

''You will when you see the phone bill next month.''

''But Margo wouldn't care about what I'm up to—not when she's so busy.''

Gramps barked out a laugh. ''Not care? That's the first thing she asks when I talk to her. Or maybe the second—she'll hold off long enough to inquire about my health. But she's not so adept at hiding her interest as you are.''

He wasn't doing a very good job of it now, Wyatt thought. Just seeing his reflection in the television set, he could tell he was alight with speculation. Did she really miss him? Even while the trial was going on?

Gramps shifted on his stool. ''If'n I were you, I'd go fetch her back now before that durn phone company bankrupts us.''

Wyatt's pulse gave a leap. It all sounded too good to be true. ''I don't know about that.''

His grandfather tsked in disappointment. ''I thought you had guts, son. I'll admit I sometimes thought you were a damn fool, like when you chased Mary Beth off and on for years, but I have admired your stick-to-itness. Now all that dogged determination of yours seems to have petered out just when you needed it most.''

Had it? Wyatt felt his heart swell in his chest. But while his heart was carrying its torch high, his mind was trying to be more practical. ''I don't want to crowd her, or pressure her.''

"Aw, don't be a lunkhead!" Gramps barked at him. "Go after her."

Just then, the TV camera flashed to Margo coming out of the courthouse behind her boss, the D.A. His heart constricted suddenly, cutting off his breath. She was so beautiful—but strangely, in this moment of triumph, she didn't look as exultant as he'd expected. Could she really be thinking fondly of him and Armadillo Bend? Could it really be as she'd said that last day, that she wanted to try to work things out between them? He couldn't say for sure...but he did know one thing.

It was worth a shot!

He turned to his grandfather and grinned. "Start passing around that Hallmark card, Gramps," he advised. "I'm leaving for the airport in ten minutes."

"I QUIT," Margo announced brashly.

And rashly. The district attorney's mouth could have caught fly balls at Yankee Stadium. But no one was more surprised than she was by her pronouncement. She'd never meant to quit her job. She was too relieved not to have lost it when she came back from Texas.

Yet when the D.A., smarting from the attention she'd received during the trial, called her into his office to tell her that, to do penance for having taken the Garcetti files, she would now be relegated to research only, the words just tumbled out of her mouth.

Of course, Robert Thomasson wasn't going to let her to stay. Instead, when her words sank in his into a big triumphant grin. "So...at the success you're running off to join Street firm! So much for being

Margo gritted her teeth. lic, or anything besides

I'm going, and I don't care. Chasing ambulances in Ohio sounds better than working another day for an egomaniac like you.''

She wasn't holding out much hope for good references.

A half hour later, Margo closed her office door and, balancing her briefcase, two shopping bags full of her stuff, a raincoat and her umbrella, began to shuffle through the hallways of the D.A.'s office for the last time. Her legs felt rubbery. What had she done? Where could she go now? It was all very well to spout off about chasing ambulances; now that she was actually faced with the prospect of doing just that, she began to get a little panicky.

She couldn't worry about a job now. Something would turn up. What she needed was a holiday. Maybe she would just sit in her apartment and read books and rent videos for a week. Maybe...

She sighed as she pushed open the door to the outside and maneuvered her bulky belongings through. Every time in the past few weeks that she'd had an idle moment, her thoughts would turn to Armadillo Bend. Now she had an indeterminate amount of free time ahead of her, how was she ever going to keep herself from daydreaming about that little town? Questions about its inhabitants already plagued her. Was Gramps still sitting in his customary spot, barking at people? Were Clarence and Nick still hanging out at the Long Neck? And what about Tom and Stacy? Would they ever get married?

And then there was Wyatt. She sighed, and tried to keep tears at bay.

She didn't regret coming back to New York. In her ___ knew that she couldn't have ever stayed away ___ iven up her chance to try the case of a lifetime. But she did regret everything that went before…that she hadn't been more honest with Wyatt. More open. He was so sincere, naturally he didn't understand why she would have acted so secretively. She also wished she'd been able to convince him, that last day, of how much she'd grown to care for him.

Care? Who was she kidding? She was in love with him. And every day she talked to Gramps, she wanted to ask him to put Wyatt on the line to tell him so. But she was just enough of a coward, and just unsure enough of Wyatt's reaction, to hesitate. He'd offered her a lifetime once, and she'd turned it down.

She rounded a corner by a huge stone pillar at the front of the building and ran smack into another body. In an instant, all the items she'd so carefully tucked in her arms went flying in all directions—purse, shopping bags, umbrella. They spilled to the ground and began rolling down the steps. Her briefcase banged open and papers began blowing around her legs as if in a wind tunnel.

What a day! She heaved a heavy sigh and looked up apologetically into the man she'd just bashed into. "I'm sorry, I—"

Light brown eyes twinkled down at her.

Suddenly, the bundles were forgotten. The umbrella could roll off the face of the earth, as far as she was concerned. Somehow a miracle had happened. Wyatt Lamar was standing right in front of her!

And this time, when he held out his arms to steady her, she didn't pull back. Instead, she ran right into them and lifted up her lips for the deepest, most passio kiss of her life. The moment they touched, she worries and regrets melt away.

"Oh, Wyatt!" she gasped when she finally came up for air. "What are you doing here?"

He looked down at her and frowned. "I've come to tell you that you were right to come back to New York. I understand that now."

She stepped back in surprise. After a kiss like that, she'd been expecting him to haul her over his shoulder and carry her back to Texas, caveman style. "But I—"

He held out a hand to interrupt her. "I watched the trial. I can understand why you think you belong here now."

"Oh, but—"

"Everything you ever wanted is probably here."

She absolutely had to refute that. "Wyatt, if you'd just—"

Before she could finish, he took her into his arms again. "But I want you to come back with me," he said in a rush, pulling her just inches from him. "God help me, I swore on the entire plane trip out here that I wouldn't do this, but I can't help it. Call me selfish. I want you. I want you to be my wife."

Her heart was beating like crazy, but she had just enough of a devil left in her to keep him on tenterhooks for a moment. "Oh dear... There might be a problem."

His expectant expression collapsed into worry. "What?"

She looked down, shuffling her feet awkwardly. "There's something you don't know about me, Wyatt."

Nervously, he held her shoulders and gave her a little shake. His expression was frantic and heartbreaking. Margo almost laughed. "For God's sake, what is it?"

She grinned. "I'm unemployed."

He blinked.

"I just quit my job. I'm afraid I'll be a burden on you."

He smiled, and to Margo, it seemed as if the sun were shining for her alone. "Don't worry, we're still short-handed at the Lonesome Swallow. And I'll help you cram for the Texas bar," he offered, his blue eyes twinkling.

"That would be heaven!" she replied, stepping into his arms again. She hadn't kissed him in almost two minutes, and she was getting restless. She wanted to spend the rest of her life kissing this man. Amazing. She'd always known she would find her soul mate in New York City, and she had. He just happened to be from Texas.

He bent down to oblige her with a kiss, but stopped just short of her lips. "Heaven? In Armadillo Bend?" He waggled his brows at her skeptically.

She laughed. "As long as I'm in your arms, anywhere could be heaven."

Wyatt smiled. "I hope you'll still be saying that when we're eighty and in our rocking chairs."

She stood on tiptoe and promised, "I'll still be saying it when we're a hundred and ten, and on water skis."

And to start off the next seventy years right, he seized her lips in a long, tender kiss while her papers blew around them like oversized confetti.

Epilogue

GRAMPS WAS FOLDING napkins at the bar with the most recent help when Margo blew into the Lonesome Swallow.

"What're you doin' here?" he barked at her. "Don't you have clients to tend to?"

She pursed her lips at him. Even though they were relatives now, she still gave as good as she got. "Sure, but I've got a stomach to tend to, too. I'm eating for two now, you know. Don't y'all serve food around this place anymore?"

Gramps grunted. "To those what pay, we do." He looked her up and down, taking in her growing belly with a shaking head. Great-grandchildren. What would they think of next! "Doesn't even look to me like you brought your pocketbook."

She planted her hands on her hips impatiently. "Next time I'll bring a sign with me that says Will Work For Food."

He laughed. "Okay, but this time you can go out and get some potatoes from the cellar. There just aren't enough hands around now that Stacy's off having that durn baby of hers."

Margo breezed towards the back door, stopping only shortly to ruffle his helper's hair. The kid shook his head and scowled after her. He was four, and didn't like to be babied.

A moment later, Wyatt came tearing out of the kitchen. "Didn't I hear Margo's voice?"

Gramps nodded. "Sure did."

For a moment, his grandson looked frantic. "Well, where is she? Is anything wrong?"

Gramps laughed. "She's off fetching potatoes."

Wyatt relaxed, then stiffened again. "She shouldn't be lifting things!" he exclaimed, then spun and ran out the back door, too. He didn't ruffle the kid's hair on the way out; he tweaked his chin.

Gramps laughed at his helper's sour expression and kept folding. He hummed along with Hank for a while to "Cold, Cold Heart." Funny how things changed. Just five years ago it seemed that all romance in Armadillo Bend was doomed. Now, judging from the marriage rate and the rising population, the place was a regular loveville.

After the record had changed to the Sons of the Pioneers, and then to Patsy—oh, that Patsy!—his little companion looked up at him with concerned, inquisitive eyes. "Gramps, how long does it take to fetch potatoes?"

The boy was at that questioning stage. Always wanting to know things. He reminded him a little bit of his own son that way. Charlie had been a big one for always asking questions. "Not long."

Even this answer didn't seem to satisfy the kid. Nothing ever did! Looking at that little face, the Margo-blue eyes framed by a shock of dark hair like Wyatt's, made Gramps almost as impatient as the boy was himself. What would the future be for this one? Would he run off, like Charlie, or would he stay like Wyatt?

Maybe in sixty years, this little boy would be minding the cigar box. There was comfort in that thought.

Gramps hoped there would always be a Lonesome Swallow for the Lamars to look after.

"Gramps?"

"Yes, sir?"

The small face was scrunched up in worry. "Should we call the police?"

Gramps nearly fell off his chair. "Good heavens! What for?"

"Because Mommy and Daddy have been out in that potato cellar a long time. Something bad might've happened!"

"I doubt it, son," he said.

Naturally, this didn't sate the boy's curiosity. "Then what do you think they could be doing out there together?"

Gramps knew from years of living with Wyatt and Margo that they were just as in love as they were when they were newlyweds. Those two would sneak a kiss anywhere!

He looked down at his namesake and barked out a laugh. "I don't know for sure, Archie, but I can guess."

SUSAN MacLAND

Lovestruck

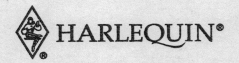

HARLEQUIN®

TORONTO • NEW YORK • LONDON
AMSTERDAM • PARIS • SYDNEY • HAMBURG
STOCKHOLM • ATHENS • TOKYO • MILAN • MADRID
PRAGUE • WARSAW • BUDAPEST • AUCKLAND

Susan MacLand credits her family and her hometown with instilling in her the dream to write romance. After all, living in small-town Georgia, the land of magnolias and moonlight, it's hard to be inspired to write anything *but* romance. And having grown up in an eccentric Southern family, writing romantic comedy comes just as naturally.

Susan's writing career has had many incarnations—from newspaper reporter to her present-day job of putting together computer manuals. When she's not working on her next book, Susan spends her time reading, bicycling and looking after her very spoiled cat, Longjohn.

This book is for Martha Kate and Howard Goggins. Thanks, Mom and Dad, for always believing in my dreams. In the parent lottery of life, I hit the jackpot.

And for Gladys O'Neill Hendrick Hardy, world's greatest grandma.

1

DRUCILLA LOGAN RAISED the high-powered telescope and searched the mountain ridge with the predatory patience of an eagle scanning the ground for an unsuspecting rabbit. She panned slowly across the landscape, one eye squinted. Suddenly, there it was—the pointed roof of an A-frame lodge, jutting out of the forest like a steeple.

Imagine that. A building that looked like a church was being used to create the most powerful aphrodisiac known to man. She chuckled at the irony of it.

The mad scientist had managed to keep his so-called love potion under wraps, refusing all interviews. But that was going to change. Tomorrow he would go up against Drucilla Logan, ace investigative reporter. The forest seemed to come alive and her pulse quickened. Her senses always became keener when she was about to move in on her target.

She had to figure out the best way to get to the chemist's compound from her rented cabin, which was nestled in a hollow farther down the mountain. She swung the telescope away from the A-frame and toward her cabin, and froze.

"No!" she gasped, frantically refocusing the scope. "It can't be!" Her extremities tingled and her pulse throbbed in her ears as the all-too-familiar image filled her view. It *was* him, the backstabbing bastard.

With a deft twist of her wrist, she zoomed in on the tall, lean form making a stealthy beeline for her cabin. She seethed, watching him pause to take a furtive glance over each shoulder. There was only one human being in the world sneakier than she was. And she was looking at him.

He'd started his career on the British tabloids of Fleet Street, where ruthlessness was a virtue. His savagery had won him a job as the top reporter on an American tabloid, the *Inquisitor,* where his motto was Nice Guys Finish Last. She knew how far he was willing to go for a story.

When he came to a break in the trees, he paused again. His hair shone blue black in the sun, and even though it was impossible given the great distance that separated them, she thought she could see the gas-flame blue of his eyes. Her heartbeat went staccato for a moment as it always did whenever he showed up. She swore savagely, not sure if the oath was for his treachery or for her own weakness. Why did such a cold-blooded, heartless rat bastard have to be such a hunk?

For years they'd been engaged in a battle of wits and one-upmanship while competing for scoops. The fiercer their competition became, the stronger their physical attraction. The results had been disastrous. She wished she was staring through the scope of a rifle instead of a telescope lens.

She retracted the telescope with an angry slap and stuffed it into her backpack. It was time to weigh her options. She could stay on the trail and avoid the undergrowth, or take a shortcut and travel as the crow flew. The mountain was steep, and recent rains had made a muddy mess of things, but she had to make good time or he would steal all her background material before she could stop him. With a last look at the comfortable hiking trail, she plunged into the forest.

As she started down the mountainside toward the cabin, her foot struck a mossy patch of unstable turf. She hit the ground and began to roll, her shout ringing in her ears. "Wait till I get my hands on you, Pierce Mountcastle!"

PIERCE CREPT TO THE CABIN window and peeked inside. She wasn't there. He leaned against the rough pine boards and released a long breath. He should be glad she wasn't home—that way, he could rifle through her background material unchallenged. Instead, her absence was an emotional letdown that throbbed throughout his body. Bloody hell! Why couldn't he get that woman out of his mind?

The door was locked, as he'd assumed it would be. Knowing Dru, she'd have brought with her a collection of high-tech gear that would put the CIA to shame. As isolated as this cabin was, she still wouldn't risk having her equipment tampered with. He reached into his pocket and removed two sharpened hairpins. Sometimes low-tech solutions worked best.

As he guided the pins into the keyhole, he felt a pang so unfamiliar that he stopped a moment to try to figure out what caused it. Was that...*guilt?* No, surely it was just a spot of indigestion. He thumped himself on the chest.

The woman was a dashed bad influence. If he didn't watch out, he'd start developing the same idiosyncrasies she had—like her insistence on truth in her reporting. When it came to getting a story, she could be as sneaky as anyone. But she refused to bend the truth when it came to her writing. What a daft way to ruin a good angle.

That was why it'd been so important to reassert his true nature the last time they had worked on the same story. Just to prove to himself that he still could, he'd resorted to some unsavory tactics while competing with Dru for the piece. The whole thing had turned out rather badly, and Dru had remained a bit sore about the matter.

But, dash it all, he had a reputation for barbarism to uphold. He also had to make sure he wasn't losing his edge. It was his edge that had long ago gotten him off the gang-infested streets of east London and into a newsroom before he had wound up in jail or worse. His edge had saved his life, and he had to keep it honed to razor sharpness. To do that, he'd learned to banish all feelings of affection and compassion. Not only had that skill kept him alive as a youngster, but it had also kept him from getting hurt as an adult.

But whenever he was around Drucilla, he felt that skill slipping. He couldn't get Drucilla Logan and the passion they'd shared out of his mind. It was enough to make a bloke think he was going soft.

There was only one thing to be done. He'd seduce her again and get her out of his system once and for all. And he'd get a good story while he was at it. Sure it was nasty. But they hadn't called him "The Shark of Fleet Street" for nothing.

He gave the hairpins a twist and felt the rusty doorknob turn. Taking another deep breath, he eased inside.

Sure enough, the one-room cabin was strewn with electronic gizmos, some of which he couldn't even identify, much less use. To his relief, he saw Dru's taping equipment, so he was relatively sure she hadn't made a move on the good doctor's compound yet. She was probably just scoping out the territory.

As he shrugged off his rucksack, he scanned the room, fervently hoping that she'd brought some hand-written notes he could nick. He spied her notebook computer and scowled. If all her material was committed to that bloody contraption, he was out of luck. Then he spotted her briefcase lying open on the rough-hewn table.

He sifted quickly through the stack of papers, discarding maps, scribbled directions and travel itineraries. He came to a slim volume of poetry and flipped through its pages. It turned out to contain love poems of the sappiest sort. That was Dru for you. On the outside, she was a hard-boiled reporter, but at heart she was a romantic. The wildflowers in a jelly jar at the center of the table were typical Dru. She loved all the standard girlie-girl things—flowers, poetry, perfume and candy.

As for him, his idea of a good romance was a nice dinner, a great bottle of wine, a few hours of terrific sex and a hasty goodbye. Whenever a woman started pushing for permanence, he was history. Love poetry, with its implied "forevers," filled him with dread. He dropped the book back into the briefcase as if it were a hot potato.

He continued his search until he found a dossier of Dr. Jackson Peel. He scanned the information, most of which he already knew. The eccentric chemist had spent most of his seventy years studying human attraction. For the past few years, he'd been holed up in an isolated mountain compound working on what he called a "love potion" that was rumored to be a powerful aphrodisiac.

The last paper—a copy of a memo to Dru's editor—proved enlightening. When Pierce read the details of her scheme to get into the compound, he laughed. "Well done, darling. I couldn't have devised a better plan myself, unless it's the one I'm going to use to get into that compound on your coattails."

The most amazing thing about Dru's plan was that it called for her to actually *lie*. Perhaps *he* had had an influence on *her*, he thought with satisfaction. Although she could devise a plan as devious as anyone could, she was completely useless when it came to lying. This was going to be fun.

He studied the map to the compound, committing it to his photographic memory. Then he replaced the memo at the bottom of the sheaf of papers exactly where he had found it. His fact-finding mission accomplished, he needed only to steel himself for Dru's arrival. It would be the first time they'd seen each other since their misunderstanding. Perhaps he should gird his loins or something—whatever that meant.

His gaze strayed to the bed. Peeking out from beneath a pile of clothing and other belongings was a tiny scrap of red silk. His heart seemed to drop into his stomach. *Steady on, lad.* He tried to ignore what he saw. His first instinct was to grab the garment, but he resisted—not for the sake of his pride, for the sake of his sanity.

He jammed his hands in his pockets and rocked onto his heels. Perhaps it wasn't what he thought it was after all. What harm could come from a closer peek? Sidling up to the bed as if he were approaching a pit viper, he leaned toward the clothing. Before he could help himself, he plucked the garment out of the pile and gathered it into both fists, savoring its slippery softness.

The wispy thing was the teddy she'd been wearing the night they'd made love—before he'd peeled it off her. A wave of regret, another unfamiliar emotion, washed over him as he buried his face in the gossamer garment, breathing deeply of her scent—lilacs. He'd swear he could feel her nearness, as if she were getting closer and closer, and his heart hammered harder. Why was he acting like such a besotted fool?

Maybe because she was the most feminine woman he knew, but as tough as nails at the same time. Dru was like the silk he held against his cheek—soft, strong and easy to let slip through his fingers.

He heard the door creak open too late to do anything but wad up the teddy and stuff it in his pants pocket. The door slammed with enough force to shake the cabin, but as he wheeled to face her, the shudder that shook him was of a more emotional variety. *Blimey.* The breath whooshed from his chest as he met her furious green eyes. She was beautiful.

Her jet-black hair, fair skin and delicate features had always reminded him of Snow White. But while her face might have been straight out of a fairy tale, she had the figure of a moll from a Raymond Chandler novel.

"You tea-swilling, crumpet-dunking, double-crossing limey bastard!"

He arranged his features into their customary guise of cool self-confidence. "Flattery will get you nowhere," he said, and with calculated emphasis added, "darling."

The blistering tirade Drucilla had composed on her way down the mountain died on the tip of her tongue, slain by *that word.* He'd thrown it down like a gauntlet, drawing it out for maximum effect in that velvety baritone and aristocratic British accent. Coming from those wide, sensual lips, that *daaahling* sound slid down her spine like a spoonful of honey, igniting each nerve ending along the way. Just as he knew it would.

"Don't call me that," she said through clenched teeth.

"I remember a night when you begged me to call you that."

She mentally flashed back to the night when, in the throes of passion, she'd begged him to say it to her. The only time she'd ever let her guard down had been with him. Big mistake. "Don't start with me," she warned.

Her earlier glimpse of him had not prepared her for the toe-curling effect of Pierce Mountcastle up close and personal. He was six feet two inches of suave sophistication and masculine elegance. He reeked of class and good breeding, even in khakis and a polo shirt. Though he'd slogged through the woods to get here, he looked as if he'd just stepped off the cover of *GQ*.

He could push her to do things she wouldn't ordinarily do, say things she wouldn't usually say. But she'd be damned if she'd let him sense the effect he had on her. With as much menace as she could muster, she said, "If you think you're going to steal this story out from under me, think again."

He feigned a wounded look. "I wouldn't dream of it. And may I say you're looking lovelier than ever. That mud on your knees and those twigs in your hair make you look like a pagan goddess."

She threw her backpack onto the dilapidated sofa and raked her hands through her hair. Her fingers came away with pine needles and lengths of vine gathered from her inadvertent roll down the mountain. She must look like Medusa on a bad hair day. "Save the compliments," she said, pulling a thorny bramble out of a lock of hair beside her cheek. "Just tell me how you found me."

Pierce watched as Dru picked at the vine entangled in her thick hair. It wouldn't do to tell her the truth—that he had a spy at the *Nova,* the tabloid she worked for, who kept him informed of her activities. Yesterday the spy had reported that Dru was on some kind of love potion story. He'd almost choked on his Darjeeling later that afternoon when his own editor, acting on a tip, had assigned him the same story. He'd hopped on a plane, and when he reached the local cabin-rental agent, the lady was only too happy to reveal Dru's whereabouts to the charming man who was—as she amusingly put it—a dead ringer for James Bond.

"You know I never reveal my sources, but since we're such good friends, I'll tell you. My editor assigned me the love potion story only yesterday. When I called for accommodations, the rental agent told me that her last cabin had just been taken by a lovely, doe-eyed wood nymph with an attitude."

Dru crossed her arms and narrowed her large green eyes. "You are so predictable. Is it even possible for you to tell the truth?"

Pierce pretended to think for a moment. "I *honestly* don't know. I don't believe I've ever tried it. Perhaps I never shall. Anyway, it doesn't matter how I got here. All that matters is that I'm here."

She'd opened her mouth, probably to deliver an angry comeback, when he noticed that one of the thorns tangled in her hair had slashed her cheek, causing a tiny rivulet of blood. He reached out to her instinctively, taking her chin in his hand.

When his fingertips made contact with her skin, she flinched as if he'd touched her with a hot iron. She tried to pull away, but he held her in a firm, but gentle, grip. With his other hand he reached into his pocket and, pushing aside the teddy hidden there, removed a pristine white handkerchief.

"You're bleeding. Stick out your tongue," he instructed, and she obeyed. He felt his breath become ragged as he touched the linen to the tip of her tongue. Close enough now to smell her perfume and see the rapid rise and fall of her breasts as her own breathing quickened, he suppressed a groan and dabbed lightly at the scratch. "It'll be all right, luv," he murmured.

She jerked away, tossing her head, her eyes flashing. "I've been working on this story for weeks. What makes you think you can move in on me and take over?"

Pierce placed the handkerchief in his pocket with a flourish. "I wouldn't dream of 'taking over.' Aren't you forgetting that both our papers were recently purchased by the same conglomerate? Since we now work for the same company, don't you think we should work together?"

"You've got to be kidding. After the acquisition, the *Nova* and the *Inquisitor* are going to be bigger rivals than ever."

Pierce allowed to himself that she was undoubtedly right, but he still had to convince her they could work together. It was the only way she'd let him stay. "On a story this big, with such far-reaching implications, I'm sure we could convince our editors to let us work as a team. That way both papers could break the story at the same time, only with different angles."

"Oh, yeah? Whose byline goes on top?"

"I thought we'd take turns being on top," he said, arching one black brow a fraction. He ignored the murderous look she gave him. "What I mean is that for each story in the series, we alternate whose byline is on top."

"How democratic of you." She looked at him evenly for a moment, saying nothing, and he could tell she wasn't buying it. Suddenly her expression turned benign and she said, "Sure. Fine. Why not? We'll go to the mad scientist together tomorrow, but until then, you can't stay here. You'll have to find someplace else."

"But there is nothing else. Why can't I stay here with you? I can't sleep in the woods."

She folded her arms across her chest in a defensive gesture. "I don't care if you have to sleep hanging upside down with the possums."

Pierce shivered. "I'm not worried about those furry creatures. But what about the snakes?"

"Snakes wouldn't touch you."

"Why not?"

"Professional courtesy."

"Very amusing. But, I say, I can't sleep outside, can I? Be a jolly good sport, eh?"

"Why is it that when you get in a jam, you get even *more* British?" She paused and looked down. "Look, after our...past history, there's no way I'm letting you stay overnight in the same cabin with me."

Pierce lifted his chin. "I'll have you know, in a pinch, I am capable of conducting myself in a professional manner without regard to any attraction we may have for each other."

"Oh, yeah?" Her gaze wandered over him slowly, and a hard, cynical smile tugged at one corner of her mouth. "Get this, Mr. Professional—your strap is showing."

Pierce looked down to see the bright red shoulder strap of her teddy trailing out of his pocket. *Blimey.*

"Where'd you get that?" Dru pointed and took a step closer.

"That? Um, that's mine."

"You're wearing women's silk underwear now? I don't remember you being quite that kinky."

"You have no idea." He gave her a leering smile, then quickly changed the subject. "But the fact remains—I don't have any other place to stay for the night, and it's getting dark." As he pointed toward the west-facing back door, Dru went toward it.

She opened the door and leaned out. He was right. Splashes of pink and orange lit up the western sky over the tops of the evergreens. Stalling for time, she leaned against the door frame and pretended to admire the sunset. Since he clearly wasn't going to go away, she had to play along with his partnership scheme and then ditch him when the time was right. But there was no way she was going to let him stay with her in the cabin. Not only did she not trust him, but how could she give him the slip when he was right here in the one-room cabin with her? It was time to give Mr. Mountcastle a dose of his own medicine, and the only way to do that was to make him sleep outside and sneak away without him in the morning.

She stole a glance over her shoulder just in time to see him snatch her teddy from his pocket and fling it back onto the pile of clothing when he thought she wasn't looking. She quickly glanced outside again and felt herself go warm all over. *He'd actually stolen her lingerie.*

"Look at that sunset. It's positively...romantic."
Pierce squeezed himself into the doorway next to her
so that they stood shoulder to shoulder.

He was right. Not long ago, the combination of a
beautiful sunset and the suave Mr. Mountcastle would
have been too much for her to resist. But that was then.
This was now. She had learned her lesson where Pierce
was concerned. *So why were her knees turning to jelly
just standing this close to him?*

"I don't suppose you brought any blankets." She
left the open door and went to the fireplace.

"No, but I do have a six-pack of beer."

She rolled her eyes and issued a humph of disapproval.

"It's imported," he added hopefully.

"Some things never change."

"What's that supposed to mean?"

She crossed over to the stack of wood on the hearth.
"Why is it that I'm always the one who comes prepared, while you waltz through life expecting other
people to do all the planning?"

He came to stand beside her as she stacked sticks of
wood onto the grate. "Don't think of it as a character
failing on my part. Think of it as the beauty of our
newly forged partnership."

"What are you talking about?" She didn't look at
him as she stood on tiptoe searching the mantel for
matches.

He put another piece of wood on the grate. "Don't
you see? Our individual strengths complement each
other perfectly. You're great at the advance work, the
research. And I'm great at the execution, the interviews."

She grabbed the stick of wood he'd just dropped and

shook it at him before throwing it back into the wood-pile. "I'll have you know I'm as good at 'execution' as you are."

Pierce backed off. It was clear that she'd be glad to execute *him* if she had the chance. Good thing there was no rotisserie on the fireplace, else he'd be roasting on it. "Of course you are. All I meant was..."

"All you meant was that you specialize in using your British charm to con people into spilling their guts, while I'm out busting my buns to get the story through legitimate means."

"Well, yes, in a manner of speaking. Ours can be a collaboration made in heaven. You're forgetting all the good times we've had together—on stakeouts, telling war stories in pubs all over the world."

She knelt and struck a match, then held it to the paper until it burst into flame. She stood up and faced him. "That's just it. I know you *too* well. That's why I don't trust you."

He watched her storm away and felt a jab at his heart. He rubbed his chest. *Hmm. Another one of those pesky pangs. Perhaps I should have a checkup.*

Dru paced to the open door and stared out at the darkening landscape. He joined her in the doorway and reached out to her. "Can't you let bygones be bygones? Let me stay tonight, darling. You know you want to."

She looked searchingly into his eyes and he could see her resolve waver. Then her head tilted to one side and her face registered a determination that told him she had made up her mind. She placed her hands on his shoulders, her touch sending shock waves down his spine and stoking his desire.

"Good show, darling. You've made the right decision," he whispered.

"I'm so glad you approve," she said in a low, throaty voice, moving her hands to the center of his chest.

She shoved him so hard he was forced to stagger outside or land on his backside.

2

HIS RUCKSACK STRUCK HIM in the midsection. "Oof," he said, dodging a tin of pork and beans. He became truly alarmed when he saw her grab a Swiss Army knife from the table. It was closed when she threw it, which in her mood was probably an oversight. He was able to catch it before she slammed the door.

He strode to the door and pounded on it. "Darling," he began, "you can't leave me out here. I'll freeze, won't I? How could you, after all the good times we've had? After all we've meant to each other? Be a good egg, eh?"

There was a pause. She opened the door, her green eyes shining. "I guess I can't leave you completely in the cold."

Pierce gave her his most brilliant smile. He'd gotten to her after all, he thought, drawing himself up straight. The Mountcastle charm was nothing to be trifled with.

A blanket sailed out the door and landed draped over his head, blinding him. He heard the door slam again.

"Blimey!" He removed the blanket and smoothed his hair. What was wrong with the woman? Didn't she know that no female could stay angry with Pierce Mountcastle for more than a fortnight? Most men he knew complained that they just didn't understand women. He, on the other hand, considered women to be entirely predictable, at least where their responses to him were concerned. Dru was proving to be an exception. Still, he had all weekend to get back in her good graces.

His immediate problem was a bit dodgy.

He surveyed his surroundings. The hilly landscape was covered with pine trees as far as the eye could see. A prickly-looking bush here and a patch of vines there alleviated the sameness of the pines, whose needles thickly covered the ground. He spread the blanket, shrugged off the rucksack and sat down. Resting his back on the rough trunk of a pine, he took a bottle of imported beer out of the pack and opened it.

Camping was thirsty work. He took a long drink and scraped up a handful of pine straw. He supposed he could make like one of the three little pigs and build a house of straw, but if memory served, that hadn't turned out too well. Perhaps it was time to ask for some support. Pierce delved into the backpack again, retrieved a cellular phone and punched in a number.

"The *Nova*, Deborah Gilroy speaking."

"How's my favorite photo editor?" he asked, but didn't wait for an answer. "I found Dru just where you said she'd be. Now I need some advice. How do I get back in her good graces?" He took another drink of beer. "Oh, and I also need to know how to build a shelter using a Swiss Army knife, pine straw and beer bottles."

There was a pause before Deborah said dryly, "I don't know which is the more difficult task." She let out an exasperated sigh. "Look. Dru is my best friend. The only reason I agreed to tell you her whereabouts is that I think you two would make a great couple if you could just work out your differences."

"Couple? Let's not get too hasty here. I'm not exactly looking for a long-term relationship. I just want a weekend of fun and a good story in the bargain.''

"If I believed that, I never would have told you where she was going. You've been bending over backward to get yourself assigned to the same stories as Dru since the last time you were with her. When are you going to admit to yourself that you're crazy about her?"

"I, um—see here…that is…" Pierce felt perspiration break out on his forehead. He'd never been the type to go mad for a woman, and he never would be. He just wanted one last fling, that was all—a weekend of passion to purge all thoughts of Drucilla Logan from his mind forever. Of course, he couldn't tell her best friend that, could he? So what the hell *was* he going to tell her? "I say, I've got to go. I think I see Bigfoot."

Deborah laughed. "I don't believe I've ever seen the silver-tongued Mr. Mountcastle at a loss for words. Relax. I'm not going to put you on the spot anymore. But, listen, if you want my advice on how to get close to Dru, just be yourself. There's a genuine nice guy buried under that ruthless veneer."

Pierce nearly choked on his beer. "Kick a chap when he's down, will you?" he said between coughs. "You and I were friends long before you went to work with Dru. Why is all your loyalty to her and not me?"

"Sisterhood, man," she said simply. "That reminds me, if you tell Dru who tipped you off, Bigfoot will be the least of your worries."

He could picture the look on his friend's face, the smooth brown skin of her forehead creased in a warning frown, her dark eyes shining. She'd known him longer than Dru and almost as well. Her belief in his humanity sometimes embarrassed and always humbled him.

And he didn't even *do* humble. "Don't get your knickers in a knot," he said, and drained the beer bottle. "I won't do anything to shake up the sisterhood."

"Let me know how things work out. Oh, and if I were you, I'd cut some saplings, lay them over a ditch and lash them together with vines. And take those beer bottles back with you when you hike out. Remember the environment, mister, and tell Sasquatch I said, 'Howdy.'"

"Cheers," he said, and hung up. Women really did stick together, he reflected. They probably had a secret handshake and held meetings in windowless flats to discuss strategy against men and to swap recipes. Still, Deborah's tip about the shelter seemed as good as any.

He looked around again and saw a depression in the ground a few feet from where he was sitting, a dry creek bed from the look of it. He opened the knife and tested the blade with his thumb. "Here goes nothing," he said, and began sawing on a nearby sapling.

DRU BUSIED HERSELF by making her bed and tried not to think of Pierce outside in the cold. She was determined not to look out the window to see how he was faring.

When she'd finished her task, she felt restless again. Why couldn't she get Pierce off her mind? She'd known good-looking men before and had dated quite a few. She'd never been fool enough to fall for the irresponsible "bad boy" type.

Not before Pierce, that was. It had to be that maddeningly roguish charm. Or maybe the accent. But was there any substance beneath that suave exterior? She doubted it.

She jumped at the hoot of a nearby owl. The thought of wild animals outside made her nervous, although she'd never admit that to anyone and be considered a wimp. She'd considered bringing along the revolver her father had once given her, but decided against it. She hated guns, a trait that had won her the disapproval of her macho dad. And, goodness knew, she craved her father's approval, even though she could never count on him.

Another hoot of the owl made her almost glad that Pierce was right outside. If there was one thing she knew about him, it was that he was absolutely fearless. He'd proven that one of the last times they'd wound up on the same story.

She and Pierce had been assigned to cover the rumor that Graceland was closing. She was in the middle of a mob of enraged fans of the King when a crazed Elvis impersonator shot a gun into the crowd. Pierce had shielded her body with his own and led her to safety. Nobody was hurt in the incident, but the perpetrator was now singing ''Jailhouse Rock'' for real.

Pierce might have saved her life that day, and now she was leaving him outside on a chilly spring night in the mountains with nothing but a blanket. Dru bit her lip. What should she do?

She saw her cell phone lying on the table and snatched it up. Another opinion from someone who was totally impartial was what she needed. She dialed a number and listened to the tone.

''The *Nova*, Deborah Gilroy speaking.''

''Thank goodness you're still there. I need some

advice—'' Dru heard a clattering sound as if her friend had dropped the receiver. ''Deborah, are you there?''

''Uh, yeah—but, listen, I was just on my way out, so I—''

''Pierce is here! Can you believe it?''

''You don't say,'' Deborah squeaked. ''Imagine that.''

''Are you okay? Your voice sounds funny.'' Deborah's voice always rose half an octave or so when she was nervous, but what did *she* have to be nervous about?

''Allergies,'' Deborah offered, and coughed weakly. ''So what's going on?''

Dru looked out the window. There was still enough daylight left for her to see Pierce sipping a beer and piling up some sticks and vines, probably to make a fire. ''He followed me to this cabin and wants to sleep here tonight. I said no way, so now he's staying right outside without a tent or anything. Do you think he'll be safe out there? From wild animals and all?''

''Hmm,'' Deborah said thoughtfully. ''It depends. It's springtime, right? That means the bears will be coming out of hibernation, and they'll be awfully hungry—and thirsty.''

Dru suppressed a gasp and dropped onto the couch. ''Ohmigosh. Do you think there are many of them around here?''

''Black bears? In the North Carolina mountains? Tons of 'em. Of course, Pierce should still be okay as long as he doesn't have much food...''

''That's a relief.'' Dru relaxed a little. ''He doesn't have any to speak of.''

''...or beer.''

''Beer?''

"Bears love beer. It's a little-known fact. Yep, you open a beer around a bear and just watch out. But I'm sure Pierce wouldn't have a beer on him. Besides, that may be the least of his problems."

"What do you mean?" Dru asked wanly.

"I have it on good authority that there have been Bigfoot sightings in that area."

"What? You're telling me that *now?*"

"The tip just came in a few minutes ago," Deborah said defensively.

"Wait a minute. Bigfoot lives in the Rocky Mountains, not the Smoky Mountains. Besides, I don't even believe in Bigfoot."

"And you call yourself a tabloid reporter!" Deborah made a scoffing sound of disapproval. "Of course Bigfoot is real, and he can migrate just like any other animal."

"That's one helluva migration."

"He can cover a lot of ground," Deborah said petulantly. "They don't call him Bigfoot for nothing."

Dru sighed. "I suppose I might as well let him sleep in front of the fireplace."

"Bigfoot? I wouldn't advise it. Pierce, on the other hand—well, why don't you give the guy a break?"

"Maybe you're right." Dru ran a hand through her hair, resigned to her decision. "See you Monday."

"Happy camping," Deborah said, and hung up.

Dru put down the phone and stared into the fire. Maybe letting him stay the night was the best thing. At least she could be sure of his exact whereabouts when it came time to sneak away without him. He wouldn't be hiding behind some tree waiting for her. She remembered him mention once that he was a sound sleeper. Maybe she could get away without waking him.

When Dru walked outside to tell Pierce he could come in, it was nearly dark, but a full moon promised to offer some meager light. She paused to let her eyes adjust to the moonlight and took a deep breath of the crisp mountain air.

There was no sign of him anywhere. Pierce, along with the gear she'd thrown at him, had vanished. Even his pitiful pile of sticks was gone. Dru felt gooseflesh rise up on her arms and rubbed them briskly. Could Deborah have been right about a monster in these woods? Had she sent poor Pierce to his doom?

She decided to make a hasty circuit around the outside of the cabin just to see if she could find any trace of him before calling for help. In case there was something wild lurking nearby, she would be quiet. Calling out might alert some evil presence to her whereabouts. Stealthily, she set off toward the side of the cabin. Glancing over her shoulder while descending a slope, she didn't see the grid of branches and vines lining the creek bed until she'd stepped right on top of it.

The sound of her scream mixed with that of splintering wood as she crashed through the roof of Pierce's lean-to shelter. She landed squarely in his lap.

"Hello, luv. Jolly glad you could drop in."

She smoothed her hair and tried to look nonchalant even as the heat of his body dissipated her chill. "Nice place you've got here. Real homey. I didn't know you were so...resourceful."

"I'm glad you approve. I'd show you my etchings, but it's a bit dark."

She scrambled away from him as he tried to encircle her with his arms. "I came to tell you I've reconsidered. You can stay in the cabin if you promise to keep your hands—and all the rest of you, for that matter—to yourself. Deal?''

''I'll be a perfect gentleman.''

Dru stood up, dusted herself off and selected two green branches from the pile of twigs that used to be Pierce's roof. ''And I have just the way to keep those hands busy.''

''YOU'VE NEVER DONE THIS before, have you?'' Dru observed as she watched Pierce's third marshmallow fall off the sharpened end of the green branch into the fireplace.

''Can't seem to get the hang of it.'' Pierce poked another marshmallow onto the end of the stick and extended it gingerly toward the fire. Who could concentrate when she was licking her fingers like that?

He watched her as she carefully pulled a perfectly toasted confection from the end of her stick. Bringing her lips together in a perfect Cupid's bow, she blew gently, then snaked out her tongue to test the candy's temperature.

''Mmm,'' Pierce groaned.

''There goes another one. You're not paying attention to what you're doing.''

''Dashed sorry. I'll try one more.'' He anchored another marshmallow to the stick. ''You seem to be an old hand at camping.''

''My dad had custody of me on weekends and we'd go camping a lot. Of course, sometimes he'd have some big story to cover and he'd have to cancel. The work always came before anything else, including me.'' Dru popped the marshmallow into her mouth and chewed thoughtfully. "Anyway, he taught me everything I know about the outdoors."

Pierce rotated the marshmallow carefully on the stick. He'd never heard Dru speak of her journalist father, the legendary Ben Logan, a man almost as famous for his drinking and brawling as he was for his pen. "I hear your dad is a hell of a newspaperman. I'd love to meet him."

Dru stared into the fire. "He'd like you."

"Oh?" Pierce inspected his marshmallow, then put it back over the flames.

"You're his kind of reporter—driven, ruthless, competitive. The type who'd do anything to get a story."

"Please," Pierce said, "you're making me blush."

"On the other hand, he wouldn't approve of your habit of stretching, bending and sometimes mutilating the truth."

Pierce glanced sideways at Dru, remembering the memo he'd read earlier that outlined her plan to get into the chemist's compound. It seemed to him like an awfully high horse she was on, given her plan. "But I heard that he goes undercover a lot. Misrepresenting who you are to get a story is hardly what I'd call honest."

She flinched and her eyes reflected the light of the fire. "That's different. He is as sneaky as he has to be to get the story, but once he has the facts, he sticks to them, unlike you."

Pierce started to retort, but thought better of it, in case she decided to put him outside again. Besides, it was too difficult to work himself up to a fight with Dru when she was looking so beautiful in the firelight. He decided to change the direction of the conversation.

"Sounds like your father is a big influence on you. Do you think you are like him in other ways?"

Dru's dark brows drew together slightly and she leveled a steely stare at him. "Yes. I don't like to lose. In fact, I *hate* to lose, just like he does."

Her meaning was clear. She didn't intend to lose the story she'd been working on to him or anyone else. His marshmallow wasn't getting brown enough, so he held it closer to the fire. "Like father, like daughter, eh?" he offered brightly.

She would have none of his cheer and only glared back into the fire. "When I played Little League, I once dropped a ball in the outfield. When we got home, my dad made me run laps around the yard until dark. Said I was too soft, and that he would toughen me up. From then on he tried to turn me into the son he never had."

"How appalling. I'm certainly glad he didn't succeed." He let his eyes run the length of her body, from her shapely legs stretched out in front of her to her small waist and perfect breasts. Only too perfect, he remembered. As he stared at her, she absentmindedly brought her marshmallow stick to her lips, where she slowly licked off a bit of the white candy that clung to the tip.

This was just too much. He longed to take her in his arms, smear her entire body with the melted candy and lick it off bit by bit. Knowing she wouldn't go for it in her present state of mind, he drew his branch with the roasted marshmallow to his mouth. Gazing at her lush profile, he lost himself in the fantasy. Sweetness upon sweetness. Lick by luscious lick.

The heat of his need grew until his loins felt as if they were on fire for her.

"Watch out!"

Pierce looked down to see a fallen bit of burning marshmallow sparking on his lap. "Ow!"

He tried to jump up, but Dru was faster. With quick, neat jabs to his crotch, she triumphantly beat out the flames.

"Bloody hell!" Pierce crumpled to the floor, less than grateful. The room swam for a moment as he struggled to speak again. "Haven't you ever heard of drop and roll?"

"Sorry." Dru's face flamed as brightly as his crotch had. "I was just trying to help."

"I think I'd rather have had the fire," he rasped. Though her quickness had spared him even the slightest burn, his surge of lust had been effectively nipped in the bud. He gulped in a deep breath.

"Are you all right?" Dru patted him gently on the back as if he'd had a choking spell instead of an assault on his very manhood. "Were you burned? Do you need to...put something on it?"

He stared at her, speechless. Something did, of course, leap to mind...and, incredibly enough, started that lust kindling within him again.

Suspecting she wouldn't buy the remedy he wanted to suggest—and not sure he was physically up to it at the moment, anyway—he changed the subject. "So why is this love potion story so important to you?" he asked in a croaking voice.

"As if you didn't know." She withdrew her hand from his back and gave him a suspicious look. "This is a story important enough to be picked up by the mainstream media. The reporter who breaks it is going to be famous—not to mention a shoo-in for a Tabby nomination."

Pierce had to admit she was right. If the advance word on the love potion was correct, the story would be big. And if the media attention didn't make the reporter famous, the tabloid industry's highest award would. It almost made him sad for Dru that she wasn't going to break the story. "The Tabby award isn't everything, you know." He stared into the fire to escape her gaze.

"That's easy for you to say. You've got two of them."

Pierce shifted uncomfortably. "I get the feeling you're trying to prove something. Is it to yourself or to your father?"

She raised her chin, a muscle working along her jawline. "I'm trying to be the best reporter I can be. I'm just as tough as you, my father or anybody else for that matter."

"Rubbish." Pierce leaned over and took Dru's poetry book off the table. "What you are is a romantic."

"Just because you're tough doesn't mean you can't have a sensitive side. Didn't you study any poetry at Oxford or Cambridge or whatever hoity-toity university you went to?"

"Oxford, actually," he said in his best upper-class voice. In reality, the only time he'd ever seen Oxford was in a picture postcard. As he looked into her eyes, there was something deep inside him that made him want to tell her the truth about his background on the mean streets of London's East End, but he saw no reason to blow his cover at this point in his life. He'd worked too hard to create the Pierce Mountcastle persona for himself. People in the industry—people like Dru—might revile him for his ruthlessness, but at least they respected him for who they thought he was.

Pierce flipped through the book's pages. "Tell me, do you think any of these love poems would inspire you to let me share that bed with you tonight?"

Dru stood up, snapped her marshmallow stick in half and threw it into the fire. "Not if you were William Shakespeare himself."

Pierce winced. "You can't blame a bloke for trying." He scrambled to his feet, sensing the evening was about to end and wanting to prolong it. His mind ticked off her favorite girlie things that might put her in a romantic frame of mind. She already had flowers and wasn't in the mood for poetry, and there was no perfume or candy at hand. What was left? Dancing!

"The night is young," he announced, joining Dru as she cleaned up the kitchen area. "Let's dance."

She looked at him as if he'd just proposed a trip to Mars. Then her gaze roamed the room. "There's no music."

"We don't need music," he offered cheerily.

"Hmm. We *are* in the Carolinas. I suppose I could teach you to shag."

Pierce grinned broadly and drew her to him. That was easier than he'd thought. Just the suggestion of dancing had done the trick. Or it could be the old Mountcastle charm kicking in. "You read my mind, darling. Only I like to think I'm somewhat of an expert already."

She pushed him away roughly. "The shag is a Carolina dance, you jerk. It doesn't mean...*sex*, like it does where you're from. I'm going to bed now. You keep to the couch and don't come near me."

He watched her as she stalked away, and scratched his head. Blimey, he thought. The Mountcastle charm was evidently still on hiatus.

BEDDED DOWN ON THE LUMPY SOFA, Pierce stared at the rough beams of the ceiling and listened to Dru's rhythmic breathing. He couldn't rest knowing that she was sleeping only a few feet away. His groin ached, and only partially from the swat he'd received earlier. This was not the way he'd imagined he would spend the night with her, but at least he wasn't out in the cold.

He sat up, every nerve cell in his body tingling, as Dru began to moan and thrash about on the small bed. Wearing only his briefs, he was at her side at once. She was obviously having a bad dream, poor luv, perhaps reliving some unpleasant incident like when he trounced her at last year's Tabby awards.

As he looked down at her troubled face, he longed to hold her and comfort her. Instead he stroked her hair gently and cooed, "It's all right, darling." His tender words sounded strange to his own ears, and he knew he'd never used that tone of voice with anyone. What was it that Dru had said earlier? Just because you were tough didn't mean you didn't have a sensitive side.

Did he? He doubted it. Was it possible for a person to change, even if he wanted to? Not that he wanted to. His toughness had served him well, had saved his life in fact, and he wasn't about to change for anyone. No, a bastard he was born and a bastard he would stay.

She had quieted now and was sleeping more or less peacefully again, curled up on her side in a short cotton nightie, exposing a tantalizing length of thigh. He longed to join her in bed, crush her to his chest and kiss her like she'd never been kissed before. Instead, he took the edge of the blanket she'd shrugged off and covered her with it, letting the back of his hand gently stroke her cheek before he finally backed away.

DRU WOKE THE NEXT MORNING before dawn, feeling as if she'd barely slept at all. She hadn't been able to relax all night knowing Pierce was in the same room. Whenever she'd closed her eyes, his face would appear to her. When she'd finally dropped off, he haunted her dreams. She awoke several times bathed in perspiration, convinced he was in bed with her, touching her everywhere with his hands, his mouth. But she was alone in bed, and Pierce was across the room, keeping to the sofa as he'd promised.

She slipped noiselessly from bed and dressed in the dark, hoping Pierce was sleeping better than she had. Shouldering the backpack she'd packed the night before, she took a deep breath. To reach the door, she had to pass by the end of the sofa that cushioned Pierce's head, so close she could reach out and stroke the lock of hair falling over his forehead. She couldn't help but pause before she crept past him.

His long, lean body sprawling across the sofa made her sigh. He'd partially pushed away the blanket she'd lent him, revealing broad shoulders and a rock-hard chest covered with a mat of black hair. Her fingertips tingled as she remembered the texture of his hair, his skin. She balled her fists at her sides to keep from touching him.

She forced herself away from him and started toward the door, but the distraction had cost her—her knee connected with a chair leg. Unable to completely stifle her yelp of pain, she made a low moaning sound instead.

As if in answer to her moan, Pierce issued one of his own—a deep, masculine purr that Dru would have recognized anywhere. She looked down into his face, which was illuminated by waning moonlight from a nearby window. His dark brow creased and his full, sensual lips parted slightly. It seemed Mr. Mountcastle was having dreams of his own. But his dreams were none of her business.

She'd tried to forget him and thought she'd made progress—up until yesterday. The best thing she could do now was to make short work of this assignment and head back to Atlanta as soon as possible. At least she'd be able to take some satisfaction from beating him at his own double-crossing game. Ditching him would be the most fun she'd had in weeks.

Dru waved her hand in front of Pierce's face, and when he didn't flinch, she eased out the door and into the dawning day.

As soon as he heard the sound of the door gently closing, Pierce opened one eye, then two, and stretched like a great male cat. A twenty-minute head start should be just about right for his purposes, he decided with a glance at his watch. He linked his fingers behind his head, closed his eyes and chuckled. He couldn't wait to see the look on Dru's face when next they'd meet.

THE GRANDMOTHERLY housekeeper peered at Dru, her vivid blue eyes lit with concern. "You must be freezing, you poor thing. I've just made this pot of tea, so help yourself. It'll warm you up. Since you've gone so long without food, I'll bring you the cucumber sandwiches we had left over from yesterday's tea."

"Oh, I don't want to put you to any trouble," Dru said, looking back and forth between the housekeeper and her host, Dr. Jackson Peel.

"No trouble at all," Dr. Peel said with a dismissive

wave of his plump hand. "We're certainly not going to let you starve, are we, Ginger?"

Ginger tugged up the waistband of her apron and grinned. "No, indeed."

Dru smiled gratefully as Ginger and Dr. Peel conferred about some housekeeping matter. Dru sipped the strong, hot tea and peered over the rim of the delicate china cup at her host. She'd been immediately impressed with Dr. Peel, a gentleman of the old school. He had class, no doubt about it. His home was forbidding enough on the outside, with its eight-foot chainlink fence and security cameras. On the inside, it was all graciousness, furnished and appointed with impeccable taste.

It had been a long hike to get here and she was starving, but she was going to have to sing for her supper. The song and dance she'd prepared was designed to convince Dr. Peel that she was a hapless waif in need of shelter for the night. Her story had impressed Ginger enough to get her past the front gate. Now she had to put on her act for the good doctor.

She chuckled at the thought of Pierce all by himself at the cabin. She almost wished he were here to see how smoothly she was going to pull off her scheme. He was always telling her what a bad liar she was. *We'll see about that.*

The housekeeper retreated with her instructions and Dr. Peel sat down across the tea table from Dru in an overstuffed velvet armchair.

"Now, child, what's this about your husband abandoning you in the woods?" He dropped two lumps of sugar into his tea with silver tongs. A portly gentleman of seventy, Dr. Peel cut a distinguished figure in a tweed jacket and bow tie. He had a full head of white hair, combed neatly back from a broad forehead, and a prodigious, matching mustache.

"Well..." She paused, casting her eyes down for effect, then continued. "We were on a camping trip, a kind of second honeymoon. A family of raccoons stole all our provisions and my husband left to get more, but he never came back. I waited for him as long as I could, then decided to hike back to the main road to get a ride. But I got lost and wound up here."

She gave him a tremulous smile and was rewarded with a look of paternalistic concern. So far so good.

"Perhaps we should organize a search party for your husband. He may have gotten lost himself."

"No, no," Dru said quickly, realizing she should have anticipated Dr. Peel's response. "I'm sure he's not in trouble."

Her forehead broke out in perspiration. Her story was falling apart already and she'd only just begun. She knew that to tell a convincing lie, you had to stick to the truth as much as possible so as not to trip yourself up. She closed her eyes briefly and tried to visualize her fictitious wayward husband. The image of Pierce Mountcastle's face leaped into her mind.

"Ow!" Dru jumped as some hot tea spilled out of her cup onto her bare knees, just below her hiking shorts.

"You poor thing, you've worked yourself into a dither," Dr. Peel said solicitously, handing her a tea towel. "What could make him abandon you like that?"

Dru set her cup and saucer down with a rattle and dabbed the tea off her legs with the towel. "The truth is, we argued," she said.

"What about?"

"His ambition. He cares more about his career than

about me.'' She should stop prattling on while she was still more or less ahead, but she couldn't seem to make herself shut up. ''We, uh, broke up over it once.''

''When was this?''

''A few weeks ago. We were separated from that time to this.''

''But you got back together and now you're on your second honeymoon. Is that right?'' The old gentleman was definitely interested now. His mustache twitched like a creature with a mind of its own, and he leaned forward on his armrest.

''Er, yeah, that's it.'' Where were those damned cucumber sandwiches?

''I hope you don't mind my inquisitiveness. It's just that human relationships, particularly of the romantic kind, are my life's work.''

''Oh, are you a marriage counselor or something?'' Dru asked the question innocently, mentally thanking Dr. Peel for the smooth opening into the subject she was really here to explore.

''I started out as a psychologist, and I still consider myself a counselor. Helping two people find happiness is extremely gratifying. A few years ago, however, I turned to medicine so I could study the chemical component of attraction.''

Bingo! Dru opened her mouth to ask him more about his work, when he interrupted her with a question of his own.

''Tell me more about this ambition problem that caused your breakup.''

''Huh? Oh, yes. Well, we were working on a story— that is, a project.''

''What kind of business are you in?''

Dru almost said ''newspapers,'' but caught herself

in time. She was carrying this truth thing a little too far. If only she were as good a liar as Pierce. "Papers," she managed to say. "That is, *paper*. You know, uh, pulp and paper."

Dr. Peel nodded and steepled his fingers. "Go on."

"So we were working on this project, a project that I had initiated and done all the preliminary work for." She rubbed her sweaty palms on her khaki hiking shorts. "So the first thing you know, he's taken credit for my work!"

Dru exhaled and for the first time felt the weariness from her long hike. She felt a kind of emotional weariness, too, as if she were in a real counseling session, which in a way she was. What she was telling the doctor was essentially true. The last time she and Pierce had worked on the same assignment, he'd seduced her and left the next morning—stealing the story as he went. When she picked up her teacup again, it seemed to weigh a ton.

PIERCE THANKED the cheery housekeeper, who excused herself and left him outside the door to the parlor where Dru was meeting with Dr. Peel. He paused with his hand on the knob and reviewed his plan once more. On the hike to this place he'd rehearsed the role of Dru's missing husband. Thank goodness he'd found the memo that had revealed the tale she would use to con her way into the compound.

It felt good to be competing against Dru again. Having an adversary as worthy as her made the chase for scoops that much more exciting. He started to turn the knob and his hand stopped. What was happening? He realized he was having mixed feelings about stepping in to take the story.

He was so unaccustomed to this guilt thing. And he just hated it. It was like a sickness. He hoped the price-less look on Dru's face when he appeared would cure him. He turned the knob and eased the door open. Dru, sitting in a chair with her back to the door, was talking to the doctor in an animated fashion. Pierce crept forward softly, trying to overhear.

It was so liberating, Dru thought as she wound down her diatribe, to talk to a professional about her problems with Pierce. She felt so much better just getting things off her chest.

"And I thought he cared for me. Tell me, Doc, what kind of dirty, rotten scoundrel would treat a woman like that?"

Dimly aware of footsteps behind her—the sandwiches, thank God!—she took a long sip of her tea.

"Darling! I've found you!"

3

DRU GASPED, forgetting her mouthful of tea, which spewed out in a fine spray. She was on her feet in an instant.

"Mind your manners, dear," Pierce said. "Don't talk with your mouth full." He patted her back, a bit more forcefully than was necessary, but his face retained a guise of concern.

"What did you—where did you—" she stammered, wiping her chin on her sleeve.

"The auto wouldn't start, and when I called for help on the cell phone, I was told it would be tomorrow before anyone could come out and look at it. When I got back to the campsite and found you gone, I was frantic. I've been searching for you for hours." Pierce hugged her—a little too warmly for her liking—then deftly reached around her to extend his hand to Dr. Peel.

"I'm Reggie MacGregor," he said, giving the name he always used when he went undercover. "Your lovely housekeeper was kind enough to let me in. Thank you so much for rescuing my sweet, precious darling." He reached out to smooth her hair and pretended not to notice when she slapped his hand away.

"How did you find me?" she demanded.

"I tracked you, of course."

"Since when did you become an Indian scout?"

He gave her a benign smile and an almost imperceptible wink.

Damn him! He must have figured out the location of the compound before she had. And how did he know the story she'd told the old man? Then she remembered the memo. Of course. He'd pilfered the memo that referred to her plan for getting into the compound.

"Now, now," said Dr. Peel in a conciliatory tone. "You're both safe and sound and that's the important thing. Since you're having car trouble, I insist that you both stay the night." Dr. Peel put one arm around her shoulder and the other around Pierce's. "You two must be starved. I'll cancel the order for sandwiches. Instead, I'll have Ginger make you a proper lunch. I'll have to work through lunch myself, I'm afraid, since my research project has reached a critical stage. But I'll join you for dinner this evening and we'll talk everything out."

Dru stared after Dr. Peel in desperation. When he'd closed the door behind him, she grabbed the tea towel, twirled it deftly and snapped it against Pierce's chest with a resounding *pop*.

"Ow!" Pierce yelped.

"Ow yourself, you brazen Brit. I should have known you'd show up here. Now I'm going to lose the exclusive on my story *and* my cucumber sandwiches!"

"I say, may I remind you that you ditched me after we'd made a deal?" Pierce rubbed his chest. "And what do cucumber sandwiches have to do with anything?"

She waved a hand, dismissing his question. "I figured you needed a dose of your own medicine." She stamped her foot. "He was about to tell me all about his research when you showed up. I had him eating out of my hand.''

Pierce looked dubious. ''We'll be even more effective working as a team. In any case, the old chap thinks we're husband and wife, so now we have to play the jolly old part.'' His dark brows rose and fell and a roguish grin played across his face.

Dru gritted her teeth. She couldn't believe he'd trapped her in her own scheme. It was bad enough that she was going to have to spend another night under the same roof with him, probably in the same room, maybe even in the same bed. She covered her face with her hand for a moment, trying to calm herself. Then she peeked from between her fingers and saw that Pierce was still wearing that maddening grin. *The same bed.* That devil must've been thinking the exact same thing.

AT LUNCH, PIERCE WATCHED DRU concentrate on her crab cake as if she thought it might scurry away sideways any minute.

''Dashed sorry about the cucumber sandwiches,'' he offered.

Dru shrugged.

He leaned forward, trying to make eye contact. ''When we return to civilization, I'll make you a whole plate of cucumber sandwiches to celebrate our success.''

She gestured menacingly toward him with her fork. ''When we get back, you'll be on a plane to the West Coast with your precious story so fast it'll make my head spin.''

Pierce sat back and sighed. Last night in the cabin he'd had to be on his best behavior lest she cast him out into the wilds. He'd hoped that the time they'd spend together today would make Dru friendlier toward him. He really hoped that tonight could be a more romantic evening. Sadly, the Mountcastle charm still seemed to be having no effect on her. What made him think he could seduce Dru again when he couldn't even engage her in small talk over the lunch table, for God's sake? It was all enough to discourage a bloke. He suddenly realized that he'd never cared what anybody thought of his behavior, until now. It was a frightening revelation.

"We make a great team, don't we? I know my behavior in the past has left something to be desired, but can't we put the unpleasantness behind us and start over?"

"You don't get it, do you?" Dru laid down her fork and tossed her napkin onto the table beside her plate. "I don't trust you because you've proven you'll stop at nothing to get what you want, even if it means hurting me. Try to get this through your head. We're finished. *Finished.*"

"Finished?" Ginger chirped. Both of them started as the housekeeper strode into the small dining room they were in. "But you've hardly touched your lunch." She set her hands on her generous hips and looked at them with disappointment. Her silver hair was wound into a tight bun and corralled by a black-and-white maid's cap.

"The food was wonderful. We just don't seem to have much of an appetite," Pierce said with a glance toward Dru, who seemed to be examining the pattern in the carpet.

"No wonder." Ginger folded her arms across her ample bosom. "You poor dears, you must've been frantic when you thought you'd lost each other.'' She bit her lip and looked from one of them to the other.

Lost each other. Pierce's breath caught a little. There was that annoying pang again. It certainly had nothing to do with the tongue-lashing that Dru had given him. He'd had a lot worse. He'd lost many an acquaintance through his ruthless behavior in the past, and he'd laughed it off every time. But this time felt different, because he stood to lose Dru. Perhaps the formerly friendly nature of their rivalry meant more to him than he'd realized. Did that have anything to do with the ache in his chest? It was the damned crab cakes, that was all.

Over Ginger's protests, Pierce and Dru helped her clear the dishes away to the adjoining kitchen. Although it had all the modern conveniences, the sunny yellow kitchen's traditional touches gave the room a homey feel. Pierce, who didn't usually notice or respond to such things, had to admit that there was something oddly comforting about the place.

When he looked at Dru, he saw that she'd closed her eyes and her face reflected pure contentment. After a moment, she opened her eyes and breathed deeply. ''What's that wonderful smell? It reminds me of my grandmother's kitchen.''

''I've got a pot of hot, spiced cider on the stove. I'll get us all some.'' Ginger opened an oak cabinet and removed three large mugs. ''I know it's spring already, but that mountain chill is still in the air. I like my hot cider to warm me up.''

As they sat at the table, Pierce noticed that Dru seemed less tense, which in turn made him feel more relaxed. She smiled and nodded as Ginger described what life was like at the compound. Dr. Peel kept steadily to his lab work while Ginger cooked for him, the security guards and the occasional part-time lab assistant. At night, she and the doctor would challenge each other to a game of chess or backgammon.

"Sounds like a jolly tranquil existence, doesn't it?" Pierce observed.

"Boring's more like it." Ginger blew the steam off her cider, took a sip and sighed. "Occasionally I try to…liven things up, but Dr. Peel likes his routine." The housekeeper turned to Dru and patted her hand. "Tell me about that grandmother you mentioned."

Pierce listened intently as Dru described her grandmother's kitchen, a haven of warmth and security, filled with cousins to play with and good things to eat. Her descriptions of the idyllic place were so vivid, he closed his eyes and could almost feel as if he were there. What he wouldn't have given for such a place as a boy. Instead of listening to stories at the knee of a loving grandparent, he'd been on the cold, damp streets of London picking pockets and dodging bobbies.

He started at the touch of a warm, broad hand on his arm. "Are you okay, dear?" Ginger asked.

"Oh, yes. I was just remembering the lovely kitchen staff we had at the country house. A bit of all right, they were." As he recalled his actual circumstances, the words stuck in his throat, causing his voice to break. He stared at the floor to compose himself. Lies like these had always been easy. Why were they becoming difficult now?

Ginger smiled and took their empty mugs to the sink. While she rinsed the dishes, Dru leaned toward Pierce and said softly, "I didn't know you had a sentimental bone in your body." She looked at him a long moment as if she'd never seen him before. "It suits you. In fact, I feel as if I've seen a whole other side of you."

"How appalling." Pierce felt himself blanch. "Don't tell anyone, eh?"

Dru rolled her eyes. "Deborah always told me you were a sensitive man underneath it all. I never thought I'd say this, but maybe she was right." She eyed him thoughtfully. "Tell me, what makes Pierce Mountcastle tick?"

His mouth went dry as he fought the urge to confide in her. If he opened up to her now, it would destroy the tough-bloke image he'd built up for himself. And that image had served him well. He put on his game face and said, "As to what makes me tick, your timepiece analogy is a good one. Instead of a heart, I have a tightly coiled spring of coldest steel." He thumped his chest, a gesture he thought would make him look tough, but only made him cough.

Dru sighed in exasperation and shook her head. *"Men."*

A FEW MINUTES LATER, Ginger showed him and Dru into the library, where they were to while away the rest of the afternoon. "I'll have your room ready in time for you to dress for dinner," the housekeeper promised. "Meanwhile, you can relax in here." She waved her hand toward the floor-to-ceiling shelves of books. "There's plenty to read." Pierce noticed that she smirked a little when she said this.

After she was gone, Dru walked over to one wall and inspected the volumes. "Oh, my God," she said, taking a huge leather-bound book off the shelf.

"What?"

"All these books are about...sex."

Pierce walked the length of the room, scanning the book titles. When he reached the bay windows at the far end of the room, he gave a low whistle. "There must be thousands of them. He must own every book on human sexuality ever written." He looked back toward Dru, who was still examining the first book she'd opened. Her cheeks and lips had reddened and she looked a bit dazed.

He walked back to her and peered over her shoulder. The pages she held open revealed dozens of drawings, each depicting a couple in a different sex position. He pointed to one near the bottom of the right-hand page. "I say! There's one we haven't done."

She slapped his hand away from the page and closed the book so forcefully that a small shower of dust flew off it.

"Don't be cross, darling. I remember now. We *did* try it, didn't we?"

Dru collapsed into a burgundy leather chair in front of the fireplace and tried to suppress a smile. She turned her head to look all around the room again. "We should make good use of our time here," she said. "We're surrounded by all the background material we'll need for this story. I've done a good bit of research already, of course, but it couldn't hurt to do some reading. We should be able to come up with a sidebar about earlier advances in this type of science."

"And what type of science would that be?" Pierce asked coyly. When she'd mentioned making good use of their time, going through dusty old books was not what had sprung to mind.

"Why, the science of sex, I suppose. Now, what would you call that? Sexology?"

"I obviously majored in the wrong subject."

"Well, here's your chance for some postgraduate study." Dru got up from the chair and handed him the book.

Pierce set the book on the end table and pulled her down on the sofa beside him. "I was thinking more along the lines of hands-on research."

Dru pulled away from him and was on her feet again in an instant. "I insist on *hands-off* research."

He sighed and held up his hands. "I just thought we could conduct a little experiment of our own—all in the name of science, of course. The experiment could be called, 'The Sexual Effects of a Six-Week Separation on a Man and Woman Who Are Mad about Each Other.'"

Dru gave him a withering glare. "I don't think so. Now start reading."

Pierce stretched out on the couch, opened the book and pretended to read. Instead, he peeked over the top of the volume at Dru as she inspected the books on the shelves across the room. He'd been kidding himself when he thought that rekindling the old romantic spark between him and Dru would be all that was necessary to make her want him again. The events of the past hour had convinced him of what he'd known deep down all along—that the issue keeping them apart was trust. In order to seduce her, he had to make her not just want him, but trust him. And that would take some doing. But that didn't mean he couldn't keep working the romantic angle until some trust-related solution occurred to him.

Dru glanced over her shoulder at him and he turned a page, rapidly refocusing on the book, which he realized to his chagrin was upside down. This was evidently not lost on Dru, who cleared her throat and pointed to it. "Unless you've developed some strange form of dyslexia and can now read upside down and backward, you might want to consider turning that book around."

"You misunderstand. The illustrations of some of these positions take some figuring out. I can't tell where some of the body parts begin and where they end." Pierce pretended to study the page, which contained only text, as he turned the book in a slow hundred-and-eighty-degree circle before letting it come to rest on his chest.

"If you've forgotten what goes where, you have bigger problems than dyslexia." Dru took another large book off the shelf.

Pierce got to his feet. "I admit it's been a while," he said, approaching her slowly. "Perhaps you'll be good enough to refresh my memory." He reached out for her, but she held the book lengthwise in front of her as a barrier between them.

"Down, boy." She backed away a step. "That picture book seems to be giving you ideas."

"I admit I find it...inspirational. However, I had ideas long before I opened that book." He took another step forward, advancing on her.

"I don't doubt it." Dru tried to step back again, but was brought up short by the wooden ladder attached to a brass railing near the ceiling. "But understand this. There's not going to be any hanky-panky tonight, just like there wasn't any last night."

Pierce pressed his advantage, putting his hands against the bookshelves on either side of her shoulders, trapping her within his arms. He leaned so close to her that he could see the fascinating flecks of gold in her wide green eyes. "But we're supposed to be married.

And we've just been through a frightening separation. We should act the part, or we might blow our cover."

"The key word being *act,*" she said, flattening her back against the books. "And 'acting' as if I'm in love with you—for Dr. Peel's benefit—is all I intend to do."

"Fine," rasped Pierce, letting his lips caress her forehead, her brow, her eyelid. "Then let's rehearse." He slipped his arms down and around her shoulders and back, gathering her to him with a rush of emotion so intense he had to lean her back against the books again to steady them both. He brought his lips against hers and kissed her as he had on their night of passion. As she began to return his kiss, he felt her body go from rigid to relaxed. So relaxed that the unwieldy book she still held slipped from her grasp.

"Ow!" Pierce yelled.

"Ohmigosh! Are you all right?"

Pierce hopped up and down on his remaining good foot. "Bloody hell." He held on to the ladder to steady himself.

"I'm sorry. I didn't mean to."

Her sweet, conciliatory tone of voice cut through the haze of pain and almost made him glad he'd been maimed. "Of course you didn't, darling."

Ginger opened the door, an alarmed expression on her face. "I heard a shout. Is one of you hurt?"

"I accidentally dropped a book on his foot." Dru put her arm around Pierce's waist to help steady him as he balanced on one foot like a tall, dark flamingo.

"I'll be fine. Really." If he'd known that getting injured would have inspired Dru to get this touchy-feely, he would have dropped a book on himself.

"I'll go and get a pan of ice water to soak your foot in." Ginger started to leave the room and then turned back to them. "I meant to tell you. I have your room almost ready. It's a good thing you two are nice and slender, not round like me." She patted her hips and grinned.

"Why?" Dru asked.

"Because the bed in your room is an antique and therefore not as big as a modern double bed. You'll really have to snuggle up close, but I'm sure you won't object to that." With a wink, she was gone.

Pierce felt Dru's arms fall away from him. She replaced her you-poor-baby look with her former stony expression.

"Look on the bright side, darling," he said. "Being together again in a narrow bed will give you a chance to make it up to me for injuring my foot."

Dru stepped away from him and crossed her arms, her eyes shining with sparks of green-and-gold fire. "And after you get through soaking your foot, you can go soak your head."

"I CAN'T BELIEVE HE'S MAKING us dress for dinner," Pierce called from the bedroom they'd be sharing that night.

"They don't call him eccentric for nothing," Dru answered from the bathroom, where she was dressing. "You go on along to the dining room. I'll be a few more minutes."

"Are you sure? I can wait."

"I'm sure."

There was a pause. "You know, if you need help with any zippers or anything—"

"Go!"

Dru listened as he limped to the door and closed it behind him. Only then did she come out of the bathroom in the vintage evening gown and slippers Ginger had given her. She hadn't wanted to be alone with him in the bedroom any longer than she had to.

She stared at the bed. Ginger hadn't been exaggerating about it. It was an antique four-poster that was so ancient it was barely big enough for two adults to sleep comfortably—not that sleep would be on Pierce's mind, or hers, either, for that matter.

She'd just have to take a pillow and blanket and sleep on the floor, or in the bathtub maybe. At least in the bathtub there'd be a door between them. She only hoped that the old tuxedo Ginger had given Pierce was some baggy monstrosity that would make him look like a clown. If it fit, she was in big trouble. No man alive looked as good in a tux as Pierce Mountcastle.

Shaking her head to dislodge the image of Pierce in evening wear, she opened her backpack and removed a tiny camera and even tinier wireless microphone. After checking the recorder in the backpack, she wrapped the camera in a handkerchief and went to the bureau mirror.

The dress was of some sheer, shimmery fabric and didn't leave much to the imagination. The best she could manage was to pin the microphone to the underside of the material deep in the plunging neckline of the dress so that it was somewhat camouflaged by her cleavage.

After fastening the mike, she smoothed the dress over her hips and surveyed herself in the mirror. The late Mrs. Peel must have been a petite woman, because the dress was a little too tight on Dru. She had bathed and pulled her hair back with an elastic band. Now she pinned it into a creditable twist, leaving a few still-damp tendrils free to do as they liked. She thought she looked pretty good for having hiked through the woods half the morning, but not *too* good. Looking too good, in this case, would definitely *not* be good.

Secreting the handkerchief in one hand, she made her way down the dark-paneled corridor until she heard men's voices. She pushed gently at one of the huge double doors and they swung inward.

She saw him a second or two before he saw her. Good thing, too, because it took that long for her to get her face, if not her emotions, composed.

Pierce stood in front of the fireplace, his injured foot resting on the stone hearth, a glass of scotch in his hand. His relaxed, casual grace said he belonged in elegant surroundings like these. The conservative tuxedo fit his lean, lanky frame as if it had been tailormade. His midnight-black hair was carefully combed back and shone with blue highlights, thanks to the firelight. The same flickering light illuminated his breathtaking profile and made his eyes the color of the deepest, bluest ocean, an ocean any woman could easily, gladly drown in.

She didn't know how long she'd stood there staring before he became aware of her. He turned his head as if in slow motion and leveled a gaze on her that seemed to warm every place it touched her—and it touched her everywhere.

"Would you join us for a drink, my dear?"

From the corner of her eye, she was dimly aware that Dr. Peel was looking from one to the other of them as if he were observing a tennis match. Perhaps the sparks between her and Pierce were even more tangible than she'd imagined. When she finally looked at Dr. Peel, she saw that he was decked out in full-dress Scottish regalia, including kilt and sporran. The rosy glow of his cheeks suggested that he'd had a drink or two already this evening.

"White wine, please," she said, forcing herself not to return her attention to Pierce. "You're looking very dapper tonight, Doctor."

Dr. Peel thanked her and launched into a brief history of the vintage outfit. Ginger had restored it, he said, and had taken particular pains with the patent leather dress shoes, polishing them to a mirrorlike shine. Thankful for the distraction, Dru feigned interest, all the while thinking about her situation with Pierce.

Maintaining an emotional distance from Pierce was going to be harder than she had realized. The more or less pleasant afternoon they had spent together had worn down her defenses enough. Now she had to sit through dinner with Pierce at his most dashing, which would bring her face-to-face with feelings she didn't want to examine. He would see the desire in her eyes and step up his assault on her willpower until the last of her resistance melted away.

There was only one thing to do. She must never show a sign of weakness, must never let him think she was softening toward him. Because once Pierce saw a chink in her armor, that armor would wind up cast aside on the bedroom floor tonight, along with the shiny dress. She mustn't show him any encouragement, even if she had to become the bitch goddess of the Western Hemisphere. And if the dinner conversation went in the direction she thought it would, she might just get some help from their host.

As Dr. Peel busied himself at the bar, Pierce watched Dru cross the room. Her gown was the color of moonlight and hugged her body like a second skin. The nearer she came to the fire, the more the dress shim-

mered with heat and motion. She looked like a waver-
ing mirage in the desert, and he felt like a man dying
of thirst.

"You look beautiful," he said simply, and was
pleased to see her cheeks color slightly.

Dr. Peel joined them at the hearth long enough to
hand Dru a glass of wine. "She does indeed." He retreated to a wing chair with his own drink and surveyed
the young couple keenly. "In fact, you make a beautiful couple."

Dru cast her gaze primly toward the fire, making
Pierce smile. "Yes, we do," he said.

Dr. Peel laughed heartily. "Hear, hear, dear boy.
I've never been an admirer of false modesty."

"That's a good thing, because modesty is not something he has in abundance, false or otherwise." Dru
narrowed her eyes on Pierce as she took a slow sip of
wine.

Pierce chuckled at the jab, along with Dr. Peel. So,
she wasn't going to let up on him for the benefit of
their host. So be it. "My wife and I know all of each
other's strengths and weaknesses, Dr. Peel," he said
congenially, stepping closer to her and extending an
arm around her shoulder. "That's what makes us the
perfect couple."

Dru raised an elegant brow. "Nice comeback," she
whispered, loud enough for only him to hear. "Although that last remark may just come back to haunt
you."

He started to ask her what she meant when Ginger
appeared out of nowhere in a fresh black uniform with
a starched white apron and cap. "Dinner's ready," she
chirped.

"Shall we?" Dr. Peel asked, and hoisted himself out of his chair.

Pierce offered Dru his arm. "My injured foot still pains me. I'm afraid I'll need some help."

She glanced hopefully at Dr. Peel, but he was already leading the way to the dining room. Without meeting Pierce's eyes, she linked her arm through his, and they started after the chemist.

"Thanks for letting me lean on you." He brought his face toward her and inhaled the fragrance of her hair. "Hmm. Lavender." His gaze traveled from her face to her throat and downward to her cleavage, where he saw the hidden microphone.

"Lucky mike," he said.

"Who's Mike?" Dru followed the direction of his gaze. "Oh, that. Never mind how I smell. Straighten up and fly right. We have a job to do."

He leaned so close to her breasts that his lips nearly touched her skin. "Help. I'm leaning and I can't straighten up," he whispered directly into the mike.

She hit him lightly on the forehead with the heel of her hand just as Ginger glanced at them. "Headache remedy," she explained, smoothing Pierce's hair back. "Works every time."

Dru needn't have worried that Ginger thought her behavior odd. It seemed the old girl had eyes only for her boss. Ginger drank in the sight of him in his kilt and black jacket, but when he paused in front of her to give her some instructions, she cast her eyes demurely downward. When it hit Dru what the housekeeper was up to, she nearly laughed out loud. Ginger was trying to see up Dr. Peel's kilt by the reflection in his shoes! If the doctor was cognizant of the old schoolboy trick she was pulling, he didn't let on. If

Ginger was successful at copping a peek, she didn't show it.

The dining room was as elegant as the rest of the house. A long mahogany table and chairs sat in front of a stone fireplace. At a matching sideboard, Ginger held camp, preparing to serve soup from a silver tureen. Dr. Peel sat at the head of the table, indicating that Dru should sit to his right and Pierce to his left.

After they were seated, Ginger placed a bowl of the steaming soup in front of each of them. When she served Dr. Peel, she leaned in close to him. Dru noticed that the top button of her maid's uniform was undone, revealing more than a bit of cleavage. Dr. Peel seemed oblivious.

"The tomato-basil bisque is divine," Pierce said with a nod to Ginger. Then he gave Dru a benign smile. "This is already better than the meal we had last night, isn't it, dear?"

"I don't know," Dru said. "I like a good wiener roast."

Pierce winced at the memory of the spark in his lap, nearly spilling a spoonful of soup on his white dress shirt.

"So tell me about the pulp and paper business," Dr. Peel asked. "Your wife says you take your work very seriously."

Pierce froze with his soup spoon halfway to his lips. He glanced quickly at Dru, who was trying to suppress a smirk. What the hell had she told Dr. Peel about his background?

"Yes, honey, tell Dr. Peel a little about our industry. I'm sure he'd be fascinated," Dru said innocently, batting her eyelashes at him.

Pierce cleared his throat. All of a sudden his bow tie

seemed to be a little tight. "Ah, the jolly old pulp and paper business," he began. "It's a demanding business, no question about it. And I do take it seriously, how could I not? After all, this business is where I met my lovely wife." Pierce favored Dru with his most adoring smile.

Dru's mouth twitched slightly. "I was telling Dr. Peel about your...ambition. And about how that has caused problems in our relationship."

"I don't know if your wife told you about our conversation this afternoon," Dr. Peel cut in. "Although I'm mainly a chemist now, my first love is psychology, specifically couples counseling. I'm very interested in people's marital problems. I'd be more than happy to listen to anything either of you would like to share about any difficulties you might have. In fact, your wife touched on a couple of areas I would really like to explore."

"She did, did she?"

"She told me about the time you took credit for the pulp and paper project she had initiated."

Dru stared at him coolly, waiting to see what he had to say for himself.

"I see." Pierce took a long drink of wine to fortify himself and buy time to think. Perhaps an apology would break down Dru's defenses. He'd heard it said that humility was a wonderful thing. He'd never actually tried it himself, but there was a first time for everything.

He set down his glass and looked at Dr. Peel earnestly. "Believe me, if I could go back and change the past I would, but I can't. I've said that I'm sorry, and that it will never happen again, but my wife still hasn't been able to find it in her heart to forgive me." He glanced at Dru, who gave him a withering look. "All I want is another chance."

Ginger appeared at Dr. Peel's side, dabbing at one eye with the tail of her apron, and began to remove the soup bowls. Dru took advantage of the interruption to compose herself. Had she heard correctly? Had Pierce actually apologized for something? He was playing along so smoothly, she could almost believe he was sincere. Well, she wasn't a fool and she wasn't through with him yet. It was time to nip this mushy talk in the bud and crush whatever hopes he might be nurturing for tonight. She thought she knew how to do that and get Dr. Peel to talk about his formula at the same time.

"So, Mrs. MacGregor, according to what you said this afternoon, this incident has led you to your inability to trust your husband, is that right?" Dr. Peel asked Dru.

"That and another big problem," she said, meeting Pierce's steady gaze with a lifted chin.

"And what would that be?"

"Frigidity."

"Frigidity?" Pierce repeated. His eyes widened with disbelief.

"You hadn't noticed this?" Dr. Peel asked Pierce in a puzzled tone.

"I say, why, I hadn't...that is, well..." Pierce looked from Dr. Peel to Dru, who narrowed her eyes on him coldly. "Well, yes, of course I've noticed that things were a little...frosty."

Dru turned to Dr. Peel and crossed the fingers of both hands in her lap. "I'm totally turned off by him. By the way he looks at me, by his touch, everything." A clap of thunder sounded in the distance, and she jumped.

"What's the matter, darling? Afraid that God will strike you dead?"

She looked at Pierce, who, to her total chagrin, had recovered from his earlier shock. In fact, he was grinning rather wickedly at her. His blue eyes gleamed with a fiery intensity that made her squirm in her seat. As she stared back at him, she realized what she'd done. She hadn't discouraged him, she'd issued a challenge! Instead of backing down, he was going to be more insufferable than ever. She moaned involuntarily and passed a hand over her brow.

"Are you quite well, dearest? Do you need to lie down? We can go back to our room, and I'll—"

"Sit," Dru hissed, "down."

Ginger reappeared with plates laden with thick slices of roast beef and vegetables. As she bustled around the table, Dru remarked on how wonderful the food looked and smelled and tried to ignore Pierce. But she could still feel that gaze on her. She didn't know how much more her nerves could take.

Dr. Peel chewed thoughtfully on a bite of beef. "This is a serious problem," he observed.

"You ain't kidding," Dru said, and gulped from her water tumbler.

"Quite so. I think we're at an impasse." Pierce sighed. "So, Doctor, you've heard our problem. My wife is indifferent to me—"

"The very sight of you makes me want to retch," Dru corrected, stabbing viciously at a new potato.

Pierce continued, unfazed. "Whereas I, on the other hand, still love her and just want our relationship to be what it once was."

Pierce bit his lip and gave the old chemist a pleading look that could have wrenched the hardest heart. From somewhere behind her, Dru thought she heard Ginger whimper. Dru crossed her arms. *And me without my hip boots.*

"So tell me, Doctor," he said haltingly. "What do you recommend?"

Dr. Peel set down his knife and fork and looked back and forth from Pierce to Dru as if trying to make up his mind. With an almost imperceptible wink at Ginger, he smiled broadly and nodded his head. "Actually, I've just completed work on a formula that I designed for cases like yours."

Pierce and Dru exchanged glances. She could see that his breathing had quickened, and could feel her own heart beating faster, as well. The thrill of capturing a news story was particularly good when she was sharing it with Pierce, she grudgingly acknowledged to herself.

"Is it a medication of some kind?" she asked, smoothing back her hair nervously. "An antidepressant, perhaps?"

Dr. Peel beamed, evidently delighted to talk about his work. "Better. It's a drug that not only puts desire back in a marriage, but enhances the sexual experience itself."

"How extraordinary. An aphrodisiac, is it?" Pierce asked, feigning surprise.

Dr. Peel chuckled. "I prefer to call it a love potion. It's passed all its toxicological and animal testing and is ready to try on humans. If you're interested, you two could be the first human test subjects. You can sign the proper consent forms and I'll give you some pills to take home."

Dru caught Pierce's eye again out of the corner of her own. They had planned to lead Dr. Peel into talking about his work over dinner, but she didn't think either of them had anticipated this stroke of fortune. They could take the pills back to their respective newspapers for analysis and then write up the results.

"Why, of course we'd be interested, wouldn't we, sweetie?" Pierce beamed. "Anything to keep our marriage together."

"Of course," she said. "Anything." A new and disturbing thought occurred to her. What if Pierce proposed that they take those pills themselves and report on the results firsthand?

"Excellent!" Dr. Peel rubbed his hands together. "Actually, I haven't synthesized the formula into pill form yet, but I'll go and get the process started and then return for our after-dinner drinks. Later on I'll take you on a tour of the lab." He dabbed at his mustache with his linen napkin. "Ginger, would you help me out in the lab for a minute?" With that, the pair left the room.

The moment the door was closed, Dru pointed her finger at Pierce. "Don't even think about it."

"Darling," Pierce said in his most languorous, honey-coated voice. "When we make love again—and we will—I don't want it to be because of a chemical, but because of the natural chemistry we have together."

"We will, will we?"

"Indeed, we will. But I must say, you had me going for a nanosecond there about that frigidity business. How clever of you to tell Dr. Peel that you don't want me sexually so he'd give us the formula. Good show. I say, you're an absolute genius." Pierce raised his glass and tilted it in her direction. "Cheers."

Dru drummed the fingers of one hand on the pristine

tablecloth. "How can you be sure I wasn't telling the truth?"

"You're a terrible liar, sweetheart. Like I said earlier, we know each other's strengths and weaknesses. That's what makes us—"

"I know. I know. The perfect couple."

"BUT I THOUGHT YOU SAID you were going to put the stuff in pill form. Why are we moving this canister?" Ginger grunted as she tried to get a better grip on her end of the heavy metal cylinder.

"I'll give them some harmless placebos to take home with them. I can't actually let them leave the compound with the drug—it might fall into the wrong hands."

"Then why did you tell them you would?"

"I needed their consent. I can't try the drug out on unsuspecting people without their knowledge. It wouldn't be ethical."

"So you're going to gas them in their sleep. What do you call that?"

Dr. Peel paused to catch his breath, the canister suspended awkwardly between them. "Scientific method."

"Huh?"

"If they know they're receiving the drug, the results might be tainted by the placebo effect."

"You mean, if they think they're *supposed* to act turned on, they will, even if the drug doesn't work the way it should."

"That's correct. If they don't know, we'll get a more accurate picture of how the drug really works." He started tottering off down the hall again, dragging Ginger and the canister with him. "We'll rig it up in the

adjoining room, slip some tubing under the door, and
I'll sneak in after they've retired for the night and turn
it on.''

"Ooh, I don't know about this, Dr. P.''

"It's all in the name of science, Gin. Besides, you
saw those two. Wouldn't you like to see that lovely
couple happy again?''

"Well, now that you mention it, they do seem perfect for each other. I was getting all misty-eyed just
listening to him talk about how badly he wants her
back. I just hope she can find it in her heart to give
him another chance.''

The chemist reached behind him and opened the
door to the room next to Pierce and Dru's. "Oh, she
will.'' He chuckled. "And another...and another...''

4

THE LAVENDER-SCENTED BUBBLES parted around her as she eased her sore legs into the hot water. The morning's hike was taking its toll on her body just as being with Pierce was taking a toll on her nerves.

"Are you sure you don't need any help in there? I could scrub your back," Pierce offered from behind the door.

"I can scrub my own back," Dru said, trying to banish visions of Pierce lathering her body.

"I could wash your hair."

"My hair is clean."

"I could give you a pedicure."

"No."

"You hiked a great distance through the woods today. For safety's sake, I think I should check your entire body for deer ticks."

"Go away!" Dru wished the latch on the door didn't look so flimsy. She sank down into the tub so far that the bubbles tickled her chin.

She hoped a long, hot soak would ease her muscles and her mind. She was so nervous just thinking about how she was going to get through the night in the same bed as Pierce, she wanted to scream. *I'm not going to think about that now.*

Perhaps listening to the tape recording she had made during the tour of Dr. Peel's lab after dinner would help her get her mind off her upcoming ordeal. He had been remarkably forthcoming about his research, and the tape contained a wealth of information. She leaned outside the antique clawfoot tub to get her microcassette tape player. She felt so naked with only a thin door separating her and Pierce that her hands shook from sheer vulnerability. Still, she managed to turn the tape on, and Dr. Peel's voice droned from the machine.

Pierce called out from behind the door, "Are you listening to the tape player in the tub? You'll electrocute yourself! You'll boil like a bloody lobster! I insist that you come out this instant!"

"No way." The tiny player was powered by a couple of low-voltage batteries, which, judging from the behavior of the machine, were about to expire. She muttered a curse as the tape ground to a halt. Setting the tape player on the side of the tub, she removed the microcassette. The tape containing all the material for her story spooled out of the cassette case like a forkful of plastic spaghetti.

"Aiieee!" she screamed in horror. A split second after her outburst, the sharp report of splintering wood gave her such a start she dropped the tape into the water.

"Great Scott! I knew you'd electrocute yourself!" Pierce burst into the bathroom, his dress shirt open to the waist, and knelt by the tub. Acting surprised to find her still alive, he asked breathlessly, "Didn't you just get shocked?"

"I'm shocked, all right." Dru drew up her knees and sank back down into the bubbles, feeling all around her for the errant tape. "You just caused me to drop the tape into the water, not the tape player. Get out now before you do any more damage!"

''Let me help you find it.'' He leaned over the tub so close to her that their faces touched, and plunged his hands into the soapy water.

''Stop it! Go away! Aiieee!'' Dru squealed as a hand that wasn't her own came in contact with something it shouldn't have. She grabbed his wrist, levering his hand away from her. ''That, as you very well know, is not it.''

''Sorry,'' Pierce said, his face looking a bit flushed and not sorry at all.

She raised her foot and kicked a generous portion of bubbly water onto Pierce's face and shirt. Mistake. The wet silk clung to his chest, making his exquisite pectorals and biceps all the more visible. Drops of water beaded on his jet-black lashes and made his eyes look like deep blue crystals.

''It's going to be like that, is it?'' He scooped up a handful of bubbles and came toward her face with it. She grabbed his arm and they wrestled for a moment until a distinct ''plop'' made them look down in time to see the tape player sinking into the water.

''I'll save you, darling!''

Dru squealed again as she felt Pierce's hand go under her bare bottom. With his other hand behind her back, he lifted her quickly from the water.

''The batteries are dead, you cretin! Put me down!'' She kicked her legs violently, but he held her fast as he carried her—dripping, soapy and naked—to the bedroom.

''You're delirious. Too much electricity will do that to you.'' He deposited her on the bed and fell onto it beside her. ''For all I know, you're still in danger. I may have to use mouth-to-mouth.''

''The only thing I'm in danger of is catching my

death of cold. You've taken me dripping wet from a hot tub to a freezing bedroom.'' She reached out and caught the corner of the cotton comforter and pulled it over herself as far as she could. But it wasn't far enough. He stared as if mesmerized at her naked body, her nipples hardened by the chill, her skin slippery and moist from the bubble bath.

She took advantage of his momentary trance to place her hand against his chest and push him off the bed to the floor. Then she tightened her grip on the comforter and rolled herself into it so that only her head was visible above a solid cylinder of fabric.

Pierce staggered to his feet and blinked. ''Nice and snug, are we?''

''*I* am, and I intend to stay this way. I can't say the same for you.'' He seemed to be almost as wet as she had been, and had begun to shiver. ''Go into the bathroom and get the tape out of the water. I might be able to get it repaired.'' *And I might be able to buy some time,* Dru thought.

Pierce did as he was told, grateful for the excuse to leave the bedroom. He needed a moment to compose himself. When he picked up the remains of the audio tape, he noticed that his hands were shaking slightly. No other woman had ever worked him into such a state of sexual frenzy as this.

Blimey! What was she doing to him? And what was he doing to himself? His goal all along was to get her out of his system, but what if it didn't work? It certainly hadn't worked that way when he'd slept with her that other time. What if he became more obsessed with her than ever? He wouldn't be able to stand it. And yet here he was, pulling every sophomoric trick in the book to get her naked and in bed. It had worked so far, but they were at an impasse. If he couldn't penetrate her defenses, he would simply die of frustration.

He splashed cold water on his face at the sink and looked in the mirror. "You pathetic sod," he said to his pale reflection. Part of him wanted to throw on his hiking clothes and walk out, but that would mean he'd have lost, and he hated to lose. It was one of the many things he had in common with Dru. If this was a game to be won or lost, the stakes were high. His whole image of himself as a man whose armor couldn't be breached—whose heart couldn't be touched—depended on whether he could make love to Dru and walk away.

He pulled himself together, dried his face and returned to the bedroom. "I put the tape on a towel to dry, but I think it's a goner. I had to fish part of it out of the drain. Good thing I have a photographic memory, eh?"

Dru winced at the thought of her precious tape having gone down the drain. "Yeah, and if you don't remember it exactly, I'm sure you'll make something up like you usually do."

"I've never been one to let the truth get in the way of a good story, that's true. You should try a little creative reporting yourself. It's very liberating." He rubbed his arms briskly and climbed back onto the bed beside her. "I say, is there some kind of mist in the air? And what's that faint odor?"

Dru looked around. Sure enough, it looked as if a light fog was settling into the room. "This bedroom probably hasn't been used in so long, it must be a little musty. The mist is just steam from my bath. Don't change the subject. I have no intention of stooping to the kind of reporting *you* engage in."

She should be able to recall enough information for a basic article, but the loss of the tape was still a set-back to creating the kind of in-depth story she'd envisioned. Her memory was not as good as Pierce's. "This is all your fault. If you hadn't pulled that stunt to get me out of the bathroom and into bed, I'd still have the tape." She scowled at him. "And stop plucking at my comforter."

"But I'll freeze," he said, not bothering to defend himself from her charge.

"Look in the closet for more blankets."

He crossed the room to the closet, where he rummaged for a few moments before coming out with a heavy Navajo-print blanket. He wrapped himself in it and solemnly held up one hand. "How," he said in a cowboys-and-Indians movie voice.

"How what?"

He pounced onto the bed beside her. "How am I going to get you to admit that you want me as much as I want you?"

"Hell will freeze over before that happens." She lifted her chin and gave him a defiant look. He'd always said she was a lousy liar. Could he tell she was lying now? Because, God help her, she was.

He sighed and then a gleam came into his eye. "Speaking of freezing, I still am. I have to get out of these wet clothes." He got to his feet again and began to strip, an impudent grin playing across his face.

She squeezed her eyes tightly shut. Pierce was very well aware of how the sight of his body affected women, especially her. She knew because she'd once had the poor judgment to show him. "Go in the bathroom and do that."

"That won't be necessary."

"I'm not watching."

"But you want to."

"You're mistaken."

His rumbling masculine chuckle mingled with the juicy sound of him removing the sopping shirt. She stifled a moan.

"I'm flexing my bare biceps now."

"I don't care."

"Liar."

She heard the sound of a zipper unzipping. The thin metallic sound set off a moist fire in her belly that spread downward and made her squirm. In her mind's eye, she could see him sliding the tuxedo trousers and his black briefs down his powerful thighs in one smooth motion. Her control was disintegrating like her plans for her story, and there was nothing she could do about it. He was right. Despite everything, she still wanted him. It was useless to deny it, but she would— for as long as she could.

Unable to help herself, she opened one eye. Surely a little peek couldn't get her anymore worked up than she was now. To her surprise, she saw that Pierce had folded the blanket to fashion a crude kilt and was wearing it proudly, his hands on his hips, just waiting for her to peek.

"I saw ye eyeing Dr. Peel this evening. I didna know that ye admired a man in a kilt so. I suspect you were wondering what was underneath."

"You suspect wrong."

"Och! What a wee liar ye are. I thought ye prided yerself on always telling the truth."

He was right. She'd always thought a man in a kilt was as sexy as hell, and he was no exception. Even the Scottish accent was getting to her, as hokey as his was.

The jaunty kilt draped low on his hips, and her gaze couldn't help but follow the thatch of hair that started out broad on his chest and narrowed until it disappeared beneath the fabric.

"You expect me to be turned on by the sight of a man in a skirt?" She tried to inject her tone with all the disdain she could muster.

Pierce whipped away the kilt in a lightning-fast motion, revealing his entire body in all its glory. And was it ever glorious. Something primitive wrenched inside her as she stared, mesmerized, at his impressive manhood. It was a good thing her arms—and legs—were restricted by the cocoon she was in, because she wanted so badly to reach out to him, welcome him. She could not, however, let him see the effect he was having on her.

She swallowed hard and sent him a haughty look. "You'd better wrap up in that blanket. You're obviously getting a chill."

Pierce looked down at himself and, satisfied she was bluffing, gave her a wicked grin. "I can think of a much better way to warm things up."

"Go jump in the loch," Dru muttered, and drew her head down into the comforter like a turtle.

She felt one side of the mattress dip as he crawled into bed next to her. She opened her eyes to see him lying on his side, propped up on one elbow, and regarding her studiously. He plucked at the comforter again with his free hand. "You're like a lovely butterfly wrapped up in this old cocoon of a comforter. You need to spread your beautiful wings so we can fly."

"Want me to spread 'em, huh? Forget it. I have a new policy—I don't sleep with scoundrels. That means you."

Pierce looked aghast. "You don't mean that."

"I do. From now on, I only want to date nice, sensitive men." Dru crossed the fingers of both hands under the comforter. She tried to cross her toes, as well, but started to get a cramp. She hated to admit it, but his persistence was so humorous that she was beginning to enjoy the game.

"I can be sensitive," Pierce said, a bit petulantly.

"Okay. Then do something sensitive."

"Like what?"

"I don't know." She thought for a moment. "Recite a love poem."

"That's easy," he said, grinning. "There once was a man from Nantucket—"

"Not *that* kind of poem. You've probably never even read a love poem." Dru wriggled deeper into the comforter and rolled away from him. She'd found herself actually wanting him to recite a poem to her.

"I was only joshing. Of course I can recite you a love poem. And if I do, will you unroll yourself from that comforter and come into my arms where you belong?"

She sighed, feeling a tad more resistance drain away as he put his lips against her neck. No way could he recite a love poem. If anyone was bereft of a single poetic bone in his body, it was Pierce. A barracuda had a more poetic soul than he did. "I don't know. What do I get if *I* win and you can't come up with a poem?"

"Darling," he purred into her ear, sending a shiver of desire down her spine, "I'll give you a night you'll never forget. Of course, that's also what you'll get if *I* win. You see, it's a win-win situation."

Dru felt the bed shift again as Pierce leaned over to turn off the lamp. The room was now lit only by soft moonlight filtered through sheer curtains. He snuggled up close to her back and wrapped his arms around her, comforter and all, drawing her nearer. She could feel his warm breath against her cheek. Then that voice, the voice like liquid velvet, warm and deep and lilting with that luscious accent, began.

> "She walks in beauty, like the night
> Of cloudless climes and starry skies;
> And all that's best of dark and bright
> Meet in her aspect and her eyes:
> Thus mellow'd to that tender light
> Which heaven to gaudy day denies.

"Lord Byron, 1815," he added for good measure.

Dru turned her head to stare at him in awe. She would never have believed it, but Mr. Ruthless *had* memorized a love poem. And what was even more difficult to believe was how much that simple act moved her. Although her instinct for self-protection caused her to weigh the possibility of betrayal, she wanted him now more than ever. "That was very...sensitive."

"Thanks." He stroked her cheek, smoothing back her hair. "That poem could have been written for you, luv. Your beauty rivals everything nature has to offer. When you walked into the parlor tonight in that silver dress, I knew you were the most gorgeous woman I'd ever seen."

The sincerity in his voice spread warmth all through her, and her body ached for him all the more. Still, she resisted. "Flattery is cheap. And as far as the poetry is concerned, you *do* have a photographic memory. Tell me something that will *really* impress me."

"You're a hard woman to please," he muttered.

"Okay, let me think." A shadow crossed his face for a moment, and he took a deep breath, as if he was about to make a costly admission. "Do you remember when you got sick on that UFO assignment in Mexico and someone left bottled water, canned chicken soup and biscuits outside your door?"

She gaped at him. "That was you? Why didn't you stay after you knocked? When I got to the door, nobody was there."

Pierce shifted his head on the pillow and a lock of jet-black hair fell across his forehead. "Didn't fit my image, I suppose."

"That was a very, very sweet thing to do." She saw him shrug and look away. "That story was much better than poetry." Had Deborah been right all along? Did the heart of a nice guy beat underneath that ruthless exterior?

Dru rubbed her temples and tried to think. She was a mass of jumbled nerves as raw and electric as live wires. She resented him for being irresistible and for causing her more sexual frustration than she'd ever experienced. Why couldn't she think more like a man, be willing to take what she wanted and damn the consequences?

Her frustration turning into indignation, she pushed herself higher in the fabric she was wrapped in. Why, she reasoned, would her consent to a casual toss in the proverbial hay constitute a win for him and a loss for her? She wanted him, by God, and she could be just as cavalier about sex as he could. It was like her father always said: *Don't be a wuss. Take what you want out of life, don't apologize, and don't look back. You're a Logan, and the world is your oyster.*

Dad was right. She was going to go for what she wanted. And what she wanted was Pierce Mountcastle.

"Well, um...I guess a deal's a deal, huh?" She writhed as his hand stroked the length of her arm, captured her fingers and was still.

He raised his head and looked at her. "Pardon?"

"We had a bet. You recited a love poem, and now I have to pay up."

"I say, darling," he began, raising her hand to his lips. "I meant what I said at dinner after the others left. I want you back, but only if you really want me. Now, if you were to give me a sign—"

She couldn't believe it. Now *he* was playing hard to get. He was still kissing her fingers one by one when she wrenched her hand away. She turned toward him and grabbed the edge of the comforter, meaning to whip it away as he had done with his makeshift kilt. But she was wound too tightly and her efforts seemed to only make it tighter.

When he saw what she was doing, Pierce said quickly, "Let me help," and took hold of the offending comforter. He yanked. Nothing happened. He braced himself on one elbow and yanked harder. Her body did a full revolution while the material slid away.

"Aah!" As her body rolled toward the floor, Dru managed to hold on to the other edge of the comforter, which landed underneath her, saving her from the cold wood floor. The force of her fall dragged Pierce, still holding fast, off the edge of the bed and squarely on top of her.

Even in the dim light, she could see his smile of triumph. He rose above her and nudged her thighs apart with his knee. "I seem to have fallen hard for you this time, Ms. Logan."

"Shut up and kiss me." Dru groaned as he slanted his lips hungrily against her mouth, his hands caressing her breasts, thumbs teasing her nipples. His mouth continued downward, pausing only a moment at the hollow of her throat before it captured the rosy peak of her breast. Pulses surfaced all over her body and throbbed with the rhythm of their thundering hearts.

Her arms encircled his neck and rested on his powerful shoulders, the muscles there straining as he moved his body over hers. She thrilled to the orchestrated muscles in his back and along his lean flanks, the feel of his skin, his hair, the insistent pull of his lips. The sounds of love he made resonated through her body, sending reverberations to the warm, wanting center of her.

With his mouth he played her body like a fine, tautly stringed instrument, drawing from it a crescendo of pleasure. He hadn't shaved in a day and a half, and the places he nuzzled with his chin came alive with a delicious tingly itch—the hollow of her throat, the arch of her foot, the tops of her thighs.

His hands captured, caressed and moved on to claim new territory. Her body writhed in instinctive response to his touch as if he were leading her in a wild, primitive dance. In the square of moonlight in which they lay, she could see that his eyes had taken on a hypnotic, unearthly brightness, and his voice washed over her, whispering his own personal poetry that only her heart understood. Under the attentions of his hands and mouth, she quivered in places she didn't know she had.

Even though she'd only been with him once before, she'd missed his touch like no other man's. She'd had lovers before, but none could make her body and soul sing the way he could. Did scoundrels always make the best lovers? It was her last thought before all reason slipped away and she dissolved into pure sensation. She felt his need against her thighs and rose to meet him as he entered her.

They moved against each other with hot, sweet urgency and spiraled upward together on a wave of sensation until Dru thought she was floating on a misty cloud that seemed to envelop them. Just when she thought she would burst with pleasure, he began to move faster and clutch her more tightly.

Their groans of passion merged as they peaked together.

They continued to hold each other tightly while they caught their breath. She closed her eyes again and wished the wonderful feeling of being one with Pierce would never fade. Although he still held her tightly to him, she felt the old vulnerability and doubt begin to creep back into her mind. Her earlier bravado now vanished, and she knew she'd never be able to look at lovemaking the way men seemed to. She was a woman, a romantic woman, and she needed gentleness and assurance.

She prayed she had not made a heartbreaking mistake—the very same mistake she'd made before. One of her father's favorite sayings was, "Fool me once, shame on you. Fool me twice, shame on me." The shame she'd felt the first time Pierce had loved her and left her was going to be nothing compared to what she'd feel if he did it again. Because this time, she risked not only her pride but her heart.

Dru raised herself on one elbow and looked into Pierce's eyes, steeling herself for some insensitive remark, some mocking look now that he'd gotten what he wanted. But he said nothing. His face glowed with a sheen of perspiration and his hair hung down over his forehead. His eyes looked like dark sapphires in the moonlight and, she was startled to see, regarded her with tenderness, an emotion she'd never seen in them before.

"Who are you, and what have you done with Pierce Mountcastle?" she murmured softly.

"What?" He smiled at her quizzically and ruffled her hair.

"Never mind." She lay back down beside him and snuggled her cheek against his fuzzy chest.

AS THE DAWN BEGAN TO BREAK, Pierce slipped from bed with the print blanket and sat in the chair beside the small desk facing the window. They'd finally made it to the bed sometime during the night. How many times had they made love? he wondered. It seemed they'd never stopped. Never in his thirty years had he spent a night like that. He didn't believe he was capable of blushing, but if he was a lesser man, he might be doing it right now, just thinking about last night. He stretched, pulled the blanket around him more closely and shivered.

Now would be the perfect time to make his escape.

Dru was sound asleep and probably would be for some time. He could be miles away before she even realized he was gone. And since Dru's tape of the material he'd committed to memory was destroyed, the story would be his. Exclusively. Seduce Dru, steal the story and split. That had been the plan, right?

So why did it now feel so wrong?

Perhaps it was because he'd learned last night that by showing some sensitivity and not coming on too strong, he could earn Dru's trust. And for some reason, he simply couldn't bring himself to betray that trust. Not after last night. *Mountcastle, old chap, you are definitely going soft.* He shuddered. His entire self-image was being shaken by that brunette in bed. What the hell was he going to do about that?

As if she sensed his turmoil, Dru tossed restlessly onto her side in her sleep, so that she now faced him. She curled her hand against one flushed cheek, her silky black hair spilling across the pillow, her face troubled as if she was having a bad dream.

He slid out the top desk drawer as carefully as possible so as not to wake her. There he found a notepad and pen. Just enough light came in through the window for him to begin scribbling the information he'd heard and seen from the night before. He turned toward the window and put pen to paper. Yes, a photographic memory was certainly useful, and not only for reporting. Dru's book of love poems he'd skimmed through had come in quite handy, too. That Lord Byron really knew how to appeal to women.

He heard a stirring behind him and turned in time to see Dru, still half-asleep, patting the covers on his side of the bed with increasing urgency. She thought he'd left her again. Seeing this, he felt that little pang in his chest again. "Over here," he said softly.

Dru let out a long breath, as if in relief, and smiled. "What are you doing?"

"Writing down what I can remember about what Dr. Peel said last night."

"I thought you had a photographic memory."

"I do." Pierce mentally thanked the powers of creation for his gift. He hoped the image he was viewing now—that of Dru propped up in bed, the rising sun casting a golden glow over her perfect hair and skin, creamy breasts visible above the comforter—would be forever etched in his memory.

"Then why are you writing down your notes? Are you afraid you'll forget?"

Pierce capped the pen. "No," he said. "The notes are not for me. They're for you."

Dru said nothing for a moment, but a look of sincere gratitude came across her face. When she finally spoke, she said, "So if your memory is so good, I guess you can do that later, huh?" Her hand stretched slowly toward him across his empty side of the bed.

He glanced momentarily back at his writing, as if torn. "Well, perhaps I could put it off until later, but what if you give me an experience so shattering that I lose my memory?"

"You mean amnesia? Like in romance novels?"

He got up and eased himself onto the side of the bed. "Yeah, that's right. We'd be a couple right out of a romance novel. The ones where they stay in bed all the time."

She held the covers up for him as he crawled underneath. When he drew her close, she snaked her arms around his neck. Her soft body warmed him as he nestled his head between her neck and shoulder. "I think we should risk the amnesia. Being in a romance novel doesn't sound too bad."

A short time later Dru collapsed onto his chest, sated. After a few moments, she raised her head and looked into Pierce's eyes. "So, how's the amnesia?"

He looked at her and blinked, his dark brows knit together. "Young woman, whoever you are, I just want you to know that those liberties you just took with my physical person are much too intimate to be borne, at least not until we're properly introduced."

Dru seized a pillow and brought it down toward his head, but he blocked the blow easily. He grasped her about the waist and rolled them onto their sides, each of them laughing amid a sprinkling of downy feathers.

DRU GAZED AT HER SLEEPING partner. Could this possibly be the same Pierce Mountcastle she'd known for the past few years? The one who'd sell his own granny down the river for a story? She'd woken fully expecting him to be gone. But here he was, stretched out next to her, sleeping peacefully. *I'll be damned.*

She snuggled deeper into the covers and ran her hand lightly across his chest, savoring the feel of the curly black hair and hard muscle beneath her fingertips. Was he really changing? Could she actually have a relationship with this man to whom she was so drawn but could never trust? Was now the time to let her defenses down?

Time. Dru sat up in bed and looked at the antique clock on the wall opposite the bed. "Look what time it is!"

Pierce woke with a start. "Blimey! It can't be 2:00 p.m.!" The last time he looked out the window, the sun was rising. Now, afternoon shadows crept across the wooded lawn. "I say, what *day* is it?"

They looked at each other in alarm before Pierce remembered his watch had a calendar. "Sunday," he said, grinning.

"Thank goodness."

They washed and dressed quickly. "What are we going to tell Dr. Peel about why we haven't surfaced until now?" Dru asked, pulling her cotton sweater over her head.

''I doubt if much shocks him. You're talking about a man who spends all day watching mice mate.''

As they made their way down the hall, they heard voices from the parlor. Dru pulled up short in front of the half-open door. ''I can't go in there.''

''Don't be embarrassed. They think we're a newly reunited married couple.''

''Who've been doing it like bunnies for the past fifteen hours. You go in first.''

Dru peeked around the door as Pierce went in and greeted Dr. Peel and Ginger. The chemist folded his newspaper and winked at him. ''So how was your night?''

Pierce, his back to her, said, ''Jolly good. We overslept.''

''Oh, I don't doubt it.''

There was something disturbing in Dr. Peel's knowing tone. It wasn't exactly lewdness, but definitely strange. Was there something going on that she didn't know about?

Ginger poured juice from a pitcher into a tumbler, then offered it to Pierce. ''Here, drink this. You're probably dehydrated.''

Dehydrated? What the—

Dr. Peel rose from his easy chair and came to stand beside Pierce. ''So, my boy, how did you like my little love potion? Was it everything you hoped it would be?''

5

HER SHYNESS FORGOTTEN, Dru burst into the room. "What? What did you say?"

"There are some cold cuts in the fridge if you want a late lunch," Ginger said nervously.

"That wasn't it."

"Oh. And Dr. Peel piped the love potion into your bedroom last night in gas form. Juice?" Ginger thrust a full glass into her hand.

"What? What do you mean he—" The tinny sound of a watch alarm interrupted Dru in midsentence.

Dr. Peel pressed a button on his timepiece and the sound stopped. "I've got to get back to the lab for the next stage of a timed experiment, but we must talk over dinner. For the record, I need to get your assessment of the drug." He clapped Pierce on the back as he passed by him. "As if I have to ask. Come along, Ginger."

Ginger looked all too happy to comply as she hustled out of the room after Dr. Peel, leaving Pierce and Dru alone and staring at each other.

"Blimey! He gassed us! That old sneak," Pierce said, and shook his head. "I say, this is the limit. I need a drink."

Dru's mind flashed back to the chummy way in which Dr. Peel had asked Pierce if he liked the formula. Then there was the wink, the slap on the back. A terrible possibility dawned on her. "It takes an old sneak to know one."

"What rot." Pierce had crossed to the bar and picked up a bottle of vodka. "You can't possibly imagine that I had any prior knowledge of this." He poured a healthy amount of the liquor into the glass with the orange juice. "Want a screwdriver?"

"No, but if I had a butcher knife, you'd be a soprano and I'd be a happy woman."

"You're being bloody ridiculous."

"Am I? So why was it that you worked so hard to get me out of the bathroom last night? Because you knew the gas wouldn't have reached me in there!" Last night was becoming all too clear. No wonder he'd been able to break down her defenses so easily!

"I got you out of the bathroom because I wanted you in bed." Pierce gulped his drink and wiped his mouth with the back of his hand.

"And to think I fell for that line about how you only wanted to make love to me if I really wanted you, not because of some silly bet. You only said that because you knew all along I'd be powerless to refuse you after you got me into the bedroom."

He abandoned his drink and came to stand facing her. "I knew you'd be powerless to refuse me because of the Mountcastle charm—and because you find me irresistible."

"Ooh!" Dru tossed the contents of her glass at him, showering Pierce with the sticky juice. "I was crazy to imagine that you'd changed! And to think I was starting to actually care for you!"

She turned on her heel and stormed out, leaving Pierce staring after her, juice clinging to his shirt and dripping from his hair. He removed his handkerchief from his pocket and dabbed his face. "Jolly good," he muttered.

What went on between him and Dru last night had seemed real enough. But what if it had been the drug? What else could explain why he had stayed and written up his notes for Dru when his every instinct had told him to cut and run, taking the story with him?

So it came down to this, he thought, licking orange pulp off his upper lip. Either he had been drugged against his will, or he was turning into a nice guy, a man a woman like Dru could actually care for. The latter was definitely the more frightening prospect.

DRU RAN INTO THE BEDROOM she'd shared with Pierce and immediately saw what she should have seen earlier. A small length of flexible plastic tubing protruded from underneath the door. Examining it, she saw that there was some condensed liquid on the inside of the tube. Maybe she could get a sample analyzed when she got back, just to make sure the drug was safe. She got the pocketknife out of her pack, pulled on the tube until several inches came free, cut the tube and tied off the ends. Then she stuffed the section of tubing, her equipment and her clothing into her backpack as fast as she could.

Of all the dirty tricks Pierce had pulled over the years for the sake of a story, this had to be the dirtiest. He probably planned to write a first-person account of their night together as part of the story. Her face burned with shame just thinking about it. And her heart ached with loss as she realized that the closeness she'd shared with Pierce last night had more to do with chemicals than with real emotional attachment.

She couldn't bear staying in this compound another

minute. She had to get out while Dr. Peel was busy in his lab. Slinging her pack over her shoulder, she remembered the notes that Pierce had written for her. She ran to the writing table, snatched the papers and started out again, only to collide with Pierce in the doorway.

"Where are you going?" he demanded.

"I'm not staying here with you a second longer." She tried to push past him, but he stood fast, his large, lanky frame barring the door.

"Don't you want to stay for dinner to see what else Dr. Peel has to say about the drug?"

"I don't care what else he has to say about it. I'm tired of your tricks, and I'm going home."

He started toward her, but she backed away from him until the bed stopped her. "I wasn't in on what Dr. Peel did. I swear."

"I don't believe you. Get out of my way!" Dru grabbed a pillow from the bed, and tried to knock him aside with it. There must have been a tear in it because a shower of down came out, settling on his face and shoulders, getting stuck in the orange-juice residue.

Looking like a man who'd been tarred and feathered both literally and figuratively, Pierce said calmly, "Very well, if you feel that way about it, I'll wash up and go with you."

"Like hell you will. I'm going to make it back to civilization first and file my story ahead of yours. The race is on, and may the best reporter win." Dru's eyes flashed the challenge and she took off down the hall.

Pierce looked after her, his frustration building. Why wouldn't she believe him? He scratched his forehead and his fingers came away sticky with juice. If he had to be perfectly honest—an activity he tried to avoid—he supposed it might have something to do with all the lies he had told her in the past. Still, was it so impossible to believe that he could be sensitive and caring if he really tried?

Sensitive and caring? Was he mad?

He marched to the bureau mirror. A sticky, feathered stranger stared back at him. What was happening to him? Why did he even care whether she believed him or not? *That bloody drug!* Well, from now on, he was going to be his old beastly self.

"NOW I KNOW WHERE THEY GOT the expression 'twisting in the wind,'" Dru muttered to herself as she swung gently in the breeze. She was suspended in midair by her backpack, which had been caught on the top of the chain-link fence.

She'd taken off her boots and thrown them over the fence so she could get toeholds in the links. Doubting that her nails would ever be the same again, she'd actually made it over when something had gotten snagged. She'd nearly dislocated a shoulder trying to wriggle free of the pack's straps, but it was no use. If only she could reach the penknife she'd used earlier and put in her pants pocket. But with her arms pinned back, she couldn't manage.

A curious squirrel scampered over and sat staring up at her. "What the hell am I going to do now?" Dru asked. The squirrel cocked its head to one side. Dru let her body go limp and closed her eyes. "I've hit bottom. While Pierce Mountcastle is stealing my story, I'm hanging on a fence talking to a squirrel. Things can't possibly get any worse."

Then she heard a sound that made her feel as if the blood were freezing in her veins.

"Well, I'll take the high road—"

She opened her eyes. The squirrel was still there. "Please say you're a singing squirrel," she begged.

The squirrel ran away and the singing grew closer, accompanied by the sound of snapping twigs. She twisted her body toward the sound and in a few moments Pierce came into view.

Dru wriggled like a worm on a fishing hook, but went nowhere. "You—you—why, I oughta—"

"Tsk. Everyone's a critic." Pierce grinned at her and started to walk away. "I'd love to hang around with you, luv, but I've got a story to file."

She took a deep, cleansing breath. "Come back here and cut me down."

Pierce shrugged. "What with?"

"I have a knife in my pocket." What in the world had she been thinking earlier when she'd thought things couldn't get any worse?

Pierce scratched his chin. "I'll do it on the condition that you give me a twenty-minute head start."

"What?"

"It's only fair. You took off without me and now I've had to slow my progress to help you out of this jam."

"Oh, all right. Get the knife."

Pierce gave her a wicked grin and probed in her pocket. "I can't find it," he lied, massaging her hip through the fabric. She aimed a kick at him and narrowly missed. "Found it!" he said.

Stretching to his full height, he cut away the snagged material with one hand and caught her against him when she fell. He held her to him for a moment, and her senses were filled with the nearness of him. Her head came to rest on his rock-hard chest and her nose caught the fresh scent of citrus. As she looked up at him, his eyes rivaled the blue of the Carolina sky. Unbelievably, even after what had happened, she found herself wanting him again.

He evidently also felt whatever spark had passed through them. For just a moment, his cocky expression gave way to one of tenderness and confusion. Then his eyes took on a flinty glitter and a muscle worked in his jaw. "Looks like the formula is still at work."

She pushed him away. Stooping to retrieve the remains of her backpack, she said, "Last night Dr. Peel said it stayed in the system for weeks."

"How tiresome. It can't wear off fast enough to suit me." Pierce made no move to help her get her things together.

His remark stung her so badly that she kept her eyes trained on the ground so he couldn't see the hurt she knew would show there. "Same here."

"Now, don't forget my head start. We had a deal."

"Oh, sure, no problem." Dru sat cross-legged and began to put one of her hiking boots back on. She had no intention of waiting any longer than it would take him to get out of earshot. "Scout's honor."

"I'm afraid that's not good enough. Think I'm a twit, do you?" Pierce scooped up the other boot, threaded one of the laces through one of the links in the fence and tied it to the other lace in several difficult knots. "It ought to take you about twenty minutes to untie that."

"You pig!"

"Oink." Pierce saluted Dru with her own knife and pocketed it. "The race is back on, and may the *trickiest* reporter win. It's like I've always told you, Dru. Nice blokes finish last. Cheers."

Dru hurled a pinecone at his retreating back, and it

bounced off harmlessly. She waited until the sound of his singing had died out before she grabbed her toiletry bag from the backpack and rifled through it. "Aha!" She held her nail file up in triumph.

As she sawed at the heavy nylon boot lace, she heard twigs snapping. Figuring Pierce had decided to come back for some reason, she stepped up her pace so he couldn't pull the same stunt again. When her boot was loose, she scrambled into it, and as she was readjusting the laces, she felt a tap on her shoulder. "Back already?" she asked without looking up. "Realized you can't get back to civilization without my help and came crawling back, eh? You really are pathetic."

Pierce cleared his throat, but it was from several feet away. Dru finally looked up and was startled by her own reflection in the tinted lenses of a large, uniformed man.

"Come with me, miss," he said without inflection. "I'm the off-duty police officer hired to guard this compound. You're under arrest for criminal trespass."

Pierce, his wrists handcuffed together, stood beside the man and tried to look nonchalant. "Hurry along, dear. We don't want to keep this fine member of the local constabulary waiting."

She groaned inwardly. If Pierce hadn't been able to finesse his way out of getting nabbed, she didn't have a chance. Still, she did have her wiles. Twisting a lock of hair around her finger, she batted her eyelashes. "But what do you want with *me,* Officer? *He* was the one who wanted to break in. I tried to tell him it was wrong, but he wouldn't listen."

Pierce rolled his eyes and the officer's mouth became a thin, hard line. "I watched you break *out* of the compound on closed-circuit TV. Dr. Peel became suspicious when you left so abruptly, and he found this in your bathroom.'' He held up the remains of the microcassette tape. ''He knows you're reporters.''

Dru groaned and held out her wrists. To her chagrin, the officer handcuffed her to Pierce. ''Hey, this is cruel and unusual punishment.''

''This is a fine, rummy mess you've gotten us into,'' Pierce countered under his breath as the guard marched them along in front of him.

''Me?'' Dru said under her breath. ''It was you who got caught and then ratted *me* out.''

''But if you had kept your cool, we could have made an orderly exit and Peel never would have been the wiser. Now, thanks to you, we're headed to the hoosegow.''

''How could I keep my cool knowing you'd just drugged me?''

''Dash it all! I *didn't* drug you!''

''Did somebody say something about drugs?'' the officer asked sternly from behind them.

''No,'' Pierce and Dru both cried in unison.

''I said he bugs me,'' Dru added quickly.

''No kidding,'' the officer muttered.

The policeman ushered the still-arguing Pierce and Dru into a cruiser that stood waiting at the compound gate and threw their packs in the trunk. ''They're all yours, and good riddance,'' he said to the officer who'd come to pick them up.

''Dangerous, are they?'' the man said, eyeing the two in the back seat cautiously.

''No,'' the first officer said. ''Just extremely annoying.''

DR. PEEL LOOKED OUT his laboratory window at the police cruiser leaving by the service road. ''I just can't believe they were reporters. They probably weren't even married. What have I done?''

Ginger hastily shut one of the human sexuality books she had picked up from his desk and fanned herself with her plump hand. ''There probably hasn't been any harm done.'' She saw Dr. Peel's shoulders shrug. She hated to see the dear, sweet man's disappointment and longed to comfort him, to lay his handsome gray head on her ample bosom.

She'd been trying to seduce the old guy for years, with no success. She'd even recently begun to peruse the sex books in the study for pointers. Lately she'd decided to take a more direct approach and she sensed an opportunity was at hand. She felt her face flush and wished she was wearing something sexier. Still, some people thought maids' uniforms were hot, didn't they? She looked down at her attire. Probably not with gravy stains on the apron, though.

''They might not have been married, but my instincts still tell me they're made for each other,'' she said. ''Don't you believe in that, Doctor? Two people being made for each other?'' She discarded the stained apron and hiked her dress up a few inches, retying the sash to keep it in place.

Dr. Peel, still gazing out the window, sighed. ''I suppose. I'm mainly worried that I can't trust the test results now that I've found out those two were here under false pretenses.''

''I have an idea.'' She removed her maid's cap, took the pins from her bun and let her long silver hair flow around her shoulders. She pinched her cheeks and bit her bottom lip for color. ''Let's test the formula out ourselves—you and me.''

Dr. Peel turned to face her and his eyes grew wide. "Ginger!" His gaze traveled from her black oxfords, up her plump but shapely legs, over her generous figure to her face. "Oh, my." The old boy's cheeks puffed out and the whiskers of his mustache seemed to stand on end. "You and me?"

Ginger approached him, catlike, and nodded. As she walked past a canister of the love-potion gas leaning up against his desk, she turned the valve on the top. The tank emitted a barely audible hiss. "In the interest of science, of course."

When Ginger reached the slack-jawed Dr. Peel, she put her hand on his chest and pushed him slightly. He collapsed into his desk chair and she settled onto his lap.

"Of course," he said right before she covered his mouth with her own.

DRU WALKED OUT OF THE COUNTY lockup early the next morning with her backpack slung over one shoulder. Her hair was plastered limply to her head, and the rumpled clothes she had on were the same ones she'd slept in the night before. Just ahead of her on the steps in his immaculate hiking outfit, not a hair out of place, was Pierce Mountcastle.

Damn. You could throw the man in jail for the night and he would still come out the next morning looking like Cary Grant.

He noticed her and paused for her to catch up to him. "How was your night, darling? Not too stressful, I hope."

"Let's just say I know a little more than I really need to about prostitutes and their unique concerns. I did make friends with some of them, though. One even said that if I ever need a job to call Big Larry and tell him Sheila sent me. What about your cellmates?''

''Believe it or not, I got in a cell with Big Larry himself. We got on famously. In fact, he offered me a partnership. Said he always wanted an operation out west.''

''Gee, I didn't know you could obtain a franchise in that kind of business.''

''He's an enterprising bloke, that Big Larry.''

''So are you going to take him up on his offer?''

Pierce squinted into the morning sun. ''It's always nice to have something to fall back on. But my heart really is in newspaper work, you know.''

''Speaking of having a heart, who talked Dr. Peel into dropping the charges?''

''Evidently our parent corporation offered him advertising consideration when he starts to market the formula.''

''Sounds like a good trade,'' Dru observed. ''I'm just glad to be out of that place.''

He leaped down three steps at once to catch up with her. ''I couldn't agree more.''

Dru spied a cab at the curb and they exchanged sidelong glances. Now that they were out of jail, the race to file the story was back on.

They broke into a run at the same instant, but with Pierce's long strides, she didn't have a chance. He hopped into the back seat and locked the door. ''See you, darling!'' he called over his shoulder. Dru pounded on the top of the taxi as Pierce told the driver to take off, and she was left standing at the curb, fuming.

Fortunately, another taxi was in sight and she hailed it by waving her arms frantically. She barely let it come to a halt before she jumped in and barked, "Airport! And you've got to get there before the guy in that other cab." She pointed at Pierce's taxi, which was almost out of sight.

"Don't get your slinky in a kink, lady. This ain't no action movie, and I'm no Mario Andretti."

Dru reached into her wallet and threw a twenty-dollar bill over the seat. "General Jackson likes to go fast," she asserted. "He says it's an order."

The driver saluted. "Anything for the general." He stamped on the accelerator and the car lurched forward as the driver started to hum the "Battle Hymn of the Republic."

Approaching the entrance ramp to the freeway, Dru saw an awesome sight and let out a whoop. Pierce was standing on the side of the road running his hands through his hair in frustration while steam boiled from under the raised hood of the cab he'd been riding in. As they passed by him, Dru rolled down the window and yelled, "Better luck next time, newsboy." He froze in place, his jaw slack and his eyes wide. Dru laughed so hard she started to cough.

The radio in Dru's taxi squawked, and the dispatcher at the cab company, which owned both taxis, directed Dru's driver to pick up a fare stranded at the on-ramp nearest the courthouse. "Are you anywhere near there?" the dispatcher asked. As the driver reached for the microphone to reply, he was already slowing down and angling toward the shoulder of the road.

Dru gave out a squeal of alarm. "No! Don't! That's the guy I'm trying to beat to the airport!"

"Sorry, lady. I've got an order from my dispatcher." He began to back the taxi toward the stranded cab.

Pierce saw what Dru's driver was doing and started to walk toward them with a smug smile.

Dru reached into her wallet again and this time pulled out a fifty. "I think General Grant outranks your dispatcher, don't you, Mario?"

"You're right about that," the driver agreed. "I always follow the chain of command." He promptly told his dispatcher he was on the other side of town.

By this time the cab had pulled almost even to Pierce, who was grinning broadly. He'd taken a step toward Dru's cab, his arm outstretched, when the driver hit the accelerator hard, leaving him in a puff of exhaust. Dru rolled down the window and, this time, blew him a kiss. The dumbstruck look on his face was priceless.

Dru settled back in her seat and watched the scenery go by. At last she felt as if she had the upper hand over Pierce. So why didn't she feel better? Probably because she'd had another lapse in sanity and had almost fallen for him again.

She let her mind wander as she stared ahead, her view of the countryside slightly obscured by the pair of baby shoes that swayed back and forth from the rearview window. How sweet, she thought. Mario's a daddy. She shook her head as she thought about the wild sex she'd had with Pierce that weekend. Thank goodness for birth control pills.

ON A SUNDAY MORNING three weeks later, Dru paced back and forth in the bedroom of her Atlanta town house in her velour bathrobe and bunny slippers. "How could the birth control pills not work? Aren't they something like ninety-eight, ninety-nine percent effective?'' She threw up her hands, one of which tightly clenched the wand of a pregnancy test kit.

"Watch where you're waving that thing," said Deborah Gilroy. Dru's best friend had come over immediately when Dru called. Tall and reed-thin, Deborah had skin the color of cinnamon and hair that framed her pretty, oval face in a pageboy made up of dozens of tiny braids. "Now, just pull yourself together. You're telling me that you were taking your pills last month when you went on that drug-induced lovefest with Pierce? So what makes you think you're pregnant?"

"I'm late. I'm *never* late. So I called the doctor and she said that I should get a kit. She also said the antibiotics I was taking for my sinuses could have downgraded the pills' effectiveness."

Deborah's brown eyes widened. "Or, it could be that Pierce's masculinity is just so potent that he can defeat contraceptives with his—his super-macho life force!" She leaned against the wall and grinned dreamily.

"Life force?" Dru stifled the urge to shake her. "Do you think he has supersonic sperm or something? You're nuts."

Deborah cleared her throat and gave her a sheepish look. "How much longer for the results?"

Dru looked at her watch. "A few more minutes." She sat down heavily on a chintz-upholstered chaise. Longjohn, the gray tabby alley cat that had adopted Dru years before, napped blissfully on the end of the chaise and barely twitched when Dru sat down.

"Does this cat always sleep with his eyes open? It gives me the creeps."

"All cats give you the creeps."

"Especially that one."

"That's a shame. He adores you."

As if he could sense he was being talked about, Longjohn roused and yawned, displaying a set of truly vicious-looking teeth. He sniffed idly at the bunnies on Dru's feet and then turned a keen green gaze on Deborah.

Deborah made a faint noise of disgust. "He's *looking* at me."

Dru gripped the cat under the forelegs and lifted him off the chaise. The animal, which had looked like a normal cat an instant before, now seemed to be made of taffy.

"When you stretch him out, that cat has got to be four feet long," Deborah observed. "He's not a cat. He's a Slinky with fangs."

"Why do you think I call him Longjohn?"

The cat wandered off at a dignified pace, but not before he rubbed against Deborah's legs, causing her slender body to go into a shudder of revulsion from head to toe. When he was gone, Deborah sat on the end of the chaise.

She looked at Dru. Dru looked at her watch. "It's time."

Deborah gave a low whistle. "This is heavy. So what are you going to do if the stick turns blue?"

"I haven't thought about anything else since I realized I could be pregnant. You know how much I've always wanted kids, and since my luck with men isn't the greatest, I probably would have gotten around to having a baby on my own, anyway. I just didn't want to have one right now. But if I'm pregnant, then I'll just have a baby sooner than I'd planned."

Deborah sighed with relief. "You go, girl. You'll be a great mom. I just hope it's later rather than sooner."

Dru covered her eyes with one hand and held out the stick with the other. "I can't bear to look. Tell me what you see."

After a moment, Deborah said, "On the other hand, sooner's good."

Dru's eyes flew open. The stick was blue. She propped her elbows on her knees and rested her head in her hands. "I guess deep down I knew all along the rabbit died." The bunnies on her slippers stared at her, silent accusation in their beady eyes.

"I'm sorry, Dru." Deborah put her arm around her friend's shoulder. "No. That's not right. I'm not going to tell you I'm sorry. I'm going to say—congratulations!"

When Dru raised her head, her eyes were bright, but no tears fell. She smiled. "You're right. You're absolutely right. No more negative thoughts. Still, can you possibly imagine how this is going to change my life? I've been thinking about it ever since I realized I could be pregnant." Dru stood up and began to pace again. She took up a pretty lace pillow from the Victorian-style sofa on the other side of the room and squeezed it. "There's morning sickness, cravings, mood swings. Then after the baby comes, that little life will be depending on me for its every need! As a single mother, every decision I make about my life and career from now on will be dictated by what's best for my baby." Dru stopped pacing and stood stock-still as the import of her own words sank in, and a crucial decision began taking shape in her mind.

Deborah leaned back on the chaise and looked up at her friend. "How do you know you'll be a single mother? Maybe Pierce will want to share the responsibility of raising the baby. Maybe he'll want to get married.''

Dru looked at her as if she'd gone insane. ''This is Pierce Mountcastle we're talking about. Pierce? Responsible?''

''Oh, yeah. What was I thinking?''

Deborah grinned apologetically and Dru couldn't help but smile back. She'd almost forgotten that Deborah used to work with Pierce on another newspaper and that they had been close friends, as well.

Dru stood up. ''Come on in the kitchen and I'll make us some brunch. I'm eating for two now, and I'm starved.''

''That's the spirit.'' Deborah laughed and followed Dru into the kitchen.

Dru's kitchen was small but efficiently organized. Ceramic tiles hand-painted in floral patterns lined the countertops and the wall behind the stove. Shiny copper pots hung from hooks attached to a decorative piece of wrought iron mounted on the ceiling. Deborah perched on the stool next to the bar-style counter across from the stove while Dru began getting together ingredients for an omelette.

Dru sniffed an onion and made a face. ''I hope you like your western omelettes without onions. Looks like some food smells are already making me queasy.'' She opened the refrigerator to get the eggs.

''Fine with me. Listen, I hate to keep harping on a sore subject, but, uh, when are you going to tell Pierce?''

''I'm not.'' Dru kicked the refrigerator door closed with her foot. ''He'd be the worst father imaginable. He's ruthless, just like my old man, and doesn't give a damn about anyone but himself.''

"Oh, no. Dru, you can't mean it. At least give him a chance. What if we're both wrong and he *does* want to be a part of your life and a father to your baby?"

For a moment, Dru's mind flashed back to that last day on the mountain when Pierce had told her the drug couldn't wear off soon enough for him. "He doesn't want me," she said flatly. "And I can't imagine that he'd want my baby, either, but I can't take that chance." Dru raised her hand to silence her friend's protests. "I've been lying awake nights thinking about this and I know what I'm doing. I was dragged back and forth between my parents when I was little and I was miserable. I'm not going to put my kid through that. I'm glad Pierce is on the other coast. We've always bumped into each other on assignments in the past. I'll just have to try harder to avoid him from now on."

Deborah wrapped a braid around her finger and bit her bottom lip. "Uh, that reminds me of a rumor I heard Friday afternoon after you left the office."

"What rumor?" Dru had picked up a knife and was chopping tomato for the omelette.

"Here, let me do that." Deborah took the knife, put it on the cutting board with the tomato and moved back to her perch at the counter bar.

"Well?" Dru broke an egg into a blue ceramic bowl. "Aren't you going to tell me?"

"Yeah, but, hey, put that egg down first, okay?"

"Why on earth are you carrying on this way?"

"Because I don't want you to kill the messenger—or pelt her with eggs."

Dru's eyes narrowed with apprehension. "Out with it."

"Pierce may wind up being a little closer than you

think.'' Deborah squinched her face as if anticipating disaster.

Dru tried not to panic. She didn't like the direction this was going. ''Do you mean he's gotten a job with an East Coast paper? Is it New York?''

''Hmm. Closer.'' Deborah pretended to concentrate on the tomato.

''Oh, no. The *National Enquirer* is headquartered in Florida. Do you mean closer as in Florida?''

''No, but you're getting warm.''

Dru tapped her bunny-slipper-clad toe and crossed her arms. ''I give. Tell me. Tell me now. Pierce is going to be closer as in—''

''As in the same office. Don't hurt me!''

The news hit Dru like a slap in the face. She sank onto a stool beside Deborah before her shaky legs let her collapse. ''What do you mean he's going to be in the same office?''

Deborah relaxed a little when it became clear that Dru would not faint or worse. ''The rumor is that he got wind of an upcoming opening in management and transferred to the *Nova* so that he could try and take advantage of it.''

''Are you saying that he's not only coming to work on the *Nova,* but he might even be our boss?''

''That's about the size of it.''

''Of all the—'' Dru's feelings of helplessness and frustration started to give way to anger. Pierce Mountcastle had been the bane of her existence for years. And now he might be in a position to ruin her career, not to mention her whole life if he ever found out about the baby, which he eventually would if they stayed in the same place for very long.

Dru felt the strength come back into her body and

stood up. She returned to the eggs, which she continued breaking—a good deal more forcefully than necessary—into the bowl.

"I think you got a little shell in there."

"Roughage is good for you."

"So what are you going to do?" Deborah handed the cutting board and a neatly diced tomato over to Dru.

"I'm going to put in for a transfer to the *Inquisitor* immediately. With any luck the transfer will come through before I start to show."

"Dru, don't be crazy. Pierce would be fun to work for. And he might even make a good father if you gave him a chance."

Dru pinned her friend with an accusatory glance. "You're just saying that because you *like* him."

Deborah flapped her skinny arms once, a gesture that made her look like a giant heron about to take flight, and let her hands come to rest on her hips. "I admit it. I *do* like him. He's handsome, he's funny, he's devilishly charming—"

"You left out manipulative, sneaky and thoroughly untrustworthy."

"Okay. Okay. So maybe he's not the greatest father material in the world. Doesn't he, at least, deserve to know the baby's his?"

Dru leaned against the counter. "This baby is depending on me to do what's best for her, to give her as happy and as emotionally stable a life as possible."

"Her?"

"Or him." Dru waved her hand dismissively. "And if that means not being completely honest with Pierce, then what he doesn't know won't hurt him, and it definitely won't hurt my baby." Dru put a dollop of margarine in the frying pan and then leveled a serious look at her friend. "Deborah, you're the only person who knows about the baby and who the father is. You've got to promise me you won't tell anyone, especially not Pierce."

Deborah gave her a pout. "Ooh, okay."

"Let me see your hands."

"Ooh, all right." Deborah displayed a perfect French manicure and no crossed fingers. "But it just doesn't seem right. Raising a baby without telling its— sorry, *her*—father and all."

Dru frowned and dumped the eggs into the sizzling pan. "Well, you know what they say. To make an omelette, you've got to break a few eggs. And if I have to break some conventions to raise a happy child, then that's what I'll do."

6

"YOU'RE MOVING INTO her cubicle with her?" Deborah shook her head so hard that the beads on the end of her braids made a clicking noise. "She's gonna kill you."

"There's not any room for me anywhere else. At least not until your editor leaves and his office becomes available." Pierce gave her a wink. "Besides, it was his idea."

"What makes you so sure you're going to get Hal Connelly's job?"

Pierce gave his new desk a final shove into position facing Dru's and steadied the vase of spring flowers he'd brought. "It's the jolly old Mountcastle charm, luv. It works in the boardroom as well as in the bedroom."

Deborah smirked. "Somebody's going to teach you a lesson one of these days, and I hope I'm front row, center."

"And just who would that someone be?" Pierce sat on the edge of his desk and stretched his long legs.

"Don't be cute with me." She gave him a stern look. "I'm the one who tipped you off to Dru's whereabouts in North Carolina, remember? And I did it because I thought if the two of you got together, you could work things out. I did *not* do it so you could take advantage of her again."

Pierce sighed. "You know me. Why do you persist in this romantic notion that Dru can kiss me and turn me into Prince Charming?"

"Because although you behave like a complete toad, underneath it all, you have a heart. And a good one. Look me in the eye and tell me you don't care about Dru."

Pierce looked away uneasily. "The truth is, I think about her night and day. I just haven't been able to get her out of my system. I feel like an absolute twit."

"Mmm-hmm." Deborah crossed her arms and nodded knowingly. "I knew it."

"It's the drug's fault. It's not me," Pierce insisted. He jammed his hands in his pockets. "I don't suppose she's said anything, you know, about...me?"

She gave him an odd look. "Oh, I think it's safe to say that she's got a little bit of you in her system, as well."

He tried not to show how pleased he was. In the six weeks since he'd last seen her, he'd been obsessed with thoughts of Dru. He missed her smile, her laugh, even her angry glares. His days were dominated with wondering what she was doing, what she was thinking. Was she thinking of him? His sleep was haunted by the fevered memories of their last weekend together and their wild night of passion. And his dreams were troubled by the fact that she'd thought he had tricked her.

"So tell me. How much of this transfer has to do with your wanting a promotion, and how much has to do with you wanting to be close to Dru all the time?"

"I assure you, Dru had nothing to do with it." He looked across at Deborah, who clearly wasn't buying it. His old friend had a most disturbing way of holding a mirror up to his heart and soul and daring him to take a peek. He never much liked what he saw, so he always tried not to look.

"Well, I'm sure she'll be overjoyed to see you."

"Sarcasm becomes you," Pierce offered, grinning. He looked at his watch. "Where is she, anyway? It's nine-thirty already and I know how punctual she always is."

"She's been a little tardy lately."

"Poor dear. Can't get her rest, eh? She's probably heartsick over missing me."

Deborah raised one sleek brow. "Oh, she's sick, all right. That reminds me, why did Hal say for you to move into Dru's cube?"

"He said he thinks she and I should work as a team."

Deborah shook her head again and her beads chimed. "I'm going to the basement."

"Are you going to get me some supplies from the storeroom? I say, good show."

"I'm going because the basement is a certified fallout shelter. Though I want to be front and center when she finally puts you in your place, I don't intend to be at ground zero when she finds out you're sharing her space."

As Deborah left, Pierce frowned and rubbed his chin. She was right; Dru would be livid. That's why he had brought a peace offering he knew for sure she'd love.

To distract himself from thoughts of Dru, Pierce stood up and surveyed the newsroom. The editors' offices were around the outside of the huge space. Opposite the offices was one row of cubicles enclosed by shoulder-high partitions. These were for the higher-ranking reporters like Dru. In the middle of the space was the open area of the newsroom with rows of desks piled high with newspapers, books, Chinese takeout cartons, photos and all the other flotsam and jetsam that came a reporter's way.

Pierce had introduced himself around first thing that morning. Of course, the staff knew him by reputation already. They seemed a right grand bunch of birds and blokes. Yes, he was going to be right at home here.

On the other side of the partition from Dru's cubicle, sitting in the open area, were Jerry Creech and George Scaggs, part reporting partners and part comedy team. Creech had a waist-high basketball hoop beside his desk. Scaggs had his own collection of sporting equipment, including foam footballs, basketballs and soccer balls. Scaggs had explained that someone had neglected to inform him and Creech that tabloids didn't have a sports page, so the two frustrated sportswriters covered Elvis sightings instead.

Right now Creech and Scaggs were debating the relative merits of bar tricks such as tying cherry stems in a knot with your tongue and rendering pennies "new" with Tabasco sauce.

"That one is tired, man," avowed Creech. "It doesn't take a genius to figure out it's the vinegar that does it."

"Oh, yeah? I think the cherry-stem trick is a myth. I tried it once and almost got lockjaw. Have you ever known anybody who could actually do that one?" countered Scaggs.

Pierce couldn't help but join in. He thrust his head over the partition and said, "I say, do you chaps know that our own Drucilla can tie a cherry stem in a knot with her tongue?"

"Wow," Creech intoned.

"Awesome," added Scaggs.

"Yes, we were in a Sherpa pub in the foothills of the Himalayas covering a yeti sighting, when—"

"Pierce!"

Pierce swung around and found himself confronting a red-faced Drucilla.

He straightened his burgundy suspenders against his white shirt. His heart pounded and his face and fingers tingled with a strange heat. So the drug *was* still at work. "Oh, there you are. Finally come to join us, have you?"

She lowered her voice and hissed, "I'll thank you not to discuss with my co-workers what I can and cannot do with my tongue." Although she'd been mentally preparing herself for days, Dru felt the same shock to her system that she always felt when she saw Pierce for the first time after a long absence. Her heart seemed to surge in her chest, at once sending heat waves to her face and robbing her extremities of feeling. Only this time it was worse. The drug!

She heard paper shuffling and then silence from the other side of the partition. Creech and Scaggs had the good sense to drop the subject of bar tricks. She forced her attention away from Pierce and took in the changes in her work area. Her desk had been turned to face an additional desk, behind which sat the grinning Mr. Mountcastle. And he had actually brought flowers.

"Sorry about rearranging the furniture, but this is the only way two desks would fit in this cubicle. Besides, this way I get to look at your gorgeous face all day long."

"Why? Why, of all the cubicles on this floor, have you moved into mine?" Her briefcase suddenly weighed a ton. Trying not to stagger, she crossed to her desk and sat down.

"It was Hal's idea. After reading how our articles on Dr. Peel's love potion complemented each other, he's decided we should work as a team on the really big stories."

"Ooh," Dru groaned. Just as she'd managed to get her stomach calmed down, she was hit with the worst imaginable news.

Ignoring her distress, Pierce pressed on. "Congratulations, by the way."

Dru froze. "Con—congratulations?" Surely Deborah hadn't told him.

"I guess our race to get the love potion story was a draw since both articles came out on the same day. Excellent piece of reporting, that."

Dru released a pent-up breath. "Are you complimenting yourself or me?"

Pierce gave her one of those chastising looks that so annoyed her. The one that said he couldn't quite believe what she was accusing him of. "I was complimenting both of us, actually. I've heard your story bandied about as a shoo-in for a Tabby nomination."

Pierce waved his hand above and to his right, indicating two plaques that he'd put up on the wall, which she hadn't noticed before. The Tabby was the tabloid industry's highest award, given for the best writing and reporting of a sensational news story. She'd been in the running for the award but had never won. Pierce had won twice and hadn't let anyone forget it since. Her mouth virtually watered looking at the plaques.

Little did he know that she had an ace up her sleeve. She'd taken the tubing with the trace of the drug to a private lab for analysis. The findings could make for a follow-up article that would give her an edge over the competition if she made it to the final round. The results would take a few weeks, but should be available just in time for her to make the final-round deadline.

Pierce's own love potion article bore the Mountcastle trademark blend of sensationalism, half-truths and innuendo. And it was riveting.

"I hear *your* version of the love potion story is a sure thing for a Tabby nomination, as well."

"May the best reporter win, eh? Now, why don't we get started on our first assignment together? I just got a tip this morning that—"

"You know, you just amaze me."

"Hmm?" Pierce looked up from his notes and blinked his impossibly blue eyes.

Dru lowered her voice. "You're pretending that our working together is just business as usual, as if nothing extraordinary ever happened between us." She lowered her voice again. "As if we're not still under the influence of a drug that distorts our reactions to each other."

Pierce leaned forward and gave her a leering grin. "So what *is* your reaction to me? Animal lust? Blinding passion?"

She narrowed her eyes. "Try overwhelming disgust and blinding nausea." She fudged on the first part, but the last was true enough. Her morning sickness was coming on strong, thanks to the stress of sharing close quarters with a man who did things to her psyche the laws of nature shouldn't allow.

"I was afraid you'd feel that way after our last encounter," Pierce said, reaching for a foil-covered plate on the far end of the desk. "That's why I brought the flowers to you as a peace offering, and I made these myself. I remember how much you said you loved them."

He uncovered a plate of cucumber sandwiches carefully made with the crusts neatly trimmed off the bread. Just as Dru was marveling at the uncharacteristic gesture, the odor of raw cucumber wafted toward her nose. Bringing her hand to her mouth, she ran toward the ladies' room.

As Pierce stared after her, Deborah reappeared in the cubicle opening. "It certainly didn't take you long to scare her away."

Pierce held up the plate of sandwiches. "You see what I mean? On the rare occasions that I try to do something good for someone, it always backfires. I'm telling you, I wasn't meant to be a nice guy."

Deborah took half a sandwich and munched it thoughtfully. "I still say there's a nice guy deep inside you just waiting to get out. And I think he's going to get his chance to bust out one of these days real soon."

"And what about wee Miss Perfect?" Pierce said, gesturing in the direction in which Dru had run. "What kind of person does *she* have inside *her* just waiting to get out?"

Deborah swallowed the last of her sandwich and looked away. "Never you mind."

LEANING OVER THE SINK, Dru pressed wet paper towels to her face and took deep breaths until the waves of nausea passed. The waves of near panic, on the other hand, still tap-danced across her nerve endings.

Could she really keep up this charade with Pierce? It was only a matter of time before he guessed the truth, especially since he would be sitting directly across from her all day, every day. But that was the least of her worries. Given the way the drug was still affecting her, it would be all she could do to keep from jumping across the desk and having her way with him at regular intervals. Her request for a transfer to the other newspaper was bogged down in corporate red tape, but it couldn't come soon enough for her.

Deborah walked into the ladies' room and joined her at the mirror. "You look white as a sheet," she remarked as she studied Dru's reflection. "Seeing Pierce camped in your cube this morning must've been quite a shock."

"Oh, Deborah, what am I going to do? It can't be long until he guesses the truth."

"Honey, he came so close to guessing it a few minutes ago that even *I* turned pale."

"Ooh, don't tell me." Dru pressed a wet paper towel to her neck. "On top of all that, the damned drug is still working. I'm so attracted to that man right now, I could fling myself across the desk and attack him."

"I can check the employee handbook, but I think we have regulations against that."

"I'm just going to have to control myself, that's all. I'm just going to have to rise above my physical urges until the drug wears off, and pray that the transfer comes through before I start to show."

Deborah inspected her own image in the mirror and fluffed her braids. "What if it doesn't?"

"Doesn't what?" Dru pinched her cheeks to give her face some color. "Ow."

"What if it doesn't wear off? Or worse yet, what if it's not the drug at all? What if you have an all-natural case of the hots for you-know-who? What if Pierce Mountcastle is *the* man for Drucilla Logan?"

Dru watched the pinch of pink drain out of her reflection, leaving her pasty pale. "That's impossible. I...I...." She turned and bolted for the nearest stall.

"I think that's my cue to leave," Deborah said, shaking her head. As she let the outer door of the rest room close behind her, she muttered, "Ain't love grand?"

THE NEXT MORNING Pierce drummed his fingers on his desk and tried to concentrate on the words on his computer monitor. He'd gone mad. That was the only explanation. Mad to have suggested to Hal that he and Dru share an office. Mad to have thought that getting closer to Dru would exorcise her from his system once and for all.

He'd figured that nearness would make the two of them sick of each other, but he'd forgotten about the drug's effects. Instead of familiarity breeding contempt for Dru, it had bred a sappy, brooding schoolboy crush. He found her every mannerism or habit—no matter how subtle, no matter how small—absolutely, disgustingly adorable. The way she nipped at a pencil with her teeth when she was concentrating. The funny way she put her thumb through the handle of her coffee cup instead of her forefinger. Oh, the way she sighed. Oh, the way she breathed. Oh, brother.

What could he do to break this spell? He rubbed his eyes and tried to think back to what Dr. Peel had said about the way the drug worked. He'd said its effects were twofold. First, the drug made the person who took it more attracted to others. Second, it caused the drug taker to emit stronger sexual signals, thus making others—even those who hadn't taken the drug—more attracted to the drug taker. Of course, the Mountcastle charm was already so devastating that it would be difficult to tell if women were more attracted to him than they already were. But he could make use of the other side of the equation. He'd just have to spend time with some of the many attractive women in the office and see if he could form a new attachment that would help him get over Dru.

His gaze strayed over the top of the monitor and he caught her looking at him looking at her. He dragged his gaze quickly back to the screen. Something had to give or he'd go entirely mad.

"Check your e-mail," Dru said. "Looks like we have a new assignment."

After a minute or so of cursing the computer, Pierce clicked into his e-mail and read the message—long-lost film and theater star Griffin Lee had surfaced in New York after fifty years of seclusion. "We're supposed to interview and photograph him, which will be tough since he's one of those 'I vant to be alone' types."

Dru wrinkled her nose in distaste. "I just hate staking out reclusive celebrities. It seems so unfair."

"You need to toughen up. I think it's fortunate that you now have me as a role model to help you learn to go for the jugular. Perhaps I can give you a few pointers."

"You? A role model for me? That's rich. You're a shining example of how *not* to do this job."

She watched him lean back in his chair and stretch, extending his arms outward. His right hand touched one of his Tabby plaques and he ran his fingers over it, as if brushing away a speck of dust. "The awards committee for the past two years might disagree with you." He smiled and linked his fingers behind his head.

That brilliant, seductive, maddening smile both irked and charmed her. The only jugular she wanted to go for was his. But that wasn't really true. To her chagrin, she found she wanted to go for his entire body. The new arrangement was torture. It was all she could do to keep from reaching across the desk to touch his face or lips, or to smooth back that unruly lock of hair that sometimes fell into his eyes.

And the jealousy was killing her. Each time he picked up the phone to speak with a female contact, his blatant flirtations and sweet talk drove her up the wall. What could she do to shake off these awful feelings?

She watched him smooth back his hair and adjust his tie and suspenders, little habits that had become annoyingly endearing in the past twenty-four hours. Something had to give. Perhaps stoking their rivalry again would take her mind off Pierce as a sex symbol and reestablish the more normal and natural image of Pierce as a scoundrel and sworn enemy. Yeah. That was the ticket.

"I have an idea," she began, trying to ignore the cute way he blinked when a conversation changed tack. "Since our race to the love potion scoop was a draw, what say we start a new competition?"

He leaned forward, his eyes keen with interest. "I'm listening."

"We're covering this new story as a team, right? I propose that you write the main article, I write a colorful sidebar and we'll see which is the most titillating."

Pierce's brows rose a fraction. "Goodness knows, I'm all for titillation. You're on."

He extended his hand over their desks and she clasped it in her own. His grip was firm, and his skin was rough and warm. For an instant her thumb brushed across the black hair on the back of his hand, its texture reminding her of the hair on his chest—the springy hair that continued in a tantalizing vee down his washboard stomach until—

"Plane tickets, anyone?" Patty Reid stopped in the entrance to the cubicle, waving two envelopes.

Patty was the editor's secretary, a petite, popular redhead with a ready smile. Even though Dru knew that Patty had a steady boyfriend named Jerry, she felt her spine stiffen when Pierce's eyes lit up with seductive charm. He sprang to his feet and went immediately to the young woman's side.

"Why, aren't you the model of efficiency? We just found out about our new assignment and here you are already with the plane tickets to New York. Isn't she amazing, Dru?" Pierce put his arm lightly around Patty's shoulders and gave her his most to-die-for smile.

"I'm amazed, all right." Dru felt her nails digging into the upholstery of the chair arms.

"I say," Pierce said, his full attention focused on Patty, "I really don't know my way around Atlanta very well. Maybe you could show me the sights this weekend."

Few women could resist Pierce under ordinary circumstances. When he was emitting vapors from eau de love potion, could any woman resist? Dru didn't relish having a hair-pulling catfight in the newsroom with anyone, much less her friend Patty, but in her present state of mind, she might not be able to stop herself. *Come on, Pats, Jerry and I are depending on you.*

For a long, excruciating moment, the slim secretary wavered, biting her glossy lip prettily. Then she grasped the hand that rested on her shoulder, firmly placed the tickets in it and stepped out of the circle of Pierce's arm. "Sorry, I have a steady boyfriend.

Thanks just the same." She was gone as quickly as she had come.

With his arm frozen in midair, Pierce looked like a mime leaning against a pretend parking meter. The expression of disbelief on his face was priceless. Dru would have bet the farm, if she had one, that Pierce getting turned down was as frequent an occurrence as a snowboarding party in hell.

Trying to act nonchalant, Pierce smoothed down his shirt front and handed Dru her ticket. "Lovely girl."

"Smart, too."

Pierce seemed to recover from his shock quickly, something she was oddly glad about.

"I'm sure." Pierce examined his ticket and shot her a winning smile. "Big Apple, here we come."

DRU LEANED on the wrought-iron railing surrounding a sidewalk café on Columbus Avenue and stared longingly at the food and drink being consumed at the colorfully draped tables. Her pregnancy was giving her a monster case of the munchies. She was so hungry she felt as if she could eat one of the hansom cab horses that clopped up and down the avenue.

Pierce had instructed her to stand at this corner to watch for Griffin Lee while Pierce stood watch one block north. He had contacted an informant in Manhattan who said that the actor was living on the Upper West Side and went to Central Park at the same time each afternoon. Since she couldn't leave her post lest their quarry get away, Dru was unable to get anything to eat.

"Where are those hot dog vendors when you need them?" she muttered. Unfortunately, food wasn't the only thing she was hungry for. She watched Pierce, who was standing just across the street in khaki trousers, navy blazer and sunglasses of the latest style. He looked as if he might be the subject of a photo shoot for a men's fashion magazine. The sight of him made her mouth water more than the smell of the lasagna that wafted to her from a nearby table.

Thanks to that damned drug, the plane ride had been hell. The seats had been so cramped, she and Pierce had sat shoulder to shoulder, thigh to thigh the whole way. The idea of cramped, sweaty sex in an airplane rest room had always seemed disgusting, but being wedged into a pair of seats with the long-limbed Mr. Mountcastle had made her wish for a membership in the "mile-high" club. The drug seemed to be removing all her inhibitions about sex.

A wave of nausea washed over her. She cursed herself for forgetting the sleeve of saltines she carried in her purse to ward off such attacks. If she didn't get something to eat *now,* she would either be sick or faint.

As a couple vacated the table next to the railing, she looked right and left, leaned over as far as she could and snatched the bread basket off the table. She pawed the red-and-white-checkered napkin inside, hoping the couple had left a roll behind. *Eureka.* She bit into the tough French bread and reached out to put the basket back.

"Thanks."

Dru swung her head to the side to see a black-clad waiter with slicked-back hair and a skinny mustache. He arched a brow and looked her up and down as he took the basket from her. "They left some calamari. Do you want that, too?"

She lifted her chin. "No, thanks. I'm trying to quit." Dru gave him the evil eye when he turned his back on her. The embarrassment was worth it when she realized that the bite of roll had already cured her nausea.

Pierce appeared out of nowhere and seized her arm. "Come on! I think I just saw him go into the park."

Clutching the roll, she dashed into the park and followed Pierce down a shrubbery-lined path. "That's him," Pierce said, pointing toward a grassy area just off the trail. Dru saw an athletic-looking elderly man jogging along the path.

"The jogger?"

"No. The one in the wheelchair."

Dru's heart sank as she saw a wizened old man being pushed along by a white-uniformed woman.

"Let's go in for a closer look. Where's that bloody photographer?"

"I haven't seen him," Dru said. The freelance photographer who was supposed to meet them hadn't shown up, and Dru was glad. She was beginning to have a bad feeling about this assignment. She allowed Pierce to lead her into the bushes, where they crept up behind the man in the wheelchair and his nurse, who sat down on a wooden bench beside him. The man wore a trench coat with the collar turned up high and a fedora pulled down low on his forehead.

"He's got to be roasting in that outfit," Pierce remarked. "He looks like a man determined not to be recognized."

Mr. Lee seemed to be watching two young boys playing soccer nearby. One of the boys kicked the ball astray and it rolled straight for the wheelchair. As the other boy came close to retrieve it, Mr. Lee covered his face with his hand until the child scampered away.

Dru frowned and took a folded photocopy out of her pocket. By way of research, she'd looked up the last

interview that the actor had given years earlier, before
he retired. He had told the interviewer that when he
quit the movies, he would drop out of sight forever.
He didn't want to destroy the public's fantasy by letting
them watch him grow old. He wanted people to remember him in his prime, in the dashing roles he created—not as an old man. He thought dropping out of
the public scene would be a good way to ensure that
his films would live on and be enjoyed by future gen-
erations.

Dru glanced up at Pierce, who was frowning at the
photocopy she held, which he'd also read on the plane.
He looked as if he was feeling as guilty as she was.
Knowing him, though, it was probably just his "killer
instinct" kicking in. Why did such a reprehensible cad
have to be so devastatingly attractive?

Mr. Lee took a bag of peanuts from his pocket and
began to feed the squirrels. "I'm hungry," she complained. "The only thing I've eaten in hours were my
peanuts on the plane."

"Your peanuts, my peanuts and everybody else's
peanuts who didn't want them. Even the peanuts of one
poor soul you caught looking the other way."

"He was asleep," Dru pointed out, "and was about
to drop them in the aisle. I ate them for safety reasons." She remembered the roll and took another bite,
showering crumbs onto her dark suit. She brushed them
off vigorously with one hand, while propping her other
hand on the ground.

The motion must have caught Pierce's eye, because
when she looked up at him crouched above her, she
saw that his attention had riveted on her cleavage, of
which he had a perfect view. Although she wasn't

showing yet, her breasts were growing by the day and threatened to overflow her bra.

She crossed her arms over her chest, realizing too late that this action only emphasized her cleavage. "What are you staring at?" As if she didn't know.

Pierce swallowed, and she saw his Adam's apple do a little jig. Not taking his gaze from her breasts, he said, "Your cups runneth over."

"I—I shrank my bra in the dryer, that's all." On top of everything, the top button of her blouse had come open, making the situation worse. She reached to refasten it, but he took her hands in his to stop her. He knelt beside her and she noticed that she was not the only one bursting out of her clothing. The drug had taken over their senses again. She felt herself wanting him so badly she could jump his bones right here in the bushes. They were certainly hidden well enough. She shook her head. What was she thinking? She'd never done it outdoors in her life, and in the daylight!

A bold squirrel came up to them and began to chatter. Dru threw him the rest of the roll. "Scram, Rocky."

Kneeling side by side, she and Pierce looked at each other for a long, lust-filled moment.

"We can't. Not here," she warned.

"Why not?" he said, his eyes glittering. "Nobody can see."

She couldn't believe what she was about to do. Before she took that drug, sex in a public place would have been unthinkable. The potion was putting her through a personality change. She was in the grip of a chemical reaction she couldn't control. So why even try?

They lunged at each other and kissed hungrily, their

hands clutching clothing to move it down, away, aside, eager to feel flesh. The intoxicating sensations of Pierce's warm, rough skin sent shock waves through her system. The hell with saltines, *this* was what she'd been starving for.

He sank to the ground and pulled her on top of him, pressing their hips together as his mouth traveled to her breasts. He nipped lightly at her nipples through her blouse until she was sure they would burst through the fabric. He reached into her cleavage and undid the front fastening of her bra, as she'd unfastened his belt.

"Can't you folks get a room?"

Pierce and Dru looked up into the scowling face of one of New York City's finest.

"This isn't what it looks like, Officer," Pierce said as they both scrambled to cover themselves.

"Oh, no? Well, it looks to me like a night in jail and a couple of stiff fines."

7

"I CAN'T BELIEVE you got thrown in jail again," Deborah said. She'd listened in wide-eyed astonishment as Dru had poured out the story of the trip.

From somewhere over the partition, Scaggs yelled, "Goaaaaaal!"

Someone from the back of the newsroom said, "Shut *up*. And keep that soccer ball in your own aisle."

Ignoring the commotion, Dru said, "Thank goodness we didn't have to spend the night in jail. Pierce sweet-talked a night-court judge and we got off with just a fine."

Deborah shook her head and fiddled with her braids. "You manage to stay out of jail for twenty-six years, and then you get locked up twice in just a few weeks' time."

"It's the drug, and it's getting worse! It's like I'm thinking with my hormones and not my head." Dru paced back and forth in the cubicle. "The New York trip proves it. It was one thing being cooped up with Pierce in the mountains in relative privacy, but now I'm doing it with him in public places. I almost propositioned him on the plane."

Deborah's thin brows shot up. "On the plane?"

Dru collapsed into her chair. "And on top of that, we didn't even get enough material for a decent story. I guess he'll just make something up like he usually does. Thank goodness I'm just doing a background article.''

"The plane, you say,'' Deborah said, fascinated.

"Poor Mr. Lee.'' Dru leaned her head back against her chair and closed her eyes. "All he wanted was to be left alone. When they were putting me in the police car, the photographer showed up and I saw Pierce point toward the area Mr. Lee had been sitting, and give him some instructions I couldn't hear. I imagine he told the photographer to take the most unflattering photo possible.''

"So how does that work exactly? Sex on a plane, I mean.''

Dru covered her eyes. "You haven't heard a word I've said.''

"Oh, sure I have. But there's nothing you can do now. The paper's out.''

Dru opened her eyes to see Deborah take a newspaper from Patty, who was pushing a cartful of them down the hall.

"Hot off the presses,'' Patty said, and continued on her way.

Deborah glanced at the front page and handed it to Dru with a smug look.

"Huh?''

"Read it and weep,'' Deborah commanded, swinging her feet back and forth as she perched on Pierce's desk.

Dru read the lead paragraph aloud.

"Dateline, New York City. Long-lost film and theater star Griffin Lee surfaced in Manhattan this week after a fifty-year absence from the public scene. Pictured here jogging in Central Park, Mr.

Lee is an exceptionally fit and healthy ninety-three.''

The photograph was not of Mr. Lee, but of the elderly jogger they'd seen in the park earlier. Relief washed over Dru and she began to laugh with delight. ''This is a lie, but it's a wonderful one. Mr. Lee has a perfect disguise now. If anyone else tries to find him, nobody will be looking for a man in a wheelchair. This is terrific. Why did you say to read it and weep?''

''Because you're going to have to admit that Pierce is not as bad a guy as you think he is. That his veneer of ruthlessness is all an act.''

Dru put the paper down and sank into her desk chair. ''One act of kindness does not make a nice guy. Besides that, it's probably just the drug. It's making him more lovable than he really is.''

''It's not the drug! You must see the potential here,'' Deborah insisted. ''If you nurture that potential, Pierce might turn into Mr. Nice Guy, the guy you've always wanted.'' With a meaningful glance, Deborah stood and left the cubicle, then stuck her head back around the partition. ''The plane?'' she said in wonder.

Dru waved goodbye to Deborah, who retreated toward her own office. Dru kicked off her shoes under her desk.

''Heads up,'' Scaggs called from over the wall as a foam football spiraled into Dru's cubicle. She caught it and sent it sailing back. ''How many times do I have to tell you, Scaggs? Keep your balls to yourself!''

''Sorry.''

She had to admit she was impressed by what Pierce had done. But was it a rare and random act of compassion on his part or, as Deborah believed, an un-

tapped reservoir of niceness? Of course, nothing would
please her more than for him to turn into Prince Charming. But she'd already kissed this toad, and as far as
she could tell, the warts were still there.

He certainly didn't care about her opinion of him.
Still, he bore watching. Maybe the niceness was a
trend. And maybe it wasn't. She'd bet herself a chocolate sundae that he wouldn't say or do one single nice
thing all day.

"Morning, luv."

She looked up into Pierce's dark blue eyes. "Good
morning."

He sat down at his desk and opened his briefcase.
He removed that morning's paper and a small white
bag. "Did you see the story? Smashing, eh?" He took
a powdered doughnut from the bag and extended the
bag to her.

"You brought me breakfast?" Dru took the remaining powdered doughnut out of the bag. "That was really...nice." She nibbled on the pastry. Okay. Double
or nothing on the sundae.

"We scooped all the competition with this one." He
sighed with satisfaction. "And your sidebar was great.
It added a lot of color and excitement to the story as a
whole."

"It's...nice...of you to say so." She gulped another
bite. So far she was in the hole several chocolate sun-
daes. "But I think you've definitely won the bet. Your
story was by far the most interesting."

He waved a hand modestly and swallowed the last
of his doughnut. "It was nothing."

Dru looked at Pierce's immaculate shirtfront and suit
coat and then glanced down at herself. He had just
eaten a powdered doughnut without getting so much as

a granule of sugar on his dark gray suit. She, on the other hand, was covered in so much white powder she looked like a cocaine fiend.

She brushed off her shirt. "Anyway, I concede victory in the competition for best article."

"Oh?" He grinned slyly. "And what do I win?"

"This sounds like déjà vu to me." Dru rolled her eyes to the ceiling. "Pick your prize. Within reason." She steeled herself for the usual lewd suggestions, but Pierce only stared at her thoughtfully and swiveled back and forth in his chair. Finally, she threw up her hands. "So, do you want me to shave my head, or what?"

"Get rid of that glossy mane of raven waves? Heaven forbid." His expression became serious. "I want you to believe me when I tell you that I wasn't in on Dr. Peel's plan to drug us."

This was the last thing she'd expected. "Why are you bringing this up again now? And why do you care if I believe you or not? You never cared before what I think of you, or what anybody else thinks of you, for that matter."

He picked up a paperweight from his desk and toyed with it. "I knew you didn't believe me, that's all. And I just wanted you to know that, although I'm capable of a lot of things, I would never do that. As to why I care what you think, well, we're partners now, you know? All for one and one for all, eh, what?"

Dru couldn't help but smile. Once again, Pierce got even more British under pressure. "So now that we're working together, you want me to trust you. Is that about right?"

He looked up at her finally, nodded and leveled a searching gaze on her. He really did want her to have a good opinion of him, she realized in surprise, and she even found herself wanting to give it to him.

She put her palms on her desk blotter. "Okay. I'll trust you—on the condition that there are no more double crosses and no more lies. Agreed?"

"Agreed."

Dru picked up the newspaper folded to Pierce's article. "So what do you call this?" Dru brought the paper down across Pierce's desk. "It was a swell gesture on your part, but it's still a lie. You just don't get this truth thing, do you?"

Pierce shrugged. "The old chap wanted people to remember him the way he used to be. I couldn't see the harm."

Dru dropped the newspaper. "The truth issue aside, why don't you do nice things more often? Give someone a break? Go for the heart instead of the jugular?"

Pierce rose from his desk and rubbed the back of his neck as if suddenly weary at ten in the morning. "That's just not how it works where I come from."

"Where *do* you come from exactly?" Dru had always assumed that the immaculate Mr. Mountcastle had an aristocratic British background, maybe even a noble one.

Jamming his hands in his pockets, he lowered his voice just enough to avoid being overheard beyond the partition. "A rundown council estate in east London."

She sat up straight, surprised. "Isn't that...sort of...?"

"The wrong side of the tracks, as you Americans would put it." He supplied the words for her, his eyes becoming flinty and hard. "Ever wonder how I got into your cabin in the mountains that time? Or how I got out of the gate so easily when we escaped? I know how to pick locks, not to mention pockets.

"I did what I had to in order to survive. Luckily, before I could land in jail, I discovered the newspaper business. At fourteen, I lied about my age to become a copyboy. From then on, I would do, say or write anything to get ahead. Along the way, I re-created myself. Reggie MacGregor, street urchin, became Pierce Mountcastle, man of the world." He held his arms out, then let them fall back to his sides.

"Reggie MacGregor. That's the name you use when you go undercover." She stared at him, wide-eyed.

"Clever, isn't it? And easy to remember since it's my real name." He laughed in a caustic, humorless tone.

Sitting back down at his desk, he returned her gaze evenly, his expression so cold she rubbed her arms. Even though his remarks had contained no pleas for sympathy or even understanding, her heart went out to him just the same as she finally realized what drove him. "That must have been rough," she said.

"Don't pity me. I wouldn't have traded it for the world. It's made me what I am today. Ever since I've been in this business, I haven't let anything tie me down or hold me back—not ethics, not romantic entanglements, not a wife and kids. My only commitment is to my work."

Dru winced, and her heart ached a little. She looked down at her desk, not wanting him to see the disappointment in her eyes. At least she had the satisfaction of knowing she'd made the right decision not to tell him about the baby. He was clearly not interested in having a family.

"But I think it might be time for a change," he said softly.

She snapped to attention. Had she heard him right? "What do you mean?" She waited, curious and uncertain.

Pierce ran a hand through his black waves. Tentatively, he said, "I'm ready to make a commitment to you."

"What kind of commitment?" Dru watched him intently, not sure what to expect.

"Well, since you're my partner now, I promise that as long as we're working as a team, there won't be any lies or tricks." Dru knew that, for him, this was a significant gesture. He looked downward briefly, long enough for her to appreciate his thick lashes. He raised his head and added, with some effort, "And in return I'd like you to trust me, if that's not too much to ask."

She looked at him as if she were seeing him for the first time. There was no doubt of his sincerity. Maybe there was hope for this guy after all. She extended her hand to him, feeling as if her reach were bridging a broad chasm instead of the width of a desk. "Deal."

A feeling of profound relief washed over Pierce. With a look of warmth and gratitude, he took her hand in his. They sat there for several moments, hands clasped, as he savored their newfound trust. He'd surely touched her more intimately, but sitting there holding her hand, he was as happy as he'd ever been in her embrace.

Patty thrust her head around the cubicle wall. "Here's your mail."

They withdrew their hands quickly, but not before Pierce saw Patty's knowing grin.

"Have a nice day, you two," the secretary said, "as

if you're not already. Though judging from the return address on those top envelopes, it's about to get even better.'' She disappeared down the hall.

Pierce looked at the envelope on top of his stack of mail. ''It's from the Tabby awards committee.''

Dru tore open her own envelope. ''I'm on the list of finalists!'' She jumped from her chair, a look of sheer elation on her face. ''We both are!''

Rather than open his own envelope, he watched her dance around the cubicle. He couldn't remember when he'd been happier than he was now, just watching her celebrate her accomplishment. Had he ever been this happy for himself? Even when he'd been nominated for the award the first time? Even when he'd actually won?

She pointed to the other two names on the list. ''You follow these things. What do you think of my chances? And of yours, of course.''

After opening his own envelope, he studied the names. He knew the other two reporters. Their work was good. Dru's was better. ''Lightweights compared to us,'' he pronounced. ''It's got to come down to either you or me.''

Dru hugged him as he sat in his chair, almost pressing her breasts to his face, taking his breath for a moment. Creech, Scaggs and a handful of other reporters peered over the partition, their disembodied heads making them look like prairie dogs.

''We heard,'' Creech said. ''Way to go!'' The others chimed in with their congratulations and then went back to their desks.

''I'm going to tell Deborah. She'll be thrilled for us.''

He breathed deeply and could still faintly smell her

scent in the air where she'd stood beside him. Studying the letter again, he glanced at the telephone. He was struck with an urge to try a little backhanded maneuvering to influence the judging in Dru's favor, but he'd given his solemn word—no more tricks.

He shuddered. What was happening to him?

Here he was, making sappy promises to be nice and never tell a lie. And not only that, he was actually happy that the one person who could beat him in the Tabby competition was nominated. Then there was what happened in New York and his ruining a perfectly good news story so as not to hurt an old man's feelings. Pretty soon he'd be helping old ladies across the street, rescuing kittens from trees. He was losing his edge…or his mind.

It had to be the drug.

Or was it? He'd been obsessed with the idea of getting back together with Dru ever since he'd loved her and left her the first time. It hadn't been easy to wrangle an assignment to get close to her again—the love potion story. And when he'd seen her, he'd been more smitten with her than ever. All that had happened *before* they'd been drugged. Maybe there was something more profound, and lasting, about what was happening to him.

Maybe he was falling in love.

He felt his throat go dry and reached for his coffee cup. His hand trembled slightly as he brought it to his lips and drank the tepid brew. His mind replayed his conversation with Dru. He'd poured out his life story, told her things he'd sworn he'd never tell a living soul. He'd laid himself bare.

He'd actually used the "C" word—*commitment.*

And why? Because he wanted her to trust him. He wanted her—God help him—to love him.

Looking down at the murky liquid in his cup, he muttered, "I need something stronger." He'd never been one for drinking on the job, but there was a first time for everything.

"I KNEW YOU COULD DO IT," rasped Deborah as Dru pulled her into a power hug. Dru jumped up and down, forcing her friend to jump up and down with her or be mortally injured. Deborah's beads clacked and she gasped for breath. "Congratulations," she croaked.

"What's wrong with your voice?" Dru asked.

"Oh, nothing. You're just choking the life out of me, that's all." The slender young woman managed to extricate herself from her friend's embrace. "I guess you're hugging for two now, huh?"

Dru brought her hands to her stomach. "And that's not all my good news. Pierce and I had the best talk just now. He came clean about some things, and even promised not to lie to me ever again. He says he wants me to trust him."

"Do you?"

Dru bit her lip and sat down in the chair beside Deborah's desk. "I want to."

"Then do it."

"It's not that easy. Not after his past behavior. Besides that, all the niceness and promises may only be the drug talking."

Deborah sank into her own chair. "So, what's it going to take for you to give this guy a chance?"

Dru thought back on her conversation with Pierce and the seed of an idea that had started to grow. "Well," she said, "as a matter of fact, there is something that might help influence me to drop my defenses and trust Pierce.''

Deborah leaned forward. ''What is it? Is it something I can help with?''

''As a matter of fact, yes.''

8

"I DON'T LIKE IT." Deborah studied the short list of questions Dru had given her.

"I can't make the call myself. Dr. Peel will recognize my voice. I have to know the answers to the questions on that list. Just tell him you're a fellow researcher and you're very interested in his work. Knowing his ego, he'll be glad to speak to you. Tell him you saw the story about the drug and want to ask him a few questions about it. Put him on the speaker phone. If you turn it down low and I close the door to your office, nobody in the hallway will be able to hear."

"Oh, okay," Deborah said grudgingly. "But I still say that you should just make the commitment to trust Pierce and then stick to it. I really think you'll be glad you did."

"And I hope to be able to do just that. But a little insurance won't hurt. Besides, at the very least, I have to get an answer to the most important question on the list. It's been bothering me for weeks. So while you're talking to him, you might as well ask him the rest."

Deborah sighed and dialed the number Dru had given her. Dru's stomach knotted with anticipation. The answers she got to the questions her friend would ask Dr. Peel could affect her future and her baby's.

The phone was answered by a cheerful-sounding

woman. Dru mouthed the name "Ginger," and Deborah nodded her head.

"This is Dr. Deborah Gilroy, with the…uh…" Deborah's voice trailed off and she got a deer-caught-in-headlights look. Her eyes darted wildly around her office until her gaze settled on a poster of her favorite actor. "The Snipes Institute. I'm with the Snipes Institute," she repeated with authority, giving the frantic Dru a thumbs-up. "I'd like to speak to Dr. Peel about his research. It'll only take a moment."

Ginger agreed to get her boss and they heard her footsteps trail off. "You scared me to death," Dru hissed.

"Hey, I'm a photo editor, not an investigative reporter. Being sneaky doesn't come naturally to everybody, you know."

They both jumped when Dr. Peel's voice came from the speaker phone. "Yes? This is Dr. Jackson Peel. How can I help you?"

"Dr. Peel," Deborah began, her nervousness forcing her voice into a Minnie Mouse squeak. "That is, Dr. Peel, I'd like to ask you a few questions about your love potion." Deborah had adjusted her voice into an unnatural alto. Dru drew a hand across her forehead. If she'd known Deborah was going to have such a hard time, she would have made the call herself. At least she could do a low voice that wouldn't sound like a bad Lauren Bacall impersonation.

"I read about your research in that tabloid and I was fascinated. But you can't believe what you read in those scandal rags, right?" Deborah winked at Dru, who rolled her eyes. "Naturally, I have some questions of my own."

"Well…" Dr. Peel hesitated, then said, "All right.

Since the story was picked up by so many other newspapers, the cat is out of the bag, so to speak. I suppose there's no harm in answering your questions. Besides, my first round of human trials has been ongoing since shortly after the story ran, and I'll be making the results public soon, anyway. Fire away.''

"Good." Deborah smiled and Dru breathed a little easier. "Have you been able to confirm your earlier suspicion that the drug stays in people's systems for several weeks?''

"The tests on animals make it quite clear that the drug stays in the system for around three months. My own experience with the drug and that of my fiancée, Ginger, confirms that.''

Damn. This was not the answer Dru had been hoping for. Before, Dr. Peel had said the drug stayed in the system for "several weeks." Now he was saying three months! By that time her pregnancy would be showing. In spite of the bad news, Dru had to smile a little. Good old Ginger got her man.

Deborah tapped a pencil on the desk and gave Dru a sympathetic glance. The next question was the most important of all. As Dru held her breath, Deborah held up her hand, fingers crossed. "Next question. Have you been able to determine if the lingering effects of the drug would be harmful to a fetus?''

"The drug is made from simple, natural ingredients and is entirely safe for pregnant women and their unborn children," Dr. Peel said with conviction. "There's absolutely nothing in the formula that could possibly compromise a pregnancy in any way.''

Dru closed her eyes and said a prayer of thanks. Deborah visibly relaxed and continued her questioning. "After the article ran in the *Nova*, I called one of the reporters to ask her some additional questions, and she told me something extraordinary. She said that you had exposed her and the other reporter to the drug without their knowledge. Is that correct?"

"That is technically true," Dr. Peel began, sounding defensive. "But I did have their signed consent. Besides, they came onto my property under false pretenses, so I really feel—"

"I'm not questioning your methods—really," Deborah cut in. "I just need to know if you're absolutely sure that neither reporter knew that the drug was being used on them. She said the drug worked on them beautifully, but naturally I'm concerned about the placebo effect."

Dru leaned forward in her chair. She felt guilty for checking up on Pierce after he'd already sworn more than once that he didn't know about the drugging. But she had to be sure.

"I'm sure that neither of them knew."

"Not even the male reporter?" Deborah raised her brows and gave Dru a pointed look.

"No, he absolutely did not know."

The answer brought joy to Dru's heart, and she felt doubly remorseful for not having trusted Pierce from the beginning. But as for Pierce's Prince Charming potential, the sixty-four-thousand-dollar question was coming up. Dru twisted her hands.

"Just one more question, Doctor. Can the drug change your personality? That is to say, does it work by making you more lovable? Can it make you nicer, if you will?" There was a pause in which neither Dru nor Deborah breathed.

Finally, Dr. Peel's answer came. "Yes," he said simply.

Deborah frowned and twisted a braid. "You mean a selfish person, perhaps an untrustworthy person, could take the drug and, while the formula was in effect, actually become...nicer?"

"That's what I'm saying," Dr. Peel said. "The drug seems to affect the personality in that way."

Dru put her elbow on the corner of Deborah's desk and propped up her suddenly aching head. Deborah slumped in her chair. "Thank you, Dr. Peel. That's all the questions I had. I'll let you get back to your work now."

"Wait a minute," Dr. Peel said. "I want to find out more about you."

"Me?" Deborah's voice returned to its former squeaky timbre. "Wha—what do you want to know about me for?"

Dr. Peel's tone turned suspicious. "How do I know you're not out to discredit me? It wouldn't be the first time one of my colleagues has tried to ruin my credibility."

"Huh?"

"I'm sure you must know about my reputation within the scientific community."

"Why, I'm sure it's the highest—"

Dr. Peel interrupted her with a snort. "Don't toy with me, Dr. Gilroy. If you know anything about me at all, you know I'm a renegade. My so-called fellow scientists have been out to get me for years. They're too shortsighted to recognize my genius. Now, I want *you* to answer some questions for *me*. Let's start with—"

"I'd love to talk more, but I've got to run. Thanks! Bye!" Deborah dropped the receiver back onto the cradle as if it had suddenly become radioactive. She leaned back in her chair and closed her eyes. "Don't ever make me do that again. It took years off my life."

"You were great, though," Dru said, chewing a nail thoughtfully. "What do you think all that talk about the other scientists was about?"

"Who knows? He sounded positively paranoid, though. Like everybody's out to get him."

"I know the feeling. You know, I never realized until this moment how potentially harmful this drug could be. I mean, when you're in a relationship, you have to be able to trust the other person and their motives. The formula distorts all that. It can really cause a lot of mischief." Dru looked her friend, who was nodding her agreement. "I've got a lot to think about."

"At least you're two for four as far as the answers you wanted. Thank God, the baby's all right."

"That's the most important thing." Dru patted her stomach. "And now I know for sure Pierce was telling the truth about not knowing that we'd been drugged. But the hell of it is, I still don't know if this transformation of his is real or the result of the drug. And since the formula will be with me for twelve weeks, I'll be showing before I find out if I can trust Pierce enough to let him know I'm carrying his baby."

Deborah gave her a hopeful smile. "That's the first time I've heard you mention telling him about the baby. Does this mean you're going to put off that transfer to the West Coast that you asked for?"

Dru threw up her hands in frustration. "I don't know," she wailed. "Not knowing what to do is hell. Pure hell. Nobody should have to go through this."

Deborah reached out and laid a hand on her friend's shoulder. "Girl, sometimes you have to go with your gut. It's like I said before. You just have to make up your mind to trust him and go with it."

Dru patted the hand that rested on her shoulder. Deborah always looked for the best in people, especially her friends. "Believe me, if it were only my feelings at stake, I would do just that. But there's the baby to consider. I have to make sure I'm doing the right thing. Anyway, I'm not going to make any decisions now. Maybe something will happen between now and the end of the twelve weeks that will help me make up my mind. Maybe I'll get a sign or something, who knows? But I'm not going to think about it now. And I have the perfect thing to take it off my mind." Dru rose to go.

Deborah bit her lip, trying without success to hide her disappointment. "You mean the final round of the Tabby awards," she said. "So what story are you submitting?"

As Dru paused at the doorway and looked back at her friend, an idea struck. A brilliant idea. The deadline for her to fax her second-round entry to the awards committee was the day after tomorrow at noon, so there was no time to waste.

"I'm writing it tonight. And when the story comes out, nobody will ever have to go through what I'm going through right now."

THE NEXT MORNING, Dru propped herself up in bed on a stack of her favorite pillows. Longjohn napped beside her on his back, his eyes half-open and vacant. She rubbed his belly and he purred like a motorboat. "Just making sure you're still alive," Dru said.

Her bunny slippers looked at her quizzically with

their beady eyes. "Flopsy and Mopsy, it's a work-at-home day."

She'd left a voice-mail message telling the ever tardy Pierce that she had a stomach virus and wouldn't be coming in to the office. She'd called Deborah and told her the truth. Her morning sickness was acting up and she'd decided to spend the day at home working on her new story—the story she planned to submit to the Tabby committee.

When she'd talked to Deborah, she'd commented on an e-mail her friend had sent her. "By the way, thanks for the e-mail, but when I said I was looking for a sign to tell me whether or not to trust Pierce, that wasn't the kind of sign I had in mind." Deborah had sent her a computerized picture of a yield sign that had filled her monitor's entire screen.

"I just wanted to illustrate that I think you should *yield* to what your heart is telling you and give Pierce a chance," Deborah had said. "Anyway, you can't blame a girl for trying, right?"

Dru took a deep breath as she clicked her notebook computer's mouse to start a new document. The story she was about to write was important but ethically dubious. She was going to write the story of a young woman who had participated in Dr. Peel's drug tests and whose life had been thrown into turmoil. In other words, she was going to write her own story.

She'd use a fictitious name, of course. And since Dr. Peel's human trials were ongoing, everyone would assume that Dru had merely gotten one of the test subjects to tell her story, only it would be Dru's own story in her own words. It was somewhat misleading, yes, but wasn't Dru's own experience with the drug as legitimate as anyone else's? Her concerns with the drug and the potential harm it could cause to people and their relationships should be put on the public record. She owed it to other women, and men, too, for that matter, to share the heartbreaking uncertainty and doubt about her future.

There was only one thing missing. She wished that the lab results of the drug sample she'd taken had been back by now, but they weren't. Maybe the data would reveal something that would back up her point of view. Oh well, she couldn't wait for the results. She had to have the story to the Tabby committee by tomorrow. She felt a bit guilty that part of her motivation for writing the story at this time was tied up with the award, but that didn't change the fact that the story needed to be told. The drug had thrown her life into turmoil, and that shouldn't happen to anyone.

She stared down at her feet and wriggled her toes. Flopsy and Mopsy fixed their shiny eyes on her. "Don't look at me like that," she said. "I'm doing what's right. At least, I think it's right."

THAT AFTERNOON, Pierce entered the cubicle he shared with Dru with a cup of steaming coffee in each hand and a bag of croissants between his teeth. He had spent the morning out of the office doing an interview and had thought to surprise Dru with an afternoon snack. She wasn't at her desk, though. She was probably off talking to Deborah or Patty about something. Depositing the food on the desk, he punched the lighted message button on his phone.

The sound of her voice sent a wave of longing through him that quickly turned to disappointment. He wouldn't see her today. He half listened to his remaining messages, making a few cursory notes, and stared at her empty chair, angry with himself for letting her absence get him down. If he hadn't already been convinced he was going soft, he surely was certain now.

"Incoming," he shouted, and tossed the bag of croissants over the partition into the newsroom. He heard what he could swear was the sound of snarling and then ripping paper. "Animals," he muttered.

The thought of going a whole day without seeing her face or feeling her touch filled him with abject loneliness. He keyed in his voice-mail password to hear her stored message once more, just to savor the sound of her voice again. When the message was through, he archived it so he could listen to it again later.

He shook his head. What a sap he was. But it felt good, it felt right, to miss somebody. It would make seeing her tomorrow that much sweeter. No, he decided, he couldn't wait for tomorrow. He would go to her later with chicken soup and saltines, the way he had done in Mexico. Only when he knocked on the door this time, he would wait for her to open it. She would ask him in and tell him she was glad that he had stayed.

In the meantime, he would keep busy by selecting an article to submit for the final round of the Tabby competition. Maybe that alien baby story would be appropriate.

He reached into his file drawer and withdrew a folder full of clippings. They were his better articles over the course of the year. As he flipped through them, he realized an important one was missing. As he often did, he'd forgotten to save one of his better stories. He'd just have to call the *Inquisitor* and get them to send him a copy, but first he had to remember when it ran.

The daily desk calendar Patty had ordered for him

had not arrived, so he reached over to Dru's desk and got hers. He knew the story had run no more than three or four months ago on a Monday, so he started four months back in the calendar and began to flip forward to see if any of the Monday dates rang a bell. As he turned the pages, he glanced at Dru's scribbled notes to herself and noted with interest that, although there were references like "dinner with Deborah" or "movie with Patty," there was nothing to indicate that she'd been seeing a man.

That thought pleased him so much that he began to whistle merrily as he turned the pages. Then his mouth went dry and his whistle warbled to a shaky halt. There, the week before he'd arrived at the *Nova,* was a note on the calendar in uncharacteristically tiny print. Print so tiny that nobody just standing over the desk could have read it. He blinked at it, comprehension warring with denial.

The note read, "First trimester appointment— 2:00 p.m."

Trimester. That terminology was only used in connection with…pregnancy. It couldn't be. Could it? No. She would have told him. Dru, the one person he knew who prized honesty above all, would have told him.

He groaned, trying to sort out his thoughts. A baby. He thought back to the calendar and its lack of social engagements with men. *His* baby! They must have conceived a child during that lovemaking marathon at Dr. Peel's cabin. Why hadn't she told him?

Perspiration beaded on his forehead and he whisked it away with the back of his hand. Still, it would explain so much. Like the queasiness she tried to hide, and the change he'd noticed in her body. Her bra had shrunk in the dryer, she'd said. Right.

But there were more signs, all in the last couple of days. She'd gotten such a craving for chocolate yesterday that he'd caught her eating hot-cocoa mix right out of the packet with a spoon—dry! When she saw him watching her, she took a breath to speak and nearly choked to death.

In addition to weird cravings, he'd heard women got more emotional during pregnancy. When Dru had gotten around to reading the rest of her mail yesterday, she'd come across a note a reader had sent her thanking her for a helpful medical story she'd written. Dru had gone misty-eyed over the note. When Pierce assumed that she had surely helped save someone's life, she'd said no, she was moved by the photo of the kitten on the front of the card. He'd asked her if the cat reminded her of a long-lost pet. "No, I just think it's cute," she'd replied.

And just last night, they'd gone out with co-workers to a nearby Mexican restaurant to celebrate the two of them making the Tabby finals. They'd ordered pitchers of beer and Dru had refused even a glass, opting for water instead. Dru turning down a beer! A free beer! With Mexican food, no less! If that wasn't a smoking gun, he didn't know what was.

He looked across the empty expanse of desk, the space over which they'd shaken hands twenty-four hours ago. He'd asked her, practically begged her, to trust him, and she'd promised that she would. Only she didn't trust him enough to tell him that she was carrying his child.

He hung his head, massaging his temples to banish the ache there. His phone rang and he jumped involuntarily. "Yeah," he said tersely.

"Hello to you, too."

"Oh, Rhonda, it's you." Rhonda Taylor was one of the editors he'd worked with at the *Inquisitor*. "Sorry. What can I do for you?"

"I need you to give me a reference on someone there that wants to transfer from the *Nova* to the *Inquisitor*. This chick must be behind in her rent or something, because she really seems in a rush to get out here."

An awful sense of dread overwhelmed Pierce. Could this get any worse? "Who is it?" he managed to say.

"Drucilla Logan. I hear she's pretty good. Isn't she the woman you collaborated with on that love potion story? What can you tell me about her?"

Pierce closed his eyes. "Nothing. I guess I really don't know her very well after all." Rhonda said something else, but Pierce didn't understand what it was. He hung up the phone.

The woman he loved was planning to leave him. Leave without telling him about her baby. About *his* baby. What had he done to deserve this? His gaze came to rest on the brass paperweight on his desk and its inscription leaped out at him. Nice Guys Finish Last, it said. Why was he kidding himself? He knew exactly what he'd done to deserve this. He'd lied to her, stolen a story from her and admitted to her that he'd been a teenage criminal and lowlife, that's all. In short, he'd made it clear that he would be abysmal father material. Who could blame her for wanting to get herself and her child as far away from him as she could?

Still, she had promised—promised to trust him, yet she clearly didn't.

He was going to be a father, something he'd never wanted to be. But he'd never been in love before, and the thought of the woman he loved bearing his child filled him with awe. That was all too bad, though, because Dru didn't want him to be a part of her and her baby's life and was going to great lengths to make sure he wouldn't be. What was he going to do?

"Mail call," Patty sang out from the hallway. "Aw, you look like you just lost your last friend. Don't worry about Dru, she'll be back tomorrow." She set a few pieces of mail on his desk and one envelope on Dru's. "She just faxed in a story to run in tomorrow's paper. Hal read it and thinks it's fabulous. He wants you to look at it."

Pierce ran a hand through his hair. "Sure. In a minute." He had to get himself together first. As Patty went on her way, Pierce's gaze strayed to the envelope on Dru's desk. The return address read, "Oglesby Labs."

"Labs," he said dully. Did this have something to do with the baby? Some kind of test result perhaps? If so, he had a right to know, and the way things were going, he knew Dru would sure as hell not tell him. He reached for the envelope and tore it open.

He scanned the cover letter briefly. This wasn't what he'd thought it was. Dru had gotten hold of a sample of Dr. Peel's drug and had it analyzed. These were the results. He turned the page of the letter and stared in amazement.

"Well, I'll be damned," he whispered.

9

DRU CAME IN THE NEXT MORNING at her usual time, anxious to see her masterpiece in print. The story she'd sent to Hal the previous afternoon was her best work ever, and she couldn't wait to fax it to the awards committee. She also wanted to see what Pierce had thought of it, but he was late.

Deborah danced into the cubicle opening and Dru did a double take. Her friend wore a policeman's hat and brandished a cardboard stop sign which read Stop In The Name Of Love.

"Don't tell me. Let me guess. The stop sign is supposed to be the 'sign' I said I was looking for, right?"

Deborah nodded hopefully, and the hat slid to a jaunty angle across her forehead.

"I hate to tell you, but you're the only black woman I know who absolutely can't dance. But I give you an A for effort."

Deborah sniffed and set the hat down on the desk. "It's not nice to make fun of the rhythmically challenged. Besides, I went to a lot of trouble for this performance. Stealing a hat from a police officer can get you into a lot of trouble, you know."

"You stole that hat from a cop?"

"No, but I had you going there for a minute, didn't I? The truth is, I borrowed it."

"I thought even that much was against the law."

Deborah held her index finger to her lips. "Sh. Don't tell anybody. It has to go back this afternoon before the second shift. I'm meeting a very cute cop at the corner doughnut shop to give it back to him. I think I can get him to buy me a cruller."

"A cop hanging out in a doughnut shop," Dru mused. "Imagine that."

"Speaking of food, did my performance give you food for thought?"

"Sorry, but as I said yesterday, that's not the kind of sign I had in mind."

"Dang, I was afraid of that."

"Say, has today's paper come off the presses yet? I've got a story in there I'm rather proud of. I wouldn't be surprised if it made the front page."

"Nope, haven't seen it, but I did hear an interesting piece of news this morning. Our editor got fired last night!"

"Hal? You're kidding. What happened?" Dru was no big fan of Hal Connelly's. Still, his dismissal was a shock. They clashed often about editorial decisions. Hal was more Pierce's kind of editor. He wouldn't know the truth if it bit him.

"I heard the powers that be have decided to make the *Nova* into a more mainstream newspaper. Hal's penchant for twisting the facts when the truth would do as well won't fit with that new image."

"Well, I'm delighted to hear about the change in focus. But this raises some interesting questions. We know that Pierce transferred from the *Inquisitor* because he heard there would be an opening in editorial here. Do you suppose he heard though the grapevine that Hal was on his way out? If what you've heard is true, Pierce may be in for a disappointment. His reputation for playing fast and loose with the truth is almost as bad as Hal's.''

Deborah frowned and reached for the hat. ''I don't know, but I'll ask around and see if I can get the scoop on who the new editor will be.'' With a parting wave of the stop sign, she was gone.

Dru got up and paced nervously. As if she didn't have enough uncertainty in her life, now she didn't know who her boss was going to be.

Dru heard the squeaky wheels of the mail cart coming down the hallway. Patty came into view, pushing the cart loaded with that day's papers. The secretary gave Dru a copy of the newspaper and a cheery good-morning and went on her way.

Brimming with excitement and pride, Dru opened the newspaper and gasped in shock. Her story was there, all right. The headline read Test Subject Tells Woes Of So-Called Love Potion. But it was what was under the headline that hit her with the force of a slap in the face. At the beginning of her story was Pierce Mountcastle's byline.

''He stole it!'' she yelled.

Creech shouted, ''Keep it down—people are trying to get some sleep around here,'' but the joke didn't register with Dru.

She sat down heavily onto her desk chair. He'd betrayed her. Just when she'd started to believe in him. Just when she'd started to trust him enough to make plans to tell him about his child.

How did it happen? Her mind raced. Pierce probably took advantage of the confusion over Hal's firing to do the deed. All he had to do was talk to the boys in the press room. *Hey, boys, there's a little mistake here. No big thing, just have to change a byline.* That's all it would have taken. And with the editor gone and no new one in sight, there was no threat of censure. It would be her word against that of the great, award-winning journalist Pierce Mountcastle.

As for his motive for stealing the story, there was only one answer. He wanted to win another Tabby so badly that he was willing to steal her work and submit it to the committee as his own.

And he'd promised her only two days ago that he'd never play another trick at her expense, never tell another lie that affected her. Just when she was beginning to believe he'd changed, he had stolen her masterpiece, her award and her heart. It was then that she realized what she'd been denying for so long. She loved him. She loved a man who was willing to hurt her for his own gain. She hung her head in despair and felt her throat constrict and bitter tears sting her eyes.

Only two days ago he had uttered the ''C'' word— *commitment*—and although he'd only been talking about their partnership at work, she'd begun to kid herself that the father of her child actually cared about her. She'd even begun to harbor absurd dreams about another kind of partnership. Now that dream was gone.

She felt someone's gaze on her and her skin began to crawl. She looked up into the inscrutable face of Pierce Mountcastle, and she erupted in fury. ''You!''

''I can explain,'' he began, but his face looked anything but contrite. In fact, he was stone-faced, she observed, but what else could he be after what he'd done? He couldn't exactly give her the old Mountcastle grin and shrug it all away.

She lowered her voice to a pained whisper so others in the newsroom couldn't overhear. ''I don't want to hear your excuse, whatever it is. I've had it with your tricks and lies. I should have known I could never trust you. I'll never believe another word you say.'' She bit her lip to stop it from trembling, and then continued. ''I'm prepared to uproot my whole life and move across the country if that's what it takes to ensure that I never have to see you again.''

Pierce had opened his mouth to reply, but had gone silent in the face of her onslaught. His face registered shock, anger and—of all things—hurt. When he finally spoke, he said humorlessly, ''I hate to see you bottle up your emotions like this. Why don't you tell me how you *really* feel?''

''Don't tempt me.'' Pierce Mountcastle had put her through the emotional wringer before, but never like this. She'd never experienced the kind of pain she felt now, looking into his face. The face that had struck her with its masculine beauty so many times before now only made her want to run away from its hard, unapologetic countenance.

He took a deep breath, and his gaze probed hers. ''It really doesn't matter what I say, does it? You'd never believe it in a million years, would you?''

''No, I wouldn't.'' To keep from having to look at him any longer, she jerked open a desk drawer and began pulling out her personal items. Her hands shook as she blindly closed them around the objects inside.

''You don't have to do that. I'll leave, and I can promise you that I shall never trouble you again.''

''Too bad your promises are completely worthless.''

At that moment, Patty stuck her head in the cubicle opening. ''Dru, you're wanted in the editor's office. Something's up with the top brass. Chop-chop.''

Grateful for any excuse to get away from him, Dru strode out of the cubicle and down the hall with Patty at her side. She felt like sobbing, but she was a professional, she told herself, and she'd damn well act like one. She'd keep her mind off Pierce and on her job. Through force of will, she wouldn't allow herself to cry until she was alone in her apartment tonight. Now she had a career to look out for, and the first order of business would be to fax in another story to the Tabby awards committee.

"Patty, would you do me a favor as soon as possible?"

"Sure. What?"

"Go to the archives and make a copy of my story about the woman with two brains."

"The one about the woman who could play 'Lady of Spain' and do long division at the same time?"

"That's the one. It ran six weeks ago. Fax it in to the Tabby awards committee."

"Will do."

Patty continued toward her desk as Dru stopped in front of the editor's office. She took a moment to compose herself and entered.

Clustered around the desk were four serious-looking men in suits, one of whom she recognized as Harold Gryfe, the publisher of both the *Nova* and the *Inquisitor*. The executives had made a rare trip from the home office. Her pulse quickened. Maybe the shake-up went further than the replacement of the editor. Maybe there was a layoff under way. Was she about to be fired? It didn't matter much since she planned to transfer, anyway. Still, her knees became a little weaker than they already were as Mr. Gryfe made the introductions and asked her to sit.

"I'm sure that by now you know that Hal Connelly has been removed from his duties as editor."

Dru nodded and steeled herself for what might be coming next. They might be about to give her the old heave-ho, although the higher-ups usually didn't handle that sort of thing themselves. What could these guys want?

"We decided to let Hal go because he wasn't a good fit with the new editorial direction we have planned for the *Nova.* We feel that the general public is dissatisfied with outlandish stories and celebrity stalkings. We want the *Nova* to make the move toward becoming a more mainstream newspaper."

Dru was stunned. Just when her newspaper had the mandate to turn into something she could truly be proud of, she was going to be forced to leave. That was, if Pierce didn't follow through on his vow to leave first. He might as well leave, she thought, almost feeling sorry for him. If he stayed at the *Nova* now, he'd be a fish out of water with his sensationalistic reporting style. Then a thought hit her. Maybe he'd had advance word of this. Maybe that's why he'd said he would leave, not because she said she never wanted to see him again, but because he'd known he would not fit in at the new *Nova,* anyway. He couldn't even be honest about his motives for leaving, she realized with a fresh pang of pain in her heart.

"Toward that end, we've selected as the new editor an individual with the very highest standards of integrity in reporting. Drucilla, we want *you* for the job."

She couldn't have heard that right. "Me? You want me?"

"Drucilla, I hope you didn't think all your good work had gone unnoticed over the years. We think you'll be a terrific editor and we hope you'll take the job. Will you?"

Her own editorship. It was what she'd always wanted. She should feel ecstatic, but without Pierce to share her triumph, she felt empty. Still, she'd be a fool not to grab the brass ring being offered. Oh well, there was no looking back now. She took a deep breath. ''I will.''

Mr. Gryfe extended his hand and she shook it. He and the other men sat down with her and went over her benefits package. The details barely sank in, but she did gather that she would be getting a substantial raise. She informed them about her pregnancy and told them when she'd need maternity leave. They congratulated her and told her that with advance planning they didn't foresee any problem with her taking all the time she needed.

After some final instructions detailing their vision for the future of the newspaper, the men wished her well and departed. Her sigh seemed to echo in the lonely office. At last, she had an opportunity to take her beloved *Nova* in the direction she'd always wanted it to go, not to mention a promotion and hefty pay raise. If she'd received this break a month ago, she'd have been dancing on the desk. It would have looked like a scene from a Ginger Rogers movie. Now, with Pierce out of her life for good, her achievement was empty. She couldn't feel less like dancing if her feet were made of lead.

Her co-workers began to stream into the office to congratulate her, flashing smiles of approval. Patty pressed a sisterly kiss to her cheek, and she felt Deborah's slim arms around her neck. She returned all hugs and kisses, shook hands and thanked everyone for their good wishes. Where was Pierce? He might be a lot of things, but he'd never been a poor sport. He must have wanted the job for himself so badly that he couldn't bring himself to congratulate her.

The crowd finally dispersed, and she was alone, feeling more heartbroken than ever, and despising herself for it.

That's it. I've had it.

She refused to let Pierce Mountcastle ruin her enjoyment of her new job. She had a fresh start to make, and she'd begin by sorting out the paperwork Hal had left strewn all over his desk—now *her* desk.

As she sorted through the papers, the phone rang, and the woman on the other end of the line introduced herself as the Tabby awards chairperson.

"I just wanted to let you know that we received your fax and you're all set for the second round of judging."

"Thanks," Dru said woodenly. *For all the good it'll do.*

"There's one more thing, though. Since Pierce Mountcastle works with you, perhaps you'd know if he meant to withdraw or if there was a postal error."

"What do you mean?"

"Well, he's won the award for two years straight, but he'll be disqualified this year because we didn't receive his entry for the second round by the noon deadline. We tried to call him earlier there at the *Nova* but got no answer."

Dru was jolted upright in her chair. "There must be some mistake. He was supposed to have faxed you a story. You're saying the story didn't make it?"

"I'm afraid not."

"I'll speak to him. Thanks so much for calling." Dru hung up. There had to be an explanation. She picked up the phone and called Pierce's desk. There was no answer.

Even if Pierce intended to follow through on his promise to leave, surely he wasn't gone already. He was probably just out having a long lunch to compose himself after losing out on the promotion. Dru rested her head on the back of her new executive chair and stared at the ceiling. She had to know why he didn't enter the story he'd stolen from her in the contest. If he wasn't going to use it, why did he bother to steal it? What was going on?

Deborah came into Dru's office bearing two salads in take-out containers. "You haven't eaten lunch yet, have you?"

"No," Dru muttered. "Too busy. Not hungry."

Deborah placed the salad before Dru on the desk, anyway, and dropped a plastic fork beside it. "Hmm. They just made you a newspaper editor and you've already forgotten about subjects and verbs. Isn't that always the way? You don't need to be skipping meals. Think about the baby."

"Deborah, sit down. Something's happened—that is, something's happening and I don't know what to make of all of it." Dru poured out the story of the article she'd written, Pierce's betrayal and the call from the Tabby chairperson.

"Now *I'm* not hungry." Deborah abandoned her own salad and slumped down in the chair across from Dru's desk. "Dru, why didn't you give him a chance to explain?"

"What explanation could there be?" She returned her friend's scowl with a sheepish look. "Well, maybe I should have, but you have to admit, it looked awfully bad."

"Are you afraid he's gone already?" Concern knit

Deborah's brow. She'd begun to nervously straighten the papers on her side of the desk.

"I don't know what to think." Dru glanced at her friend, who seemed mesmerized by a paper she'd just unfolded. "What is it?"

Deborah's eyes darted back and forth across the page and then became as wide as saucers. "You'd better have a look."

"It's the lab results from the formula sample." Dru turned the page and quickly scanned the data. "How did it get to Hal before it got to me? But—but these results are impossible! How can this be? This means— this means—"

"The formula is totally worthless," Deborah finished for her.

10

THE NEWS SANK into Dru's consciousness with the full force of a blow. Her feelings for Pierce were real all along. "Oh, no."

"I'll bet anything that what Pierce did has something to do with that lab report," Deborah asserted. "You have to get to the bottom of this."

Dru took another look at the report. "The time stamp says this was sent early yesterday just before deadline time." She felt a deep sense of dread that she'd made a terrible mistake. But she felt a tiny blossom of hope, as well. What if she *had* made a mistake? What if Pierce *did* have a good explanation?

On the one hand, the test results suggested that the change she'd observed in Pierce was real. On the other hand, his most recent treachery seemed to prove that he was the same low-down sneaky bastard as always. She had to know if that lab report had anything to do with Pierce stealing her story.

The wording of the report was clear. The formula was no good. That meant that her feelings for Pierce were real—the passion she'd felt for him on that weekend in the mountains, and every feeling of longing for him since. She realized then that deep in her heart she'd known she loved him all along.

But what about *his* feelings? Sure, he was attracted to her and had come to enjoy their partnership, but was that all there was? Surely he couldn't love her and be willing to betray her the way he'd done just yesterday. But again, what if there *was* an explanation, as he'd claimed?

"You're right. I have to get to the bottom of this, and if Pierce has gone AWOL, then maybe Hal can shed light on what happened yesterday." Dru picked up the phone and asked Patty if she could get Hal on the line.

While they waited, Deborah said, "What do you make of the note the lab manager wrote at the end of the report?"

"I didn't get that far. I only read as far as the results."

"Well, go on," Deborah urged.

Dru read aloud.

"Dear Ms. Logan,
I think you should know that Jackson Peel is well-known in the scientific community as being a kook. He keeps trying to publish his harebrained ideas in the leading journals and they just laugh at him. His so-called revolutionary ideas don't stand up to the more rigorous testing of respected scientists, and each has been disproved. He once even claimed to have discovered the fountain of youth! And the formula he devised for that was little more than springwater and vitamins."

Dru tossed the paper onto the desk.

Deborah said, "So now we know what Dr. Peel meant when I spoke with him on the phone. You know, the part about his fellow scientists trying to discredit him. Looks like they have the goods on him and he knows it. What a crazy old coot.''

''And we fell for it,'' Dru groaned. ''This is awful. The story we did was picked up by so many other newspapers that it's only a matter of time before the truth comes out. Pierce and I are going to look bad.''

Deborah steepled her fingers, and her wispy brows drew together. ''Actually, I don't think you'll look all that bad because of your first story. After all, you were simply reporting what you were told by a man who billed himself as a great research scientist. But think of how Pierce is going to look now after the story that came out yesterday.'' Deborah's eyes widened again. ''The story went on and on about how harmful the formula's effects could be to people, and now we know that it doesn't have any effects. Think of what would have happened to *your* reputation if that story had come out with *your* name on it as you'd planned.''

Dru swallowed hard. It would have been goodbye promotion. And it undoubtedly would have come to light that *she* was the subject of her own story. That would really have put the nail in the coffin of her career. Now more than ever, she couldn't shake the feeling that there was more than met the eye where Pierce's actions were concerned. An entirely new thought struck her. Could it be? Was it possible he'd done it for her?

When the phone buzzed, she jumped.

''Hal on line one,'' Patty said. Dru activated the speakerphone so Deborah could hear the conversation, as well, then with a deep breath pushed the button to connect.''

''Hal, it's Dru. I need to know what happened with the story I turned in yesterday. How did Pierce's byline get on it?''

"Mountcastle was hit by an uncharacteristic bolt of journalistic integrity." Hal indulged in a bout of laughter and continued. "He showed me a lab report that proved the chick you wrote about was either lying or completely nuts. He tried to talk me out of running the piece. Said it would destroy your reputation, ruin your chances of winning the Tabby if the truth in the lab report came out before the winner was announced. Then I said to him, 'Mountcastle, you crazy son of a bitch. Wasn't it you who always said it's a crime to let the truth stand in the way of a good story?'"

Dru squeezed her eyes shut as the picture became clear. Pierce *had* been trying to help her. She imagined him sitting in this very office, pleading her case, having his own words thrown back at him by his editor. "Go on," she said hoarsely. "What then?"

"I told him it was a great story and there was no way in hell I wasn't going to run it. He begged me to print it without a byline, but I refused. I told him since it was a story the two of you had broken in the beginning, it had to have a byline on it from at least one of you for continuity's sake. Then he put his own name on it, and that's how it ran. So, as the man says, now you know the rest of the story."

Dru thanked him and hung up. She brought her hands, which had gone cold, to her cheeks, which had gone hot. "What have I done?" Tears stung Dru's eyes and she pulled in a ragged breath. "I finally start to see a kinder, gentler Pierce, and then I alienate him because I think he's betrayed me when he only tried to save me.

"And not only does the lab report and what Hal said prove that the change was the real thing, but all my feelings for him were real, too. He didn't tell me about the report and the byline because I said I'd never believe another word he said and jumped to the very worst conclusion about him. Since Hal wasn't here to back up his story, he probably thought there wasn't any use in wasting his breath. I've got to find Pierce before he makes good on his promise to leave!''

Dru got up from the desk and strode down the hall, breaking into a run before she reached her cubicle. As she entered the opening, she drew up short. Pierce's desk was completely empty. His awards, photos and memorabilia had been removed from the walls, and his briefcase was gone. She opened his file drawer. No files. Nothing.

Where was he? Where would he go? The father of her child, the man who had sacrificed his own reputation to save her career, was gone. But it was more than that. The man she loved was gone.

On top of his otherwise empty desk was a hastily written resignation letter. A lump formed in her throat as she looked at the terse statement. He was leaving to ''pursue other opportunities,'' it said. The letter was addressed to Hal. When he'd left, Pierce hadn't known Hal had been fired. That proved he'd left because of her, not because he'd found out he'd been passed over for the promotion or because of the *Nova*'s new direction.

The last words she'd said to him were that his promises were worthless. Of all the hateful things she'd said, that caused her the most pain. Because in the end he'd made good on his promise to leave her, and she might never be able to get him back. She trudged slowly to her new office and told Deborah what she had found—or rather, not found.

Deborah squirmed in her seat as her friend issued a choked sob. "Look on the bright side, Dru."

"What bright side? I've just lost the man I love, a man who might have actually begun to care for me. A man who was willing to take the rap for a disastrous mistake in order to save *my* reputation and career. What, pray tell, is the bright side?"

Deborah offered a wan smile. "Things can't possibly get any worse."

As if on cue, Patty appeared at the doorway again. "A courier just showed up with this. Said to see that you got it right away."

Dru looked at the address on the outside of the envelope and her spirits buoyed. "It's Pierce's handwriting!" She ripped into the manila paper, and a check floated onto her desk. "What?" She picked up the check and saw that it was for a substantial sum and made out to her. Then she saw the edge of a small note sticking out of the envelope.

For the baby. Love, Pierce.

"Oh, no!" Dru wailed. "He found out I'm pregnant! How?"

Deborah crossed her heart against the bodice of her linen dress. "I swear I didn't tell him."

"This means that when he left here, he knew that his trusted partner, whom he'd just promised never to be dishonest with, was running out on him without telling him that she's pregnant with his child." She buried her face in her hands and gave in to sobs.

Patty stared at Deborah, who reached across the desk to pat her friend's shoulder. "She's pregnant? Why am I always the last to know these things? And what did you mean when I first came in and you said things couldn't get any worse?"

"Wah!" Dru wailed.

"Never mind," said Deborah, still patting. "You know how emotional pregnant women are."

PIERCE MOUNTCASTLE WALKED unsteadily out of the airport bar and looked left and right. It was hard enough getting around Hartsfield International Airport sober. When you were entirely blotto, it was exceedingly difficult indeed. The alcohol was affecting him more than usual—probably because he hadn't eaten in so long. If he wasn't careful, he'd probably wind up on a plane to Timbuktu. Actually, considering the past twenty-four hours, that didn't sound too bad.

He picked a direction and fell in with the stream of fellow travelers. He stopped to check his gate number and found himself standing in front of a shop window. A strange reflection stared back at him. Dru had always said he looked as if he'd just stepped off a magazine cover. Well, he didn't look like that now. In fact, he looked like hell. His eyes were bleary, his black hair hung over his forehead, and his suit looked as if he'd slept in it.

"Bloody hell," he muttered. "I look as knackered as I feel." He ran a careless hand through his hair and his gaze traveled to the merchandise in the window. In one corner was a collection of baby toys, no doubt put there so that busy moms and dads could bring a pretty present home to their baby after a business trip that had allowed no time for shopping. Plush pink and blue rabbits, nubby terry-cloth bears and various dolls sat in a pleasing artistic display.

Babies. He'd never given them much thought before now, although he'd certainly grown up among many of the wee nippers. There had been plenty of squalling infants here and there in the council estate, but he'd never been responsible for one, and had never wanted to be. He'd never had to consider the possibility of becoming a father.

He considered it now, and his throat ached. He thought of his beautiful Drucilla, and what a gorgeous baby they'd make. If he was hurrying home from a trip right now, should he select the blue bunny or the pink one? Would the baby like it? He pictured a charming toddler flinging chubby little arms around his neck and putting a sweet-smelling cheek to his. The display became a little blurry.

Pink, blue, what difference did it make? Dru didn't want him, and she didn't want him as a father for her baby. To ensure that he wouldn't demand a part in her or her baby's life, she was prepared to move across the country without telling him about their child. He'd once thought her an inept liar. Now she'd proven herself better at deception than he'd given her credit for.

Since she'd obviously deemed him unworthy father material, she probably wouldn't even let him see the child. And who could blame her? He'd lied to her so many times in the past that when it had come time to tell her the most important things he'd ever had to tell, she hadn't even been willing to hear him out. Knowing that the love potion formula had been fake wouldn't have changed any of that.

She could believe what she wanted about him and his motives. She wanted him out of her life, so he'd go, even though it was killing him. All the good times they'd shared probably didn't mean anything to her, anyway.

He sighed and continued to trudge toward the concourses. It was funny how life worked, all right. Just when he felt himself finally ready for the responsibilities of fatherhood, the opportunity to be a father was jerked out from under him. Dru's influence—not that of the drug, he now knew—had made him into a different man. All those times he found himself wondering if he was going soft—well, he was, in a sense. Thanks to Dru, he had turned into a man who could give and receive love. A few days ago he might have finally been able to revel in that realization. But knowing what he knew now, it only caused him pain, for when he'd turned into a man who could love, he'd also become a man who could be hurt.

"I guess I do have a heart," he murmured to himself. "I feel it breaking."

"You MEAN THE PA SYSTEM isn't fixed yet?"

The harried airline clerk gave Dru a practiced, apologetic look. "That's right, ma'am. It's the same as when you called a while ago. We still can't page him. The phones to the gates are down, too."

"Damn!" Dru and Deborah had rushed to the airport after having determined that Pierce was on the passenger list for a flight to London. "Okay, tell me the gate number then."

The clerk looked up the flight number on his computer screen. "Gate twelve," he said. "And you'd better hurry. They're boarding right now."

Dru squinted down the crowded corridor. The sign for gate twelve was a tiny speck in the distance.

"How can we make it in time?" Deborah asked with a groan.

Dru seized Deborah's slender arm. "Come on." She set out at a dead run, dragging Deborah with her.

They weaved in and out of the slower traffic, dodging luggage carts, meandering tour groups and tots in strollers.

"You run fast for a pregnant woman," Deborah said, gasping as she struggled to keep pace with Dru. "You're so fast I'm surprised you got pregnant at all."

"I guess he was a little faster." Dru jumped over a pet carrier, causing a small dog to yap furiously.

They finally drew even with the sign for gate twelve. The two women sped between two rows of chairs and past the desk, behind which a lighted sign twinkled: Flight 1241 to London. A gate agent was about to close the door to the loading platform as they reached it.

"I've got to stop that plane," Dru said as she squeezed through the heavy door. Deborah darted in behind her.

"Wait! You can't do that!" the agent called after them.

"Ooh! We're going to get in trouble." Deborah craned her neck to see if the agent was gaining on them as they charged down the ramp.

"Never look back. It slows you down," Dru called over her shoulder. But she couldn't help it. She had to look, too. The agent was running toward them while speaking into a radio.

Dru went through the plane's hatch, ignoring the greeting of the flight attendant. Frantically, she scanned the first-class cabin, knowing Pierce would be nowhere else. He sat in the back corner, eyes closed, wearing headphones. Her heart leaped and sank at the same time. Was that sorrow she saw on his face? Thank God she'd reached him in time. When she told him how she felt, it could make all the difference. That was, if he felt the same way. There was only one way to find out.

"Pierce!" she called, starting forward.

Strong arms clasped hers from behind and dragged her backward. Dru looked from side to side to see that the pilot and copilot meant to remove her from the plane. "Wait! I have to talk to that man!"

"She forced her way past me." The agent's voice came from somewhere behind Dru. From somewhere else behind her, she heard Deborah's frantic protests.

"Come along with us, ma'am," said one of the men who had hold of her.

"You don't understand. This plane can't take off until I speak to that man. Pierce!" Dru dug her heels into the carpet beneath her feet, but it did no good. The men were still dragging her backward and Pierce couldn't hear her because of the headphones.

The last she saw of him, his head rested on a pillow, his eyes closed, his brow furrowed, as if with worry or regret.

"No," she moaned as she was escorted off the plane and handed over to two security guards who already had Deborah in hand. Dru made one last lunge for the plane's door as it was slammed shut.

Dru's shoulders sagged as she saw a stern-looking security guard crook his finger to beckon her over.

"Dru! What are we going to do? I've never been to jail!" Deborah wrung her hands.

"I have," Dru said dejectedly. "It's not so bad."

"I CAN'T BELIEVE WE'RE STUCK in here," Dru wailed. "I should be on the phone with Pierce's pilot or with Heathrow airport, making arrangements for someone to meet him and tell him to call me. He'll be almost impossible to trace if he gets away. I don't even know what name he'll be using, for goodness' sake. I may never see him again!'' She took hold of the bars and shouted, ''I demand my phone call!''

''Keep it down. A working girl needs her beauty sleep.'' A woman in a micromini, caked-on makeup and a tiara sat up on the bench where she'd been reclining and leveled a menacing gaze at Dru. ''Don't make me come over there.''

Deborah, who'd been worrying her beads nervously in a corner, put her arms protectively around her friend. ''Leave her alone. She's had a bad day. The father of her child just left for Europe without her and she has no way of ever contacting him again.''

''Ran out on ya, huh? That's rough. Listen, if you need a job, I can set you up with my boyfriend.''

Dru rolled her eyes. ''Big Larry's already got dibs.''

''Huh?'' Deborah asked.

''Never mind.''

Deborah straightened her shoulders. ''She's already got a job. This woman is the new editor in chief of the *Nova*.''

Tiara Woman looked at them dully. ''Humph. And I'm Miss America.'' She shrugged and lay back on the bench.

An idea leaped into Dru's mind. ''That's it! That's the answer!'' Dru seized her friend's narrow shoulders and nearly lifted her off the concrete floor. ''If I can't find him before then, the Tabby awards are in a few weeks. What do the Tabby awards and the Miss America Pageant have in common?''

Deborah looked at her as if she'd lost her mind. ''If you want to plead insanity, you'll have to wait until you get before the judge. I don't know what you're talking about.''

''Deborah, think!''

Deborah looked into her friend's joyous face, and then understanding dawned. "Of course! Last year's winner always presents this year's award. Dru, there's still hope!"

"Hallelujah," muttered Tiara Woman as Deborah and Dru jumped up and down in each other's arms.

11

"HE'LL BE HERE," DEBORAH SAID as she craned her neck along with Dru, looking from banquet table to banquet table, hoping that one of the tuxedoed men would prove, on closer inspection, to be Pierce Mountcastle. She nervously took a sip of water from a stemmed glass. "It's a tradition."

Dru was almost beside herself, twisting this way and that, trying to see everyone at once. "Yes, but he's nowhere in sight, and the ceremony is about to start. The awards coordinator said she hasn't spoken to him—she just assumes he'll be here."

"He'll be here," Deborah said again.

But Dru could tell by the concern in her friend's eyes that she didn't necessarily believe it. "He has to be," Dru murmured, her hand going to her belly. Several weeks had passed since she'd seen Pierce, and she'd recently begun to show. In those weeks, she'd tried her best to contact him, but couldn't find him anywhere. It was as if he'd vanished off the face of the earth. The awards banquet tonight was her last best hope. She needed to see him, to tell him that she loved him, to ask him to forgive her. And most of all, she needed to know how he felt about her and their child.

She tossed her napkin onto her plate. "I can't just sit around. I've got to know if he's here. I'll sneak up on the stage and peek through the curtain. From that vantage point, I should be able to see everyone in the banquet hall.''

''What if they announce the award and you're not back?''

''Screw the award. I've got to find my man.''

''I'm glad to see you finally have your priorities straight,'' Deborah said, grinning.

''My priorities have been off-kilter for a long time. My father always tried to make me tough, and as a result I've been too tough on other people. I haven't been willing to forgive myself for my own mistakes or anybody else for theirs. Well, no more. I love Pierce, warts and all, and I'm going to get him back.''

''You go, girl.''

PIERCE MOUNTCASTLE SAUNTERED up to the cash bar in the corridor outside. ''Whiskey,'' he said to the bartender, laying a bill on the bar. Just knowing that Drucilla Logan was somewhere in that hall had his nerve endings tingling. Taking a gulp of his drink, he walked to the doorway. What would they say to each other?

She was aware that he knew about their baby. Maybe she'd be showing by now. His heart felt as cold and desolate as the ice in his drink. Why had he even come here? He didn't give a damn about the silly award. He snaked a finger inside his shirt collar to loosen it. Who was he kidding? He'd come here to see her one more time.

It wasn't long ago that seeing her, touching her, loving her one more time was something he wanted to do to ''get her out of his system.'' He now knew that was impossible. She'd always be a part of him, and thanks to their baby, he'd always be a part of her. Whether she liked it or not.

He took a final drink and set the glass aside, savoring the numbing burn of the whiskey as it traveled down his throat. But all the whiskey in the world couldn't make the pain in his heart go away.

He'd let his tough-guy image get in the way of opening up to the only woman he'd ever loved. Because of Dru's influence, he'd spent the past few weeks trying to right some of the wrongs he'd done to people over the years. In this way, he had proven to himself that he could actually be a good man. Too bad he had lost the opportunity to prove that to Dru. If he'd come to his senses earlier, perhaps the happily-ever-after ending he'd never believed in could have come true.

His reverie was broken by the public-address system crackling to life. It reminded him of the official purpose of the evening's festivities.

"And now, ladies and gentlemen," a voice boomed, "the moment you've been waiting for—the presentation of the Tabby awards."

Pierce took a deep breath and entered the banquet hall. "Good luck, darling," he whispered.

BACKSTAGE, DRU COULDN'T FIND the part in the curtains, so she'd had to feel her way to the far corner of the stage in the dark. Her progress was hampered by the theatrical props and other junk that were stored backstage. She finally reached the end of the curtain and peered around it. Frantically scanning each row from right to left, she heard the awards presentation begin. The first awards to be given would be for things like best tabloid news photography.

She continued to scan the crowd as a couple of editing awards were presented. Her heart sank—he wasn't here after all. The man she loved was lost to her forever. She'd been a fool, and she'd lost him. She stepped back behind the curtain and blinked away tears.

As she started toward the other end of the stage, she heard the announcer say, "To present the award for best tabloid reporting, I give you last year's winner, Pierce Mountcastle."

He had come! Dru cried out with joy and rushed for the entrance to the stage, but the darkness forced her to feel along the curtain. She stumbled, then righted herself, but when she tried to continue, she realized that her ankle was caught in something.

She strained to hear Pierce's voice amid the hubbub and tinkling silverware and crystal from the banquet tables. Then she heard it—the smooth baritone that sent chills down her spine. "And the nominees are—"

Dru made a final lunge toward the light at the end of the curtain, but it was no use. Her ankle twisted painfully. "To hell with it." Dru took a deep breath and shouted as loud as she could, "Pierce! Help!"

A shaft of light cut through the darkness as the end of the curtain was pushed back. In a sleek black tuxedo, Pierce appeared in the middle of the artificial moonbeam like a dark angel. Her breath left her body as he rushed toward her. "What are you doing back there?" he asked, blinking his eyes of bluest blue. On the other side of the curtain the crowd noise hushed to the gentle hissing of mingled whispers.

"I was looking for you and I caught my ankle."

Pierce bent forward and gently placed his hand on her calf, then swept it downward. He pushed away the small pile of lumber and metal she had stepped into and massaged her ankle. "Are you all right?"

As he stood up, Dru nodded. Then she took a deep breath and opened her heart. "Physically, I'm fine. But

I was sick with worry that you wouldn't show and that I'd never get a chance to thank you for what you did for me and ask you to forgive me for not hearing you out the day you left. Pierce, you put your career on the line to save mine.''

He smiled slowly, warily. "I forgive you."

She saw his eyes sweep her from head to toe and come to rest on her expanding belly.

"I—I've been searching and searching for you. I thought I'd never find you again."

"You've found me." His gaze delved into hers, as if waiting to see if there was more she had to tell him.

"Oh, Pierce, I would never have left without telling you about the baby. I was planning to keep it to myself, but I couldn't have gone through with it in the end."

"I believe you." He reached for her and put one arm around her shoulders. His other hand went out tentatively to touch her belly, but he withdrew it as if he didn't know if he should. Instead, he smoothed her tousled hair and stroked her cheek with his fingertips. "But what then, Dru? Would you have wanted me?"

He stared at her with the same earnest longing that she felt in her own heart, and hope bloomed inside her. She took a deep breath. "I want you. I love you. And I want you to be a father to our baby!"

A smile of pure elation spread over Pierce's face. "You mean you want me after everything that's happened?"

"The past is past. I want us to make a new start. No more secrets, no more lies, and no looking back. But— but how do *you* feel? Do you want me...and our baby?" Her eyes searched his, hoping to see the love and commitment she knew he was capable of.

"I've never wanted anything as much in my entire

life. I'm never leaving you again.'' As she felt her body relax at his words, he held her to him and pressed a kiss to her lips that told her he was finally hers. She twined her arms around his neck and drew him closer to feel the thrill of his body she'd been craving for so long.

''Would you two get out here!'' called the announcer, who'd stuck his head behind the curtain and just as quickly disappeared.

Pierce gave her a blinding smile and held out his arm for her. She linked her arm through his and they walked out from behind the curtain. They looked out over the crowd and were shocked to see the entire audience of tabloid reporters frantically scribbling on their notebooks, programs, even the tablecloths. Dru looked at Pierce. ''Blimey,'' he said. ''I forgot about this.'' He indicated a tiny microphone attached to his lapel. Their heartfelt reunion had been broadcast to everyone in the hall. ''Hell of a story, eh?'' he said sheepishly.

''They can have it,'' Dru said, laughing. ''As long as I have you, I don't care if I wind up on the front page.''

The announcer's voice rang out from the podium right beside them. ''And the winner is—Drucilla Logan!''

Dru stepped to the microphone, leading Pierce with her. She raised his hand in hers and said, ''I sure am!'' Ignoring the plaque that was being held out to her, she turned to Pierce and stepped into his arms.

They became so lost in their kiss that they didn't even hear the applause from the audience, or see the slender young woman doing an awkward dance of victory on her banquet table.

Epilogue

DEBORAH SIDESTEPPED the giant gray tabby on the top step of the front porch and shuddered as it tracked her with its huge amber eyes.

She rang the bell. "Good kitty. Don't hurt me."

"Come in!" Pierce flung the door open wide. "Welcome to the new digs." He led Deborah through the foyer, past the framed front page of a tabloid newspaper emblazoned with Pierce and Dru's photo and the headline, Reporters Conceive Love Potion Love Child.

"I can't believe that you guys had the baby and bought the house without me," Deborah said. "I guess that's what I get for going on vacation for two weeks."

Dru's voice came from around the corner. "I told her she had to wait for her godmother to be there, but she had other ideas."

Deborah, laden with baby and housewarming gifts, halted in the doorway to the den, face-to-face with Dru and the baby. Her brown eyes misted. "Godmother?"

"Meet Deborah Logan MacGregor Mountcastle." Pierce took the packages from Deborah's arms and set them aside. "Want to hold your namesake?"

"She's a lucky little girl to have you two as parents." Deborah wiped away a tear and carefully took the sleeping baby from Dru. "And to think you guys almost didn't get together at all. That reminds me,

Pierce, you never told me where you were during those weeks that Dru was searching for you.''

Pierce took a deep breath and locked eyes with his wife. ''Falling for Dru made me realize what was really important. After I resigned, I went back to London to make amends to the people I hurt the most in my younger days. It took some time, and in some cases money, but it was the best thing I ever did.'' Pierce ran a hand through his hair. ''But, of course, all that meant...changing my image, shall we say. I'm a new man in more ways than one.''

''He's always been an old softy. Now he's man enough to admit it.'' Dru winked at Deborah. ''You were right about that all along.''

''I seem to recall that during the time you lost touch with Pierce, you did some soul-searching of your own,'' Deborah said.

Dru glanced at Pierce. ''That's right. I realized that my inability to trust people and take them for who they were had possibly cost me the greatest thing that ever came into my life. Nobody's perfect, especially not me. That's why I decided to patch things up with my dad. Things had been strained between us for too long because I hadn't been willing to forgive him for not being a perfect father.'' Dru laughed. ''Now he seems determined to be the perfect grandfather.''

''I'll tell you who *is* perfect. This little baby here,'' Deborah said between coos.

''We're glad you think so, because we're going to count on you for a lot of baby-sitting,'' Dru said as Pierce walked to her chair and draped his arms around her. ''Not that we're going to be doing the kind of globe-trotting we used to do.''

Deborah shook her head and laughed. ''I can't believe the change in you two, especially you, Pierce. Who'd have thought you'd be perfectly happy to forgo your ambition to be an editor and report to your wife as your new boss?''

"Just call me the ultimate nineties man," he said, smiling down at Dru. "Changing my reporting style has been a bigger adjustment, but I'll manage."

Dru took his hand. "I think you'll be the first reporter from the *Nova* to win the Pulitzer prize. Forget the Tabby. We're going to report the truth and nothing but the truth from now on. By the way, how are the guys at the paper getting along with both of us on parental leave?"

"We're scraping by, but we're looking forward to you both coming back."

As if on cue, the baby woke up and issued a howl.

"I think she needs changing." Deborah handed the baby back to Dru and pointed again to the stack of presents. "I've got something you can use for diaper time." She reached for a tall package and handed it to Pierce. "You know, I just can't imagine the suave Mr. Mountcastle taking care of a baby and still maintaining his immaculate every-hair-in-place image." She looked at his stylish all-black outfit—a turtleneck, close-fitting corduroy jeans, leather belt with silver buckle.

"It's the Mountcastle know-how," he said with authority. "I have everything under control."

He opened the package, but squeezed it too tightly trying to get the last of the paper off. A small eruption of baby powder burst from the top of the container and settled in a fine white powder all over his black outfit.

The three of them burst into laughter. "Well, look on the bright side, honey," Dru said, going over to her husband and sliding her arm about his waist. "At least you still have the Mountcastle charm."

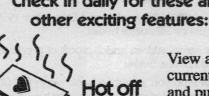

EXTRA! EXTRA!

The book all your favorite authors are raving about is finally here!

The 1999 Harlequin and Silhouette coupon book.

Each page is alive with savings that can't be beat!

Getting this incredible coupon book is as easy as 1, 2, 3.

1. During the months of November and December 1999 buy any 2 Harlequin or Silhouette books.

2. Send us your name, address and 2 proofs of purchase (cash receipt) to the address below.

3. Harlequin will send you a coupon book worth $10.00 off future purchases of Harlequin or Silhouette books in 2000.

Send us 3 cash register receipts as proofs of purchase and we will send you 2 coupon books worth a total saving of $20.00 (limit of 2 books per customer).

Saving money has never been this easy.

Please allow 4-6 weeks for delivery. Offer expires December 31, 1999.

I accept your offer! Please send me (a) coupon booklet(s):

Name: _____

Address: _____ City: _____

State/Prov.: _____ Zip/Postal Code: _____

Send your name and address, along with your cash register receipts as proofs of purchase, to:

In the U.S.: Harlequin Books, P.O. Box 9057, Buffalo, N.Y. 14269

In Canada: Harlequin Books, P.O. Box 622, Fort Erie, Ontario L2A 5X3

Order your books and accept this coupon offer through our web site
http://www.romance.net

Valid in U.S. and Canada only.

PHQ4994

Of all the unforgettable families created by
#1 *New York Times* bestselling author

NORA ROBERTS

the Donovans are the most extraordinary. For, along with
their irresistible appeal, they've inherited some rather
remarkable gifts from their Celtic ancestors.

Coming in November 1999

THE DONOVAN LEGACY

3 full-length novels in one special volume:

CAPTIVATED: Hardheaded skeptic Nash Kirkland has *always*
kept his feelings in check, until he falls under the bewitching
spell of mysterious Morgana Donovan.

ENTRANCED: Desperate to find a missing child, detective
Mary Ellen Sutherland dubiously enlists beguiling
Sebastian Donovan's aid and discovers his uncommon abilities
include a talent for seduction.

CHARMED: Enigmatic healer Anastasia Donovan would do
anything to save the life of handsome Boone Sawyer's
daughter, even if it means revealing her secret to the man
who'd stolen her heart.

Also in November 1999 from Silhouette Intimate Moments

ENCHANTED

Lovely, guileless Rowan Murray is drawn to darkly enigmatic
Liam Donovan with a power she's never imagined possible. But
before Liam can give Rowan his love, he must first reveal to
her his incredible secret.

Silhouette®

Available at your favorite retail outlet.

HARLEQUIN®
SUPERROMANCE®

By the Year 2000: BABY!

What have *you* resolved to do by the year 2000?
These three women are having babies!

Susan Kennedy's plan is to have a baby by the time she's forty—in the year 2000. But the only man she can imagine as the father of her child is her ex-husband, Michael!
MY BABIES AND ME by Tara Taylor Quinn
Available in October 1999

Nora Holloway is determined to adopt the baby who suddenly appears in her life! And then the baby's uncle shows up....
DREAM BABY by Ann Evans
Available in November 1999

By the year 2000, the Irving Trust will end, unless Miranda has a baby. She doesn't think there's much likelihood of that—until she meets Joseph Wallace.
THE BABY TRUST by Bobby Hutchinson
Available in December 1999

Available at your favorite retail outlet.

HARLEQUIN®
Makes any time special ™

Visit us at www.romance.net

HSR2000B